PRAISE FOR

DON'T KILL THE MESSENGER

"Riveting adventure . . . One of the best books I've read in years! Melina is an edgy, kick-ass protagonist."

—Alyssa Day,
New York Times bestselling author

"A strong and sassy heroine shines in this exciting, sexy and hilarious debut. Melina's charisma and wit, interesting side characters and dashes of hot romance will keep readers wanting more."

—*Publishers Weekly* (starred review)

"Amusing urban fantasy . . . Fun [and] lighthearted."

—*Midwest Book Review*

"Rendahl has a really distinctive voice. Her writing's nicely detailed, and with a little sarcastic wit thrown in, I felt [it] was great . . . Fantastic."

—*Night Owl Reviews*

"Her first stab at the paranormal world is off to an excellent start. She comes out with the big guns, ready to take gold! This book will have you screaming for more."

—*Manic Readers*

"[A] highly entertaining start to a new series . . . Melina is a sarcastic yet lovable heroine . . . Rendahl has a winner on her hands!"

—*Romantic Times*

Berkley Sensation titles by Eileen Rendahl

DON'T KILL THE MESSENGER

DEAD ON DELIVERY

EILEEN RENDAHL

THE BERKLEY PUBLISHING GROUP
Published by the Penguin Group
Penguin Group (USA) Inc.
375 Hudson Street, New York, New York 10014, USA
Penguin Group (Canada), 90 Eglinton Avenue East, Suite 700, Toronto, Ontario M4P 2Y3, Canada
(a division of Pearson Penguin Canada Inc.)
Penguin Books Ltd., 80 Strand, London WC2R 0RL, England
Penguin Group Ireland, 25 St. Stephen's Green, Dublin 2, Ireland (a division of Penguin Books Ltd.)
Penguin Group (Australia), 250 Camberwell Road, Camberwell, Victoria 3124, Australia
(a division of Pearson Australia Group Pty. Ltd.)
Penguin Books India Pvt. Ltd., 11 Community Centre, Panchsheel Park, New Delhi—110 017, India
Penguin Group (NZ), 67 Apollo Drive, Rosedale, North Shore 0632, New Zealand
(a division of Pearson New Zealand Ltd.)
Penguin Books (South Africa) (Pty.) Ltd., 24 Sturdee Avenue, Rosebank, Johannesburg 2196,
South Africa

Penguin Books Ltd., Registered Offices: 80 Strand, London WC2R 0RL, England

This book is an original publication of The Berkley Publishing Group.

Cover illustration by Tony Mauro.
Cover design by Diana Kolsky.
Interior text design by Laura K. Corless.

PRINTING HISTORY
Berkley Sensation trade paperback edition / March 2011

Library of Congress Cataloging-in-Publication Data

Rendahl, Eileen.
Dead on delivery / Eileen Rendahl.—Berkley Sensation trade pbk. ed.
p. cm.
ISBN 978-0-425-23878-3
1. Messengers—Fiction. 2. Supernatural—Fiction. I. Title.
PS3618.E5745D43 2011
813'.6—dc22 2010045589

PRINTED IN THE UNITED STATES OF AMERICA

10 9 8 7 6 5 4 3 2 1

To the BDBC,

for the laughs and the hugs and the wine.

ACKNOWLEDGMENTS

I lead a charmed life. At no time is it more evident to me than when I set about to write acknowledgments. My life is full of people who sustain me and give me joy and make sure that I'm never lonely even when following a somewhat solitary pursuit. My family and my friends are absolutely the best. Thank you to everyone who listened to me, laughed with me, drank with me, biked with me and ran with me.

A huge thank-you to the very patient Leis Pederson, who suffered with me through some missteps in the early production of this book, and as always, I don't know where I'd be without the guidance and support of my agent, Pamela Ahearn.

"DO YOU WANT TO EXPLAIN THIS?" TED DROPPED A FOLDED copy of that morning's *Sacramento Bee* onto my kitchen counter and jabbed a finger at an article in the Our Region section.

I picked up the paper and looked at the article. Some dude in Elmville had died under suspicious circumstances. Crap. Another one had bitten the dust. Neil Bossard was the second person I'd made a delivery to in Elmville in the past two months who had ended up dead. Coincidence? Possibly. I wasn't crazy about the odds, though. Elmville was tiny. It had been weird enough to make two deliveries there within such a short time period—and both of them to 'Danes, to boot. To have both of the recipients wind up dead? Not likely to be a wacky fluke. Still, I didn't know for sure and there was no point in upsetting Ted before I knew that there was something to get upset about.

"Why do you ask?" I avoided looking up into his cornflower blue eyes. Not because I couldn't look directly into them and lie, though. I could do it. Probably. The real problem was the way my heart did that weird flip-flop thing in my chest every time I looked directly into his baby blues. The flip-flop thing made it hard to lie. I needed to focus to lie and Ted was nothing if not distracting to me.

"The case is weird, which always makes me think of you." He took a step closer and lifted my chin. A smile quirked at the corner of his lips.

Now I had no choice but to look into his eyes and there went the damn flip-flop. "Is that a nice way to talk to your girlfriend?" That gave me a shiver. I was someone's girlfriend. Who'd a thunk it was possible? It never had been before.

I am twenty-six years old, nearly twenty-seven. Ted Goodnight is my first boyfriend ever. There have been a few dalliances before but never a boyfriend. I still can't decide if it's the best good fortune that has ever befallen me or the worst mistake of my short life, and there have been some doozies, starting with the day I decided to sneak into the swimming pool behind my mother's back and drowned. That was pretty much the mother of all mistakes. It's the one that started me down the road to all the rest.

On that day, I was legally dead for three minutes. They resuscitated me and everyone said it was a miracle that no harm had been done. The doctors couldn't detect any brain damage. I would be "normal." Ha! If only they'd known. Apparently, the ability to sense supernatural creatures and see all the crazy-ass paranormal doings that go on around most people without them noticing doesn't show up on an MRI.

No other guy has been able to get past the freaky things that happen around me or my crazy schedule or what my mother refers to as my "moods." In fact, the only guy I can remember making it past two dates was David Bounds in eleventh grade and he was bipolar. Even he couldn't hang in there with me, not even with medication to help him.

I'm not saying Ted hasn't had his occasional problems with who and what I am. The first time he saw me truly in action almost killed our relationship before it ever really started. Maybe it's because he grew up in such a crazy family (seriously clinically crazy). Maybe it's because he's amazingly accepting. Maybe he really, really likes me. I am the Sally Field of Messengers. Could be worse.

Whatever it is, it's working and while I am not the type to skip joyfully through fields of daisies, I'm feeling pretty good about the whole thing. I do try to keep most of the woo-woo things I'm up to separate from him so I don't freak him out too much, but I'm used to compartmentalizing.

The big drawback to having Ted Goodnight as a boyfriend? He's a cop.

I have always mistrusted cops. Cops mean trouble. It's not that I'm into breaking the law; it's the order part of the police department that I have issues with. Or maybe order has issues with me. My very existence is about the disorderliness of things. I don't fit neatly anywhere. Trust me, I wish I did. I think I've spent most of my life wishing that, but this beggar isn't riding and I never quite belong anywhere. All of which makes it even more interesting that I'm now dating a cop, especially one who I'm pretty sure wanted to hear that I had nothing to do with some guy running into traffic on Highway 120 and being turned into road pizza by a semi, which was exactly what had happened to Neil Bossard. According to the article, they didn't know what he was doing running onto the highway. I didn't either. I didn't like it, though.

"Looks like a traffic accident to me, Ted. What could I possibly have to do with it?" It did look like a traffic accident, but one that made me a little bit itchy and uncomfortable.

"Not every detail made it into the paper. The local cops think that maybe somebody was chasing the guy. Or, at least, he thought he was being chased. Someone saw him running down the road, screaming that something was after him, but he was all alone. Before the witness could do anything to help, the dude had run out onto the road and gotten creamed by a big rig." Ted smoothed my hair back behind my ear and I felt a little gooey inside. "They were canvassing the guy's neighborhood to see if they could figure out who might have been chasing him and somebody mentioned seeing a car that sounds an awful lot like yours. Weird plus an old Buick tends to equal you in my book, babe."

Fabulous. What more could I want than to be the solution to a funky equation? He wasn't wrong, though. I weighed my options. I could lie. Chances were that this whole thing would completely blow over and he'd never know. Of course, if it didn't and Ted found out that I'd lied to him . . . well, suffice it to say, I didn't think he'd be pleased. I could tell him the truth, as far as I knew it, which really wasn't all that far. I didn't have to mention Kurt Rawley, the other guy I'd made a delivery to who was now six feet under.

Come to think of it, his death had been weird as well. Had it been arson? I remember it had something to do with a fire.

"I made a delivery to him," I blurted. "It was days ago."

"What was it?" Ted leaned back against the counter and crossed his arms over his chest.

I shrugged. "Hell if I know."

"You don't look?" He looked incredulous.

I shook my head. It wasn't a rule, as far as I knew. Nobody had ever told me I couldn't look inside the packages that were left for me to deliver. I chose not to peek. Peeking signaled curiosity and perhaps an interest in becoming involved. I generally had neither. Or, at least, I hadn't had.

If someone handed me something, all unwrapped, then I knew what it was. If someone had taken the trouble to put it in an envelope or wrap it up in a little box, like whoever had needed me to make a delivery to Neil Bossard had, then I didn't know. I didn't care. Or, at least, I didn't want to care. With information comes responsibility and I've spent almost twenty-seven years avoiding as much of that as I can and now have more than I ever wanted.

My last experience in getting involved with a delivery hadn't gone well. I'd lost someone very dear to me and damn near gotten killed myself. It didn't make me want to change my habits now. The fact that this particular package had given off a little hum of power didn't exactly make me more interested in opening it. It did needle at me a little bit, though.

"How did you know where to take it?" He wasn't quite using his cop voice on me, but it was getting close. I liked that about as much as I liked it when my vampire buddy used his vampire voice on me, which was not much.

I smiled at him, even though I didn't totally mean it, and said, "Gee, I don't know. Maybe it was some special magical divining process. Maybe it spoke to me. Or maybe I used the address that was written on the package."

His eyebrows went up. "I don't think sarcasm is called for."

Norah, my roommate, strolled into the kitchen, hair disheveled and a pillow crease across her cheek. "She always thinks sarcasm is called for." She made straight for the coffeepot and poured herself a cup.

I attempted not to let my jaw hit the floor. Norah hadn't been herself lately and poisoning her body with the evil drug caffeine was one more hint that all was not right in the sunshine and rainbow-strewn world of my yoga-loving BFF. "You want some cream or sugar for that?"

She shook her head. "Black is fine."

I looked at her closely. Had she been possessed by some other being? Would I find a Norah-shaped pod in the basement of our apartment building if I ever got up the guts and energy to go through it? Stranger things had happened and some of them had happened right here at our apartment. My Norah had a sweet tooth and I couldn't imagine her drinking coffee without girlying it up at least a little.

"Hey, Ted," she said, and gave him a weak smile.

No, my Norah was not herself at all. She likes cops less than I do, or she had until Ted saved her soy-bacon last summer when we were fighting off Chinese vampires as they rose out of tunnels beneath Old Sacramento.

Now? Now she not only tolerated him but often seemed happy to see him and not in an icky I'm-going-to-steal-your-boyfriend way.

"Hey, Norah." He smiled at her but then turned directly back to me. "Who gave you the delivery?"

I shrugged. "I don't know. The box was sitting on the hood of my car when I came out of the dojo one night." Which was pretty much exactly how the package for Kurt Rawley had come my way, come to think of it.

"Was there a note?"

"No. Just the box with the address marked on it."

"That was it. There was a box on your car, so you drove it all the way out to Elmville and . . ." He hesitated. "What did you do with it once you got there?"

"I left it on the doorstep." *Both times*, I added silently.

"And then hung out long enough for someone to notice your car." His eyes narrowed a bit.

"I hung out on the street for a little while and watched to make sure some guy who at least looked like he could be Neil Bossard picked it up. I don't exactly ask for ID." Again, contact with message recipients might constitute some kind of caring beyond fulfilling what was basically expected of me. Not my thing.

"Did he open the box?"

I was so done with the third degree. I threw up my hands. "How the hell should I know? And if I did know, what difference would it make? Someone needs something taken someplace, I take it there. End of story."

"Until someone ends up dead." Ted's eyes narrowed.

Norah's head shot up. "Who's dead?"

I shot Ted a nasty look. Now he had upset Norah. Who knew how long it would take me to calm her down? "No one you know. No one I know. Some guy that I happened to deliver a box to last week got hit by a car."

She blinked at me, her eyes big and round. "That's it? No undead creatures ate him or anything?"

"Not according to the *Bee*. It was a simple case of man versus semi. The semi won. They pretty much always do." I'd seen that a few times in the Emergency Department of Sacramento County Hospital where I work. It was never pretty.

"Well, okay then." She went back to swirling her coffee.

"It's a coincidence," I said, with way more confidence than I felt. Ted started to open his mouth, but I shook my head at him. "Not now," I mouthed at him and tipped my head at Norah.

He pressed his lips together in a tight line and headed back toward my bedroom. As he brushed past me, he whispered, "I don't believe in coincidence."

I didn't bother telling him that I didn't either.

TED LEFT AND NORAH SETTLED IN ON OUR FUTON COUCH WITH a bowl of Cocoa Krispies, making me increasingly convinced that an intervention was in order. I headed off to River City Karate and Judo to teach the Saturday morning Little Dragons classes. Out on the street, the Buick awaited me. It's not an entirely good thing when the place a person feels most at ease is in their car. It used to be the dojo for me. I'd walk into River City Karate and Judo, my feet would hit that slightly scratchy gray mat and all my troubles would drain away. Or if they didn't, they would seem more manageable. Like maybe I could roundhouse kick them into submission. I knew who I was there, what was expected of me and how to meet those expectations.

Now the dojo caused as much stress as it offered solace. In a move that had both honored and terrified me, my mentor Mae had left her karate studio to me in her will. I'd practically lived at the dojo before Mae's death. Now it seemed like I really did. Small business owner was not a title I'd ever aspired to. My mother was inordinately proud and it wasn't terrible to throw her the occasional bone, but it was a lot of freaking work.

I'd had no idea what kind of crap Mae had dealt with for all those years. It wasn't only scheduling classes and training people and shaking hands. There were bills: ones that had to be paid and ones that had to be sent out. There were cranky parents and hyperactive second-graders and everything in between. There was insurance and business licenses and forms to fill out. The responsibility for making it run was all mine now. I'd always thought of myself as

Mae's apprentice, but apparently that was only true when it came to the actual martial arts part of the equation. The business-running part had escaped me completely.

I didn't think there was ever going to be a day that I didn't miss Mae, that the thought of something she'd said or taught me or done wouldn't catch me unawares and startle me into missing her again. Walking into the dojo and having her not be there brought a special kind of pain, though, something both sharp and sweet.

I rubbed at the cold spot under my breastbone that formed whenever I thought of her, and pulled into the strip mall parking lot in front of the building.

I wondered if I should just close the studio, but I couldn't bring myself to imagine that. Mae had spent so much of her talent and time building it. I felt that I would be dishonoring her memory if I didn't keep it open.

Plus, without the dojo, what would I do with Sophie?

The question was ever present in my mind, but only more so at the moment as she opened the door to the dojo and greeted me. I'd made it her job to get to River City Karate and Judo by eight fifteen every Saturday morning to open the studio, make a pot of coffee and sweep. I figured if nothing else, it meant she'd be getting home early on Friday nights and maybe it would keep her out of trouble.

Plus, it had been my job at the studio for years. I really didn't know what more to do with her than what Mae had done with me, since I'm pretty sure Sophie is my replacement.

She'd shown up at the dojo this past summer, the scars on her face and neck from the car accident she'd been in nearly healed. She wasn't entirely sure why the odd things she'd been seeing were telling her to come to River City, but Mae and I were pretty sure we knew.

Like me, Sophie had died for a few minutes and then been

brought back to life. Like me, she'd started seeing and hearing things that no one else seemed to see or hear or sense. Like me, she was a Messenger.

Unlike me, Sophie was sixteen. I'd only been three when I'd drowned in the backyard. Her learning curve was going to be different. I'd barely figured out my own, so trying to figure out hers was a bit of a problem for me, especially since the only person I'd ever gone to for advice on matters of the Arcane had died.

I stepped in the door and immediately felt a buzzing in my skin. The hairs on my arm lifted ever so slightly.

"Good morning, Sophie. How's it going?" I glanced around. I didn't see anything that would set off my freaky radar, but there are many more senses than sight. I'd been working on mine, honing them and developing them. Or maybe I was just paying more attention to them. It used to be as if I had only one channel and it was either on or off. Something was out there or something wasn't. Suddenly I'd gone cable. My supernatural palate had become more sophisticated. I'd started to notice subtle differences between, say, the feeling I got when a vampire was lurking around the corner and the feeling I got when a troll was hunkered down under a bridge. Being able to differentiate was helpful. Not everything out there is out to get me, but some things definitely are. It was good to be able to sense the difference.

"It's great." Sophie gave me a big beaming smile.

See how different from me she is? A big beaming smile at eight forty-five in the morning? I would never in a million years have done that. I'd loved Mae with all my heart and soul and the best I could usually produce was a lack of scowling.

I did feel like I'd made some progress, though. Sophie no longer wore her hair hanging down over her scars. Right now, her hair was pulled back into a low ponytail at the back of her neck. The high pony might be cute and swingier, but it was also a potential handle hold for your opponent in a fight. It was unlikely that any of the Little Dragons that Sophie would help me teach this morning would grab her by her hair. It was actually unlikely that any of them would be able to reach it. The oldest Little Dragon in the beginning class was only seven and less than four feet tall. As Messengers, however, we had to be ready for a fight at any time. It wasn't like we got to choose the times and places of our deliveries. We never knew where we were going or whom we were going to meet there. Speaking of which . . .

"So," Sophie said. "There's, uh, someone in your office."

I raised an eyebrow. "Someone? Like a parent? Or a student?" I wouldn't say I was a disaster with the administrative side of things, but that was because I was usually very generous with myself.

"Not exactly." The smile stayed fixed on her face.

I stopped for a second. That must be the source of the buzzing. Whatever was in my office wasn't particularly powerful, but it had some magic to it. It felt . . . earthy. "What exactly is it?"

"I'm not positive. I think it might be a Basajaun." She paused and scuffed one bare toe against the tile floor of the foyer. "At least, I think that's what it is. I'm still getting confused between Yetis and Basajauns."

Totally understandable. Every time I thought I'd learned most of what was out there in the universe of the Arcane, something came along and bit me on the butt. Occasionally literally. I had the scars to prove it. It could have been worse, though. I never really liked wearing thongs anyway and I did learn to never ever turn my back on a Tailypo. Never ever turn your back on something that's demanding the return of its tail. It may well take a chomp out of yours.

"So whatever this thing is, it's in my office?" I asked.

Sophie nodded.

"And fifteen seven-year-olds will be here in ten minutes?"

She nodded again. "Do you want some coffee?"

"Definitely." I walked into my office and shut the door.

The Basajaun sat behind my desk, running its long hairy fingers up and down the shaft of a hefty looking axe.

"Hey," I said. I'd read about Basajauns, but this was my first in the incredibly hairy flesh. He—at least I think it was a he, it's a little hard to tell with all that reddish brown hair hanging down to its knees—was close to seven feet tall. Or would be if it stood up straight. Still, when it rose from behind my desk, shoulders hunched and shambling, it was easily a foot taller than me.

It nodded and held out the axe, handle first. Lovely, a Basque Lord of the Woods who believed in Safety First. I took the axe. "Thanks."

It nodded and headed toward the door. "Whoa, big fella! Where am I taking this?" It was one thing not to look a gift Basajaun in the mouth; it was another to take its axe without knowing what I was supposed to do with it.

"Ginnar." It turned back toward the door.

"Help me out, big guy. Is that a place or a person?"

"Dwarf." So, a supernatural creature of few words. I was down with that.

"You want a return receipt?"

It stared at me. At least, I think it did. It was hard to tell with the hair. It shook its head slowly and opened the door to my office.

I heard a high-pitched scream from the other side of the door and ran.

I was too late.

The Basajaun was backed into a corner, hands thrown up in front of its face. Advancing on it was all three foot two inches of a very determined Parvinder Gundar. I'd be frightened, too, if she was going after me. That is one resolute seven-year-old.

I jumped in front of her. "It's okay, Parvinder. He's with me."

"What is he?" She scowled up at me.

"Yes. What is that thing?" Parvinder's mother demanded from on top of the chair that she'd apparently jumped on.

Think fast, Melina. Think fast. "He's, uh, a character I've been thinking of hiring. You know, for birthday parties. Too scary?" I mustered up my brightest smile, which didn't hold a candle to Sophie's, but you had to go with what you had, right?

"He smells funny." Parvinder stopped advancing.

I sniffed. She was right. He smelled like the slightly rotten layer of pine needles that lay on most forest floors. "Good point." I turned to the Basajaun and pointed toward the back door. "Go out that way. Next time you come for a job interview, take a shower first."

It shambled away across the mat. I took a deep breath and tried to relax.

Mrs. Gundar stepped down off the chair and smiled at me. "You're going to do birthday parties? We were just wondering what to do for Parvinder's party next month. What do you charge?"

Please, someone, kill me now.

A LITTLE OVER TWO HOURS LATER, SOPHIE AND I HAD USHered out both the Beginning and Advanced Little Dragons. We had about two hours for lunch and then the sparring classes for teenagers and adults would start. Saying good-bye to the parents and kids, I felt yet another jab. I used to stand where Sophie stood now, a step back from Mae. Now I had to stand in Mae's place.

That's what it still felt like to me. I was standing in Mae's place, trying to be her and falling so incredibly short of the mark. In all the years I had been coming to River City, I had never once witnessed a meeting between a Mundane being—or 'Dane, as we cool kids called them—and a 'Cane—the down-low way to refer to an Arcane, or supernatural being. I'd managed to screw that one up damn fast.

"That was pretty quick thinking with Mrs. Gundar and the Basajaun," Sophie said as she straightened out the chairs.

"You think so?"

"Sure."

"Great. You can figure out what to do about Parvinder's birthday party, then." I stalked toward the office.

"Sorry," she said. Damn. Was that hurt I heard in her voice?

I turned back around. Her face was flushed.

"I guess I should have put him in the back or maybe out by the Dumpsters."

"Ya think?" Could I not stop my own sarcastic mouth?

The flush spread farther up Sophie's face and a knot formed in my stomach. I don't mind being a pain in the ass, but I don't like being mean and that's exactly what I'd just been. Mae had never been mean. Occasionally disappointed. Often exasperated. Never mean.

"No, Sophie. I'm sorry. I never thought about making some kind of protocol for handling the creatures that might come here. I'll think of something so we don't have another incident like this one." I gave myself a little kick in the pants. Just because I was feeling defensive about being incompetent didn't mean I needed to take it out on Sophie. She hadn't asked for this life any more than I had and was generally a lot more gracious about it.

She smiled. "Thanks. By the way, I do have some ideas about birthday parties. I think they could be fun."

I stared at her. She was serious. Fun? She thought birthday parties for seven-year-olds could be fun? I knew she was naïve, but this was beyond the pale. Still, I'd already been a bitch once this morning. Perhaps I could learn to have a B.Q. (Bitchy Quotient) of only one per day. That would be livable for everyone, wouldn't it?

"I'd love to hear about it," I said. "But right now, I need to do a little research about some deliveries I made."

She frowned. "What about the axe, then? Will you leave it here? Or do you want me to take it somewhere?"

I thought about that for a minute. I'd let Sophie make a few simple deliveries on her own. Nothing big. She'd taken an envelope to some elves and dropped a package off in the Delta for a water spirit. All close by. All easy. She'd done a great job. This one would be a little trickier. Was she ready for it? "That's not a bad idea, Soph. The axe is supposed to go to Ginnar the Dwarf."

"Where does he live?"

"Not sure." I had a few ideas but nothing definite.

"How am I supposed to find him then?" Her eyebrows drew down.

I gestured for her to follow me into the office. I sat down behind Mae's desk and then twisted a bit. Mae had been a small woman and while I'm not an Amazon, I am close to five foot eight. Her chair didn't fit me and I was constantly trying to adjust it. Nothing seemed to work. I was going to have to bite the bullet and buy my own. That would be about number nine hundred and twenty-seven on my priority list, though.

The axe, on the other hand, had made it to about five or six. I moved the *gi* that I'd quickly thrown over it when Mrs. Gundar had started screaming.

"Wow," Sophie said.

It was a wow-worthy axe. The metal hasp gleamed. Carved runes and dwarven figures intertwined their way down the wooden handle. "It's going to tell you how to find Ginnar."

She looked up at me, eyes wide. "It talks?"

Fabulous. She'd believe almost anything these days. I couldn't really blame her. To suddenly find out that so many things you thought were the product of feverish imaginations and fictional geniuses were actually roaming the earth and possibly next to you on the bus made a person wonder what to believe and not to believe. Sophie had clearly taken the route of acceptance.

"No. It doesn't talk. At least, not with words."

She nodded and waited while I tried to find words for what had become innate for me. I'd become a Messenger when I was practically still a toddler. Explaining how to figure out where to make a delivery was like trying to tell someone how to breathe.

"Put your hand on the axe," I said.

She looked at me, her eyes wide. "Are we going to swear some kind of blood oath?"

I shot her a look. "No. We're not going to do each other's nails or give each other facials either. Just put your hand on it."

She set her hand on the hasp and pulled it away as if the thing were hot.

"I take it you felt something?" I sat back in the chair.

Sophie nodded. "What is that?"

Objects of magic contain power. I realize that sounds simplistic, but it's true. Rarely do they have power of their own, however. They're like containers. They become imbued with power. Sometimes only one being places the power in the object. Sometimes it's layered on over generations or heaped on by groups that believe in it. Either way, the farther the objects are from those that imbue them, the less powerful their magic becomes.

The magic in the axe wasn't strong enough, at this point, to feel across the room, but place your hand right on it and you'd feel the buzz. Well, you would if you were sensitive to such things. I'm pretty sure my brother could have hauled this thing around for weeks and not received a single spark from it. Sophie had certainly felt it, though.

Until now, most of her deliveries had been safely ensconced in packages and envelopes. I hadn't let her handle too many objects of power mano a mano, as it were. It was wise to be careful about handling these things. They can take power as fast as they give it. "It's the axe talking to you."

She crossed her arms over her chest. "I'm not sure I speak its language."

"You do. Maybe not fluently yet, but you do." I saw the stubborn set of her chin and felt a little bad. I did know how she felt. Once you become a Messenger—and it's not like you apply for the job—you discover abilities and information inside yourself that you might not really like or want. I suppose I could have offered some words of understanding or comfort, but they would be meaningless. The reality of the situation was that the universe pretty much said tough cookies to what you wanted. You are what you are, and if you're a Messenger, you speak fluent Dwarf Axe whether you want to or not.

"Now, scoot. I need to figure some stuff out." I held the axe out to her to take.

She took it, holding it away from her as if it had cooties or something. "Can I help?"

Her face was so open and so earnest, but she knew nothing. No. The person who generally helped me was gone and I needed to figure out how to handle stuff on my own. "I wish you could, kiddo."

It would have been nice to have Mae here to talk to right now. What was I supposed to do about this situation with Bossard? I didn't like that someone had remembered my car, but I'm pretty sure if they'd had the plates, Ted would have done more than make me look at a newspaper article. There might have been discussions with local authorities and other things that didn't sound like any fun at all to me.

Who was this guy, anyway? Maybe if I knew who Bossard was, I'd be able to figure out who was sending him neatly wrapped little packages with careful block printing on the front. Maybe I'd find that the package had nothing to do with him being spread like peanut butter on toast down Highway 120.

I turned on the computer on Mae's desk and waited for it to come to life.

It really could be a coincidence. There might be no connection with me or with Kurt Rawley. Come to think of it, I'd better look into him, too. His death looked as accidental as Bossard's. I think the paper said something about a house fire. If somebody was orchestrating these deaths, they were damn clever.

I typed Neil Bossard's name and Elmville, California, into the search engine. The usual bazillion results came in the standard nanosecond. The first entry was an account of Bossard's death in the local newspaper. It didn't tell me much more than had been in the *Bee*, except it gave the time and place of his memorial service. Tomorrow at three P.M. at the Svoboda Family Mortuary. I jotted the address down. The *Bee* article was listed. Then came Bossard's MySpace profile and Facebook page.

I logged onto Facebook, but couldn't access the page without friending Bossard. Since I doubted he would be accepting new friend requests in the near future, I switched over to his MySpace page.

Bingo! His profile was hanging out there for everybody to see, including me.

I enlarged the picture. Yep. I was reasonably certain that was the dude who'd scooped the package off the porch and walked into the house in Elmville. At least I'd gotten the right guy.

He was a Libra and he liked Sublime and Bad Religion. That didn't help much. I scrolled through some of the messages. They were all recent, all posted within the last six weeks. Jbone had posted, "Welcome home, bra! Good times ahead." Cshelty08 had posted, "Good to see you back, homey. When we gonna hoist some brews?" The other messages ran along the same lines. I checked through his list of friends, but couldn't find Kurt Rawley.

I typed Rawley's name and Elmville into the MySpace search. He popped up, too. Did these children have no concept of protecting their own privacy? I'd made his delivery long enough ago that I didn't have as clear of a mental picture of who had picked up the package. It definitely looked like the right guy, though I couldn't swear to it. He was just your standard white boy.

Rawley's page had several "welcome home" messages and a few "good to see you on MySpace" messages, too. I looked at the message dates; they were all from this summer. I'd made Rawley's delivery a couple of months later and he was dead within a few weeks. He liked some of the same bands as Bossard and he was a Cancer.

I drummed my fingers trying to figure out the connection. I looked at the messages again. There were a couple of "happy birthdays" mixed in with the "welcome homes." Kurt Rawley had turned twenty-one on July 18. I flipped back to Neil Bossard's page. He'd turned twenty-one in October.

Okay. They were the same age and lived in the same town. They must have known each other; Elmville wasn't that big. If nothing else, they would have gone to the same high school. Elmville only had one.

I scrolled through the messages on Rawley's page again. Hot damn. Jbone and Cshelty08 had left messages on both boys' pages. I clicked to their pages. Both Jbone and Cshelty08 had graduated from Elmville High and had gone on to Modesto Junior College. I'm not sure their mamas would have been too happy to see exactly how they'd celebrated their accomplishments. At least, my mother would have been horrified to see me with a beer bong, but she was a tad on the old-fashioned side.

I clicked back to Bossard's page. Nope. No graduation photos and nothing about where he'd been going to school. Come to think of it, there was nothing about where he was being welcomed back from. How far away could a kid his age go?

I clicked back to Rawley. It was the same deal. No graduation information and no word on where he was returning from either.

Crap. There was going to be a connection between these two and whatever it was, I was pretty sure I wasn't going to like it.

2

BY THE TIME I LEFT RIVER CITY, I WAS TIRED, HUNGRY AND A little bit cranky. Plus, T. J. Hamilton, in an effort to prove once and for all that he was the biggest swinging dick at the dojo, had left a bruise the size of a football on my thigh when we were sparring.

It had been a close thing. I was pretty sure actually killing a student wouldn't be a good thing for the dojo. I'd call it one of Mae's unwritten rules or perhaps a universal assumption.

I knew how to control myself. I had to. I'd spent years at the dojo not letting my fighting skills show completely. I had to fight well enough to win the respect of my fellow students and to justify being Mae's pet, which I obviously was to anyone with half a brain. But I couldn't fight inexplicably well, and left to my own devices, I do fight way better than most people would assume.

It's not like I'm not fit, but I'm a girl, which is one strike against me in the very macho and masculine world of martial arts. I also look a little younger than I am. I'm guessing it's part of the Messenger gig. I heal fast. I move fast. I'm likely to still be getting carded when I'm forty, assuming I live that long.

Most of the students at the dojo had accepted me as Mae's successor, if not her replacement, when I'd inherited the dojo. I was still fighting for recognition from a few of them. T.J. would be among that few and it was starting to get on my nerves.

To be honest, those nerves were already a bit frayed anyway. Between the studio, my job at the hospital, Sophie, Norah and my regular Messenger duties, I was stretched thinner than a supermodel during Fashion Week. When T.J. landed his kick to my thigh, it was everything I could do to keep myself from taking him out right there and then.

It wouldn't have been hard to do. He had six inches on me and probably close to one hundred pounds, but that just made him cocky. I had to content myself with a leg sweep that left him on his back gasping for air. He was lucky I hadn't snapped completely and broken his larynx while he was down. It was my first instinct and my hands had been in motion when I'd stopped myself.

Clearly, I needed a vacation.

I was not going to get it, though. Instead, on my day off, I was going to Elmville to attend Neil Bossard's memorial service. I didn't think I was going to find too much more on the Internet. It was a wondrous place, the World Wide Web, but it did have its limits. This smelled distinctly like something that was going to require some actual sniffing around. I was pretty sure the best time and place for that was going to be Bossard's memorial service on Sunday. Don't TV cops always go to the victim's funeral?

I started the engine and rolled down the windows. It was a beautiful night. Fall was here. I let the playful wind blow across my face all the way back to the apartment in Mansion Flats.

I did the standard drive around the block for ten minutes, looking for a parking place, but finally got one within what I considered a reasonable non-grocery-carrying distance.

I pulled the collar of my jacket up and walked down the sidewalk, whistling a little to myself as I went. I made sure to glance up and down the street, checking into all the dark shadows between the parked cars and the darkened houses. There was nothing on the streets in my neighborhood that was going to jump me that I couldn't take tonight. Anything that could kick my ass would have set off my internal alarm system by now. My fingertips would be tingling. The hair on the back of my neck would be standing up ever so slightly. I was getting nothing. Still, it didn't do to not look concerned. If I wanted people to treat me like a regular girl, I had to act like a regular girl.

It was an interesting lesson to have learned after all these years. I'd learned it from an interesting source, too. Alexander Bledsoe, M.D., my coworker at the hospital, my cohort in my fight against supernatural crime, my favorite vampire and . . . my friend? I didn't know quite what to call Alex. He wasn't my lover. Things hadn't gone that far between us, although only because of a bizarre show of forbearance on his part during a moment of weakness on mine.

It had pissed me off at the time. I'd been looking for comfort and solace and had felt like he'd been denying me for no good reason. When I realized he'd been doing it for my own good, it pissed me off even more. One of the countless issues between Alex and me is the age difference. He'll never give me an exact count of how old he is, but he did mention having seen Benjamin Franklin once, which meant that he had to be at least three hundred and fifty years old.

I'm going to be twenty-seven this year. It's kind of a big gap. Yet they say that age is just a number.

Alex's forbearance, on the other hand, had made it so that I could look Ted in the eye and say nothing physical had ever happened between Alex and me and be 100 percent honest. And, honestly, probably still at least 25 percent curious. I've heard a lot of rumors about vampire sex. I'm not sure why physical congress with something cold-blooded is supposed to be so damn hot, but that's what all the kids say.

I let myself into our apartment building. It's an old Victorian that's been split up into flats. Norah and I are on the third floor. Ben and his mother, Valerie, are on the first. The rosemary and sage that Valerie had planted last summer were still green and going strong in the planters on the porch. It still amazed me to think about what they'd survived. Then again, I was a little amazed that any of us had survived last summer and still a little in shock about the one person in my life who hadn't.

I stamped my way up the stairs to the apartment, turned the key in the lock and opened the door as far as the chain would allow. "Norah," I called through the crack. "It's me. Let me in."

"Coming."

The chain was a new thing. Norah had installed it after our little adventure last summer. I'm not sure what she thought it was going to keep her safe from. I'm pretty sure even the pudgiest Seventh-day Adventist lady could kick the door right off that chain.

She let me in.

"You know that chain won't keep him out if he wants to come in," I said as I brushed past her.

She crossed her matchstick arms across her chest. She'd lost weight in the last few months and Norah had never been exactly hefty to start with. "I know."

"It does, however, present an issue for me." I got it that she was afraid. She should never have seen what she saw that night at the Bok Kai Temple in Old Sacramento. I'd tried to keep her from going, but she'd insisted. In fact, I'd spent years trying to protect

Norah from knowing who I was, what I was and what kinds of things I dealt with.

Turns out I'm not so good at keeping secrets from her. I'm pretty sure she wished I had been better at it now.

"I'm sorry." She marched back to the couch and flung herself into it.

I sighed. It wasn't that I wasn't sympathetic, but I'd been being sympathetic for months now. Apparently, I have a finite amount of sympathy and Norah was dangerously close to having used more than her share. Perhaps for the decade.

"As vampires go, he's really not bad." I sat down next to her. She was watching *So You Think You Can Dance*. I grabbed the remote and turned it off.

She held her hand out like a cop stopping traffic. "He drinks blood. Human blood."

I scratched my nose. It was a difficult point to argue. That's pretty much what vampires did. "Only what people come in and spray at him, for the most part." And a bit from willing partners, met anonymously and left mainly intact. They might end up with the tiniest of puncture wounds on a neck or a wrist or some other highly vascular body part, but he'd never drink enough to harm them and never ever enough to turn them. Of that, I was reasonably certain. It was one of the ways that Alex was different than most of the other vampires I'd met and was one of the reasons I could stand to be around him.

She glared at me, grabbed the remote and turned the TV on again. "He's more like them than like us."

Unspoken between us was the fact that Norah was the one who had invited him into our apartment. As much as I like Alex, and there are times when I like him a confusing amount, inviting him into the apartment was not a mistake I was likely to make. Despite hours on the Internet and watching old *Buffy* DVDs, I couldn't for the life of me figure out how to uninvite a vampire from a home. Therefore, Alex could pretty much come and go in our place as he pleased.

The irony was that Alex had not taken advantage of the situation. Not once. He had not fluttered through the windows, slid like smoke under the door or simply busted his way in. He hadn't even shown up and knocked. The even bigger irony was that until Norah had seen the *kiang shi* in action, she'd thought Alex was pretty cool.

Which he is. What with the being undead thing, his temperature stays way below us 98.6-ers. But Nora hadn't thought it literally. She'd thought it flirtatiously, but flirting with a vampire is flirting with danger to a very high degree. She had no idea how lucky she was.

Alex hadn't done anything that night to put her off. In fact, he'd done pretty much nothing. It wasn't his fault. Everything went down in a temple and it's a little tricky for vampires to set foot on sacred ground. In fact, they can't. Somehow, watching Alex do nothing and watching Ted Goodnight save the day had shaken my little New Age-y, tofu-eating, yoga-posing BFF right down to her rainbow-loving core.

"Couldn't we just stock up on garlic and crosses and leave the chain off the door until I come home?" I pleaded.

She gave me a hard stare. "Once you're home, I don't need the chain on anymore."

There was that. Nora had also seen me in full action for the first time, too, and now knew what I was capable of. There wasn't much that could come through our door that I didn't have a good chance of taking.

The doorknob to the front door started to turn. Norah's hard stare turned into a look of horror and she damn near jumped into my lap. I pushed Norah behind me and stood. The doorknob jiggled again. Something was definitely trying to come in and it didn't seem to feel a need to be too stealthy about it.

I rolled my shoulders, making sure they were loose and easy. I closed my eyes, reaching out with my senses to whatever was trying to get into the apartment. My skin didn't prickle. My hair didn't stand up like I was too close to a lightning strike. Nothing buzzed in my brain or my flesh.

On the other hand, I was pretty sure I smelled pizza.

"Ted?" I called.

"Hey," he answered from the other side of the door. "Could you let me in? My hands are full and I can't find my key."

WE POLISHED OFF MOST THE PIZZA IN RIDICULOUSLY SHORT order. Well, Ted and I did. Norah picked at olives and peppers and took some tiny bites of cheese and crust.

"Thanks." I leaned back on the futon couch and contemplated undoing the top button of my jeans. I decided against it. It seemed unladylike. I may not be well-versed in the ways of girlfriending, but I'm pretty sure popping open the top button of your 501s has to wait until after the first anniversary.

"I figured you'd be tired and hungry." He leaned back and smiled at me.

He'd been right about that. I'd been both of those things and my night wasn't over. I needed more information, the kind that most definitely would not be available on the Internet. I needed underworld gossip and I knew where to get it. The question was, how was I supposed to get it without alerting Ted?

If I could just maneuver him into deciding to take me where I wanted to go, I'd be golden. People call boxing the sweet science. I think it's manipulation. It's way harder to do.

"So what's the plan?" I asked, picking desultorily at a mushroom and not looking him in the eye.

"Plan for what?"

Norah made a disgusted noise in the back of her throat. "It's Saturday. It's date night. Dinner was good, but now what are you going to do?"

Ted looked from one of us to the other. "We could go to a movie or something."

I wrinkled my nose. "There's nothing I really want to see."

He drummed his fingers on his knee for a second while he thought. "How about a drink? We could go out for a drink."

This was almost too easy. I felt a pang of guilt. "That might be fun. Where would you want to go?"

"How about McClannigan's? We could stop by and say hi to Paul." Ted gave me a sweet smile.

"Great idea!" I said. "I'll go change."

That had been some low-hanging fruit I'd just picked. Still, I mentally patted myself on the back for an excellent job of covert boyfriend manipulation as I headed down the hall to my room.

NORAH WOULDN'T GO WITH US. I COULDN'T REMEMBER THE last time she'd gone out.

"She doesn't look right to me, Melina. Don't get me wrong. I'm pleased as punch that she doesn't hiss and spit every time she sees me anymore, but she's not herself." Ted looped his arm around my shoulder as we walked to his truck.

I tensed for a nanosecond. I was still adjusting to casual public displays of affection. My usual reflex to an arm across my shoulder was to grab it, whirl beneath it and give it a strong chop at the elbow. I have it on the best authority that that is not the route to getting more dates, although it is damned effective at shattering a bone. I forced myself to relax. This was nice, right? Cozy, even. "Tell me about it. I mean, what the hell is she doing home on a Saturday night? I think I can count on one hand the Saturday nights she's stayed home since high school. Since the *kiang shi*, I'm not sure she's been out on one and I don't think she's been down in Old Sacramento at all. She used to love it there."

He unlocked the truck door and held it open for me, yet another alien experience that I was adjusting to. "She has some bad memories associated with that place. She might never want to go back there." He kissed me as I slid into the truck. "Are you okay going back there?"

I nodded. He shut the door and went around to his side. I am well aware that I am not wired like other girls. It's not like I had pleasant memories about last summer's adventures in Old Sacramento. If anything, mine might be worse than Norah's. She might not have ever seen anything like the *kiang shi* before, but I related to them more than a little bit.

What had they been really but unthinking tools in someone else's cruel and vicious game? And what was I? What had happened to them? Well, I'd destroyed them. Maybe someone or something would come along and decide I was too dangerous to have around and destroy me. It wasn't completely out of the question.

Most of the time, I didn't know what I was delivering or to whom or why. I was a tool that got used and, I imagine when the time came, would be discarded when I was no longer useful.

It had pained me to destroy the *kiang shi*. Their making had not been their fault, nor had their demise. Still, they had had to be destroyed, as surely as a dog trained to kill had to be put down.

I had been trained, within an inch of my own life, to act and react without thinking. I had to fight my reflexes to get along in an everyday life and not snap my boyfriend's arm when he pulled me close as we walked down a street on a chilly night. Was I any better than they were?

I sighed. I didn't see any way out of it for the time being, so I smiled at Ted when he got in the truck and settled back for the short ride to Old Sacramento. It still felt odd and alien to lean back and let someone else drive the situation, both literally and figuratively. I wasn't entirely sure why I was okay letting Ted take that role. I certainly didn't let many other people. I bristled at people telling me what to do, even if it was something I'd wanted to do in the first place. I once rode all the way from San Jose to Sacramento with my knees practically around my ears because my mother told me to move the seat back.

I peeked over at him as he drove. I'd learned a lot about him in the last few months. I realize you're supposed to do that before you jump into bed with the guy, but our courtship was anything but normal, what with the Chinese vampires and the triad from San Francisco after us. It had seemed prudent to gather our rosebuds, so to speak, and he had gathered mine in ways that no one else had ever even bothered to try.

He'd gone into the army right after high school and had ended up as an MP. He'd gone some places that he preferred not to talk about, although whatever had happened OCONUS, or Outside the Continental United States, as they say, occasionally leaked out in his dreams. I hadn't brought it up, but then again, he hadn't brought up my occasional thrashing in the arms of Morpheus either. We all have our baggage, it seems.

Anyway, after five years in the military, he'd gotten out with enough money to go to school. After getting his degree in criminology at San Jose State, he'd landed a spot in the Sacramento PD. Which had led to him looking into an anonymous phone call about a gang fight, which had led him to my doorstep.

And the rest, as they say, is history.

MCCLANNIGAN'S WAS HOPPING. IT ALWAYS WAS ON A SATURday. It was one of those places in Sacramento that the young and the beautiful could come to meet and greet. It had also been in business for more than a hundred and sixty years. For well over a hundred of them, our friend Paul had bartended here.

I keep waiting for someone to figure it out. A manager. An accountant. Somebody at some point was going to notice either that his work history with the bar stretched back into the 1800s or that there was a faded sepia-toned photograph of him tending the bar in a starched white collar and bow tie gracing the hall down to the bathroom. So far, however, no one had.

I also wondered if some day someone would notice that Paul was a werewolf. I knew it the second I laid eyes on him, but then again he tripped my sensors at a pretty high rate of vibration, and werewolf is a very definite signature. For a regular person, he'd be hard to detect.

The Sierra pack's Alpha, Chuck Winterthorpe, wasn't a fool. He didn't let werewolves from his pack out to play with the general populace unless they had a high degree of personal control. Paul made playing human look effortless. Every once in a while, in moments of stress, I could see the beast inside him, but I think most people just thought he was a little grumpy.

Right now, however, despite the fact that the bar was packed with guys and girls wearing an overload of perfume and cologne and exuding a thick miasma of pheromones that made my eyes start to tear up, I saw Paul scent the air the second that Ted and I walked into the bar. It was kind of cute how he wrinkled his nose when something made him take notice.

He raised his head and his gaze swiveled to us in a heartbeat. He smiled and waved. Ted waved back and guided me through the crowd to a narrow space at the bar with his hand on my back. More than a few women looked our way as we wove through the throng. I controlled my urge to hiss at them, but just barely. It really wasn't their fault. Ted was hard not to look at. He, however, seemed entirely oblivious to the attention. I supposed I should be grateful it didn't go to his head.

"Hey, Paul," Ted said. They bumped fists.

I shook my head. The two of them had bonded during last summer's adventures. It didn't sit well with me. It messed with my ability to compartmentalize when my boyfriend was fist-bumping with my favorite werewolf (which was truly damning with faint praise) and general source of all good supernatural gossip.

Paul set a beer down in front of Ted and mixed a white wine spritzer for me. I looked at the drink and then back at him. "You can't be serious."

Paul always micromanages my drinking. He has a tendency to hand me light beers and diet colas, which is insulting enough in its own way, but a white wine spritzer? Seriously? It was something one of my mother's bridge partners would drink.

"I thought I'd give you something girlier tonight. You look a little girlier than usual." He grinned at me, and I could see a touch of the wolf in the glint in his eyes.

I did look a little girlier than usual. Norah had refused to come out with us, but she had sent me out dressed as her proxy. Instead of my usual jeans, boots and black turtleneck, I had on a top with a very deep V-neck that flowed from a high waistline down to the top of my low-cut jeans. It was light blue and had something sparkly in it. Oh, and heels instead of my usual boots or sneakers. I was even wearing mascara *and* lipstick. It had earned me a low wolf whistle from Ted when I'd come out into the living room. I didn't need one from an actual wolf.

Ted leaned on one elbow and looked back and forth between the two of us. "She's not driving," he offered.

Paul shook his head. "She still needs to keep her senses sharp." He bared his teeth at me. It might have looked like a smile to someone else, but I knew better. It was a show of power and a message about who was in control.

Paul was all about power and control because a werewolf in a pack was all about them. The Pack taught discipline, respect and restraint, all things werewolves need if they're going to be around 'Danes, as we call those people who think they inhabit a world without magic or mythical creatures. You wouldn't want a werewolf without a pack around other Arcanes for that matter either. Without the qualities that the Pack taught and enforced, a werewolf would most likely go rogue, which would be like letting a feral dog loose in a crowded theater and then setting it on fire. Lots of blood. Lots of tears. Probably a dead werewolf and lots of dead people. It wasn't a scenario that anyone would want to see happen. And talk about a public relations nightmare! Werewolves aren't supposed to exist, after all. Then again, neither are vampires or goblins or Messengers like me.

Still, the idea of the Pack got under my skin a little. The idea of handing over my freewill and offering unquestioning obedience bugged me. I get the heebie-jeebies at Disneyland when I feel like I'm being manipulated into having fun. Try to explain this to my mother, who paid perfectly good money just to have me cringe away from the pretty princesses as if they had STDs. She's still irritated with me and that was fifteen years ago.

I considered growling at Paul to give him as good as I was getting, but thought better of it since I was planning on asking him for information the second I could do it without Ted hearing.

So we chitchatted at the bar. Or, to be honest, Ted and Paul chitchatted while I pretended to listen and looked for an excuse to send Ted off somewhere on an errand so I could talk to Paul alone. Luckily, he decided to head to the little cop's room. The second he did, I leaned over the bar to get Paul's attention.

"Easy there, girl," he said. "Your ta-tas are spilling out on my bar."

I reached down and readjusted my top. That would never have happened if I'd been wearing a turtleneck, not unless my boobs acquired a life of their own and crawled out on their own accord. Which I suppose was possible. I'd heard of weirder things than someone's boobs becoming possessed. My point is, it would have taken more than just a little gravity to have them spilling out on the bar. "I need to ask you a question."

There were reasons I often went to Paul for information. First of all, as a werewolf, he covered a pretty large range of territory. Paul's wolf form was larger than your average wolf and he could and did travel long distances over rough ground just for the sheer joy of it. Second, he was tapped into whatever the Pack was tapped into, and that was pretty much everything. Chuck didn't get to be six or seven hundred years old without learning to appreciate the value of a good intelligence network. He was probably one of the best-informed leaders of any of the supernatural groups in the area. The vampires were generally only interested in information that pertained to them directly. As the two most sentient groups, they were always my first choices for information and the Pack was definitely superior to the Seethe in that regard.

Third, the dude was a bartender at an absurdly popular nightspot. He was crazy observant, because hunters have to be, and trust me, if you don't think a werewolf is a hunter, you've never seen one take down prey, human or otherwise. A guy can learn a lot by being observant in a place like McClannigan's. He can notice trends and hear about all kinds of funny little things before they hit the awareness of the general populace.

"Shoot," he said. "What do you need to know?"

"Are you hearing about anything weird down around Elmville?"

Paul frowned. "Where the hell is Elmville?"

"A little east of Manteca."

He snorted. "Beyond freakin' Egypt, then."

I nodded.

Paul polished a glass, a thoughtful look on his face, then he shook his head. "Not that I can think of. Why? What's up?"

I shook my head. "I'm not sure. Recipients of two deliveries I've made up there have turned up dead under strange circumstances. It made me a little nervous. I thought I'd check into it."

Paul's polishing slowed. "Have you ever heard the phrase 'once bitten, twice shy,' little one?"

It seemed like a funny phrase for a werewolf to mention. In their case, it was more like 'once bitten, never shy again.' Seriously. Shapeshifters will get naked in front of anyone at almost any time. They have no modesty whatsoever. "Of course I have. What are you trying to say?"

He set the glass down very carefully and leaned across the bar. I could feel his warm breath on my bare neck. Yet another reason to wear turtlenecks. "You're a Messenger. Your job is to deliver the messages. It is not your job to stick your pretty little nose into whatever happens after that. I would think you would have figured that out by now."

His teeth, although still very human-sized and -shaped, were way closer to my jugular vein than I was completely comfortable with. I stayed still as a statue even though every survival instinct in my dinosaur brain was screaming for me to run. Run from a natural predator and you're likely to get chased. It's hard as hell to stay still sometimes, but it's often your best avenue to survival. "Are you threatening me?"

Paul took one more sniff of my neck and stood back up. "I don't have to. I'm just reminding you of how the world—our world—works."

"That'd be peachy if I only lived in one world. I've got my feet pretty firmly planted in both," I reminded him.

He spread his arms wide, taking in the bar. "And I don't?"

As if I had the choices he had. He didn't have to work here. He chose to. "It's not the same and you know it."

"All the more reason for you to keep your nose clean in both worlds and the best way to do that is to not stick it where it doesn't belong."

I leaned across the bar and asked what was really bothering me. "What if what I took to those boys got them killed?"

Paul shrugged his thick shoulders. "What if it did?"

His nonchalance left me thunderstruck. "Then I'm somehow responsible."

"You're no more responsible than the Western Union is when they deliver bad news in a telegram. Let this go, Melina. No good will come of you meddling in whatever it is. It could just be a coincidence, anyway."

I gave him a baleful look. "Do you really believe that?"

"Nope," he said and grinned. "I thought it might make you feel better, though, and then you might be willing to drop it."

I saw Ted shouldering his way back through the crowd. Time to wrap this conversation up. "I will take it under advisement."

"You do that, Melina." His eyes softened. When the wolf left him completely, they were like dark pools of chocolate, and the wolf was completely gone now. "It would pain me if something happened to you."

I knew what it meant for Paul to say that to someone who was not Pack. I was left momentarily and uncharacteristically speechless. I set my hand on top of his on the bar. He covered it with his other hand, large and warm and rough. He moved away as Ted returned to the bar.

"Another beer?"

Ted shook his head. "She may not be driving, but I am."

Fabulous. Caught between a wolf and a Boy Scout. I almost wished there was a rock nearby.

"You ready to go?" I asked.

He nodded and we both slipped off our bar stools.

"Hey," Paul said, stopping me before I turned to go. "Say hello to Alex for me if you see him. He hasn't been around lately."

Another surprise. "Alex has been hanging out here?" During our problems with the *kiang shi*, Alex and Paul had developed a somewhat improbable friendship as well. Improbable because vampires and werewolves generally don't care for each other. I've yet to decide whether it's because they're too similar or too different. Both tend to be dominant, controlling and passionate, but where a werewolf is all hot-blooded animal instinct, a vampire is all cold-blooded charm and manipulation.

Paul looked around the room. "This is as good a hunting ground as any."

True that. The room was filled with beautiful young people out on the prowl. The pheromones were so thick in the air, a person could choke on them. It would be a sweet perfume for Alex. I'd seen him turn on the charm. He hunted with seduction, not brute strength.

"I'll tell him you've been looking for him when I see him," I said.

"You do that. Tell him I said that all work and no play makes for a very hungry vampire and you know where that can lead."

Actually, I wasn't sure, but I didn't think it was to any place particularly good.

AS WE GOT IN BED, TED ASKED, "SO DID YOU FIND OUT WHAT you needed to know from Paul?"

I froze in the act of reaching for the alarm clock. "What do you mean?" Playing stupid is one of my first fallback positions. It works with insulting frequency.

He shrugged and kissed the top of my head. "It's why we went to McClannigan's, isn't it? Because you needed to ask Paul something?" He settled back on the pillows.

I finished setting the alarm. I could dissemble, pretend I didn't know what he was talking about, but I didn't want to insult him. "What gave me away?"

He pulled me over on top of him and kissed me. "Pretty much everything. You're a good liar, but I've spent some time watching you."

"Oh, you have, have you?" I kissed him back, letting my lips linger on his for a delicious moment.

"Mmm-hmm. I have. Plus, I spent a reasonable portion of my life needing to look for underlying motivations in people's reactions." He slid his hands up under the oversized T-shirt I wore, and I felt a trail of goose bumps rise under the trail of his touch.

I trailed my fingers down his chest. "I like it when you use big words."

"Don't change the subject." His hands circled my waist and settled me more firmly onto his lap. I let out a small gasp and he smiled. "I'm not crazy about being manipulated."

I bit my lip and rocked a little. He groaned. "I'm sorry," I said, and leaned down to kiss him again.

"I'll consider accepting your apology if you'll consider being truthful with me." His hands slid up my body, cupping my breasts. His thumbs began to make lazy circles around my nipples. I rocked against him again, this time completely as a reflex.

He kissed my neck. "Why are you setting the alarm? I thought Sunday was your morning to sleep in."

Usually it was and I treasured it, but Elmville was a longish drive and the memorial service started at three. Not exactly anything I wanted to explain to Ted. "No rest for the wicked, you know?" I let my head fall back. It was getting hard to concentrate on my witty banter, such as it was.

"Mmm," he murmured. "I like it when you're wicked."

He was already naked, so it was perfectly evident that he liked it. He slid his hands along my back, pulling me closer and then he froze. "You've got a delivery to make." He let his hands drop and looked at me, his eyes narrowed slightly.

I wiggled closer and nipped his chin. "Not exactly."

He pushed me away and held me at arm's length. "But it's Messenger business, isn't it?"

I stopped trying to use my feminine wiles to distract him. I didn't have a lot of practice with them and apparently they weren't all that distracting. Perhaps Mae should have taught me eye-batting along with fist strikes. "Yes. It's Messenger business."

"Where are you going?"

I didn't say anything. I barely even breathed. If I told him where I was going, he was going to know it had something to do with Bossard's death. If I told him I was going somewhere else and he found out . . . again, those flat-out lies into those blue eyes didn't sit well with me.

He sighed and kissed me. "How am I supposed to protect you if I don't know where you are?"

It took some effort, but I didn't laugh. "I don't need any protection. It's not a big deal."

Truth was, smart money would bet on me in any fight. Oh, sure, not at first glance. At first glance, it would be smart to bet on the six foot three inch surfer god with the abs of Ryan Reynolds. Spend a few minutes watching us in action, though, and you'd change your bet faster than I could get him in a headlock, which is pretty darn fast. I am faster, stronger and most definitely meaner than Ted.

I was also not used to having anyone trying to protect me. In this particular case, I was worried that having someone there trying to protect me would put everyone in more danger. I was planning on being discreet.

I kissed my way down his chin to his neck and then to his chest and then lower still. I paused. "I think I might know a way to make it up to you."

He slid the T-shirt over my head. "They do say that to forgive is divine."

Maybe my feminine wiles aren't so bad after all.

THE NEXT MORNING, TED LEFT FOR HIS SHIFT WHISTLING AND I hit the shower. Afterward, I stood in front of my closet wrapped in a towel. It was like I'd been preparing my wardrobe to attend memorial services my whole life. I had plenty of appropriate choices. Black pants. Black skirts. Black dresses. You name it, I had it in black. I settled on a knee-length black skirt and soft gray sweater that belted at the waist. I pulled on black hose and a pair of kitten-heel pumps. I wasn't much for stilettos. They messed too much with my sense of balance. I said a small prayer of thanks to Michelle Obama for making low heels fashionable again. I brushed my hair into a low ponytail, glossed my lips and was ready to go.

Neil Bossard would be laid to rest at the Memorial Lawn Cemetery in Elmville at three o'clock this afternoon. A reception would follow at his parents' home. I should be able to make it to both and still easily make it back for my shift at the hospital tonight. It was a good thing I didn't need much sleep.

Norah was in the kitchen reading the Sunday paper and drinking coffee. She looked me up and down. "You look like you're going to a funeral."

"Don't I always?" I poured myself a cup of coffee and sat down next to her.

She tapped her mug against mine. "True that. So where are you going?"

"To a funeral."

She snorted, which was infinitely better than having her panic over who had died and why and if any vampires had been involved.

"How about you? You getting out of here today?" I grabbed a section of newspaper.

Norah pressed her lips together in a straight line. "Where would I go?"

I shrugged. "I don't know. Yoga class, maybe. The grocery store. Over to Tina's. Someplace besides the apartment or work."

"You're seriously going to lecture me about holing up in the apartment? Do you want me to get you a kettle to talk to, Pot?"

She had a point. I had some hermit-ish qualities myself. It was, however, different. I wasn't staying in because I was scared to go out. "It's daytime. He's not out there. He's home, hidden behind blackout curtains, and will be until the sun goes down."

"Fine. He's not out there, but what else is? I know there's a bunch of stuff that can come out in daylight."

"True enough, but they were out there before and it never bothered you," I pointed out.

She flung her hands in the air. "Because I didn't know any better! Now I know."

But she didn't really. That was part of the problem, too. Most of what was out there was never going to go near Norah. The majority of 'Canes didn't want anything to do with 'Danes. Mundanes were to be avoided. Detection could cause major inconveniences at best and death or total eradication at worst. Of course there were exceptions. Alex and his fellow vampires were a good example of that. 'Danes were food. They were there to be stalked, hunted and preyed upon. The trick was to do it without detection. But while vampires and werewolves were hunters, not everything else was. A lot of the Arcane world were just folks trying to get along. Weird folks. Folks with magical abilities, but in the end, folks not much different than most of the folks in the Mundane world.

For Norah, her little bit of knowledge of what was out there in the Arcane world had scared her half to death. If she really understood, she might not be quite as afraid. "You don't really know what's out there, though, do you?"

"I know enough." She took a long swig of coffee and grimaced.

"No. I don't think you do. If you did, you wouldn't be letting it screw with your head like this." I couldn't believe it hadn't occurred to me before. What was scarier than the unknown? Poor Norah's whole perception of the world had been thrown out of whack. She didn't know what to expect around the next corner. A little bit of knowledge was a dangerous thing. A whole lot of knowledge, however, could be quite helpful.

I went back to my room and dragged a box out from underneath my bed. The book I was looking for was near the bottom, underneath a collection of the various belts that I'd gone through in my years as Mae's student. I fingered the frayed edge of my white belt with its orange stripes. I remembered the day that Mae had tied it on me, showing me how to loop it properly. I'd been so little, she'd knelt on the floor in front of me to tie it. "This is a new beginning for you, Melina," she'd said.

I'd nodded. I'd been seven, but not stupid. This lady was different from other people. She didn't make my skin feel funny the way the strange things that nobody else seemed to see did, but she made me feel different than my mom or my teachers or my aunt. I'd felt safe with her in a different way.

I put the belt back in the box, shut it and shoved it back under the bed. Mae had changed my life when she had come into it. She'd made things make sense. Her leaving my life had made everything make a little less sense, but there was nothing I could do but cope with it. The knowledge that she'd given me had helped me be less afraid. Maybe a little more knowledge would help Norah, too.

I came back out, plopped the book in front of Norah and said,

"As long as you're not doing anything today, I think you should read this."

She picked up the book and read the title. "*A Grimoire of Northern California*." She looked up at me, her head tilted to one side.

"It will help you make sense of a lot of stuff. At least you'll know what you should be afraid of and what you don't need to worry about."

She still looked doubtful.

"Just try it," I said. "It can't hurt you to try."

And with that, I hit the road.

I WASN'T SURE WHO HAD MENTIONED MY CAR TO THE COPS and if they would be at Neil Bossard's memorial service or not, but I didn't think it was wise to take chances. I parked on the other side of the cemetery and hoofed it over to where the service was taking place. As a result, I was late. This is not exactly a news flash. I'm late a lot. It's rarely my fault, or so I maintain. It's hard to be on time when you never know what's going to pop up and insist you deliver something to the opposite side of town right away.

This time was my own fault. I shouldn't have spent so much time with Norah this morning, but it wasn't exactly right to let her sit there in the apartment and stew.

When I got there, it wasn't hard to blend in. There was a huge crowd. Elmville wasn't that big. Half the town must have turned out for young Neil's burial. There was a fairly large age range, with quite a few young people present. Lots of pretty young girls holding tissues to their faces. Lots of young men staring resolutely at the horizon and not meeting anyone's eyes while they clenched their jaws.

"That Neil should be taken from us so soon after he had been returned to us seems like the greatest cruelty," the minister intoned from the graveside. I made a mental note. I needed to find out where Neil Bossard had been. "So many times when someone as young as Neil dies, people ask me how God can be so cruel."

I figured the middle-aged couple standing nearest the minister must be Neil's parents. His mother's face was chalk-white, her pain etched indelibly on her face. My own heart clenched a little as I watched her try and control herself. His father was a somewhat older version of the clench-jawed young men around us. He had the added duty, however, of making sure that his wife's knees didn't buckle beneath her. Next to him was an older woman in a wheelchair. Of the three, she seemed most clear-eyed and in control. Perhaps when you got to a certain age and had seen death enough times, it was easier to put it in perspective.

On the other hand, I didn't think there was any perspective where it would seem right for a parent to bury a child. It was one of those moments in the universe where one felt everything must have been turned upside down. Even someone who had seen a lot of death would see that.

One thing I didn't see as I looked around the crowd was much in the way of brown skin. In fact, I was pretty much the brownest person there and I'm not all that dark. I'm an olive-skinned gal, and in the summer I darken to a nice light mahogany. In California, that does not generally entitle me to a brown designation.

Everyone comes to California from everywhere. We're a popular destination worldwide. We've got everything: mountains, oceans, valleys, agriculture, show business, computer geeks and hippies. Not everybody stays. Generally about a hundred thousand or so more people leave than put down roots, but that still leaves a pretty diverse group. As a result, I don't often see a really homogeneous crowd like the one I was looking at right now. This group was white and nothing but white. When I stick out as looking ethnic, you know the crowd is vanilla. I shrugged it off. I hadn't studied the demographics of Elmville. Maybe I was seeing a reflection of what the town was like.

I'd stopped listening to the minister and was somewhat startled to realize he'd stopped speaking. The crowd had started moving. Person after person made their way to the graveside to toss in a single flower, say a few words to Bossard's parents and grandmother and then walk down to where the cars lined the road. I decided to circle back to the Buick and then follow the crowd, at a discreet distance of course, back to the Bossard home.

There have been moments when my continued well-being depended on catching a movement from the corner of my eye and reacting quickly. As I crossed the cemetery, the breeze picked up and something swirled in the corner of my vision. I whirled into a defensive crouch. Well, not quite a crouch. My skirt was kind of straight and that pretty much took crouching out of the stance equation, but I lowered my center of gravity enough that I'd be able to take on anything that came from any direction.

Then I felt like an idiot. A young woman who was crying stood behind a tree down the hill a short distance. The breeze had blown a few strands of her jet-black hair into the wind. I straightened back up. I doubted I needed to take on hair. The woman whose head it was attached to didn't seem like much of a threat at first either. Her face was soft and unlined and she seemed as afraid of being seen as anything else. I pretended I hadn't seen her and that my sudden change in stance was due to having my heel sink into the soft ground of the cemetery, which was not a total stretch of the imagination. I'd been walking on my toes already to keep my shoes from sinking down with each step.

I kept walking now, keeping my gaze steady and forward. I let my other senses reach out toward the woman and nearly stumbled.

Whoever she was, she wasn't an ordinary bystander. There was definite power there. It wasn't the kind of sensation I got when I was near Paul or Alex though. I didn't think she was a werewolf or any other kind of supernatural being. She had magic in her, but she was fully human. Whatever she was, she was powerful and she was full of hate.

I FOLLOWED THE LINE OF CARS TO NEIL BOSSARD'S PARENTS' house. I knew where it was already. I'd been there once before, after all. It was where I'd delivered the package that I'd found on the hood of the Buick, address neatly printed in block letters. The house looked pretty much as I remembered it. It was a nice house in a nice area, kind of like my parents' place. Two stories, big well-tended yard, rose bushes along the clapboard siding, a driveway leading to a detached garage. The backyard was fenced. I'd lay odds there was a pool back there. My aunt Kitty would have called it neocolonial. I felt a little suffocated just looking at it and I drove past. I still didn't need my car being noticed again.

I cut over a few blocks south on Atlas Drive and then another two on Dixon Drive and parked. I kicked back and waited a bit. I didn't want to be one of the first guests to arrive or one of the last. I needed to arrive as part of that pack that seems to always get to an event at the same time. I'd slide in with a group and no one would even notice me.

I wasn't sure what I thought I was going to find, but I needed to start somewhere. It's not like anybody was likely to dish the dirt about a young man who died under such tragic circumstances at his memorial service, but I was betting that enough crumbs would fall to guide me to my next step.

I walked the few blocks to the house. My timing was perfect. Several clumps of people were heading toward the house from various directions. All of them walked along without talking, heads down. A few people held hands. It was easy enough to fall into step with one group. I chose one that looked vaguely like a family: a middle-aged couple and a young man and a young woman who looked like they might be in their late teens or early twenties. I stayed a few steps back so I didn't crowd them, but I was still close enough to look like I might be part of them. As if I were maybe the petulant daughter who was being dragged along against her wishes. I knew the part inside out. Just ask my mother.

It's easy enough to attach yourself to a group like that. If anyone in the group notices you, they simply assume you're going to the same place they are and belong there. Anyone outside the group assumes you're with the people you're entering with. The key is to blend. I've spent a lot of my life trying to blend with varying degrees of success. As long as it's purely an external thing, I do okay.

Blending at a funeral is apparently second nature to me. My outfit looked identical to pretty much everyone else's and no one was flashing big white-toothed California smiles. Perhaps I had finally found my people? The dour-faced somber-colored clothes people? I shook my head. Didn't it just figure? I'd spent a lifetime looking out of place in my black clothes while living in perpetual sunshine, with people always telling me to smile. I should have just hung out at the mortuary. My mother would definitely not have been thrilled.

I slid in with the group and edged my way into the crowded living room. I felt a little like I had at the one junior high dance I'd been coerced into attending. I was in a room full of people and didn't have a word to say to any one of them. I did pretty much what I did then, too. I leaned against the wall and watched.

The old lady in the wheelchair was holding court in one corner, a cup of tea on the side table next to her and a plate of untouched cookies in her lap.

"Can I get you anything, Mom?" Bossard's father asked her.

"No, dear. I'm fine." She patted the hand he'd placed on her shoulder. "Or as fine as I can be, I guess."

Mr. Bossard nodded, his Adam's apple jerking up and down in his throat. It didn't look like he was fine or would be for quite some time. I felt a stab of pity followed by a quick twist of guilt. I'd like nothing more than to find out that the package I'd delivered to Neil Bossard had nothing to do with his death. I so didn't want to be associated with causing anyone this kind of pain.

I edged along the room, picking up bits and pieces of conversations. "A shame, really. One mistake and he never gets a chance to come back from it," a woman my mother's age was saying to another woman. They both wore knee-length skirts and sensible shoes. One's hair was bobbed and silvery blonde, the other's was longer, darker and pulled back in a low ponytail.

"It was a pretty big mistake, Diane," Ponytail pointed out.

Bobbed Blonde shook her head and took a sip of tea. "I never thought that he was one of the ringleaders. He got caught up in something and didn't know how to get out of it."

Ponytail sighed. "And now look at poor Georgia. I thought he'd broken her heart before. He's smashed it now." They both looked over to where Mrs. Bossard stood near the dining room table, serving tea, then both looked down into their own cups.

They had a point. Mrs. Bossard looked like a zombie. Not a real zombie. They generally had rotting flesh hanging off them and lurched around trying to eat people's brains. Perhaps "sleepwalker" would be a better description of Neil Bossard's mother at the moment. Her face had settled into a stunned expression, her movements seemed automatic and a little jerky as she passed people cups and gestured toward the cream, lemon and sugar.

I shifted farther along the wall. A clump of younger people massed in one of the corners. My best guess is that they were only a few years younger than me, probably friends of Neil's. I thought I recognized one or two of them from his MySpace page.

"It's creeping me out," one of the girls said, swinging her dark blonde hair back over her shoulder. "First Kurt and now Neil? I don't see how that can be a coincidence."

Fabulous. I wasn't the only one who had put those two deaths together. I wondered who else had and why.

"Do you think it was a suicide pact?" another girl asked.

One of the boys brushed the question aside. "How could it be a pact? Neither of them could stand to even be in a room with the other one after they got back. How would they have made a pact?"

Tears filled the girl's eyes. "I don't know, but there's got to be a reason they both, you know . . ."

"Offed themselves?" The boy finished for her. He crossed his arms over his chest and glared. "They were a couple of whiney little bitches, is what they where. Only cowards kill themselves."

"Eric!" The blonde put her hand on his chest. "Don't talk like that."

"I'm just telling the truth. First, there was all that skulking around and talking about people looking at them. They both did that. Of course people were looking at them. They'd been gone for six years. Even people who didn't know what happened knew they'd come back from someplace else. Then all that weird shit about someone cursing them. Nobody cursed them. There isn't any such thing as a curse. They did it to themselves. All of it."

Eric turned and stomped away from the group. The blonde started to follow him, but one of the other boys stopped her. "I'll go."

So both boys had thought someone had been following them. Both boys had thought someone was cursing them. But why? What had they done? What had happened six years before? Where had the boys gone and why had they come back?

The group broke up. Everywhere else I inched I heard conversations about the weather and real estate prices, both hot topics at most cocktail parties. I thanked my lucky stars I didn't have to attend many.

I decided it was time to put the riskier portion of my plan into play. It was time to do some actual snooping and not just eavesdropping. I inched my way along to the staircase leading to the second floor.

I was halfway up the stairs when I caught the first faint hum of the vibration. It wasn't very strong, but it was definitely there. There was something on the second floor. I flattened myself against the wall as two women made their way down the stairs. It gave me a second to evaluate what I might be facing. One of them smiled at me as she went past. "Second door on the left," she whispered.

I smiled and nodded. It never hurts to know where the bathroom is. Then I refocused my attention on the vibration. It felt like a thing, not a being. Perhaps what I'd delivered to Neil Bossard was still in the house. I made my way to the top of the stairs. I stood for a second, feeling with my senses which way to turn. The room at the end of the hallway felt right. I glanced down the stairs. No one else seemed to be making their way to the bathroom, but with all the tea-drinking going on, I might not have a lot of time. I walked quickly down the hall and slipped into the room.

It only took a few seconds for my eyes to refocus in the dim light. I glanced around the room. There wasn't much on the walls, and the shelves and desk were bare. The bed had a blue plaid bedspread and a wooden headboard. It seemed so generic. Then again, Bossard hadn't been home long from wherever he'd been. I guess wherever it was, he hadn't wanted to bring home any souvenirs.

The hum was stronger here. I closed my eyes and let my senses guide me. I headed toward the bed. There was nothing on the bedside table. I opened the drawer and found nothing there. I got down on my hands and knees and lifted the bed skirt to look beneath the bed.

Bingo.

It was still in the box I'd delivered it in. It was small. No bigger than an index card and not much thicker than a deck of cards. Neil had never even opened it. I wondered how it had gotten under the bed and then shook my head. I didn't even know what was in the box, but I knew how objects of power worked. Seemingly inanimate, seemingly with no will or volition of their own, they often ended up exactly where they needed to be. Someone dropped a box on the floor. Someone else accidentally kicked it. Suddenly it was under the bed of whoever it was intended for, working whatever magic, good or ill, that its maker intended.

I reached for it. Damn. It was just out of reach. If only my arms were another inch or two longer, I could get it. I craned my head under the bed. I could almost slip it under the frame. My fingers brushed the box. I scraped my fingernails along the edge and caught a fold in the brown paper that covered it and pulled it toward me. I slumped with the relief of my success.

"Hey! What the hell are you doing?" a voice demanded from behind me.

I then executed a complicated series of maneuvers that I don't think I could possibly reproduce or even explain. Suffice it to say that I managed to both bash my head against the underside of the bed and scrape my face along the carpet. I also, however, managed to palm the box up into the sleeve of my sweater.

I stood. The voice belonged to a young man and I use the term *man* loosely. He was maybe seventeen at the most, but he was tall and solid looking.

"Hi," I said, giving my most disarming smile. "How's it going?"

"What were you doing under there?" He crossed his arms over his chest and scowled.

Apparently my most disarming smile was about as effective as my feminine wiles. "I was, uh, looking for the bathroom."

"Under the bed?" The scowl turned to a look of incredulity. I couldn't decide if that was progress or not.

"Well, of course not. Don't be silly. I, uh, came in here by mistake and then I, uh, dropped an earring." He was standing smack dab in the center of the doorway. The only way out was straight through him. I could definitely take him. First of all, he wouldn't be expecting it, and surprise was always a wonderful weapon. Second, despite him looking solid, he was only solid for a seventeen-year-old. That's not all that solid. Still, it wasn't a course I really wanted to take. I'd planned on being discreet. I like to stick to the plan whenever possible. Barreling over a seventeen-year-old on the second floor and then hightailing it out of the house didn't really sound discreet to me.

He squinted. "You've still got both your earrings in your ears."

I reached up to check my lobes. "Yep! Found it! Isn't that great?" I started walking toward him, hoping he would shift out of my way.

"Who are you anyway?" He didn't shift. Bummer.

"I'm Melina. I'm, uh, I was a friend of Neil's." I tried to put just the right hesitation on it so that I sounded still surprised and regretful that he was dead.

"A friend from where? I don't recognize you from around here."

I guess I didn't get the spin right. "No," I said. "Not from around here."

"You're from there, then?" It didn't sound like it would be a good thing to be from "there," wherever and whatever it was. It sounded a little like it might be a leper colony.

"Not exactly," I said, figuring it was best to be as noncommittal as possible.

His eyes still narrowed, he finally stepped out of the door. "I think you'd better go," he said.

"Well, okay then," I said.

I slipped past him into the hallway, which was when the commotion started downstairs.

One voice said, "Don't you see? They're coming for me next. Somebody's got to help me. Why won't you help me?"

I couldn't make out what the answer was, but it was a deep male rumble that didn't sound welcoming.

Bouncer Boy brushed past me and took the stairs two at a time. I followed more slowly, but not by much. I wanted to see what was going on just as much as he did, but I didn't want to rip my skirt.

A young man stood at the doorway to the house. A ring of men prevented him from entering any farther. The entryway was virtually invisible from the living room because of the retaining wall on that side. No one could really see what was going on and the buzz inside the house from dozens of conversations masked any noise.

"You have a lot of nerve showing up here, Littlefield," Mr. Bossard said, keeping his voice low regardless. "You need to leave and you need to leave now."

"Please," Littlefield begged. "Listen to me. They've cursed us or something. You've got to see that. This can't be a coincidence. I'm next. Don't you see I'm next?"

"All I see is the person who ruined my son's life now here tainting his funeral. Get out." Mr. Bossard shoved the boy back. "Get out before my wife sees you. She doesn't need your sorry ass here reminding her of what started all this in the first place. I knew I should have forbidden Neil to be around you. You're nothing but bad news, Littlefield."

Littlefield stumbled backward, holding his hands up in front of himself to ward off any more blows. "Please, Mr. Bossard. You gotta help me. Somebody's gotta help me."

"Like you helped my boy end up in prison? I said get out and I meant it, you little piece of shit." Bossard advanced. The group of men around me closed ranks behind him. Whatever Littlefield wanted, he wasn't going to get it, and no one from inside the house was going to help him.

He must have figured that out because with one last desperate look, he turned and fled.

My friend from the upstairs bedroom then whispered something in Mr. Bossard's ear. He turned and looked at me where I stood, halfway down the stairs. The look he gave me was unmistakable. I'd worn out my welcome here.

I held up my hands in front of me and said, "I got it. Time to go."

I headed directly to the door, walking past the line of men standing with their arms crossed and glaring.

Right before I crossed the threshold, someone gave me a little shove to send me on my way. I stumbled and righted myself.

Now I was on my way out the door. What's more, I was doing it peacefully. That little shove was just plain mean and as far as I'm concerned, mean people suck.

I whirled. One of the men reached toward me as if he were going to grab me by my jacket. I knocked his hand to one side and gave him an uppercut to the solar plexus. He doubled over and gasped for air.

Another one tried to grab my arm. I twisted my arm around his and broke his grasp and then swept his legs from underneath him.

They hadn't expected a girl to fight back. The other men backed away, their hands raised in front of them. I didn't wait around for them to marshal their forces. I whipped the door open and ran down the steps.

The door slammed behind me and I fell directly into the arms of Officer Ted Goodnight.

I looked up at him. He looked down at me. In unison, we said, "What the hell are you doing here?"

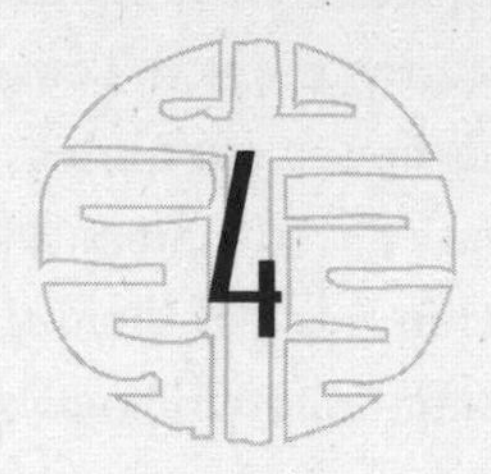

"YOU FIRST," TED DEMANDED, RIGHTING ME AS I STUMBLED on those damn kitten heels. I knew better than to try to be fashionable. I should leave that stuff to Norah.

"Why? Why don't you go first?" I craned around him to see if I could get a license plate or something to identify the young man who was running away. I didn't hear a car, though. The sun had already begun to set and the light was growing dim. It was often a good thing that I could see like a cat in the darkness, but if there was nothing to see, then it didn't help much.

Ted put his hands on his hips and said, "Because I'm the law."

I snorted and stood tall in front of him until we were nearly nose to nose or, more accurately, nose to chest. He had a solid six inches on me height-wise. "Not in these parts, you aren't, Mr. Sacramento PD. I think you're way out of your jurisdiction, in more ways than one."

He looked down at me, not budging, and shook his head.

"They'll understand why I'm here faster than they'll understand why you're here."

I took a deep breath and blew it out slowly. Sometimes I could distract him, but not if I went into full confrontation mode. "Fine. I'm willing to make a deal, but first, did you see the kid who came running out of the house ahead of me?"

"The one who got tossed from the memorial service right before you did?" He squinted a little. It was his deep-thought face. He got the same look right before he picked a flavor of ice cream. Bless his heart, he almost always went with chocolate chip cookie dough, but he gave it serious deliberation before he did.

"The very one."

"Why'd he get tossed?" He relaxed his stance a little. I was going to get my way. I rubbed my mental hands together with evil glee. I figured it was bad form to do it for real.

"I don't know. He was ranting and raving about being cursed and they booted him out. They booted me out right afterward." That little shove on the doorstep had been totally unnecessary. I wondered if Bouncer Boy was the one who'd done it. It seemed kind of petty for the grown men that had been surrounding the door.

"Oh, yeah. Why did you get the boot?" Ted squinted at me now, as if trying to make his mind up.

I sighed. "Someone caught me looking under the deceased's bed."

He pivoted toward the street and slung his arm around me. "Is it any wonder that I love you? Now, where are you parked? I didn't see your car anywhere close."

I froze. Unable for a moment to take a step forward, perhaps maybe to breathe. Had he just said what I thought he'd said? Was that a declaration of love?

In all fairness, the man had literally risked his life for me. And his job. And had been put in doubt of his very sanity. Those are all good indicators that a guy is pretty into you. Still, he had never used the actual *L* word. Like I said, long-term romantic relationships haven't exactly been my forte. Did that count as an actual *I love you*? Or was that more something a person would say the first time they bit into my mother's noodle kugel?

"Are you coming?" Ted looked down at me, bemused.

I was glad darkness had fallen, so he couldn't see the expression on my face. Or, at least, I assumed he couldn't. He did not see like a cat and I was glad of it at the moment. "Yeah, sure," I said, and stumbled forward.

"So spill." Ted kept his arm around my shoulders as we walked.

A deal was a deal. "You know how Bossard died not too long after I made a delivery to him?"

"You mean that coincidence thing you mentioned the other day?" His tone was more than a little sarcastic. I knew I deserved it, so I let it go.

"I was afraid that maybe whatever I'd delivered had caused his death somehow. I wanted to sniff around the situation and make sure I didn't have anything to do with it."

He stiffened but kept walking. "And do you think your delivery did have anything to do with it?"

"I'm not sure yet. I found the package I delivered for him unopened under his bed. Some guy—his brother, I think—caught me as I was fishing it out. I haven't had a chance to open it and see what it is."

He nodded. "And you were going to let me know about this when?" He picked up his pace a little.

His legs were a lot longer than mine and I was wearing heels. I took a few jogging steps to keep up with him. "When I knew if there was something to be concerned about or not. I mean, why get everyone all upset before anyone knows whether or not there's something to be upset about?"

"I don't know. Maybe because I thought we were intimate on more than a physical level." He picked up the pace a little more.

I dug my heels in and came to a full stop. Darkness had fallen completely now and we stood in a pool of light from the street lamp. The shadows played over his face. "What the hell is that supposed to mean?"

"It means that we're supposed to share things with each other. It means we're supposed to trust each other. It means you're supposed to let me into your little club." He threw his hands in the air.

"What club? There is no club. There's just me. It's always been just me. The only other person there's ever been was Mae and she's gone. If there ever was a club, the membership card can apparently be deadly. So be careful what you wish for." I poked his chest with my index finger.

"Wish for? You think I wished for this? You think I wished to fall in love with the girl with the craziest story I've ever heard? And don't forget, I was raised by the guy who had me sleep in the aluminum foil hat so the aliens couldn't read my thoughts, so my crazy-story rating system is pretty highly tuned." He grabbed my index finger and held it.

I glared at him. "That is the second time in the last five minutes that you've alluded to being in love with me. If you don't say it right the next time, Ted Goodnight, hand to God, I'm going to bitch slap you down this sidewalk."

He was breathing fast and furious now, as if he'd been running hard. He grabbed me around my waist and pulled me to him. His breath was warm and sweet on my cheek, his chest hard against mine. "Melina Markowitz, I am head over heels in love with you. I am so crazy about you that I'm worried that you put me under a spell."

"I can't do spells," I said.

He lowered his lips to mine and the rest of the world fell away. For a few moments, there was nothing but him and me and our bodies pressed together. Heat bloomed inside me and trailed fire from the very center of me to my toes.

Then, from the very edges of my perception, I heard a growling noise. I ignored it, hoping it was my imagination. Then the buzzing in my flesh made it clear that I couldn't. Something was out there. Something nasty. I disentangled myself from Ted just as the dog lunged at us.

"WHAT THE HELL?" TED SWUNG AROUND AND INTO A CROUCH.

I peeled around so I was back to back with him. We both cautiously circled, keeping each other's backs covered. It felt as natural to me as when we were front to front, but different. This had its own thrill, but I think I like the front to front stuff better.

The dog circled us, too. If it was actually a dog. At the very least, it wasn't only a dog. I could tell that much by the electrified hum I felt from it. The glowing red eyes were the next dead giveaway.

It lunged again, snapping its teeth inches away from Ted's throat.

"Bad dog," he yelled. "Down."

Unbelievably enough, the dog-thing backed away a little. "'Bad dog'? Seriously?" I asked. "That's all you've got? 'Bad dog'?"

"Well, he's not a good dog." Ted took off his jacket and wrapped it around his left arm.

True that. The thing lunged again. This time at me. I smacked down on its snout with my fist. It whined a little as it backed away.

I growled a little in the back of my throat. That close, I could smell the sulfur coming off it. "He's not a dog, either. Careful, don't look him in the eyes."

"Got it. Any idea what it is?" He glanced over his shoulder at me.

"I think it's a cadejo."

He snorted. "I don't think name-calling is going to help at this moment."

"Not *pendejo*. Cadejo. It's a demon that takes the form of a dog. This one isn't quite right though." I looked at it hard, something that wasn't all that difficult to do since I was not going to take my eyes off it at the moment. "Sometimes the cadejos mate with regular dogs. This might be the offspring of one of those hook-ups."

"You can tell just by looking?" The dog circled and we circled with it.

"Yeah, I'm getting a supernatural vibe off it, but it doesn't have goat hooves or chains that glow in the dark."

"Is that good news or bad?"

"Good. It means we can probably kill it."

He made a funny noise in the back of his throat.

"What?"

"I don't know. I've always hated killing animals."

"It's not an animal. It's a demon."

"It's a hybrid. You just said so." His tone was way too reasonable for someone being stalked by the son of a demon dog.

I felt myself starting to growl again. "Fine. It's still going to come down to us or it."

"Got it," he said. "Give me your jacket."

I took it off and handed it over my shoulder to him. He wrapped it around his arm on top of his own jacket. As the cadejo lunged at him again, Ted lunged forward with his left forearm braced in front of him like a battering ram. He practically shoved his arm into the thing's mouth as it lunged toward him. Then he braced his other arm on the back of its neck and, with a quick jerk, snapped the dog's head up.

I heard the crack as its neck broke and it fell slack to the ground before him. Smoke started to rise from the body. Then the body began to disintegrate, as if it were on fire from within. Within seconds, all that was left was a black oily stain on the sidewalk, with a horrible smell like rotten eggs.

I turned to Ted. "Are you all right?"

He nodded, breathing hard. "I'm okay."

I unraveled the jackets and looked at his arm. The red stain on his sleeve grew. "No, you're not okay."

He looked down, looking almost confused as the blood began to drip from his hand. "Hmm. Guess you're right." And then his knees began to buckle underneath him.

TED LET ME DRIVE HIM BACK TO SACRAMENTO IN GRANDMA Rosie's Buick. Officially, the Buick has been mine for three years now. Unofficially, it will never fully be mine. I like to think it's inhabited with a bit of my grandmother's feisty and tenacious spirit. Ted, on the other hand, views it as past its prime and prone to break down. I'll grant the *past its prime*, but it has never failed me when I needed it. Regardless, it was a testament to how he was feeling that he allowed me to drive him at all, much less in my old-lady car.

"How will we get my truck back?" he asked.

"I'll have Ben help me. Or Sophie. They both have their licenses now." Ben was my downstairs neighbor's kid. He and Sophie had a bit of an on-again/off-again teenage romance thing going, which I wasn't entirely thrilled about. On the other hand, he'd gone from total screwup to a pretty responsible young man and I had to grant him that. Plus, it was handy to have someone around who knew a little about what was going on. I hadn't approved of Sophie telling him who and what she was, and who and what I was by extension, but it had ended up being more helpful than not. Still, it was another blurring of the neat compartments in which I'd kept my life up to this point. I didn't much like it most of the time.

"I don't want either of them driving my truck." Ted had started to shake a little.

I touched his forehead. "You're burning up."

"I don't feel great." He slumped against the window.

I glanced over at him. His face was pale and shone with sweat. "You don't look great either."

He swallowed hard. "Boy, you sure know what to say to a guy."

"How about this? Take my cell phone. Call Alex. Tell him we're on our way."

"I don't need your cell," he said, fishing his own phone out of his pocket with his left hand and dialing awkwardly. "I have him on speed dial, too."

"Since when?" I wasn't exactly sure why it bothered me that Alex and Ted might have been talking without me, but it did.

"Since last spring."

"What do you talk about?"

"Stuff."

"What kind of stuff?"

"Melina . . ." Ted held the phone up to his ear.

I glanced over at him. He really didn't look good. "Got it. We'll talk later."

I gritted my teeth and drove.

ALEX MET US AT THE DOOR TO MY APARTMENT BUILDING holding an old-fashioned leather doctor's bag. He slung one arm under Ted's armpits and helped me hoist him up the stairs. It was one of those times that I really questioned the intelligence of living in a third floor walk-up. Could have been worse, though. We could have been walking into Sacramento County Hospital trying to figure out how to explain what had happened to Ted. "Thanks for not making me take him to the hospital," I said.

He shook his head, dark hair flopping over his forehead. "I get it. The less questions, the better. Now what exactly happened? Prince Charming here wasn't exactly totally coherent on the telephone."

"Mexican devil dog," Ted said, his eyes burning. "'Tacked us out of nowhere. Crazy!"

Alex looked at me. "Delirious?"

I shook my head. "Nope. A cadejo. Or the son of a cadejo."

He whistled. "Any idea why?"

"Not really," I admitted.

Alex glanced at me from around Ted. "I'm betting you're going to want to know now."

"Pretty much." I grunted as we hoisted Ted up another stair.

"You realize someone probably sent him after you as a warning." We stopped for a moment on the second-floor landing to rest.

I was reasonably certain that Alex could have carried Ted the rest of the way up the stairs without my help, but I appreciated his discretion in letting Ted do as much as he could. It wouldn't do to emasculate the one actual living breathing man I had in my life. "I hate it when they do that. It just makes me want to dig deeper."

Alex smiled. "You think they'd learn by now."

"Why?" Ted asked. "She hasn't. Someone warns her. She sticks her nose in farther. It's the Melina Way."

Alex chuckled. "It is at that."

We were almost to the apartment. I figured I could defend my honor later. "I think I better go ahead and clear the way. You okay here on your own for a few minutes?"

They both nodded. I glanced at Ted's bloody arm. The bleeding had stopped, but there was still some oozing. I glanced back at Alex again. "You're sure?"

"What? You think your boyfriend's blood is so tasty and delicious that I can't control myself for a few minutes? Dream on, sister. He's not that special." He leaned against the wall, looking like the picture of casual nonchalance.

Ted looked affronted. "My blood's not good enough for you? I'm B positive. Only like ten percent of the population has that."

"I'm sure it's delicious," Alex assured him. "But I already ate."

I grinned and bounded up the last flight.

My grin faded as I tried to open the door and was stopped by the chain again. I opened the door as far as the chain would let me. "Norah, it's me," I said, with the slightest soupçon of guilt over the fact that it wasn't just me. Then I sneezed. A little cloud of smoke came out of the door. I banged harder. "Norah! Are you okay? I smell smoke."

She took the chain off. "What's wrong? Why are you out of breath?"

I countered with, "What's that smell?"

"Sage. I'm smudging the apartment." She opened the door the rest of the way. Our little entryway was a maze of crystals.

"And that?" I asked, pointing.

She turned and walked back into the apartment. "It's our first line of defense."

"Against what?"

She picked up the copy of the grimoire I'd given her that morning. "Against whatever is trying to get in here." She dropped it on the breakfast bar with a thud.

"About that . . ." I said, and launched into my explanation of what had happened.

"So is Ted okay?" Norah asked, gnawing at a fingernail.

"That's the thing. Not really. I'd really like Alex to take a look at this bite, but I don't want to take Ted into the hospital. I wouldn't want to try and explain what happened to anybody. It's not something that most people would understand, you know?"

"So where do you want to go?"

I gave her my most engaging smile. "Here."

She took three steps back and almost tripped on a crystal. "There has to be someplace else. Why can't you go to Alex's place?"

Truth was, I'd never actually been to Alex's place. I had also wanted to end up here at my place with Ted. Moving him was an issue. For a relatively slender guy, he weighed a ton. He was solid muscle. "This seemed like a better choice."

Norah cocked her head and looked at me. "They're right outside, aren't they?"

"On the landing."

"Listening."

"Well, probably Alex is. He can't help it. He hears really well."

She threw her hands in the air and shook her head. "Then they might as well come in."

I hugged her. "Thanks. It'll be okay. I promise."

She picked up the grimoire and headed toward her bedroom. "No need to promise. I'll make sure of it myself."

I watched her door close with a twinge of unease. I needed to deal with the situation, but Ted's situation was more dire. Norah would have to wait. I threw the door open. "It's safe to come in."

Alex and Ted made it the rest of the way into the apartment. Ted sneezed and groaned. Alex looked over at me. "You're smudging? At a time like this?"

"Norah is." I got under Ted's other arm. "Where do you want him?"

"Kitchen will do."

We plopped Ted down on one of the breakfast-bar stools. Alex opened up his medical bag and began rummaging in it. First he pulled out a pair of bandaging scissors and sliced away the rest of Ted's sleeve.

"Hey," Ted protested. "I liked that shirt."

"Relax, big guy, Melina will buy you another one for your birthday. When is your birthday, anyway?" Alex examined the bite mark, turning Ted's arm from side to side. He motioned for me to get him some water.

"February. I'm an Aquarius. What's your sign, Alex?"

I brought the bowl of hot water over and looked at Ted. How out of it was he?

"I would be a Gemini," Alex said. It didn't look good, but it also wasn't as bad as I'd been afraid of it being. It didn't look like the cadejo had managed to make a deep puncture wound, but it was puffy and swollen and red.

"Very compatible, you and I." Ted winked at Alex and then tried to pull his arm away as Alex began to clean the wounds.

"We knew that already." Alex kept a tight hold on Ted's arm.

"You know that hurts, right?" Ted said, wincing.

"I figured." Alex didn't look up from his work, but he smiled a little.

Ted twisted a little on the bar stool. "Are you going to be done soon?"

"I'll be done when I'm done."

"But that'll be soon, right?" Ted twisted some more.

"That'll be now." Alex stood up and stripped the latex gloves off his hands. "When was your last tetanus shot?"

I looked at him. "It was a cadejo. Not the Chihuahua next store. I don't think a tetanus shot will fix whatever it could have given him."

"Or the son of a cadejo, so it would have all the properties of a regular dog bite on top of all the magic," he reminded me. "And a puncture wound is a puncture wound. You ever see lockjaw?"

I shook my head.

"Well, I have and it's not pretty." His face looked grim. Whatever he was remembering wasn't pleasant.

"It was two years ago. My shots are all up-to-date. The force insists on it," Ted interrupted.

"Okay. So no tetanus needed. That's good. How about a nice healthy dose of antibiotics, then?" Alex smiled.

"Sounds fabulous." Ted's head began to droop toward the counter.

Antibiotics? I could have gotten those from the nearest Doc in a Box. What was the point of having a vampire doctor if he didn't treat the supernatural part of the wound? "The dog was at least part demon, Alex. Are you really sure that all we need is antibiotics?"

He handed me a piece of paper from his prescription pad. "They're very wide spectrum."

"Ha ha. How about something to deal with the demonic poison that's clearly in him?" Ted's head dropped all the way to the counter.

Alex picked up Ted's hand and started taking his pulse. "You mean my special magic salve that sucks evil out of bodies?"

I squirmed. It sounded stupid when he said it like that. "Yes. That's exactly what I mean."

"It doesn't exist." He didn't even look up from his wristwatch.

"There's got to be something." I insisted.

"You could try dried slippery elm. It can be helpful. Not as good as a nice wide-spectrum antibiotic, but it wouldn't hurt."

Now we were talking. "I don't suppose you have any on you."

He snorted. "No. I don't carry powdered slippery elm or lobelia or goldenseal around with me."

Fabulous. Where the hell was I supposed to get slippery elm at this time of night? Or any time of day or night, for that matter? "So where am I supposed to get it at this time of night?" I asked out loud.

"I have some," Norah said from behind me.

I turned. Alex barely glanced up. He must have known she was there all along. He has a way better sense of smell than I do. Now that I was looking for it, I caught a whiff of her lavender scent. It probably smelled like a huge spray of Glade to him.

"Why exactly do you have powdered slippery elm?" I asked.

She looked a little defiant. Or as defiant as you can when you've got arms that look like spaghetti strands akimbo on your hips. "It was in the book. It said it was something you should always have on hand, just in case, so I went shopping this afternoon. Melina, have you read that thing? I don't think you have, because you are woefully unprepared."

WITHIN A COUPLE OF HOURS, TED LOOKED SIGNIFICANTLY less glassy-eyed. Alex had taken off with Ted's keys and a promise that the truck would be in front of Ted's condo before sunrise. Some of the stiffness had gone out of how Norah was holding herself as soon as he left.

I had been surprised that she hadn't gone back to her room and locked the door as soon as she handed over the slippery elm. She'd stayed out in the kitchen with us, almost as if once she was in Alex's presence, she didn't want to separate from him again. My best guess at the moment was that she wanted to keep an eye on him as long as he was in our apartment. I know I like to keep any enemies that are nearby in clear view. It hadn't felt like that, though. It had felt like they were doing some kind of complicated dance, something sexy and tango-like. If one advanced, the other retreated, only to advance again in the face of the other's retreat. Or maybe I was just tired and thinking too hard.

"You okay?" I asked her as she slumped down onto one of the bar stools.

She nodded. "Yeah. It wasn't as hard as I thought it was going to be to see him again. I felt okay, especially since I have this now." She pulled a tiny silver cross out of her shirt.

"Another helpful hint from the book?" I asked.

"Yep. I don't understand why you don't wear one." She gave me a funny sidelong look.

I rubbed my face and pondered how to explain it. "The cross only works to ward off a vampire if you believe in it." I didn't mention that it helped a whole lot if the person who had made the cross also believed in it and wasn't, say, a political prisoner making mass-produced cheap jewelry in China.

"You can believe in what the cross stands for even if you were raised Jewish, Melina." Norah fingered the little piece of jewelry. "It can be about the spirit of Jesus's teachings."

"Plus, it's kind of my job to associate with vampires, at least on occasion. It would be a little rude to be warding them off." I also knew that a little piece of metal was unlikely to stop a marauding vampire in his or her tracks. A nice big, fat stake aimed right at the withered remains of a heart? A much more satisfactory deterrent. Even holy water wouldn't do much more than slow one down. Still, if it made Norah feel safer, then who was I to argue? It's why I'd given her the book in the first place, wasn't it? "For you, though? I think it's a great idea."

I patted her on her bony back and went to check on Ted, who was sprawled on our futon couch, clutching the remote and flipping through channels. "How you doing, big guy?" I touched his forehead and was relieved to find it back to a close-to-normal temperature.

"Fine. I think if I keep my sleeve pulled down, no one will even see the bandage tomorrow." He smiled up at me. Unbelievable. I manage to get the guy bitten by a Mexican demon dog and he still smiles at me. Let's not forget: he loves me. He actually said it. Out loud. Maybe we didn't get to finish the conversation, what with the whole attack of the demon dog and everything, but I wasn't going to forget what he'd said anytime soon. It would make a wonderful story to tell our children.

Children? Egad! What was I thinking? Next thing you knew I was going to be doodling my name as *Mrs. Ted Goodnight* on my notebook and mooning over bridal magazines.

"When do you have to be at work?" I asked, instead. Stay focused on the here and now. Be pragmatic.

"Not until seven tomorrow morning. How about you?"

"I've got to go in tonight." A thought occurred to me. "Hey. How did you end up in Elmville anyway? I thought you had to work."

He looked up at me and smiled. "I traded with Jimmy. He was looking for a way to get out of going to his wife's cousin's wedding anyway. Call it a mutual favor."

"That still doesn't explain why you were there." I sat down on the couch next to him and searched those pretty blue eyes for an answer.

"I told you. I don't like coincidences." He looked back at the television. The Kings were getting spanked by the Lakers. It wasn't that interesting. I shut off the TV.

"Hey!" he protested. "I was watching that."

"No, you weren't. You were avoiding me."

He turned the full force of his gaze on me and I shivered a little. "I knew you weren't telling me something, so I wanted to check it out myself. I figured the kid's memorial service would be a good place to start. I'm guessing you were doing the same thing. Now can I watch the game?"

"Not here. I have to work. I'll give you a ride home on my way to the hospital."

5

I STILL WORKED TWO OR THREE NIGHT SHIFTS A WEEK AT Sacramento County Hospital as a receiving clerk in the Emergency Department. I wasn't quite ready to put all my eggs in the dojo basket, plus I got a pretty groovy array of benefits, even as a part-timer.

The work was boring and repetitive. It brought me into contact with some of the most outrageous elements of the underbelly of the city—the truly crazy and dispossessed wander through big city emergency rooms in the wee hours of the morning. The hours were brutal and my coworkers were often surly. Is it any wonder I couldn't bring myself to quit? It was my kind of place.

Tonight was relatively quiet. Sundays often were. Most of the city got their yayas out on Friday and Saturday night. Still, we had one guy who'd been picked up drunk as a skunk while waving a broken bottle around and threatening anyone who came near him, a guy who'd been stabbed in the neck with a fork by his girlfriend while they made dinner plus a little old lady with chest pains. I desperately wanted to know what the guy did to get his girlfriend to stab him with a fork, but no one seemed to know and he wasn't talking. I'd see if Ted had heard anything later.

Around two A.M., I ran into Alex in the hallway. He handed me the keys to Ted's truck. "Everything's delivered, safe and sound."

"Thanks. Who helped drive?"

"Paul. I figured Ted would trust him with his truck."

I nodded. "So I guess Paul was glad to see you, then."

Alex raised one eyebrow. "Any particular reason?"

I shrugged. "I'm not sure. He made some comment about you not coming around McClannigan's lately when Ted and I were in there the other night. He seemed unhappy about it." Actually he'd seemed worried, but I wasn't sure if Alex would want to hear that.

"Is our faithful puppy dog lonely?" Alex made a face.

"You know he hates it when you refer to him as a dog." I walked through the door and back toward my cubicle.

Alex chuckled. "That's why I do it."

Maybe the odd nature of Paul and Alex's friendship made it take the form of a lot of poking at each other's sore spots. Or maybe that was just a guy thing. I'd certainly watched my brother and his friends trade insults the way girls traded compliments. I was hard-pressed to say whether I didn't understand their relationship because of their supernatural statuses or simply because they had penises.

My friendship with either one of them? Way beyond improbable. They were both good-looking strong men, with the added bonus that they knew what and who I was. That made them very attractive. The domination and control thing? Very difficult for me to take on my best days and I don't have all that many best days.

I sat down at my desk and Alex settled on my desk. "He asked after you, said you hadn't been around lately. Found a new and fresher hunting ground?"

Alex made a show of inspecting his fingernails. I wasn't buying it. Alex was the cleanest vampire I knew. I don't know what it is about drinking blood that makes someone think they no longer have to wash their hair, but based on purely anecdotal evidence, they did precisely that. Not Alex, though. His hair is never greasy, although he did look a little paler than usual. Anyway, he'd more likely have a heartbeat than grime under his nails. "I wouldn't say that. I'm trying something new, though."

"Care to share?" I wasn't sure I liked the sound of that.

"Nope." He didn't meet my eyes.

"Well, okay then." I knew when I'd been dismissed.

He started to get up and then settled back down on my desk. "What's your next step?"

It was an excellent question. I thought about the box that I'd found under Neil Bossard's bed. I wasn't exactly sure what it was or who might have made it, but I knew someone who might be able to help. "Research," I said.

He slid a lock of my hair back behind my ear, leaving a cool tingle in the trail of his fingertips. "Good. How much trouble can you get into doing research?"

I FELL INTO BED THE SECOND I GOT HOME, BARELY GRUNTING at Norah as I walked past her in the kitchen. She was brewing tea and humming. It seemed like progress, but I was too damned tired to bother to investigate it.

At around ten thirty, I woke. I looked at the clock and groaned.

The alarm wasn't set to go off until noon. I don't need much sleep—a boon of being a Messenger—but I did need some. I lay back on my pillow and shut my eyes, willing sleep to come swallow me up again.

As I stilled my breathing and began to drift, I heard a faint scratching sound in the living room. I stiffened, then tried to relax again. Maybe it had just been a branch scraping against a window or the sound of something on the street.

No. There it was again. A definite scratching noise accompanied by a snuffling. Whatever was making the noise was breathing and I was pretty sure it was in my living room.

Slowly, slowly, slowly I sat up in my bed and slid from beneath the covers. Without a noise, I stood. I can be very quiet when I want to be and I wanted to be super-silent now. I waited a few seconds, letting my breathing still. There wasn't much I could do about the fluttering of my heart. Adrenaline does that. I didn't know for sure that I was under attack yet, but sneaky sounds in my living room did not bode well.

I wasn't crazy about meeting whatever was waiting out there while wearing nothing but a pair of panties and a camisole top, but I wasn't going to stop and get dressed either. I looked around the room for a handy weapon. My eyes lit on my kendo stick. It was light, maneuverable. A good choice when you didn't know what you were facing. I sniffed the air and caught a slight animal smell. I didn't think that whatever was out there was human, yet I didn't have the tingling in my skin that I should have felt if it was supernatural either.

Luckily, I hadn't shut the door to my room all the way and was able to ease it open without a telltale click of tongue and latch. I stayed tucked behind it, back against the wall, looking over my shoulder into the hallway.

Nothing. I stayed still and listened. Was that the sound of a claw clicking against our hardwood floors?

Once I entered the hallway, I'd be exposed. I wasn't thrilled about that, but I didn't see that I had much choice. I wasn't going to spend the morning pressed up against the walls of my room, waiting for whatever was in my living room to head this way. I didn't have that much patience.

I eased into the hallway. I didn't want to linger there. I wouldn't have much room to fight if whatever it was attacked me in that space. I certainly wouldn't be able to swing my kendo stick with full movement, making it an even less effective weapon. Nor did I want to rush the living room without a little more information, either.

I made my way down the hall, pressed up against the wall as quickly and silently as I could. As I got closer, the animal smell got stronger. I breathed shallowly through my mouth.

I glanced quickly into the living room and drew back. Damn. A cadejo. This time, a real one, with goat-like cloven hooves and a chain draped around it. It would be harder to kill than the animal/demon hybrid that Ted had taken out the day before, but it could still be done.

I glanced into the living room again, peeking quickly around the corner. The cadejo's head was up and alert. I wondered if it was here to avenge the death of the other dog. Perhaps this was the demonic father of the one we'd already killed. Fantastic. Mexican demon dogs bent on revenge. Just what I needed.

It still seemed unaware of my presence. Perhaps I could use the element of surprise to my advantage. If I could quickly jam the kendo stick into its mouth and then use the same maneuver Ted had to break its neck, maybe I could have this thing polished off before it even fully registered I was in the room. Not to brag, but

I am that fast. When you're getting ready to fight a demon dog in your living room, it is not the time for false modesty.

I turned the stick so it was horizontally across my chest and hurled myself into the room. I rushed the cadejo. Its head came up and its jaws opened. I jammed the stick deep into the creases of its mouth, screaming as I went.

I pushed down and back, but the cadejo bunched its hindquarters and leapt, sending me flying backwards. I hit the ground on my shoulders and did a quick back somersault onto my feet, kendo stick still in front of me.

The cadejo and I circled each other, each looking for an opening. I didn't like the intelligence I could see sparking in its eyes. This was no dumb dog. This animal had cunning.

It leapt at me, snarling, saliva dripping from its fangs. I swung the stick and knocked the cadejo away. I kept the stick twirling, smacking the dog on its sensitive snout and ears as I advanced on it. It backed away, trying to get enough distance to launch another attack at my throat. I kept crowding it so it wouldn't have the space.

Finally, I had it backed into the corner. Luckily, not the one where we kept the television. I rammed the stick down into its mouth again and lunged forward.

Behind me, the door to the apartment opened. "Melina!" Sophie screamed.

I couldn't turn, but my focus flickered. The cadejo pushed forward and then . . . disappeared.

I sprang backward. Where had it gone?

I whirled. Sophie stood in the doorway, Ben behind her. Both of them stared at me, their eyes wide and their jaws a bit slack.

"Where did it go?" I demanded. "Did you see where it went?" Just because I couldn't see the threat didn't mean it wasn't still there. That was a lesson I'd had to learn a few times before it sunk all the way in. I whirled again. The living room wasn't that big. There weren't that many places to hide. It had to be here somewhere.

"Where what went?" Sophie took a step into the apartment. "What are you talking about?"

"The cadejo," I said, then realized she might not know what that was. "The big dog-like thing I was fighting. Did you see where it went?"

Ben took a few steps into the apartment now, too. "There wasn't a big dog-like thing, Melina. There wasn't anything."

"Very funny, wise guy." I continued to turn, trying to use all my senses to relocate the cadejo. I'd never heard of one vanishing like that, but it wasn't like I was a total cadejo expert or anything.

"He's not making a joke," Sophie said. "There wasn't anything here. There was just you with the kendo stick in the corner."

"No big dog with goat hooves?" I turned now to look at Sophie, right in her big hazel eyes.

"No big dog. No goat hooves." She looked me right back in the eyes and answered with no hesitation.

"Just me in the corner with the kendo stick looking like a lunatic in my underwear?" I was beginning to understand the total looks of horror on both their faces.

"Pretty much." Ben bobbed his head.

"And you're not in school right now because . . . ?" I'd heard asking leading questions was a good technique with teens.

"Of a teacher in-service day," they said in unison.

Whatever the hell that meant.

"And you guys showed up because . . . ?"

Ben sat down on the edge of the couch. "We heard yelling and crashing and thought you might need help."

Well, wasn't that just the understatement of the day.

I COULDN'T GO BACK TO SLEEP. THE ADRENALINE SURGE I'D woken up with wouldn't leave my body. Even after my heart stopped pounding, I was beyond hyper. I was still tired though. The few hours sleep I'd gotten were not enough. It was the worst combination of hyped up and exhausted that I could come up with. I took a shower and got dressed while Sophie and Ben picked up the things my imaginary devil dog and I had knocked around. Then I made a pot of coffee and loaded it up with sugar and milk. Protein, sugar and caffeine. If I'd had a piece of chocolate to eat with it, I would have hit every food group I really found necessary.

"Are you sure you weren't dreaming?" Sophie asked as she sat next to me, sipping a cup of Norah's herbal tea.

"If it was a dream, it was the most realistic dream I've ever had." I took another gulp of coffee, hoping that the caffeine would start coursing through my system soon.

"Did you eat something spicy?" Ben asked. "I always have weird dreams after we eat Thai food."

I didn't even bother answering that one. I wished it would be something that simple. It had seemed so real. I had heard the cadejo, smelled it and seen it.

I hadn't sensed it, though. Something about that was off. I rubbed the back of my neck and turned to Sophie. "Do you want a ride to the dojo? It's almost time to head over there anyway."

"No. I've got my mom's car. I'll meet you there."

Ben and Sophie left, and I went to gather my stuff up for the rest of the day. I'd need my *gi* and I'd want a snack. I'd probably also want some clothes to change into after I was done teaching. I might as well take the little box I'd found under Neil Bossard's bed, too.

I pulled it out of the pocket of my blazer, where I'd stuffed it the night before. It looked innocuous enough. Brown paper wrapping. Cellophane tape. Neil Bossard's name and address written in Sharpie in block letters on the front.

I set it down on the counter and sat in front of it. The vibration off of it was weaker here than it had been in Elmville. Whoever had made it was probably farther away now than they were when I'd been at the memorial service. Like Ginnar's axe, whatever was in the box was losing power as it got farther and farther from its maker.

The buzz might be less, but it was still there. I closed my eyes and let it wash over me, and a cold shiver ran up and down my spine. I didn't like whatever was in there. It didn't have a nice feeling to it, not nice at all. I snapped my eyes back open and closed off my senses a little. I like a little buffer between me and malevolent things and this thing definitely felt malevolent. And witchy. It didn't do anything. It just sat there, humming its little hum of power that felt distinctly witchy to me.

I used to not be able to distinguish between various kinds of power. A buzz in my head, the lifting of the hair on my forearms—it all felt the same, whether there was a vampire nearby or a ghost or a troll. Well, generally I can smell a troll, but that's not any big power. Pretty much anybody can smell a troll. Most people think a sewage system is backing up somewhere or that someone is dumping garbage under a bridge, but it's a troll.

Over the years—and while I'm only twenty-six years old, I have been at this job for close to twenty-three of those years—I have become more of a connoisseur. The subtle gradations of different supernatural beings are hard to describe. There's a coppery tang that reminds me of blood to a vampire vibration. Werewolves have a bit of a musky scent. Witches tend to have a bit of a cinnamon taste to their vibration. I got a bitter cinnamon bite from this package.

I don't know how else to describe it. I could be wrong, but while this item had been made by someone who wielded power, I didn't think that person was supernatural. I thought about the woman I'd seen crying behind the tree at the graveside service. I'd gotten a similar feeling from her. I wished I knew who she was. I hadn't exactly had a chance to follow up on that, what with being kicked out of the memorial service, having my boyfriend tell me he loved me and then immediately afterward being attacked by a cadejo.

The next best thing would be to find out what this thing was and I knew just who to ask.

I stuffed everything into a bag and dialed Meredith's number. "What do you need, Melina?" she said, without bothering with a hello. Sometimes I hated Caller ID. At least, I'm pretty sure Meredith has Caller ID.

"I want you to look at something I found." Two could play the up-front and honest game. I don't know what it said about me that up-front and honest was now some sort of maneuver, but I didn't run into it nearly as frequently as I wished I did.

"Found where?" she asked. Interesting that she was more interested in where it came from than what it was.

"Under a dead man's bed." "Man" might be stretching it a little. Bossard was barely a man. "Dead boy" didn't sound right to me either though.

"Nine o'clock at McClannigan's?" she suggested.

"Sounds perfectly lovely." It could potentially be a little tense, depending on where in Meredith and Paul's on-again/off-again relationship we were these days, but that would add a little spice to my night. We hung up.

I dialed Ted's cell number as I grabbed my bag and keys. "Is it urgent?" he answered. Great. Another person who was dispensing with hellos when I called.

"Nope. Just checking in. Where are you?" I could hear the sound of traffic in the background.

"At work," he said, as if explaining things to a rather slow person.

I'd sort of expected him to take at least a day off. "You feel well enough for that?"

"Wouldn't be here if I didn't. Can we talk later? I'm kind of in the middle of something." He sounded distracted.

"Sure. How about McClannigan's at nine?"

"What now, Melina?" Now I had his attention.

"I thought you wanted to talk later." I teased.

He made a funny noise, but then apparently whatever was going on caught his attention again. "Fine. McClannigan's. Nine o'clock," he said, and hung up.

I left the apartment and bopped down the stairs, feeling slightly more energetic than I had any right to. It wasn't until I was on the street and headed toward Grandma's Buick that I became aware of the distinct feeling of being watched.

I didn't get the buzz of anything supernatural, but I did get that uncomfortable sensation that makes the hair on my neck stand up a little. I whirled around and examined the street behind me. Nothing. No one was out. The street was a sunny panorama of a perfect northern California day.

I turned back around and started walking again, listening for the scrape of a footstep or the sound of breathing behind me. I thought I caught the slight tap of a boot. I turned again. Nothing. Maybe it had been an echo of my own footstep. I hurried the rest of the way to the Buick and leapt inside. The solid thunk of the door as it closed reassured me.

I stayed quiet in the car for a few moments before I started it up and let my senses open. Damn it. There was nothing. But I knew I'd been watched. I'd felt it too many times before not to know the sensation and I'd learned to ignore it at my own peril.

I started the Buick and headed to the studio, keeping a careful watch on my rear- and side-view mirrors.

"STOP CROWDING ME!" CONNOR HILL TURNED AND GAVE WILL Greer a good hard shove.

Will stumbled backward, keeping his balance but knocking down Cassie Trebatchnik behind him.

"Hey," I waded in, not waiting for the melee to escalate. The class had not been right from the second they'd walked in today. I'm not saying thirteen-year-olds were the easiest group of human beings to keep a handle on. I personally think that all junior high teachers deserve some kind of special combat pay bonuses, but this group was generally pretty respectful of one another, at least inside the studio.

"He keeps coming up right behind me." Connor turned to me, arms flung out, trying to express his frustration.

"I do not." Will was clearly just as frustrated. "You keep saying that. I'm nowhere near you, dude."

"Don't 'dude' me!" Connor advanced on Will.

This would not do.

"Both of you. Opposite corners. Now," I said in my very best sensei voice, then thanked any lucky star I might have that it worked. I wasn't all that much bigger than them and wasn't sure what I'd have had to do if they hadn't listened. Oh, I could take them, but it wasn't the way I wanted to run my dojo. In the end, both boys were still steamed, but at least it wasn't about to escalate into a fistfight.

"Take a moment. Breathe. Count to ten. You can come back to the mat when you think you can behave in a way that's appropriate." I marched back to the head of the classroom, rubbing the back of my neck. The feeling of being watched hadn't left me all afternoon.

"Yes, sensei," both boys muttered from their corners.

I looked over the class. Everyone was tense. Were they getting it from me? If they were, maybe they could get rid of it the way I usually did. I hung the heavy bags and had them line up. We proceeded to drill. More precisely, I proceeded to lead them in beating the crap out of the bags. By the end of the hour, even Connor and Will were smiling again. Heck, I was smiling a little again. There's nothing like the release of endorphins brought on by really pounding on an inanimate object to make a person feel that all is right with the world.

The class bowed their way off the mat. I gave the parents a few weak smiles as they took their now tired and significantly less aggressive teenagers home.

"What's wrong here?" Sophie asked, as she started shoving chairs back into neat rows, as she had to do after every class. I don't know what possessed people to always need to move chairs around, but they did. It was a fact of life, as immutable as gravity, that if the chairs weren't bolted to the floor, someone was going to shift them into little groupings.

"I'm not sure. Everybody's cranky today. It happens." I sat down on the mat to stretch a little.

Sophie marched across the floor with the broom to sweep the entryway. "It's more than that. Don't you feel it?"

I looked up at her. She wasn't exactly the most physically impressive specimen. I don't think she was much more than five foot two and with her reddish blonde hair pulled back into a ponytail, she didn't look much more than fourteen. Of course, she wasn't much more than fourteen. In some ways, that was a boon to our kind. We didn't look threatening. People—or things other than people—tended to underestimate us.

She did, however, have good instincts. It would be foolish of me to ignore them when they were offered up like that.

"What are you feeling?" I asked, still pancaked on the floor.

"I keep feeling like there's somebody behind me, but when I turn, there's no one there." She shivered a little.

That was in keeping with the fact that I felt like I was being watched and, come to think of it, with Connor and Will's spat. "Go on."

"It's not much more than that. Maybe a little like someone's watching me. I just know I don't like it and it's making me all jumpy. What is it?" She started sweeping.

"I'm not sure what it is, but I'm pretty sure I know where it's coming from." It was coming from the little box I'd taken from under Neil Bossard's bed. Didn't Ted say he'd run into the road saying something was behind him? That he'd thought he was being chased?

I explained the box to Sophie. She stopped sweeping and sat down on the mat across from me, hazel eyes wide. "What do you think it is?"

"Nothing good." I straightened my legs in front of me, grabbed my insteps and touched my nose to my knees.

"What are you going to do with it?"

"I'm going to take it to Meredith and see if she knows what to do with it. It feels witchy to me," I said to my knees.

"Witchy?"

I straightened back up and spread my legs in a V. "Yeah. You know . . . how the axe spoke to you a little about what it was and where it needed to go? This box speaks to me in a witchy accent."

Sophie sat back on her heels. "Can I come with?"

I shook my head, shook out my legs and stood up.

She scowled, clearly gearing up for a fight. "Why not?"

"Because you're too young to go to a bar." I love it when the law is on my side.

6

I CLEANED UP IN THE BACK OF THE STUDIO AND CHANGED INTO jeans and boots and a shirt Norah had helped me pick out on one of the infrequent occasions she had been willing to leave the apartment. It wasn't quite as revealing as the one she'd had me wear the other night, but it was a step up from my usual plain T-shirt. I even dabbed on some lipstick and mascara.

It was kind of pointless. No one was going to look at me, anyway. I had a disturbing ability to melt into the background. In all fairness, it served me well. I was better off if no one remembered me coming into the room—or leaving it, for that matter. A Messenger was safest when no one even remembered the delivery. But the real reason no one would notice me tonight was because Meredith would be there.

Meredith was one of those women who everyone turned to look at when she walked through a room. More so even than Norah, and Norah attracted plenty of attention all on her own. Norah had a glow about her. Granted, that glow was a little dimmer these days and for that I felt way too much responsibility. It wasn't quite an aura, although she had one of those, too. This was more like the incandescence of her goodness shining through.

Meredith, on the other hand, had presence.

Oh, sure, she was a good-looking woman, but someone with the exact same looks wouldn't get a second glance. There was something in the way she walked through a room. A waft of power seemed to stream behind her. Most people had no idea what they were responding to when they turned to watch her go. I wasn't even sure that Meredith was always aware of it. It was there, though.

I grabbed my purse and shoved Neil Bossard's box into it and headed out the door. All the way down to Old Sacramento, I kept repeating to myself, "There's no one behind you. There's no one behind you." Giving in to the sensation would only make it stronger.

Magic existed whether we wanted it to or not, but believing in it definitely made it stronger. The less power I gave whatever was in the box, the less power it would have.

It wasn't easy, though. The hair on the back of my neck was standing up so hard that I felt like needles were being poked into me. A spot between my shoulder blades itched with the sensation of eyes boring into it. In my determination to not look behind me, I nearly creamed into another car changing lanes to exit onto J Street and drive into Old Sac. The horn blared and I nearly jumped out of my comfy seat in the Buick. Maybe not using my rearviews was taking my don't-look-back dictum a little too far.

I managed to make it into McClannigan's without a traffic accident or tripping over my own feet, but only just. I breathed a sigh of relief as I walked in and Paul looked up and saw me. If there was anyone I'd trust to have my back, it was Paul.

Well, as long as the Pack didn't ask him to do something at the same time. Then I was probably screwed.

I plopped down on a bar stool. The place wasn't as crowded as it had been when I'd come with Ted the last time. Even McClannigan's was a little slower on a school night.

"You look worried," Paul said.

"I feel worried. I'm just not sure what I'm worried about."

He poured me a club soda with a twist of lime. I didn't argue, but I did look at it sadly. He added a maraschino cherry. I sighed. He added a triangle of pineapple. I looked up at him and fluttered my eyelashes. He added a wedge of orange. I figured that was the most I was going to get out of him and started to munch on the fruit.

He was right most of the time. Alcohol wasn't exactly a good refuge for me. I didn't need anything that was going to make me a step slower or delay my reflexes even a fraction of a second. As unsettled as I felt tonight, I was fine with the club soda. I did like to get what little I could from him, though. A little fresh fruit seemed the least he could offer as a concession.

I felt more settled watching people come and go behind me in the big mirror behind the bar. The prickle of unease was still there, but it was lessening.

Ted got there before Meredith. I hardly needed the mirror to know he was in the room, though. I'd like to think my first hint was the subtle pickup in the speed of my pulse, as if I reacted to him even when I wasn't even fully aware that he was there. But it could also have been Paul lifting his head and sniffing the air. Ted did smell really good, like cookies baking on a cold day. It was sort of a vanilla-y thing. Of course, Paul could have also sensed the speed up in my heartbeat and be looking for its cause. Shapeshifters had crazy good senses that made even my heightened perception look like night goggles from a Cracker Jack box.

Either way, Ted walked up behind me, landed a kiss on the side of my neck and I felt another little notch of tension give way. I knew Ted had my back whether a Pack called him or not. I was his Pack and he was mine. Of course, he didn't have superhuman powers, but I'll take loyalty over super-strength on almost any given day.

Almost, mind you. Sometimes there's nothing that can trump super-strength.

Paul pulled a draft beer for Ted and slid it to him across the bar. I considered grumbling for form's sake but didn't. Paul would be plenty annoyed with me when he found out why I was here. I didn't need to pre-piss him off.

"How's your arm?" I asked Ted.

He flexed it. "It's okay."

"Can I see?" I reached for it.

He pulled away and shook his head. "Not here."

"What did you do to your arm?" Paul asked.

"I was bitten by . . ." Ted look over at me, clearly at a loss. Apparently information didn't stick with a person well when they were feverish and half out of their head.

"A cadejo," I finished for him. "Or, more likely, the son of one."

Paul sniffed again. "Black?"

I nodded.

"What are you doing for it?" He leaned in.

"Alex prescribed an antibiotic and Norah had some powdered slippery elm to pack into it."

Paul arched a brow at me and grinned. "Norah had powdered slippery elm? What's up with that?"

I sighed. "She's still freaked out. I lent her my copy of the grimoire. I thought if she had some real information about what she should be frightened of, she wouldn't have to be frightened of everything."

"Not bad thinking, Melina." Paul looked at me appraisingly.

"I am more than a pretty face," I agreed.

I was still deciding how to broach the subject of why we were really here when Meredith walked in.

Paul's head had risen when he'd scented Ted. When Meredith entered the bar, Paul's head snapped up like it was spring-loaded. I watched him watch her walk through the room. His face was a study in conflict. I saw desire and irritation and guilt and anger play across the handsome planes of his face before it settled into the grumpy frown he wore most of the time when Meredith was in the room. I'd be grumpy, too, if my undies were in that much of a twist. I wished I understood what had bunched his up that much.

Ted poked me and gave me a "what gives" kind of shrug. I shrugged right back. I had some suspicions but really didn't completely understand what was going on between those two.

She slid onto the bar stool on the other side of me and gave me a quick squeeze. "How are you, darling? Feeling okay?"

Meredith had been around when Mae had died. While Paul and Alex had been sympathetic, Meredith seemed to go that extra step. I wondered if in addition to her skills as a witch she was also an empath. It certainly wasn't unheard of.

"I'm okay."

"Are you sleeping?" she asked.

I shot her a look.

She made a little face back at me. "I know you don't need much, but you do need some."

"I'm fine, Meredith." I turned to Ted. "Tell her I'm fine."

"She's fine." He echoed.

Meredith shrugged. "Good. You're fine. Case closed. Why am I here?"

"Yes." Paul leaned across the bar and bared his teeth a bit at me. "Why is she here? Why do you always have to meet her here?"

I had originally thought that Meredith had always wanted to meet at McClannigan's because it was a handy excuse to see Paul. The desire on his face when she walked into a room was so obvious, not to mention the musk rising off both their bodies the second they were around each other, that it seemed like a pretty clear-cut goal to me.

Then I'd watched Meredith walk a hedge circle in the storeroom one night.

While I'm pretty sure that Meredith was happy to remind Paul on regular intervals exactly how much he wanted her, I was also reasonably certain that there was a center of some power under McClannigan's.

There are places of power. Everyone knows about the energy vortices in Sedona and the Haleakala Crater in Hawaii. Those are big kahunas. There are also smaller areas of power all over the place. Everyone's felt them. That corner of the house where you feel especially cozy. The spot near the street corner where you're always nervous. Maybe even that particular seat at the movie theater that makes you want to make out with your boyfriend. Most of us shrug them off as moods or ambience or figments of our imagination.

They're not.

They're real. Sometimes it's possible to trace back how a spot became a place of power and why. Sometimes it's not. There's an alley near an old record shop in Sacramento where a girl committed suicide back in the fifties. My flesh rises up in goose bumps every time I walk past it. I don't know if it became a place of despair because she committed suicide there or if she committed suicide there because it was a place of despair. I just know I'll walk more than a few blocks out of my way to avoid walking there.

In the back of McClannigan's, there's a source of power that Meredith is adept at bending to her own whims and ways. How it got there, I can't say. Whether the fact that Paul has been a bartender at McClannigan's for going on one hundred and thirty years now has anything to do with safeguarding this particular place of power or not, I can't say either, although I have my suspicions.

I took the box out of my purse and plopped it onto the bar. "I wanted you to look at this."

She did. Literally. In fact, we all did. The four of us sat there at the bar and stared at the little box like it was suddenly going to start doing tricks.

"Can I open it?" Meredith asked, looking up at me.

"Be my guest." She reached for it and I stopped her hand with mine.

"I'm not sure you want to do it right here on the bar, though. The man whose bed I found this under committed suicide." I thought about it for a second. "Well, he ran out into traffic in front of a speeding semi. It sounded pretty suicidal. Something's not right with this, though."

Meredith nodded. "Let's take it to the back room."

I swept the box back into my bag and we stood up. Ted stood also, as if he were going to follow us. Meredith shook her head. "Not you. You wait here."

He looked like he was about to protest, but I shot him a look and he sat back down. He did know when to pick his battles.

Paul merely growled at us as we walked away. "Clean up after yourselves back there."

Meredith had me sweep the area under the one swinging lamp back in the storeroom. "Set the box in the center."

I did, nearly dropping it. I didn't like to hold it in my hands. Something about it felt very wrong.

Then Meredith began to walk her circle. Three times she went around, murmuring her spell as she went. Each time, I felt the magic of her hedge circle grow. By the final circle, I could see the trail of bright blue light behind each of her footsteps. Her auburn hair crackled around her head and the fine alabaster of her skin glowed. Her eyes were shadowed dark circles in her pale face.

Kneeling next to the box, she crossed and uncrossed her arms over it three times. "Three times the circle I have connected. I beseech you, Goddess, to be protected. I've cast my sight in the directions four. Let this object have power no more."

Then she opened it. From outside the circle, I held my breath. Inside the wrapping was a simple cardboard box. Nestled inside that on a bed of cotton was a little doll, no more than six inches tall. It was crude. The body was no more than a fabric suggestion of a body with arms and legs. The face was drawn on with a marker and looked more like a skull than any individual person. The most notable thing about it was the fact that the head faced backward, looking over its own shoulder, as if something were following it.

MEREDITH HAD RECALLED HER CIRCLE, STEPPING BACKWARD carefully over the outlines. We crouched over the doll.

"Voodoo, Meredith? Who around here practices voodoo?" I asked. It was a foolish question and I knew it. One of the things I loved about northern California was that you could find anything here. Anything at all. Everyone from all four corners of the known world had emigrated here at some point. For the weather. For the opportunity. For the gold. For the computers.

And one of the things that made me crazy about northern California was that everything was here. Everyone who came brought their gods and goddesses, their angels and their demons. There would be someone here who practiced voodoo.

Meredith shook her head. "Not voodoo. Or not voodoo per se."

"What does that mean?"

She looked up at me, her head cocked to one side. "*Per se* is a Latin phrase. It means 'by itself.' "

I glared. "I didn't want a grammar lesson. I wanted to know what you meant by that."

"This doesn't look like a classic voodoo doll. It doesn't feel like it either. This has something else going on with it. Can't you feel it?"

She was right. I could feel it. It didn't have the sort of tropical feel that I associated with voodoo. It had more of a spice to it. "Santeria?" I suggested.

She shook her head again. "No, but not far off. You don't know who made it?"

I thought of the woman in the cemetery. The one with eyes full of tears and a heart full of hate. "Not really."

"What do you want to do with it? It's a powerful little poppet." Meredith looked at it with interest.

Didn't I know that? "What would happen if we threw it away?" I looked as closely as I could at it without touching it. Whatever cooties it had, I didn't want. It looked a little like I remembered Neil Bossard looking. Tall. Brown hair. It was holding a little guitar. Maybe it was specific enough to him that we could just toss it in a garbage can and walk away.

Meredith winced. "I don't think that's a good idea. It may have been intended for a particular person, but there's enough mojo on this thing to affect anyone around it. Have you felt it?"

"You mean, did I wake up in the middle of my living room fighting off an imaginary devil dog and spend the whole day thinking something was following me? As a matter of fact, yes." I sat back on my heels.

She raised her eyebrows. "And you have some knowledge about what you're dealing with. Imagine what havoc this thing would wreak bouncing around the average neighborhood."

I did not want to imagine. It sounded nasty. I'd rather think about rainbows and unicorns. "So how do we get rid of it?"

"That will take some doing, but I think we can do it tonight." She glanced at her watch. "We'll need to gather up some things, but we should have enough time before midnight."

Good thing I didn't have to work at the hospital tonight. Since I'd taken over the dojo, I'd cut my hours down there and didn't need to be in at eleven tonight. "Let's do it, then."

"Go get a clean white-linen napkin from Paul. And I do mean clean. It needs to be fresh from the laundry. Then we'll head down to the river."

IT WASN'T LIKE PAUL WAS GOING TO GIVE ME A CLEAN LINEN napkin and then let Meredith and I waltz out into the night on our own. I knew him better than that. I was pretty sure Meredith did, too. He might, for whatever reasons, be trying to avoid Meredith, but it was pretty clear how he felt when she was around. I'd seen him terrify men with a glare just for watching the sway of her backside as she sashayed by, and Meredith sashayed pretty much everywhere she went. She was his woman. He just didn't seem to want her. Or maybe he didn't want to want her. Any way you colored it, I was confused. I could only imagine how he must be feeling.

I hadn't been entirely sure how Ted was going to take the proceedings. He always wanted to be my knight in shining armor, but like I said, I do try to keep him out of the more woo-woo things I encounter each day and he'd already been bitten by the spawn of a demonic dog this week. He wasn't about to be left out, though.

Which was how it ended up with the four of us down at the boat launch in Discovery Park, about where the American River and the Sacramento River meet. The park was closed, but it takes more than a few padlocks and gates to keep a determined werewolf and an irritated Messenger out. Neither of us have the patience for being picklocks. Both of us can snap your average chain while barely breaking a sweat.

Ted had made a little sound of protest when I snapped the first chain we'd encountered, but Paul growled at him. "In or out, Boy Scout?"

He'd gritted his teeth and said, "In." He looked unhappy, though.

Now we crouched over the doll at the river's edge. Meredith had used the linen napkin to pick the doll up from the storeroom floor without ever letting it touch her skin, in much the same way I'd seen people picking up after their dogs. It was still wrapped up. I don't think any of us really wanted to see its nasty little skeletal face.

She'd also brought along a case from the trunk of her car. Out of it, she pulled a set of thick white candles and a long crescent-shaped silver blade. I craned to see what else was in the case, but she gave me a dirty look and turned it away from me. "What?" I asked.

"It's none of your business." She angled the top of the case so that I couldn't see anything inside.

"Do you keep that in your car all the time?" Was it some kind of special witches' survival kit, like a supernatural version of having blankets and water in your trunk when you drove up into the mountains?

She shook her head. "The candles would be nothing more than a pile of wax in the summertime."

"So you keep it in there in the winter?" I frowned. It would be seasonal, wouldn't it? Wicca was tied closely to nature and if nature was about anything, it was about cycles. Seasons turning. Death and birth. Baseball giving way to football.

"Melina. Let it go. I need to concentrate. Stop pestering me."

Paul grabbed me by the back of my shirt and dragged me back a few feet, as if I were a misbehaving puppy. Ted knocked Paul's hand off me and the two squared off. I leapt up between them.

"Yo. I'm trying to make a hedge circle here. Could the three of you stop roughhousing for ten seconds so I can think?" Meredith stood with her hands on her hips, her hair already starting to crackle with static. We all muttered apologies and stood quietly, although I noticed that Ted made sure he was standing between Paul and me.

Meredith drew a circle around the doll in the sand, and Paul and I picked up all the stray cigarette butts and bits of candy wrapper that we found within its perimeter. Then she cast her circle again. On her final journey around the edge, as the blue fire trailed behind her, Ted made a funny sound. I took his hand. "It's okay, Dorothy. She's a good witch."

Paul snorted.

Ted shook his head.

Meredith unwrapped the doll and laid it on top of the napkin. She raised her arms in the air. Sparks danced around her fingertips. "That which has been made, let be unmade. From rag and bone, by fingers sewn, let evil fly back to its home." She picked up one of the bottles she had removed from her case, uncorked it and poured it over the doll. My nose twitched with the sharp scent of vinegar.

As the liquid hit the doll, it began to smoke, slowly smoldering down into a pile of ashes.

"So let it be done," Meredith said as the smoke began to clear. Carefully, folding the cloth away from her and toward the water, she rewrapped the remains of the doll.

Again, she walked her circles backward. Ted's fingers laced through mine and tightened as the blue lights glowed and dimmed behind her steps. I'd seen Meredith cast a circle or two, and it was still impressive. I wondered what it was like to watch it for the first time, reconciling that it was actually happening with how damn good she was at it all at once. Poor guy. I wondered if he ever regretted knocking on my door and barging into my life.

Once she was done, she carefully picked up the napkin, walked to the edge of the river and cast the doll away into the moving stream. She turned to face us, brushing off her hands, and said, "Well, that's done. Who's hungry?"

TED HAD BEEN LOOKING A LITTLE PALE BY THE TIME MEREDITH had finished getting rid of Neil Bossard's voodoo doll for me, so we passed on getting an early breakfast with her and Paul, despite Paul's desperate looks in my direction.

On the way back to the car, I finally worked up the nerve to ask Meredith what was up between the two of them.

She sighed. "Think about it, Melina."

I thought for a second and still came up empty-handed. "Nope. Got nothing."

She sighed. "Do you think Paul is a good hunter?"

Paul was powerfully built, both as a man and as a wolf. His senses were sharp and he knew how to stay focused. "Oh, yeah. I think he's a great hunter."

"Do you think he's smart?"

Since I regularly went to him for advice for everything from how to make a really good dry martini to how to get rid of Chinese vampires from beneath the streets of Sacramento, I had to say, "Yeah."

"What qualities does a Pack look for in an Alpha?"

I slowed down a little. Smarts and strength made for a good Alpha, but the Sierra pack already had an Alpha. Chuck was older than Paul, but not by enough to make him old and toothless yet. Werewolves aged, though not like humans. It took centuries, but they did get old. Chuck hadn't yet. "Chuck is stepping down?"

"Nope. And he doesn't want to."

I digested that for a few minutes. Chuck must be seeing Paul as a threat. "But Paul always stays out of Pack politics." It was one of the things I loved about him. While his devotion to the Pack was never in question, he clearly saw the absurdities of the intrigues and alliances that were brokered in smoke-filled back dens.

"Doesn't make him less of a threat. It almost makes him more of one. If there's a power struggle, he could be seen as a neutral party." Meredith kept her pace slow so that we were well behind Paul and Ted. "And can you think of something that could make him more of a threat than an alliance with a powerful witch?"

I stopped walking all together and gawked at her. "So they've forbidden you and Paul to see each other?" I cast about for an analogy. "You're like the Romeo and Juliet of the supernatural world?"

Meredith rolled her eyes. "Hardly. The big bad wolf up there isn't exactly committing suicide over me."

"He is pretty frustrated, though."

"Only when he actually lays eyes on me," Meredith observed wryly. "Which I make sure he does as often as possible."

We fist-bumped in the dark.

TED AND I WENT BACK TO MY APARTMENT. IT WAS LATE. THERE wasn't a single decent parking space nearby. We ended up walking about three blocks to get back. By the time we got to the apartment door, Ted was really flagging. Then there were the three flights up. Perspiration dotted his forehead by the time we got to the door. I fished my keys out of my bag, unlocked the door and hit the chain.

I nearly cried. Well, not really. I'm not much of a crier. Norah actually hit me when we watched *Up* and accused me of being made of stone when I didn't cry during the opening montage. Now, though, I kind of wanted to cry. I wanted to get the man I loved into my apartment and into bed before he fell on the floor. I also wanted to do that without kicking down my own apartment door.

"Norah," I whispered through the door, trying to wake her but not the neighbors across the landing. The weaselly guy who used to live there had moved out and now there was this nice couple who seemed to do nothing but go to work and come home.

"I could kick it in, if you wanted," Ted offered. It was a nice offer, but he honestly didn't look like he could even stand on one leg, much less kick a door with the other. I didn't want to hurt his pride, though.

"And you think that would make Norah less fearful how?" I didn't think doors being kicked in during the night was going to make her issues any better. Besides, if I wanted the door kicked in, I could do it myself.

"Norah," I whisper-shouted more urgently. "Wake up."

"I'm coming," she said. "Keep your panties on."

"Bad advice," Ted whispered in my ear, making me shiver a little.

"Could you let us in? It's late." I called to her.

"I'm coming." The door shut and then reopened sans chain. Norah scowled at us. "Why are you coming in so late?"

"Why are you trying to keep me out of my apartment?" I shot back, not really feeling like explaining my whereabouts to her for oh so many reasons. First and foremost, it was none of her beeswax. Second, it was likely to freak her out more.

"I'm not trying to keep you out. You know who I'm trying to keep out." She stalked away from the door and plopped down on a bar stool.

"He's not so bad. The two of you were fine last night." I followed her in and then closed and locked the door behind Ted and me.

"That's part of the problem, Melina. It's part of why I don't want to see him." She slumped down on the counter and pillowed her face on her arms.

"I don't get it." I sat down next to her. That made no sense whatsoever. Of course, I was tired and not thinking all that straight.

"Neither do I. He scares me." She turned her head so she could see me.

I sighed. "He should. He is what he is. It's important to remember that. He has better control and more of a conscience than any other vampire I've ever met, but he's still a vampire."

"I know that. I don't want to have anything to do with that." She sat up now.

"That's good. That's fine. Just forget about him, then."

"I've tried to. I want to. Then why do I dream about him, Melina? Why do I have to fight myself not to run to him when he walks into the room?" Anxiety made her voice rise in pitch.

"Wait a second. You want to run to him? I thought you wanted to run from him?"

"That's exactly why I want to run from him. When I see him, I feel all hopped up. My heart beats faster. I breathe harder. I can't take my eyes off him. All I want is for him to touch me, but I know what he is. I know what he's capable of. I don't want that, Melina. It scares the hell out of me." Her eyes were huge and wide in her too-pale face.

"I'll talk to him. Maybe he's doing it. Maybe he's compelling you." I didn't have a good feeling about this. The last time I'd accused Alex of invading my dreams on purpose, I'd found out it was my own damn subconscious that was conjuring him up.

"What if he's not doing it? What if it's me?" A little bead of sweat formed on her upper lip.

I wasn't sure what the answer to that was. Keeping one's blood from going into a vampire was much more within my sphere of capabilities than getting a vampire out of one's blood.

"Then we'll figure that one out, too." I assured her.

Norah hugged me and shambled back to her room.

Ted started rummaging through the cabinets. "Do you have any booze in here? I could use a drink."

I pulled a bottle of Scotch from the bottom cabinet.

He took it from me and poured two fingers into a short, fat glass. He took a deep drink of it and then asked, "So is that like a normal Monday night for you?"

I considered. "Nearly."

"How come you need Meredith to do that . . . stuff for you?" He set the glass down on the counter.

"I can't do magic." It was a little embarrassing, but it was the truth. I can't cast a spell worth a damn. Ask me to jump over a twelve-foot wall? No problem. Take down a gremlin? I'm your gal. Cast the simplest spell? No freakin' way.

"Aren't you kind of magic yourself?" He set the glass of Scotch down.

I didn't blame him for being confused. It wasn't like I understood it. It frustrated me to no end. "I'm not really magic. Spells and stuff are their own brand of supernatural spookiness. I don't have the knack. Some people are just born with it." I, on the other hand, was born—or reborn, really—with a knack for seeing weird shit. It wasn't nearly as useful.

"I guess that sort of makes sense." He nodded to himself and then rubbed his face. "Can we go to bed now?"

"You bet, tiger." I slid my arm around his waist and leaned against his chest, reassured by the steady thump of his heart.

"Do you think Meredith is casting spells on Paul?" he asked as we swayed down the hallway to my room.

"No. I don't think she has to. I think she's got him all shook up without casting a single spell." I thought it might be a whole lot easier for both of them if she couldn't cast spells.

He stopped in front of my door and kissed me. First with tenderness and then with growing urgency. I sighed and melded my body into his, loving the feel of his taut muscles against me, of his arms around me.

He lifted his head, looking down at me, his eyes dark with desire. "That's just you and me, right? No tricks."

"No tricks," I assured him. I slipped my T-shirt off over my head. "Look. Nothing up my sleeves."

"That's a relief." He took my hand and led me into the bedroom to show me a few tricks of his own.

I WAS GOING TO HAVE TO GO BACK TO ELMVILLE. I SAT AND mulled over my morning coffee after Ted left and tried to figure out how to get around it. I couldn't come up with anything.

I needed to snoop around Kurt Rawley's place. I'd delivered a package to him. Had it had a little doll in it like Neil Bossard's? I'd be willing to bet on it. I tried to remember the circumstances of Rawley's death and came up blank except for something to do with fire.

I sighed and started up my computer. I'd be better off figuring out everything I could before I went down there again.

According to what I could find on the Internet, Kurt Rawley had died in a house fire. There was some speculation that Rawley had set the fire himself, but the newspaper articles didn't make it clear whether they suspected Rawley had set the fire by accident or on purpose.

I wasn't sure it mattered, although I did have the address. I glanced up at the clock. If I drove fast, I could be down to Elmville, have a few minutes to poke around in the daylight and be back in time to teach at the dojo by four thirty. There wasn't time for more dawdling, though. I got dressed and headed out.

On my way into Elmville, I decided to drive past the place where Neil Bossard died. I parked the Buick in the lot in front of a Quik Stop on Highway 120 and walked toward the road. I'd been a little concerned that I wouldn't be able to locate the exact place that Bossard died. Usually I'm aware of anything supernatural around me at the moment, in the here and now. Sometimes if a presence is strong enough, I can sense where something has been. Not always, which is something of a relief, otherwise I'd be bombarded constantly. Without some kind of power signature, I didn't think I'd be able to find the exact spot where he died and somehow I felt it was important that I did.

It turned out not to be a problem. Someone had erected a *descanso* on the spot. They dot the highways and byways of the Southwest and California with sad regularity. Little white crosses twined around with plastic flowers, teddy bears and trinkets around the base. They mark the spot where someone has died, usually in a traffic accident, like miniature shrines to those that have passed. There can be several at really dangerous intersections. There was no doubt this one was for Bossard. Someone had stuck a photo of him to the cross.

Thing is, they're not so much for Anglos, which Bossard definitely was. *Descansos* are more of a Latino tradition. I shrugged. One of the nice things about living in northern California is that everybody mixes and mingles. It's easy to get exposed to other traditions and make them your own. Somebody who missed Bossard, and there were quite a few candidates based on what I saw at the memorial service, had erected a *descanso* for him. It was sweet in a sad way.

I crouched down next to it, closed my eyes and cast my senses wide. I tried to sense if there was anything supernatural here. I got nothing.

I waited, willing myself to relax and quiet my mind. I focused on my breathing. Still nothing.

I stood up. There was nothing here. It didn't mean that nothing supernatural had been here. It could have either been here too long ago for me to sense it or not been powerful enough to leave an energy signature.

Or there really hadn't been anything chasing Neil Bossard and the little voodoo doll under his bed had messed with his head so much that he had run into traffic and gotten himself killed.

All in all, it was a damn handy hands-off way to commit murder.

I FOUND MY WAY TO KURT RAWLEY'S HOUSE. OR WHAT WAS left of it. The fire had taken out most of the front of the house. The neighborhood wasn't anywhere near as nice as Bossard's. The houses were smaller and much more likely to have aluminum siding. The yards were small and the grass was not always all that green. There weren't many of those fancy well-tended flowerbeds that I'd seen all over the place in Bossard's hood.

Which isn't to say that Rawley had lived in a slum. It was just a little more working class than upper middle class.

I was a little surprised that no one had done anything with the lot yet. There were danger signs posted on the edges of the property and someone had strung fencing around the perimeter of it, but a person wouldn't need even the piddly powers of a Messenger to clear the fence.

I glanced up and down the street. Someone was pulling into a driveway in a beat-up brown station wagon a few houses down and I walked on past the Rawley place, trying to look nonchalant. I do nonchalant pretty well. I'm even better at indifferent. I consider it a specialty.

The neighbor went into her house, and I did a one-eighty and headed back to the Rawley house, clearing the fence with a quick leap before anyone else could show up and spot me.

The place smelled terrible. It had been weeks since the fire, but I could still smell smoke under the damp smell of mold and rot. I'd probably be smelling it all day. Sometimes it's not a blessing to have extra-sharp senses.

I made my way around to the back of the house. Enough of the fence around the backyard still stood that I wouldn't be visible from the neighboring houses on the street. Then I repeated what I'd done by Neil Bossard's *descanso*. I closed my eyes, stilled my breath and opened all my senses.

At first I felt nothing. I'm a little prone to impatience, but I've learned that things don't always speak on my timetable and I have to corral my own unruly tendencies. Mae used to say that the skills that come to us the least naturally are often the ones we end up being the best at because we have to work at them so hard. I focused on my breathing some more and tried to still my restless mind by listening to the steady drum of my heart.

I don't know how long it was before I felt the first flicker. It could have been two minutes. It could have been ten. When I get into that state, time gets very relative. It can stand practically still or race past. But regardless of how long it took, I'd felt it. I could picture Mae smiling at me. It felt good.

I stayed calm, not wanting to break the connection until it was stronger. I was rewarded with another flicker, this one a bit longer.

I risked opening my eyes and took a few steps toward the ruins of Kurt Rawley's home.

The flicker grew stronger. I walked up what was left of the porch stairs, careful to watch my step. My reflexes were good, but I didn't want to have to leap off a collapsing porch if I could avoid it.

The stairs held and I walked farther off what had been the back porch into what had clearly been the kitchen. I felt like I'd walked through a spiderweb. I brushed at my face, but the feeling stayed the same. I ignored it as best I could and kept walking, feeling the growing strength of the flicker like a divining rod.

I picked my way through the rubble of what had once been a home, careful to step over the remains of furniture and walls, guessing at what had been here before. The heap to my left looked like the remains of a sofa, with the lump of what could have been a chair at one time next to it. The living room, clearly. A hallway led off to the right toward the bedrooms. I stepped that way and the flicker grew into a flame. I kept going.

I could tell which room had been the bathroom. Tubs and toilets don't burn that well. I was pretty sure the other rooms had been bedrooms, but the damage in this area was even worse. Floorboards creaked under me and I stepped as lightly as I could. The flame was strongest at the doorway to the second room on the left.

I did not want to go in there. The energy coming from the room was nasty. It wasn't precisely evil, not like a demon or something like that, but more like that one little bit of sour in an otherwise good bunch of grapes that sticks to your tongue. I could taste it in the back of my mouth, like bile rising. I swallowed hard and walked into the room.

If there was any doubt about whether or not I was in the right place or if Kurt Rawley's death was connected to Neil Bossard's death, it was erased when I saw the *descanso* shoved into the sodden wreckage of the bed. It was nearly identical to the one erected on the site where Bossard died. It was white. Plastic flowers twined around it. The only difference was that Kurt Rawley's photograph was stuck in the center of it rather than Bossard's.

I picked up a piece of wood that might once have been from a dresser or a wardrobe—it was hard to tell—and poked at the pile of sodden ashes in the center of the room. Nothing leapt out at me, physically or metaphysically. I poked some more, trying to turn over some of the mess to see what was underneath.

Then I saw it. A little flash of something white. Or at least whitish. I dug around it with the stick. It was soaked and dirty, but it looked like one of the legs of the voodoo doll that had been under Neil Bossard's bed. I fished it out, using my stick plus another one like a pair of giant chopsticks. It was definitely part of what had been another voodoo doll, but this one had little plastic bugs glued all over what was left of it.

I'D MANAGED TO GET THE DOLL CORPSE—I COULDN'T HELP but think of it that way, as if it had had a life of its own to lose—out of the nasty ashen mess of what had been Kurt Rawley's bedroom without actually touching it. If anything ever had a severe case of cooties, it was this thing. I nudged it out of the mess with the sticks and then I wrapped it up in tissues and shoved it in the baggie that had held the sandwich I'd packed for myself to eat on the way down. Maybe a really good Ziploc could contain voodoo vibes, or whatever these things were. I sort of doubted it, though. I have it on the best authority that plastic is actually porous. I have no idea if voodoo molecules can sneak through Ziplocs, but it was all I had and I am all about trying to use whatever's on hand. It's part of my whole self-reliance thing.

I picked my way back through the house and out the back door with my nasty little bundle. My mission accomplished, I wasn't being as careful about being spotted as I'd been on my way in and as I strolled out of the front yard and vaulted the fence, I saw a curtain twitch in a window across the street. Must there be a Gladys Kravitz on every block in America? I frowned. It was too late now and I figured the best plan was to simply hightail it out of there before someone called the cops on me. Again. Complacency does have repercussions, doesn't it?

I did my best to stroll nonchalantly back to where I'd parked the Buick a few blocks away. It wasn't easy. That curtain twitch in the window made me uneasy. Couple that with the feeling that I'd somehow walked through spiderwebs and I wanted to break into a hard healthy run and sweat all the bad feelings out. I fought it and managed to keep my pace to business brisk. I couldn't slow it further than that.

I'd rounded the last corner and could see the Buick sitting solid and sure up ahead when a woman darted out from between two houses, planted herself in front of me and said, "What the hell were you doing in my house?"

I guess I should have run.

She didn't look like a threat. She looked like someone's mom and not one of those California yoga-toned sitcom moms on television or even one of those over-educated no-makeup university moms like mine. She did, however, look spitting mad.

"I'm sorry. Which house is yours?" I asked, as if I'd been in more than one.

"Don't play stupid with me," she spit.

It was a little bit of a relief to have stupid not work for once. I'd have to find a new fallback position, though. I cast around for another option.

I was pretty sure I could drop this lady in about ten seconds. She was easily twenty years older than me and obviously a bit out of shape. There was nothing supernatural about her and she didn't hold any weapons, as far as I could see. It didn't feel right, though. It felt, in fact, a little like I'd be being a bully, not a role I relish. Just because you can physically take another person doesn't mean you should.

"Why can't you people leave him alone? Haven't you done enough?" Tears filled her eyes.

"Leave who alone?"

"He paid his dues. He went to jail. Wasn't that enough? Now he's dead. He's gone. My baby's gone." The tears overflowed her eyes and she began to shake.

I moved to go around her. Her pain was so plain and so raw, it rushed through me like a knife. She wasn't going to let me go so easily, though. She shifted to block me. "What more do you people want? What more can you take? My boy is gone. My house is gone. It's all gone. Isn't that enough? What more could you take from me?"

I put my hands up in front of me, as if I could shield myself from her hate and anger. "I don't know who you think I am, but you're mistaken. I was just in the neighborhood and I'm leaving now." I looked around. What people was I a part of? Who was it that wanted to take everything from this woman? And why?

She moved out of my way now. "You'd better leave. Don't think I won't call the cops on you, though. They've got a word for what you're doing. It's called harassment. It's illegal, too, you stupid spic." She spit on the ground in front of me and then let me pass.

I didn't wait for her to change her mind. I rushed to the Buick and took off. In the rearview mirror, I could see her jotting down my license plate number on her hand.

Fabulous. If she did call the cops, it would take them seconds to figure out who I was.

That would be a big enough problem. The bigger problem would be if they figured out what I was.

THE ADRENALINE FROM MY CONFRONTATION SEEPED AWAY slowly. I would have probably felt better faster if she'd taken an actual shot at me. A fist strike to my chin or a kick to my ribs would have been easier for me to deflect. Physical fights were so much more straightforward than emotional ones and I knew how to deal with them better.

All that hurt and anger thrown in my face? I had no idea how to counter-thrust, how to deflect. I wasn't even sure what it all meant.

The "spic" thing was pretty clear. I don't have the most clear-cut features. With my dark hair and olive skin, this wouldn't be the first time that someone thought I was Latina. My Spanish sucks, so people rarely labor under that misapprehension for long. The woman I was pretty sure was Mrs. Rawley hadn't been listening for my accent, though. She had enough hate and hurt stored up inside her that it probably roared in her ears nonstop. She probably couldn't even hear herself think anymore.

I thought about the look on Mrs. Bossard's face at her son's funeral. Or, I guess, the lack of any expression on her face. Would that numbness turn to hate eventually? And why toward Latinos? There was a lot I didn't know.

I brushed at my face. That cobweb sensation still hadn't left me. Whatever I'd walked through was sticking to me like glue. Didn't spiderwebs have some kind of sticky stuff on them to trap the bugs? It was probably what was keeping it stuck to my face. I pressed down a little harder on the accelerator. With a little judicious speeding, I might have time for a hot shower before I had to teach.

I wonder what the Latino angle was going to be in all this. I had put the *descansos* down to local custom rather than belonging to a particular ethnic group until Mrs. Rawley started hurling incorrect racial epithets at me. It still made no sense. A *descanso* was a remembrance, a memorial, not a desecration or a curse. They implied regret and sorrow over whatever had taken the life they memorialized. Why put them up if you were the one who murdered the person? Why murder a second boy if you already regretted the first one? It wasn't making sense to me.

I rubbed at the cobwebs again. This time I flipped down the vanity mirror. Maybe if I could see them, I could get rid of them, but no. There was nothing visible. The strands must be too fine. A horn honked to my right and I quickly corrected course. I must have swerved a little into the other lane. I flipped up the mirror and told myself to pay attention to the road.

I switched on the radio, hoping to find something to distract me. Oldies, oldies and more oldies, and a couple of stations pretending to be something other than oldies but really just playing oldies. I flipped it back off.

Something started to crawl along my neck. I slapped at it, but my hand came away with nothing. I could still feel it, though, skittering under my hair. I shook myself, trying to dislodge it. Another horn beeped at me. I had swerved again. This wasn't safe. I pulled off at the next rest stop and raced into the bathroom.

I peered at myself in the tinny mirrors. The light was bad, but my eyesight is exceptionally good. I couldn't see anything. No webs. No bugs. Now that I was out of the car and not driving, the sensation of something crawling on me was gone. I scrubbed at my face and neck and arms with the rough paper towels anyway. Satisfied that I'd done everything I could in a public bathroom without getting arrested, I walked back to the car.

A breeze lifted my hair off my damp neck. It felt damn good, clean and bug-free.

I got back in the Buick and eased myself back onto Highway 120. I chose the least objectionable oldies station and set the cruise control on the Buick. I had already turned onto Highway 99 when I found myself brushing at the nonexistent cobwebs on my face again.

I willed myself to keep my hands on the wheel and my eyes on the road. I was going to kill myself if I kept trying to get rid of that sensation.

That's when the lightbulb went off in my head. Who had killed themselves? Neil Bossard and Kurt Rawley. I looked over at the seat next to me. One of the legs of the little voodoo doll peeped out of its tissue covering inside its protective baggie, a little plastic spider stuck to its foot. Apparently voodoo molecules could seep through plastic. Stupid polymers. Couldn't trust them farther than you could throw them.

I jammed my Bluetooth into my ear and dialed Meredith on my cell. "Meredith, I've got another one."

I QUITE CLEVERLY LEFT THE DOLL IN MY CAR WHEN I GOT TO the karate studio. The last thing I needed was fifteen twelve-year-olds rolling around the mat, thinking they had spiders crawling all over them. I didn't know what the reach of the nasty little thing's powers were, although I did notice a number of people wiping their faces and slapping at their necks as they walked past my car in the parking lot.

I felt pretty safe inside the studio. Sophie showed up about a half an hour after I got there. The few moments to myself had been nice. I'd caught up on e-mail, paid a couple of bills and tried to figure out my bank statement, which still pretty much defeated me every month.

"I brought you a Diet Coke and a Luna Bar," she said, dropping her offerings on my desk and flinging herself into a chair.

"You're a peach." I grabbed the food. I could use the calories and the caffeine.

"Not a very good one," she said, looking at her shoes. "I can't figure out what to do with that axe. It's not talking to me. Can you help me figure out where it's supposed to go?"

"What have you done so far?" I leaned back in my chair and popped open the Diet Coke.

"I googled Ginnar." She didn't look up.

"And?"

She shook her head. "Nothing remotely useful."

"He's not going to be listed on whitepages.com, Sophie." I know. I know. I'd pledged to cut down on the sarcasm. It was hard, though. It's been my default for so many years now.

She flung out her hands. "Then where?"

"Well, think about it a little. What is he?" I could do this. I could be reasonable and help her think this thing through just the way Mae used to help me think through problems on my own.

"I don't know. I don't even know that he's a he, to be honest with you."

With dwarves that tended to be kind of a moot point. I'm pretty sure they knew which gender they were, but it was pretty hard for anyone else to tell. Female dwarves' beards could be just as long and lustrous as the males'. Little dwarves had to come from somewhere, though. Not that I planned to think about that very hard. "We know he or she's a dwarf, right? Where do dwarves live?"

"Inside mountains?" Sophie looked up.

An excellent first step. "Are there mountains near here?"

She nodded. "Lots."

"Maybe you should start there. Take it for a drive up into the Sierras. See if it starts talking a little louder. The closer an object gets to the place it needs to be, the more powerful it gets." Maybe I should drive that little voodoo doll up to Oregon and ditch it there.

Sophie gave me one of those fabulous teenage girl looks that spoke volumes on what she thought about me and my ideas. "Seriously? You want me to take an axe for a drive?"

"It's my best suggestion for the moment." I got up and stretched. The afternoon classes would be arriving soon. "Do me a favor and let me know if you start feeling like there's anything crawling on you, okay?"

Another stare. Soon I'd have this girl rolling her eyeballs and standing with her arms crossed over her chest like a barrier. Did I know how to be a mentor or what? "Like bugs?" she asked.

"Exactly like bugs." See? I'm a great teacher.

She lifted her hands in a gesture of supplication. "Any particular reason?"

"A very particular reason, but not one I'm willing to explain right now." I gave her a big smile.

"You know, it's a little frustrating when you do that." She scowled at me.

I felt a sudden shock of recognition. I knew that face. I knew that scowl. I could feel its echo on my face. I'd made that scowl a hundred times. Maybe a thousand times. I'd made it at Mae right here in this very office and I'd made it for the exact same reason that Sophie was making it at me now.

The way Mae would lead me through solving my problems used to irritate me to no end. My argument was that if she knew the answer, she should just give it to me. Her argument had been that I would actually be learning something if I reasoned it out on my own. As irritating as that had been, it was ten times more irritating to realize that she'd been right.

I stared at her. "I'm sorry. I know it's frustrating. I'll explain as much of it as I can as soon as I can. Okay?"

"I guess it's going to have to be okay, isn't it?" She got up from her chair and went out to help the kids coming in get ready for class.

I stared after her and thought about all those times that Mae had given me the inscrutable master routine. Had she been trying to keep me safe? Right now, I didn't want Sophie involved in whatever was happening in Elmville because I wanted to protect her from it. I'd thought Mae was doling out knowledge in little bite-sized bits for her own entertainment half the time. It had never occurred to me that she'd been doing it for my own good.

Maybe she'd been protecting me as much as she could. I looked down at her desk, which I now sat behind. The view was mighty different from the other side.

I MADE IT THROUGH CLASS WITHOUT ANY CHILDREN GETTING imaginary bug bites, through sparring class without me coming anywhere close to killing one of my students and through my shift at the hospital. I'd gotten the first decent night's sleep I'd had in days and had woken up Wednesday morning all fresh and ready to take on the world.

There are no evening classes at River City on Wednesdays. Ted and I had started using that night to work out together. I used to spar with Mae. Obviously that wasn't happening anymore. Sophie was learning fast but was still light-years from where she could give me a good workout. Ted had stepped up to take Mae's place as a sparring partner. At first I'd scoffed at his offer, but he'd talked me into trying it and, honestly, he was pretty good. He had some moves. I was still stronger and faster, but he had some stuff that I hadn't seen before and it was good for me to stay flexible.

He showed up at the studio at about seven and gave me a kiss hello. I kissed him back. With enthusiasm.

He pulled away. "Wow. That was a nice welcome. What's up with you?"

"Can't a girl just show appreciation to her boyfriend?" Or perhaps butter him up a little because she wants something from him?

His eyes narrowed. "A girl can. You can't. At least, I don't think you can." He walked onto the mat and took a fighting stance, left leg forward, guard up. He bounced a little on the balls of his feet.

"I could!" I roundhouse-kicked his stomach.

Well, I didn't actually get there. Ted blocked down and scooped his arm under my leg and did a fist strike at my chest. "You never have. Plus, you're using that tone of voice you use when you've done something you think is going to piss me off or you want to ask me for a favor. Or, come to think of it, sometimes it's a combination of the two. Which is it this time?" He kept lifting my leg until I was off balance.

I sighed and went over backward, landing in a backward somersault and coming up in a crouch. It was weird to have someone know me this well. The only other person who came close was Mae and she was a little more cryptic about her observations. I launched myself at him, sending a flurry of uppercuts and punches toward his abdomen to knock him off balance and then spun on my left leg, raised my right knee and sent a spinning hook kick at his chin. He went over backward to avoid me clipping him. I pounced on top of him. "You want fries with that combo, sir?"

He chuckled. "You know, it's a good thing you're cute."

I blushed. I wished I was as sure of myself in the boyfriend/girlfriend give and take as I was in a fight. I knew how to take a punch. I didn't know how to take a compliment.

"Stop blushing and tell me what's going on and what you need," he said.

"I went back to Elmville . . ."

"Goddamn it, Melina." He snaked an arm through mine, trapped my left leg with his right, twisted his left leg around my neck and twirled me to the ground beneath him. "Alone? After what happened to us the last time we were there? What the hell were you thinking?"

"That I needed more information and the best place—maybe the only place—to get it was in Elmville." And that I was capable of taking on the sons of cadejos by myself. I reached between us, grabbed his thigh, swept my leg and brought us back into a mount position with me on top. "I was careful."

"Did you go back to the Bossards' place, Melina? Please tell me you didn't. Someone didn't want you there. I realize you think that's like an engraved invitation to come back whenever you want, but it's not."

I decided not to linger in the mount. We'd end up rolling around on the floor all night. I leapt up and back into my fighting stance. "I didn't go back to the Bossards," I said quietly.

"Well, that's some small measure of solace. Then where did you go?" Ted was up in a second as well.

"I went to a house where I made another delivery a few weeks before I made the one to Neil Bossard." I came at him with a series of sidekicks to his ribs.

He tried to catch my leg like he had on my first roundhouse, but I'd sped up my pace. Who says I can't be taught? "Another delivery? In Elmville? Did you talk to the person you made the delivery to?" he asked.

"No. He's, uh, sort of dead. It makes conversation tricky." It does not make it impossible. I have run across a ghost or two in my time. I didn't get any kind of feeling that Kurt Rawley's spirit still inhabited the area around his house and even if it had, ghosts generally don't make the best conversationalists. They tend to have unfinished business and finishing whatever that business is ends up being the only track that they want to run on. If the information you want happens to be on that track, then everybody ends up happy. If not, you tend to be out of luck.

Ted swept my standing leg from beneath me. "How did he die?" Ted asked, his voice a little too calm.

"I was hoping you could look into that for me. It had something to do with a fire, possibly arson. I'm sure there's a police report. I don't really want to waltz into the Elmville station and ask for one, though. I thought you might be able to do it without anyone noticing." I asked from the floor. I thought it might be a good position from which to ask a favor.

"So you made two deliveries to Elmville and both the recipients are now dead and you were going to tell me about this when?" He danced away from me, bouncing on the balls of his feet.

"Pretty much now." I stayed still.

"Anything else you might want to let me know? Anything else besides you connecting the two cases, for instance?" He danced a little closer now.

I didn't move a muscle. "Funny you should mention that."

"No, Melina, not funny." He danced a step closer now.

I was a still pool of water on a canyon floor. "Okay. Not funny, but interesting."

"What is it?" He took the next step closer.

"I found another voodoo doll at Kurt Rawley's house. Well, part of one, anyway. Most of it was burned up. Plus, I found two *descansos*. One at Rawley's house and one at the spot where Bossard died. Their deaths are linked, Ted, and not just by me. Something's going on here and I feel like I'm being played." I twisted my legs through his and brought him down next to me.

"Not so fun when the manipulation is on the other foot, now is it?" What was I hearing in my boyfriend's voice?

"Excuse me, but I believe that unnecessary sarcasm is my specialty. You're on my turf, man." I turned on one elbow and looked at him.

"Get used to it," he said, still sounding gruff but with a hint of a chuckle in there somewhere. "You bring it out in people."

"Touché."

"So riddle me this, bat cat, if you don't like getting involved with whoever's dropping off the delivery or whomever you're making the delivery to, why are you getting involved in this? They can't play you if you don't play, Melina." Now he turned on his side so we were facing each other.

I thought about how to explain what I was feeling. "I don't like getting involved. I don't need any more responsibilities. But if I make a delivery that brings about someone's death, I feel . . ." I trailed off.

"Guilty?" he suggested.

"I guess so. Something like that, anyway."

"You didn't kill those two boys, Melina." He tucked a tendril of hair that had come loose from my braid behind my ear.

I ducked my head. "I know that. I just want to know who did."

"It looks like Bossard pretty much killed himself." His voice was so reasonable now, so reassuring. I wanted to accept what he said, but I couldn't.

"With pretty heavy prompting from whoever sent him that doll!"

"Prompting is just that—prompting. It's not anything you could take into a court of law." His hand skimmed down my body, from my shoulder to my hip.

"As if anything I'm involved with here could ever make it into a court of law. Can you imagine what kind of jury they'd have to pick for a case like this?" I looked back up at him.

He smiled. "No. I can't. I also can't imagine what it would do to me if you got yourself hurt poking around in this. I get why you're doing it. I just want to help."

"Then find out what happened to Kurt Rawley, okay? Maybe it's not as related as they look. Maybe it's a total coincidence that they both died right after I made deliveries to them."

"You know how I feel about coincidences, Melina. I don't like them." He kissed me, softly, his lips barely brushing mine.

I kissed him back. Harder. "I'm not crazy about them either, but I'm rooting for them this time." My breath was coming faster and way more uneven than it had when we were sparring.

"I don't think you're really cut out to be a cheerleader. Although I can kind of picture you in a short skirt." He trailed his fingers along my collarbone.

I hooked my leg around his waist and pulled myself closer to him. "You want a big set of pom-poms to go with that?"

"Nah. Your pom-poms are perfect the way they are." He smiled and kissed me again.

"You know I think you're pretty perfect, too," I said.

Ted's face went to a careful blank. "Thanks."

"You remember that thing you said to me the other night? The thing you said right before the cadejo attacked us?" I asked, hardly able to breathe and not knowing if I was going to be able to say what I wanted to say without shaking apart.

"You mean when I told you that I loved you?" He drew a finger along my jawline and I shivered a little.

"Yeah, well, me, too. Okay?"

"Yeah. Okay." And then he got down to some serious kissing.

I STILL HAD TO WORK MY SHIFT AT THE HOSPITAL THAT NIGHT. I tried to remember when my life had turned into a rat race. Then I remembered. The night that Mae died. That was when the bottom fell out of everything.

I sat for a moment in the Buick in the parking garage. I'd pulled all the way up to the top. It was nice to see the stars, even if it was a pain to spiral down when it was time to go home. I glanced at my watch. I was, miracle of miracles, a few minutes early. I got out and perched on the hood, leaning back against the windshield. The air was a little cold, but it felt good against my face. I could pick out the scent of drying leaves with only a touch of their eventual disintegration underneath.

I lay back and closed my eyes, letting the night air wash over me. I felt the first prickle of awareness seconds after I'd closed them.

Someone—something—was up on the roof with me. I stayed

still. Often one of the few things I had going for me was the element of surprise. I wasn't about to give that up without knowing a little more about what I was getting into.

The prickle got stronger. Definitely vampire. I could taste the coppery tang on the back of my tongue. Something was off with it, though. It wasn't as strong as it should be.

"Come here often?" he said from right next to me.

I let out my breath. Alex. Who else, really?

"That's a pretty weak pickup line. If that's what you were using at McClannigan's, it's no wonder you had to move on." I still didn't open my eyes.

"Ah, Melina, you've always known just how to build a man's ego." He sighed.

"You're not a man, and in my experience, your ego hasn't needed much building." I opened my eyes now. He didn't look quite right to me. He seemed a little too thin.

"You've got me on the first. The second, well, things change, don't they?" He propped one hip onto the car, next to me.

My skin tingled. I pulled my jacket closer around me. I trusted Alex way more than I trusted any other vampire. He was different. I still didn't exactly want to be alone with him in a deserted parking garage close to midnight. "Things don't change much, in my opinion, and if they do, they don't change for the better."

He glanced over at me. I avoided looking into his eyes. "That's awfully cynical for someone so young."

"I may be young in people years. In Messenger years, I'm getting older by the second." We didn't always have long life expectancies. It's not like there's a database or anything that tracks Messengers, but we end up in too many questionable situations to be around forever.

He stretched and shoved that thick black hair off his forehead.

"I remember that. I remember aging. Don't knock it. The alternative is not so fabulous."

I sat up and looked at him, really looked. "Do you regret it? Do you wish you'd never become . . . what you are?" It was more than tacky to use the *V* word in public with Alex. I kept who I was in the shadows for the sake of self-preservation and I wasn't even dangerous.

It's easy to teach someone to hate someone else. It takes almost nothing to turn one group against another. Logic and rational thinking have very little to do with it. Creating a sense of "other" is really all it takes. There've been studies. Teachers can get little blue-eyed children to hate little brown-eyed children in a few days, and vice versa, with nothing more than a few carefully chosen words and actions. Neighbors slaughter neighbors because of radio broadcasts. Hate seems to run in people's bloodstreams, just waiting for opportunities to be brought to a boil.

I don't know how people would treat me if they found out how "other" I really was. I don't have a good feeling about it, though.

Alex was beyond "other." Human beings generally consider themselves to be at the top of the food chain. They don't much like the idea of anything that might use them for food. It's the stuff of nightmares and horror movies. Soylent green, anyone? They are also generally smart enough and skilled enough to figure out how to get rid of anything that's too dangerous to them. Things like Alex, for instance.

His continued existence depended on him keeping a low profile. Hence, the not wanting to bandy about words like *vampire* in public.

"Do I regret it?" He shook his head. "You're assuming I made an informed choice, Melina."

I leaned toward him, realizing how very little I really knew about him. I didn't know how old he was, where he came from or how he'd become a vampire. "Were you turned against your will, Alex?"

He turned toward me now as well and braced his arms on either side of me on the car. It was an odd sensation, not totally because of what I felt, although the tingle and buzz in my flesh from him being so close was near deafening at the moment. The more disconcerting part was what I didn't feel. His mouth was inches from mine, but I didn't feel his breath on my cheek. Why would I? He didn't breathe. His body, so tantalizing close, didn't warm mine. There was no scent from him, no masculine musk, just the faint perfume of his laundry detergent.

"Not everything is about will and choice, Melina." His voice had dropped very low. "Some things are about need, about passion. They're about desire. They don't make sense. They just are."

I swallowed hard. He was so close to me now, I could feel the slight chill coming off him. I drew my knees up to my chest to force him back away from me, but made the mistake of looking into his eyes. They weren't their usual deep pools of melted chocolate. They'd turned golden and had the slightest touch of red at the pupil. I shrunk back from him and he smiled. The very tips of his fangs had started to protrude.

"Stop it." This wasn't funny. I trusted him. I let my guard down around him. I didn't like this little vampire game he was playing.

"Stop what, Melina? Being who I am? Being what I am? You of all people should know the toll it takes to constantly pretend to be something you're not." He pressed forward, forcing me back against the car, arching my chest toward him.

His gaze traveled the column of my throat and he ran his tongue over the tips of his fangs. I stayed as still as I could, not sure whether to scream or run, but instinctively feeling that any movement at all on my part could send him over the edge.

After what felt like an eternity, he backed away. "Go to work, Melina. You're going to be late for your shift. Again."

I didn't need to be told twice. I slid off the hood of the Buick and ran down the stairs.

WHEN I GOT HOME, I VERY CLEVERLY DID NOT BRING THE LEGS of Kurt Rawley's voodoo doll into the apartment with me. It had the same little malevolent witchy buzz to it as the intact voodoo doll, and I didn't want it sneaking into my dreams or messing with my head.

I hoped it wasn't strong enough to mess too much with the people walking past the car, but I figured their exposure would be quick enough to not cause permanent damage.

I dragged myself up the stairs to the apartment and let myself in. It took me a few seconds after I was already inside to realize that the chain hadn't been on. I looked behind me. Something white and gritty was scattered on the floor. I looked over at Norah, who was drinking coffee in the kitchen.

"What's on the floor?" I asked.

"Salt." She barely looked up from her newspaper. "It's on the windowsills, too."

I looked over at the windows. Sure enough, there was white gritty stuff there, too, plus a few red candles. "Any particular reason? Or did you just feel like the woodwork needed more seasoning?"

"It's supposed to keep evil spirits out. I did a whole ceremony last night. Coffee?" She offered the last as if everything she'd said before it had been perfectly normal. She actually sounded pretty normal. Well, except for the part where she was offering me coffee. That still wasn't normal for Norah.

I shook my head. "No. I'm sorry I missed the ceremony. How'd it go?"

Her lips pressed tighter together. "I don't think it worked."

"An evil spirit came in during the night?" That was not good news. An evil spirit coming into the apartment was bad news. An evil spirit obvious enough for Norah to see it or sense it was even worse news.

"Close enough. I'm trying to get him to cut it out." She looked pissed.

The only "him" in our apartment lately had been Ted. What had she been trying to get him to cut out with her ceremony? Had he been leaving the toilet seat up? Drinking the last of the milk? Not leaving enough hot water for the next person to shower? That didn't sound like him. Who else would she be talking about, though? "Tell who to cut what out?"

"Alex." She ground his name out between gritted teeth.

I poured myself a glass of milk. "What has Alex been doing that he's supposed to cut out?"

She gestured with her head toward her room and then walked to the door. I followed. She pointed, her finger shaking a tiny bit at the vase on her dresser.

I counted five long-stemmed red roses in the vase. "He sent you flowers."

"It would almost be okay if he was sending them. Almost, but not quite. He's leaving them. On my pillow."

I felt like cold icy fingers were creeping around my heart. This was definitely bad news. "When?"

"You've got me. Sometime during the night. They're not there when I go to sleep, and when I wake up in the morning, they're there. It's creeping me out. You know what it means, don't you? It means he's been in my bedroom while I'm sleeping. He's watching me and I don't even know it." She sounded pissed. That was good. It was better than sounding terrified and helpless. I could work with pissed.

I swallowed hard. Most vampires don't just watch beautiful young women sleep. "Norah, have you, uh, checked yourself?"

"Checked myself? What do you mean?" She looked confused.

"You know, for, uh, puncture wounds?" It was hard to say it out loud. It was going to be even harder to check her over.

"Ewwwww!" She started ripping her clothes off as fast as she could. "Do it. Check me. Do it now."

I did. In a scene probably worthy of a soft-core porn women's prison movie, I went over just about every inch of Norah, with special attention to highly vascular areas.

"Well?" she demanded, pulling her yoga pants back on as angrily as a person can yank on yoga pants.

"Nothing." I sat down on the bed. Relieved that I'd found nothing but confused by it all the same. What the hell was he up to?

"So he is just watching me and leaving flowers." She sat down next to me. "That's weird. Creepy and weird. Make him stop."

I nodded. "I'll talk to him about it."

"You do that." She put her head in her hands. "I'm sorry," she whispered.

"I know." I sighed and patted her back, worried at how prominent her shoulder blades felt under my hand.

"I'm so confused." She kept her head down, not looking at me.

"About what, in particular?" I spent much of my life in a state of at least a little befuddlement. I'd gotten good at it.

"He scares me."

"He should. He's dangerous." And based on what I'd seen

that night at the top of the parking garage, getting more so by the minute.

"And he fascinates me, too." She looked up now, her distress clear on her face. "Is it something that he's doing to me? Is he making me feel this way about him? I want him gone, but at the same time, the thought of him really being gone makes me . . . way more than sad. I don't even know how to describe the feeling. It's a little like how I felt about Pablo. Remember him?"

How could I have forgotten Pablo? He'd been a Spanish yoga instructor and Norah had gone head over heels for him the summer after we'd graduated from high school. When he'd left to go back to Spain, she'd cried for three solid weeks. "I remember."

"Maybe if he just leaves me alone, it'll be like it was with Pablo, too. It'll just take a little time and this feeling will go away. Can you get him to leave me alone?"

"Is that what you want?"

"I think so. I'm not sure. I'm so confused. I need to think." She shooed me out of the room and practically slammed the door behind me.

I considered giving it a kick but decided to try and be mature. It wasn't my fault, though, damn it. I was not the one who'd invited him in. She was, and now she was suffering the consequences.

This was the problem with people who dabbled in the occult. Norah had thought she could dabble. She had thought she could sit on a couch and drink red wine with a vampire. She thought she could flirt with a vampire and tease and remain in control of the situation, and it would all be fun and games.

Guess what? It wasn't. Vampires are predators and as decent as Alexander Bledsoe was, he was still a vampire somewhere deep down in his core.

What was worse was that he now seemed to be a depressed and erratic vampire. I thought about the bloodred roses on Norah's pillow and Paul's comment about hungry vampires and our encounter on the parking garage roof. My head started to throb.

I did the only thing that made sense to me at the moment. I went to bed and pulled the covers over my head.

I MANAGED TO SLEEP UNTIL ABOUT NOON. A GENTLE KNOCK AT the door immediately followed by the sound of a key turning in a lock woke me up. The scent of vanilla had me scurrying to brush my teeth and hair.

"I brought lunch," Ted called from the kitchen. He did love me. He really did.

"I got the information you wanted on Kurt Rawley." Ted was sitting on one of the bar stools at the kitchen counter already eating his panini. I sniffed. It smelled like the roasted chicken one from the co-op.

I grabbed the unwrapped package sitting on the counter and got on the bar stool next to his. "Okay. How did he die?"

"They think he doused himself with kerosene and then lit himself on fire." Ted kept munching, but I could see from the set of his shoulder that it bothered him.

"Why would someone do something like that?" I shook my head. I unwrapped my sandwich. Turkey with Monterey Jack unless I missed my guess and I rarely did when it came to sandwiches.

He sighed. "Apparently someone who thought there were bugs crawling on him all the time would do something like that." He popped open a bag of chips.

"How do we know that?" I grabbed one chip from the bag. One bad thing I was noticing about having a boyfriend was that it was really messing with my diet. I have a good metabolism but not quite good enough. My jeans were starting to feel a little bit snug. I could have one potato chip, though, couldn't I?

"His mother told the cops. He'd been complaining about it for days. He felt like there was something crawling on him all the time. He tried creams and ointments. He'd been to the doctor twice. They'd started him on something called Risperidone, but it hadn't really had time to work. Apparently it's a syndrome. It's called delusory parasitosis."

It's always nice when things have a name. Too bad this one was probably more of a symptom than a cause. I didn't think antipsychotics would help in this particular case. Not with the nasty little doll under his bed. That was a gift that was going to keep giving and giving and giving.

Ted took a chip and shoved the bag back toward me. "Here's something else you might find interesting. Rawley had just been released from the California Youth Authority."

So that's where he'd come back from. No wonder no one was bringing up the particulars. I shoved the bag back without taking a chip. "How about Bossard? Same thing?"

Ted nodded. "Yep. Both of them were released on their twenty-first birthdays."

"What were they in for?" Now we were getting somewhere. I was convinced that if we could find the link between them, we would understand why both these boys had died.

"Murder." He said it the way he might have said *grape* if I asked him what kind of Popsicle he wanted.

I sat up straight. "Whose murder? When?"

Ted shook his head. "There's a limit to what I have access to. They were tried as juveniles. I can give you dates, but not too many other details. I'm guessing you can dig around in the newspaper archives and figure it out. Rawley's and Bossard's names won't be in the accounts because of their juvenile status, but how many murders can happen in Elmville at a specific time that involve two juvenile suspects?"

He was right. He'd probably found out as much as he could from official channels. I'd need to do some digging on my own now. At least I knew what I'd be doing this afternoon. "It would help if I knew who was making those voodoo dolls."

"I can't help you with that." He rolled up his empty sandwich wrapper and stood up.

"There is something else that you might be able to help me with." I twirled on the bar stool so I was facing him. "There's something wrong with Alex."

Ted's eyebrows went up. "What kind of thing?"

"I'm not sure. He's gone all moody and brooding." *And might be stalking my roommate*, I added silently.

"Isn't that kind of par for the course with a vampire? They're sort of known for moody broodiness, aren't they? It would be kind of his thang, wouldn't it?" Ted smiled.

"No." I crossed my arms over my chest.

Ted just looked at me.

"Fine. Yes. It's a vampire thing, but this feels different."

"What do you want me to do about it?" He gathered up our garbage and took it into the kitchen.

"I'm not sure. You have him on speed dial. You guys are special buds now. Has he said anything?" Like when they were doing each other's nails and having pillow fights? What was I even asking?

"About what?" Ted finished throwing out the remnants of our lunch and came back with a sponge to wipe down the kitchen counter.

"I don't know. Feeling blue? Being obsessed with someone?" I tried to sound nonchalant.

Ted stopped wiping the counter and looked over at me. "Obsessed with whom?"

I dropped the nonchalant. "Norah, maybe?"

"That could be a problem." He sat back down. "How bad is it?"

"He's leaving roses on her pillow. Paul mentioned him not hanging out at McClannigan's to pick up take-out food, if you get my drift, and he's acting weird at work. Can you talk to him?"

"Isn't there some kind of vampire therapist he can go to? Vampire antidepressants? Bloodzac? Zoglobin?" Ted smirked.

I punched his arm. "This isn't funny."

"I didn't say it was. I just have no frame of reference here." He rubbed his shoulder and shook his head at me.

"I don't know that I do either. I am pretty sure I don't want one, though."

TED HAD BEEN RIGHT. NOW THAT I KNEW WHAT DATES TO LOOK for, it didn't take much to figure out who Rawley and Bossard had murdered. As ugly as their suicides were, what I found was even uglier.

Jorge Aguilar, a Mexican immigrant, was beaten to death on the streets of Elmville by white teenagers about six years ago. The reason they attacked him was a little murky. After reading several newspaper accounts, it seemed like it could have been that he was walking with a white girl, that he'd yelled insults at the boys or that he had simply been at the wrong place at the wrong time. I suspected it was a lethal combination of all three. Well, lethal for Aguilar at least.

The rest of it wasn't so murky. Aguilar had been knocked to the ground, pummeled with fists and finally kicked so hard in the head that he lost consciousness. He never regained it. Four days after the beating, he'd been taken off life support and allowed to die.

The boys, honor students and athletes, had been tried as juveniles, sparking protests that received national media coverage. I jotted down the name of the man who had seemingly led most of the protests. Luis Pelayo's name came up over and over in interviews, listed as "a leader of the local Latino community."

It was an ugly story. I vaguely remembered the controversy when it happened. So many of the remarks that I'd heard at the memorial service began to make sense. The talk of Bossard not being able to come back from making one mistake. Rawley's mother's comments about her son having paid for what he'd done started to make a certain kind of sense, too, although how you pay for taking another person's life so cavalierly was difficult for me to calculate. There wasn't a credit limit in the universe high enough as far as I was concerned.

The part that didn't make immediate sense and that worried me the most, though?

The news reports all stated that there were three boys involved in the attacks. Two of Jorge Aguilar's murderers were dead by their own hand. One was still out there.

There was one more thing that I remembered about Neil Bossard's memorial. The kid who got thrown out of the house right before I did, the one who kept screaming about being cursed. I tried to remember his name and came up with a blank. I wondered if Ted would remember.

While I was still mulling over what to do about the third man, Sophie whirled into the apartment, her hair scented with leaves and rain. Ben trailed after her. "I did it!"

"Did what?" Sophie was nothing if not industrious. The answer could have been almost anything. She could have mastered the spinning back kick, with which I'd been helping her, or she could have passed her Algebra II/Trig exam, with which I'd been no help at all, or she could have managed to deliver the damn axe the Basajaun had given us for Ginnar the Dwarf.

"I found Ginnar!" She spun over to me and gave me a hug.

I did my best not to tense up. I have one of those touchy-feely families that is forever hugging. They all want to be in constant physical contact with each other. Except me. It's not that I don't like being touched. I'm just wary of it. It doesn't always feel good. "That's great. Was he happy to get the axe?" Not everyone was always happy to see us. We didn't always deliver good news or tokens of esteem and love. We were not always greeted with open arms and open hearts. In this particular instance, I'd been relatively sure that Sophie would get a positive greeting.

She made a funny face.

"She didn't exactly give him the axe," Ben explained for her from the kitchen, where his head was in my refrigerator.

I was confused. "Did you forget to take it with you?" Actually taking the item on the delivery run was one of the first rules of Messengering. I'd been relatively sure I'd hammered that point home. Sometimes people needed more than one refresher, though. In the heat of the moment, it's easy to forget little details, like the object that was actually supposed to go someplace.

She shook her head, letting her hair spill over the scarred part of her face. "I took it."

"Did he not want it?" It was possible. The Basajaun hadn't exactly been chatty. He could have had less than honorable reasons for giving Ginnar that axe. I couldn't figure out what they might be, but who knew what ran through the mind of a Basque Lord of the Woods?

"I think he might have wanted it." Sophie chewed on her lower lip. Ben came in and plopped down on the sofa next to her, a piece of cold pizza in each hand.

I glared at him.

He got up, went into the kitchen and got a plate.

I turned back to Sophie. "But you're not sure that Ginnar wanted the axe?" I was getting more and more confused.

"Not entirely."

A vein in my forehead started to throb. I decided to share my pain. "You're making my head hurt."

"Well, stop giving me the third degree and let me explain what happened. You don't have to make it into the Spanish Inquisition." She threw her hands in the air in frustration.

I shut up, largely because I was speechless. Sophie had never spoken to me that way. I wasn't sure if I should take her to task for insubordination or be relieved that we were actually communicating honestly. I decided on the latter.

"I drove the axe up to the Sierras like you said I should." She sprang up from the couch and began to pace. Nervous energy flowed off her like hot caramel off a scoop of cold French vanilla ice cream. Ben watched her every move, looking like a spectator at a tennis match.

"Interstate 80 or Highway 50?" I asked.

She whirled and glared at me. Shutting up was so not my forte. "Fifty." Her brows drew together for a second. "I don't know why I chose fifty. I just knew it was the right way to go."

I smiled. I knew that feeling. I pressed my lips together and tried to get better at the shutting up thing. It wasn't bad to add to one's skill set. Mae had often said that there was always room for growth.

"Anyway," Sophie continued, "I felt it. I totally felt what you meant. I knew where I was supposed to take the axe. I knew which exit to take, and the farther I went, the more sure I was that I was going in the right direction."

This time I didn't try to hide my smile. "I know it's freaky, but it's kind of cool, too, isn't it?"

She sat down again and grabbed my hands across the coffee table. "Totally cool. I could feel the axe's power building. I could feel how much it wanted to be back with the person who owned it."

I leaned forward toward her. "So why exactly didn't you give it to the person who owned it then?"

She dropped my hands. "I'm getting to it. Jeez, you're so impatient."

I took a deep breath and tried to relax into the papasan chair.

"I pulled off onto this little road that went into the woods. It narrowed way down." Sophie's hands flew through the air. It was like watching an interpretive dance of her delivery.

"After about a mile, it really wasn't much more than a dirt track. Then I saw this little turnout and I knew, I just knew, that was where I was supposed to be."

I let her catch her breath and didn't say a word although, quite honestly, it was killing me.

"So there I was. Deep in the woods. All alone. It was a little spooky, Melina."

I knew that feeling, too. It didn't lessen over time either.

"I got out of the car with the axe and walked into this clearing. There was nobody there. I sat down on a tree stump and waited. I guess I must have dozed off or something because when I woke up, I felt like my skin was on fire and there was this . . . this crazy-ass bearded thing trying to grab the axe out of my hands."

It was a fair description of a dwarf trying to get something from you. Manners weren't their best thing. "I'm guessing that was Ginnar."

"Well, I'm guessing that right now, too, but he didn't exactly introduce himself. He just tried to grab the axe." Sophie stopped pacing and faced me, hands on hips.

"And you didn't let him." It wasn't a question. I knew the answer.

"It was reflex!"

She was right. It was reflex. Try to grab something out of anyone's hands, even a baby's, and their knee-jerk reaction will be to grab it back. Try to grab something out of a Messenger's hands and our better-than-the-average-bear reflexes will grab it back hard and fast. Try to grab something out of the hand of a Messenger who has been receiving martial arts training . . . well, I just hoped Ginnar didn't need too many stitches.

"How bad did you hurt him?"

"I think it was only a flesh wound." Sophie's pretty face crumpled and her big hazel eyes started to fill with tears.

"It's not your fault," I said. "If he'd been polite and asked, it would have gone a lot smoother, now wouldn't it?"

She nodded. "You're not mad?"

"No." I cringed inside. I'd made Sophie frightened of me. It hadn't been my intention. It hadn't been how I'd been taught, either. I had respected Mae. I'd wanted her approval and love. I'd been sad when I'd disappointed her.

I had never, ever been afraid of her.

I leaned back in the chair and took a good hard look at Sophie. I really wasn't that much older than her. It was weird to be her teacher, her mentor, when I didn't feel like I really knew enough to tell shit from shinola myself. I covered up my lack of self-confidence with a thick layer of sarcasm and sass. It had worked for me before, but I didn't think it was so effective in the present situation. I decided to try a new approach.

"I'm sorry, Sophie. I suck at this." Brrr. Honesty. It was a cold and heartless thing.

Her forehead creased. "What do you mean? You're a great Messenger. Mae told me you were the best pupil she ever had."

I felt my forehead bunch up to mirror hers. "When did she tell you that?"

"Before she, uh, you know . . ."

Before she died. Before she was killed. Before she was ripped apart by Chinese vampires at the behest of a San Francisco tong before my very eyes. Even Sophie shied away from saying it. The memory of that coupled with the idea that my teacher had thought that about me made tears well up in my eyes.

I don't cry. It's not my thing. I'm not saying I'm fantastically stoic and choke back sobs or rein in torrents of tears. They just don't well up on me. I don't have to blink them back. They never rise up. I had no idea what to do with them now. I was really falling apart.

"Are you okay?" Sophie handed me a tissue from the box on my own coffee table.

"Uh, yeah. Sorry." I blew my nose. Sophie averted her eyes. "I didn't mean I was a sucky Messenger, though. I think I'm a sucky teacher. It never occurred to me that I was going to have to teach this stuff to someone else. I barely have a handle on it myself."

"You're doing fine," Sophie protested.

This was one of the things I hated about tears. They make people say and do things they don't really mean. I know. They do it to me. Someone starts crying around me and I instinctively want to make them stop. I will do anything to make the water stop pouring out of their faces. I held up my hand. "Don't," I said.

She sat back in her chair. I got myself together. "I don't want you to be afraid of me or to be afraid to tell me when something didn't work out the way you planned. To be honest, things rarely work out the way I plan and I've been doing this for close to twenty-four years in one way or another. Can you find that clearing again? The one where you saw Ginnar?"

Sophie nodded. "I'm pretty sure."

"Go back next week on the same day and at about the same time that you were there this last time. Do everything the same except lay the axe on the ground near you instead of holding on to it. Dwarves have miserable manners. They're greedy and aggressive and grasping. He won't ask politely for the axe. He'll make another grab for it. You need to let him take it without hurting him or you."

"Okay. I can do that." She stood up and started out of the apartment, Ben right behind her.

"Sophie," I said as she got to the door.

"Yeah?" She turned around.

"You did a good job. That was a big hurdle to let the axe guide you. You cleared it with no problem."

Her shoulders straightened just the tiniest bit and I felt a little warm spot form in my heart. First tears and now warm fuzzies? I was totally losing it in my old age.

9

SOPHIE AND BEN LEFT AND I TURNED BACK TO THE PROBLEM AT hand. Who was making these dolls? I imagined there were a lot of people who weren't all that happy to see Bossard and Rawley out of prison. They'd taken a man's life and thrown an entire community into turmoil.

Who hated them enough to make those dolls and send them? Or to have them made or sent? There were a lot of services that could be had for a price. I was pretty sure that would be one. Still, whoever it was would have to know where to go to purchase those kinds of services and goods. That wasn't something that every average citizen knew.

I wondered, too, about the Jorge Aguilar case. I should probably see if I could get in to talk to that Pelayo guy. He seemed to know a lot about it. Maybe he'd have some insight that would help me figure it all out.

My mind wandered as I thought about it. It had been nice to see

Sophie walk out of here with her shoulders back. I remembered that sense of pride when Mae had told me I'd done a good job. My life had seemed so complicated back then. I'd had no idea how much more complicated it was going to get. I hoped like hell that I wouldn't look back on this time of my life and think about how good I had it.

Sometimes, however, things were simpler than they seemed when you were in the middle of them.

That was the moment that it dawned on me. Maybe finding out who made the dolls was simpler than I realized. I'd delivered them once. Granted, there'd been an address scrawled on the label. Still, they were objects of power. Maybe the burnt legs of Kurt Rawley's voodoo doll could guide me to the person I sought in Elmville.

In the meantime, I could drop by and chitchat with Luis, too. What could be better than killing two proverbial birds with one Messenger stone?

I grabbed my keys and headed to my car.

IT WAS SURPRISINGLY EASY TO GET IN TO SEE HIM. LUIS Pelayo had started a foundation to help immigrant families make the transition to living in America. All I had to do was intimate that I was working on a freelance article about immigration issues and his assistant set up an appointment for me immediately. I met him at the foundation office. It buzzed like a busy beehive with a little bit of happy Thursday afternoon giddiness added in.

"You led the protests when Judge Moffat made the decision to try the Elmville Three as juveniles," I said. It wasn't phrased as a question. It wasn't exactly confrontational either. I kept my gaze right on Pelayo's face. As an opening gambit, I didn't think it was half bad.

"I did." Pelayo leaned back in his chair. "I thought it was a travesty. Those boys murdered a young man in cold blood, just for the fun of it. At fifteen, they were damn sure old enough to know that it was wrong. It was an adult crime. It was a hate crime. It should have been tried as such. If it happened today, all three of them would have been tried as adults."

"I believe you were arrested at the time." Again, it wasn't a question, just a flat statement of fact in a neutral tone of voice. I kept my hands down, my feet flat on the floor.

Pelayo smiled, his teeth shining white against his brown skin. "Inciting a riot. I paid a fine."

"Did you? Incite a riot?" I leaned forward now.

Pelayo shook his head. "This town was a riot waiting to happen when that decision came down. Even the white folks were upset. No one wants to be from the racist town. They wanted—needed—those boys to be portrayed as a few bad apples that would be punished. Instead, it looked like they were golden boys getting a slap on the wrist."

"And you were just the helpful guy who threw the match in the gasoline?" My tone stayed perfectly pleasant. If anything, I was being even more friendly and conversational than I was being before, but the words I was saying weren't all that nice.

"There are all kinds of ways to help people." Pelayo spread his arms out to indicate the space around him. "For instance, this place would not have been possible without the Elmville Three. In some ways, those three hate-filled, violent sociopaths were the best things that could have happened to the Latino community of Elmville."

I blinked at that. "They viciously murdered a young man. How can that possibly be a good thing?"

Pelayo smiled that charming smile again, the one that made me want to finger a protection amulet. Or possibly see if he wanted to have a drink with me after work. Some guys just have it, you know?

"When they made the decision to try those three boys as juveniles, the entire country was outraged. Money poured into the community from all over the world. Everyone wanted to help. There was no way I could have founded Projeto Latino without the funding that started coming in after the riot."

"So it meant big money for you?" I asked.

"Me?" Pelayo held his hands up in protest. "Not me, per se. My cause? Absolutely. Look around this place. We are always busy. We help set up English tutoring. We help navigate the legal system. What those boys did was the essence of evil, but we turned it into something else here. We turned it into goodness. We're on the side of the angels here and the Elmville Three made it possible."

"So have you forgiven them?" I asked.

"It's not my job to forgive them or not," Pelayo said. "That's between them and their gods. I know what they did was evil. I'd guess they know that themselves. It's a matter of fact, if not public record. But let me tell you something else. What those boys did? It was like when there's an infection under your skin and someone has to cut into you to let the disease out. What they did? It hurt. It hurt bad. In the end, though, it let the hatred out into the open. When you pull that stuff out into the sunshine, it can't live."

I leaned forward now, totally interested in what Pelayo was saying. "You're saying it was cathartic? That it helped the community?"

"I am. I'm saying it exposed a lot of the closet racism that made those boys think it was okay to roll a Latino for entertainment on a Saturday night. I'm saying this is a better town for what the Elmville Three did. It changed everything. It changed the way the schools deal with the children of illegal immigrant workers. It changed the way health-care workers care for Latinos. It changed the way restaurants and banks and stores deal with my people. I'm sure it was the last thing on their mind that night, but the Elmville Three did all of us—the white community, too—a favor."

"You know two of them are dead, don't you?" I asked.

Pelayo's face went somber. "I'd heard. Guilt can do strange things to a person. Shame can make it even worse."

It wasn't a bad assumption to make. Officially, both boys had committed suicide. Factually, both boys had committed suicide. I was one of the few people who knew that there was more to it than met the eye. "You think that's what made them do it? Shame and guilt?"

"What else could there be?" Pelayo shrugged. "I'd be guilt-ridden and ashamed if it were me. Of course, I'm not anything like them, so maybe I have that wrong."

It still didn't make sense to me. "Then why wait until now? It's been six years. I'm sure they could have found some way to kill themselves before now if they were so filled with anguish."

Pelayo shrugged. "They guard those places pretty well. Maybe they didn't have a chance. Maybe they were too busy fighting for their lives in there to think about taking their own."

"What do you mean?" I broke in.

"Well, it's not like there are no Latinos incarcerated by the CYA. There are an awful lot of members of the Latino gangs in there. It's practically a badge of honor to have a juvenile record. It might be an even bigger badge for a *cholo* to beat the crap out of someone who'd rolled an innocent man just for having brown skin."

I wondered about that. "Are there any gang members here that might have been happy to take out those boys now that they're home?"

Pelayo looked alarmed. "Look. Our community isn't perfect, and the gangs are very active all over California. I don't think those boys would be very popular with the *cholos*, but I also haven't heard they were being specifically targeted. Besides, those two boys committed suicide. No one killed them. If it had been a gang-related killing, I would have heard about it by now."

"Anybody else who might not have been so happy to see them home?" I asked.

Pelayo shrugged. "I heard the three of them weren't such good buddies once they went away. There were a lot of bad feelings between them. The cops questioned them all separately and it's a little unclear who broke first. Whoever did was responsible for all of them going down. There was a lot of mutual suspicion between them."

"So you think it's possible that the third boy might have had it in for the other two? The two that are dead now?" That was an interesting thought. We needed to find that third boy.

"Maybe, but so what if he did? He didn't kill them. They killed themselves." Pelayo leaned back in his chair.

"I still don't understand why they would do it now." I shook my head.

"Maybe it was being home, back at the scene of the crime so to speak, that drove them to it. Having to face all the people who knew what they did and hated them for it. I can't say I know what went on in those young men's heads. I didn't understand them when they murdered Jorge Aguilar and I don't understand them now when they murder themselves. It's not how my mind works."

"So who hated them the most?" I asked.

"Pardon?" Pelayo's brow furrowed.

"You said they had to face all the people who knew what they did and hated them for it. Who hated them the most?"

Pelayo rubbed his chin. "That's an interesting question. You've got a few candidates."

"Name a few." I took out a notepad.

"What exactly are you after? Those boys committed suicide. There's no question about that." Pelayo started to look suspicious.

"I'm as interested in the why of it all as I am in the who. Something just doesn't seem right about it," I said.

"Claro. Does it really matter, though? You won't bring them back. Dead is dead."

He had a point. There was still one boy who wasn't dead, though. Was he a murderer? Or another potential victim who needed to be protected? "Humor me."

"Aguilar wasn't married and the girl he was with that night moved away a few years ago. He had an aunt in the area." Pelayo rubbed his thumb along the furrows in his brow.

"What's her name?" I asked.

Pelayo thought for a moment. "Lopez, I think. Rosita Lopez. She lived over by the cemetery. I heard she died a few years back, though. Cancer."

"Anybody else?" I asked.

"I can't imagine their own families were too thrilled with them. Rawley wasn't from a prominent family, but Bossard was. His dad owned a car dealership, among other things. He tarnished the family name and damn near bankrupted them with his legal expenses. I doubt they were all that thrilled."

"They seemed pretty broken up at his memorial service," I observed, then hoped that Pelayo wouldn't ask what I had been doing there.

"Yeah, well, the kid's dead. What are you going to do? Plus, he clearly won't be around reminding everybody in town that you raised a racist sociopath anymore."

He had a point. "Anyone else?"

He leaned forward on his desk.

"Maybe. But there are a lot of people who owe them thanks,

too. Now, if you don't mind, I'm done talking about those three devils and I'm ready to get on with my work of the angels."

I HAD LEFT THE DOLL LEGS IN THEIR ZIPLOC PRISON AND PUT the bag inside a little lead box that Mae had given me as a gift. Lead stopped radiation. Surely it could at least slow down voodoo or whatever this was. I had put it in the trunk of the Buick as far from me as I could get it. I hoped that and a healthy dose of self-awareness would keep it from driving me crazy all the way to Elmville. I had driven down on autopilot, chewing over what I'd learned.

Right after I left Pelayo's office, I pulled the car over on the side of the highway. With a certain amount of distaste, I retrieved the box from the trunk and brought it up into the front seat with me. I opened the box and the bag. If I wanted to listen to the legs, I was going to have to let them out in the open.

I pulled back onto the street.

I'd gone about two miles when I felt the spider crawling across my neck. I kept my eyes on the road and my hands on the wheel. It wasn't easy and I was guessing that I'd be taking a scalding hot shower the second I got home, but for now, I was going to live with the sensation.

I managed to drive into downtown Elmville without leaping around in my car, swatting at imaginary insects. If only they gave out awards for those kinds of things. I tried to open my senses more to the legs. It wasn't easy. The more open I made myself, the more real the sensations of ants crawling on my arms, spiders down my back and cobwebs across my face became.

I gritted my teeth, which quite honestly is very counterproductive to the whole opening process, and tried again. Through the creepy crawlies, I felt a push toward F Street. With a huge sense of relief, I closed myself off enough so that I could drive, and found a parking spot.

I sealed the legs up, shoved them in my pocket and started down the street. I kept my hands clenched at my sides, fighting the urge to slap at my arms and brush things off my face. I didn't need to call any more attention to myself than was absolutely necessary. Finally, I felt the urge to walk into the Canyon Café. It was just the way Sophie had described it. I knew that was where I was supposed to go. Nothing whispered in my ear. No unseen force shoved me. Something in me responded to something in those nasty half-burnt legs and I knew I needed to go into the café. The hostess seated me and I ordered a cup of coffee and waited.

I'd been there about five minutes when the woman at the table next to me began to scratch at her arm. The guy across from her began brushing at the back of his neck a few minutes later.

Then it spread to the booths along the wall. One woman actually peeled up the leg of her jeans to try and get whatever she was sure was crawling there. Then a man two booths down jumped up and begged his dinner companion to get whatever was there off his back.

I could hear plates dropping back in the kitchen. After a particularly loud crash, a young woman came darting out through the double doors. I caught my breath. It was the crying woman from Neil Bossard's graveside service. I was pretty sure I'd found my doll maker.

By now, half the restaurant was up, slapping at themselves, shaking and peeling off items of clothing. I left a dollar on the table for the coffee and slipped out unnoticed in the bedlam.

I'M NOT CRAZY ABOUT SURVEILLANCE, BUT I CAN DO IT. OFTEN times, it's wise to know the lay of the land before you attempt to make a delivery. Since I'm not always delivering happy tidings and gifts of joy, it's good to have an exit strategy before entering. It's also not a bad idea to know who's there and what threats I might face. Or maybe I was just naturally nosey. It's hard to tell sometimes. I've become so good at rationalizing my own behavior it's often difficult to tell what's real and what I've made up.

Tonight, however, I wasn't assessing threats or evaluating who or what was in the area. I was parked near the Canyon Café, nasty little doll legs back in the lead box in the trunk, waiting for my voodoo-wielding waitress to finish her shift so I could follow her back to her lair and figure out who the hell she was and what she was up to.

There are about a million things I love about Grandma Rosie's Buick. There's the totally wicked air-conditioning system that I think could give you frostbite in the middle of the Sahara. There's the solid, smooth ride. And then there are the seats. It's like driving around on a big comfy couch. Actually, it was more comfortable than my present living room couch. Futons can be really hard.

If you have to sit for hours waiting for something to happen, you might as well be comfortable.

It was close to eleven when my waitress finally left the café. I'm pretty sure I wouldn't have had feeling in any of my lower extremities if I'd been sitting that long in a Toyota or, God forbid, a Hyundai.

Crying Woman walked down the street, entered a Honda Civic that had seen better days and drove off. I followed. She wound her way past the cemetery toward the east side and parked in front of a well-kept ranch house on the edge of town. I continued on past as she pulled into the driveway, next to a Ford Taurus that was already parked there. As Crying Woman pulled in, someone got out of the Taurus. I couldn't linger long enough to see who, though.

I circled back around as soon as I felt I could without calling attention to myself and found a place to park a few blocks away. The area was just on the edge of rural. There were enough houses to make it feel like a neighborhood, but the yards were large, and Crying Woman's house seemed to back up onto some kind of greenbelt.

The farther I got from the car, the more I felt myself relax. One thing I was certain of was that I wasn't driving back with those doll legs in my car. Even if I had to resort to tying them to my antenna and letting them fly like some wicked freak flag all the way back to Sacto, I wasn't sharing space with them again if I could help it.

It was easy to access the greenbelt area behind the house. There was an actual bike path that made the walking easy. It was slightly trickier to figure out which house belonged to Crying Woman from the back. With the doll legs a few blocks away, I found it easier to get myself to open up to my surroundings. Once I did that, I was able to pick up the faint trill of her power from the path. Following that was a little like following the scent of a barbecue through the streets. I made a few missteps, but I eventually found it.

Crying Woman had landscaped her backyard for maximum privacy. The back fence was lined with Italian cypress. Thick, tangled bushes spread down each side. I found a scrub oak tree on the greenbelt side of the fence that looked sturdy enough to hold me and climbed up so that I could have a vantage point down into whatever it was she clearly didn't want people to see.

It was a nice backyard. I could see where she'd had her garden during the summer. There was a patio with a table and chairs and a hot tub over to one side. Right in the center of the yard was an open pit dug into the dirt about the size of a medium-sized woman. I knew that it was the right size for a medium-sized woman because at the moment, a medium-sized woman was lying in the pit, while Crying Woman covered her with dirt.

At first I thought the woman might be dead and Crying Woman was burying her, but then Buried Woman spoke. It didn't make me feel any better to think that Crying Woman might be burying the other woman alive. I tensed in my tree, ready to spring over the fence when the first shovelful of dirt landed on the other woman's face.

It never happened.

Crying Woman buried the other woman right up to her neck. Not a speck of dirt landed on her face, which shone in the moonlight like a pale orb. After the woman was buried up to her neck, Crying Woman got up and began walking a circle in the dirt. It wasn't exactly like one of Meredith's hedge circles, but it wasn't totally different either. There was no blue light. No electricity danced through her hair or shot from her fingers. I felt the power of it, though, low in my belly. It was like a soothing warm pool.

As Crying Woman walked, she sprinkled something behind her. At each cardinal point, she would stop, raise her arms and say a brief prayer. When she'd completed her circle, she took an egg and passed it up and down over the woman, chanting in a low voice the whole time. Then she lay down in the dirt next to the buried woman.

For the next hour, she talked softly to the woman. I strained, but it was hard to hear their voices. I know that at several points, the buried woman cried. Crying Woman wiped away her tears, brushed her hair from her forehead and gave her sips of water. All the while, they talked. At one point, the buried woman's voice rose into a wail. "Why? Why, Papa, why? Why are you doing that to me?" Her voice sounded different now. Younger, more vulnerable. She sounded like a child crying and I felt something in my chest clench up.

Crying Woman soothed her, murmuring softly.

I'm not sure when I've felt more uncomfortable and I'm not talking about the tree limb sticking into my back. I was witnessing something private, something painful, yet I couldn't move.

After the hour, Crying Woman stood and unburied the other woman. When she was free of dirt, the two women stood back to back in the center of the circle, raised their arms and chanted, "Oh, my Lady of Guadalupe. Behold your daughter. Let her give her pain back to the earth. Let the earth give her solace. May the sins committed against her be nothing more than dirt beneath her feet. Plant within her seeds of joy. I beseech you, Queen of Heaven."

Crying Woman handed Buried Woman a broom and had her sweep away the perimeter of the circle. Then she wrapped her in a blanket and sent her into the house. Once the door had clicked shut behind the formerly buried woman, Crying Woman came to the edge of her property. She scanned the area where I sat. I stayed as still as I could. While I could see her, I was pretty sure she couldn't see me. Not many people can see in the dark as well as I can. Still, I had the bad sensation that I had been noticed.

What happened next confirmed that. "Whoever you are," Crying Woman called out into the darkness, "you should be ashamed. That woman's pain is not for your entertainment. Tonight she gave her heartache and worries back to the earth despite your interference. Go home now. Be gone and stay gone."

Then she turned and walked back into her house.

AS MUCH AS I WANTED TO DO EXACTLY WHAT CRYING WOMAN asked, I couldn't. At least, not right away. I waited until I heard a car start and drive away, figuring that would be the buried woman leaving. I waited a little while longer and watched the lights in

Crying Woman's house go out one by one. Finally, I crept down from my tree.

I was over Crying Woman's back fence in a matter of seconds. Italian cypress might block the view, but they weren't much of a deterrent. Of course, hopping a ten-foot fence was less of an effort for me than it would be for most people. The casual breaker and enterer would move on to a different house. I was definitely not casual.

I crept to the pit in the center of the yard. It still pulsed with magic. Unlike the voodoo dolls, though, this felt different. The malevolence was gone. In its place was an energy that pulsed, almost like a heartbeat. Slow and steady and strong. The magic here was warm and alive. I didn't know what pain the buried woman had left in the soil and I didn't want to know. I felt guilty enough for having witnessed the ritual at all and deeply sad. Someone had done something to that woman a long time ago and had never made amends for it. I hoped that whatever had happened here tonight had brought her some small measure of peace.

I ran my fingers through the edge of the circle, sifting through the dirt to see what Crying Woman had sprinkled to make her circle. I sniffed at it. Cornmeal.

I made my way carefully and quietly through the rest of the backyard. The garden had contained herbs. The rosemary was still blooming, and I could smell the faintest echoes of sage, mint and henbane. I wasn't sure what else I could learn here. I vaulted back over the fence and made my way back to the Buick. I stayed to the shadows. There was no one else around and that alone made me conspicuous. I didn't want to draw any more attention to myself in Elmville than I already had.

I sighed as I slipped into the seat of my car. An hour on the branch of a scrub oak is not kind to a girl's behind. I pulled up to Crying Woman's house and popped the trunk. I took the legs out of the lead box and slipped up to the front door. I shook the little legs out of the baggie and onto the front porch. I could feel the sensation of their homecoming course through me. I ran to the Buick and drove away.

I STUMBLED INTO THE HOUSE AT ABOUT FOUR A.M. AND DIRECTLY into bed. I wasn't sure what was exhausting me the most, the driving, the splitting of my time and attention or the emotional raggedness of what I'd been witnessing. Rawley's mother's anger. Bossard's mother's grief. The buried woman's pain. I like to keep emotion at an arm's length. It's safest that way. I don't get hurt. No one else does either.

Ever since I let Ted into my life, however, emotions had been seeping in all over. It was as if I'd thought I was only opening the door a crack and had instead thrown it wide. I wished I could figure out how to shut it again. I'd learned how to keep my senses under control. My emotions had never been a problem. They'd been easy to keep neatly tucked away. Not anymore. It was as if letting myself feel a little bit had opened up a whole world of feeling that I wasn't sure I wanted.

I woke Friday morning with a pit of dread in my stomach. Every other Friday night from six to eight we have a sparring class at River City. Learning forms and perfecting kicks is great. Learning to actually use them when push comes to shove can only come from putting oneself in a combat situation. You may have the most graceful kick on the planet, but if you freeze up when an assailant is coming toward you or have to count to ten before you can get in position, it won't do you a darned bit of good in protecting yourself.

Fighting isn't the only reason to get involved in the martial arts. There's a lot to be learned about self-discipline and control and respect. People have all kinds of reasons to come to the dojo and I try to respect that. While I do require some sparring for upper-belt candidates, I try not to shove it down everyone's throat. Some people, however, do martial arts as a way to release hostility.

Sparring class generally attracts the most macho of my students. Women, for the most part, don't like the confrontation of sparring. Oh, a few still show up from time to time, but they're not my regulars.

T.J. is a regular. So is his buddy, Jackson Hughes. When you walk into the dojo on a Friday sparring-class night, you can practically see the testosterone dripping from the walls. It's a heady mix of excitement, aggression and anticipation. It takes a lot of effort on my part to stay separate and maintain the calm. It would be too easy to get swept up into the emotions swirling around me and let things spiral out of control. The end result of that? Somebody could end up getting hurt, really hurt.

It's a fine line to walk. I have to encourage the participants to really fight each other but not hurt each other. I have to stay in control of myself and the room. It's an effort. I come out of sparring class exhausted most nights.

I so wished that this night was a sparring-class Friday. It wasn't though.

On the Friday nights that I'm not overseeing the sparring class at River City, I'm expected to show up at my mother's house for dinner. Shabbat dinner at my mother's was torture enough before I started dating Ted. It had now devolved into a special kind of hell.

I say we're going to my mother's house. It's not like she lives alone. My dad lives there, too, and I am pretty sure he pays the majority of the mortgage. It is, however, definitely my mother's house. I don't know if it's a tribal thing or if we're just matriarchal by nature, but it's her house in much the same way that Grandma Rosie's house was hers even when Grandpa Ed was still playing two hours of doubles tennis every Saturday morning, which he did until he was seventy-four, thank you very much.

I lay back on the pillow and tried to think happy thoughts. I had to get through the evening and since I could spend most of it shoving my mother's admittedly good cooking into my mouth, it wouldn't be that bad. It couldn't be that bad. Right?

Ah, the beauty of wishful thinking.

I vaguely heard Norah getting up and getting ready for work, but I didn't have the energy to go out and talk to her. I hadn't spoken with Alex yet. I had to work tonight, so maybe that would be my opportunity.

I dragged myself out of bed at noon and called Meredith. "I found our doll maker."

"How interesting! What can you tell me?"

I described the Crying Woman and the rite I'd seen her perform.

"You've got yourself a bona fide *bruja*, Melina," she said when I was finished.

"I know *bruja* is Spanish for 'witch.'"

"Well, yes, but there's more to it than that. *Brujeria* is its own brand of witchcraft. It's actually fascinating. Is there any chance I can meet this woman?"

I sighed. "Sure, Meredith, why don't I invite her for tea?"

"I don't think sarcasm is called for," she said, with a hint of coolness to her voice.

"Why do people keep saying that to me?" I wondered out loud.

"Think about it. You're a smart girl. I'm sure you'll figure it out."

I gritted my teeth. "Fine. Can you explain to me about *brujeria* at least a little bit so I know what I'm dealing with?"

"You know how the Spanish weren't exactly the most super-tolerant people on the planet when it came to religion?" she asked.

"Meredith, I was raised Jewish. It's a little hard not to know exactly how intolerant the Spanish were. Remember that part where they threw all the Jews out of Spain? They covered that in Sunday school." I poured myself a cup of coffee from the pot that Norah must have made this morning and stuck the cup in the microwave. It would taste like crap, but I could put enough sugar and milk in it to counteract that.

"So you wouldn't be surprised to learn that they weren't really nice about native religions when they came to the New World, then."

"Not surprised at all." I'd made it too hot. I cursed a little under my breath and put more milk in it.

"A lot of native religions went underground. One of the easiest ways to do that was to pretend to worship the gods the Spanish wanted them to worship while secretly worshipping their own. Over time, the two religions sort of conflated themselves. What we think of as a personification of the Virgin Mary in Our Lady of Guadalupe is actually a form of the Aztec goddess Tonantzin."

"You mean like the way the whole maypole thing is actually a pagan fertility rite?" I remember sharing that little tidbit with Aunt Kitty. It delighted her. It hadn't been what I was going for at the time, but in retrospect, I liked it.

"Exactly. The Aztecs took all those Catholic saints and used them as sort of a curtain over their original gods. They were incredibly flexible and adaptive. It was quite clever, really," Meredith said with admiration.

"So you're saying this woman is really an Aztec practitioner?" Would there be blood sacrifices? I hated those. Just the laundry issues afterward were enough to make me cringe.

There was a pause. "No. And yes."

"Way to be decisive, Meredith."

"If you think a black and white answer like that exists, you're not listening. They sort of combined into a whole new religion, often practiced both in secret and in the wide open. When people began to immigrate to the United States and meet up with even more religions, especially some of the voodoo cults, they continued to adapt and take those practices and make them their own. It's really quite remarkable." Meredith paused in her explanation. "You're sure it's the same woman, though? The woman you saw last night is the one who made those dolls?"

"Reasonably certain. Why?" Those doll legs definitely belonged to her in some way. I would be super-surprised if it turned out she wasn't the one who made them and imbued them with power.

"It doesn't make sense. The rite you described is a healing rite, a very positive thing. The dolls have lots of purposes, but all of them are malevolent. They're used to hex people and curse them. Most of the *brujas* I've met deal in either healing or hexing, one or the other, not both."

Wow. Witches who specialized. Nice. "Why can't they do both?"

"We all have our skills, right? I'm sure there's some kind of martial arts that you're better at than others?"

That was certainly true. I excelled at anything that required speed and agility. Things that required brute strength tended not to be my forte. "Sure."

"Witches are the same. I'm pretty good at summoning and protection. Scrying on the other hand? I can do it, but it's not always pretty. You know what I mean?"

I couldn't quite imagine Meredith doing anything in any way that wasn't at least damned attractive, but I didn't think that was what she meant. "Got it."

"*Brujas* are much the same. They tend to specialize. Healers are especially gifted. It's truly a calling. Not everyone can do it. So when someone is adept at healing, that's what she tends to focus on. To be honest, the hexing stuff is a little easier. Gather a little cemetery dirt. Throw in a knife and some chicken bones. Light some black candles. Voila. You've got yourself a hex."

"So you're saying that we have an unusually versatile *bruja*?" Lord knows I appreciated someone who could multitask, but perhaps not in this particular instance.

"That and I'm guessing we still don't really know what's going on. It would take something big to make a *bruja* work that far outside of her comfort zone."

I thought about Jorge Aguilar. That was big, but I bit my tongue and didn't offer Meredith the Understatement of the Week Award. I didn't want to be accused of being sarcastic again.

After I got off the phone with Meredith, I powered up my laptop. After a cursory check of my e-mail, I plugged Crying Woman's address into a reverse address lookup. In about two seconds, I had a name. Emilia Aguilar. Age twenty-eight. Possible relatives: Rosita Lopez and Jorge Aguilar.

So much for Jorge not having any family in the area.

10

"PUT ON A SKIRT, MELINA," NORAH SAID WHEN I WALKED OUT of my bedroom wearing jeans and a long-sleeved T-shirt.

I'd taught the afternoon classes at River City, come home and showered again. Wasn't that enough? "Why? It's my mother's house, not a five-star restaurant. I spent most of the time I lived there in sweatpants. Jeans are practically black tie in comparison."

"You don't live there anymore and it's a matter of showing respect by dressing appropriately." She didn't budge from the hallway. I wondered if she'd been waiting there for me to come out inappropriately dressed.

I opened my mouth, but before I could get a word out, Norah held up her hand. "I don't want to hear it. Just go change."

I made another noise, but she cut me off again. "Enough." She turned and walked down the hallway, saying, "Talk to the booty 'cuz the hand's off duty."

I went back into my bedroom and changed.

I came out a little later in a long black skirt, boots and a top. Norah sighed and put a scarf around my neck and pronounced me suitable. Ted arrived a few minutes later wearing a sport coat and a dress shirt with jeans.

"We look ridiculous," I complained. "This is not us. It's like we're putting on costumes."

"Yes," Norah agreed. "You're wearing a costume. Tonight you will be playing the part of the loving daughter. Do you want me to give you your lines?"

I glared at her. "Let's go get Grandma."

NORAH AND TED WAITED WITH THE BUICK WHILE I WENT INTO the Sunshine Assisted Living Facility to pick up Grandma. I signed in at the front desk and dutifully put on a Visitor sticker even though I was only going to be there for about five minutes and I was relatively certain that no one would mistake me for a resident. I look young for my age, and the minimum age for getting into Sunshine was fifty-five and then you had to have a spouse who was over sixty-five. I so did not qualify, although it was tempting sometimes. Grandma Rosie didn't have to cook anymore; someone came and made her bed every morning; there were art classes and language classes, field trips to museums and weekly buses to the shopping malls. It didn't sound like a bad life to me at all.

Grandma was already at her door with her coat on when I got to her room. I glanced at my watch. I was not late, for once.

"I would have helped with your coat," I said. It seems like a little thing, but her having to hold on to her cane and reach up for her coat on the hanger at the same time took a bit of balancing.

She waved me off. "I'm fine. Let's go. I'm starving."

They served dinner early at Sunshine. Like five o'clock sharp.

Grandma was often headed down to the dining room for dinner by four forty-five. Six o'clock was stretching her appetite a little bit and she didn't like to snack.

"After you," I said.

She sailed out as grandly as you can when you have a cane with four feet.

We checked back out at the front desk. I was tempted to put my Visitor sticker somewhere obnoxious, but Grandma was watching and I didn't want to embarrass her.

"I'm going to my daughter's for dinner," she told the girl at the front desk. "I won't be back until quite late."

"Have a nice time," the girl said, and off we went.

I suspect it's a bit of a status symbol at the assisted-living facility to have your family whisk you away. Grandma makes sure to announce it whenever I come to pick her up.

Ted straightened up from where he was leaning against the car as the doors to the facility whooshed open in front of us and opened the front passenger door of the Buick.

"You took your time in finding one, Melina, but when you did, you picked a fine-looking one," Grandma said to me.

I'm pretty sure she thought she was whispering, or at least speaking under her breath, but when you're hard of hearing, those whispers tend to be kind of loud.

Ted fought back a grin. "At least someone in your family likes me," he whispered in my ear as I helped Grandma into the car. Gone were the days that she hopped in and out of the car without effort. Now it was a laborious affair of careful pivoting and terrifying balancing. I held my breath through most of it. Luckily, she was a tiny little thing, and I was pretty sure that my reflexes were fast enough and that I was strong enough to catch her if she fell.

If she fell on my watch, however, I'm pretty sure I would never be able to set foot in my mother's home again. I might rail against Friday night dinner, but I didn't want to be banned from it either. It was kind of like not wanting to be excluded from a club you didn't want to join. It didn't have to make sense. It was just human nature.

"Hello, Norah," Grandma said once she was settled.

"Hello, Ms. Silverstone," Norah said from the back. "How are you tonight?"

"Sitting up and taking sustenance, dear. Sometimes that's as good as it gets."

Amen to that, sister.

NORAH USED TO COME WITH ME OCCASIONALLY ON FRIDAYS, but now that she no longer wants to leave the apartment without a guard or stay in it alone without protection, she almost always comes. That part is actually okay. My mother loves Norah. Norah is the normal girl I'm pretty sure she wishes was her daughter. Norah is an awesome buffer between the two of us. It's a good thing my mother doesn't know that Norah is being stalked by a vampire and isn't entirely sure that she wants it to stop.

We pulled up to the house. My parents live in a Spanish-style stucco house in Land Park. It's two stories with an enclosed patio in front, a guesthouse over the garage and a pool in the gated backyard. The roof is red-clay tiles, and bougainvillea twines around black iron gates. My mother keeps it immaculate.

From the driveway, I could smell the chicken roasting. It was Friday night, after all. I helped Grandma Rosie out of the Buick and handed her her quad cane. "Ready?" I asked.

"Of course," she said, but she waited to take Ted's arm before we walked in. Norah and I marched behind them. Norah elbowed me. "You make it worse than it is. Smile."

"There are limits to what you can ask of me. If you wanted me to be cheerful, you shouldn't have insisted on the skirt." I actually didn't mind the skirt. It was being told what to wear that rankled, even if Norah was right. My mother would appreciate the effort of dressing appropriately. It would be one less thing for her to sigh over. One of these days, I was going to end up making her hyperventilate and then how would I feel? Supremely successful, I suspect.

We got to the front door, and Ted and Grandma stopped. I slipped around them and opened the door. "Mom! Dad! We're here!"

Dad met us in the entryway. "Come in, come in." He kissed my grandmother's cheek and helped her out of her coat.

"How's my favorite girl?" he asked, giving me a hug. I may have mentioned I have a very touchy-feely family. It's one of the reasons I don't come home more often than I do.

"I'm fine, Daddy." I handed him my coat, too. Yes. I call him Daddy. Say something about it and feel my wrath.

"Theodore, how are you?" He shook Ted's hand.

"Fine, sir. And yourself?" Ted smiled down at him. I have no idea how Ted feels about being called Theodore. If it makes him grit his teeth, you'd never know it. If it makes my father grit his teeth that Ted towers over him like a blond Adonis, you'd never know that either.

"Couldn't be better." Which was my father's stock response to everything. According to him, the glass is permanently half full. I've never done a DNA test, but I am his daughter. I totally have his nose. I'm just not anything like him on the inside. "Good shabbos, everyone. Theodore, would you care for a beer?"

"Thank you, sir. I'd love one."

Daddy hung the coats up and we all migrated into my mother's kitchen. The smells were already making my mouth water. "Can I help with anything, Mama?" I asked as we walked in.

"Yes, dear, make a salad." I got an air kiss. "The rest of you get out of the way."

"Even me?" Norah asked.

My mother eyed her. "You should sit down and eat. You're much too thin. Harold, put out that cheese and crackers. Set it in front of Norah."

"Yes, dear," my father said, and winked at me as he went by.

My mother then turned to Grandma Rosie. "Mom, do you want a glass of wine? Some iced tea?"

"Tea would be good, dear." Grandma Rosie settled herself on one of the bar stools out of the way.

At no point did my mother directly address Ted. I didn't miss that fact and I doubt he did either, although he never complained about it.

I'm not crazy about cops. They make me nervous. My mother is also not crazy about cops. She hates them.

Okay. *Hate* may be too strong a word, but she's damn sure suspicious of them. My mother was twelve during the Summer of Love and actually used to take the train into San Francisco to look at the hippies in The Haight.

Cops were the pigs, the fuzz, the enemy, the man.

Having her daughter date a cop was sending my mother into a very unattractive tailspin. On the one hand, she was so grateful that I was actually dating someone that she practically wanted to take out an ad. On the other hand, I was dating a cop, a pig, an enemy. It was pretty much enough to make her head swim.

Of course, if mom knew what I was, her head might well explode.

I grabbed stuff out of the crisper in the refrigerator and took the big wooden bowl out of the cabinet and started chopping and tearing.

"Tear the leaves smaller, Melina. Bite-sized. I don't like watching people try to stuff oversized leaves into their mouths." She hadn't even turned away from the stove. Seriously, how did she know how big the lettuce leaves were?

"Yes, Mama."

"And not too much cucumber. You know it gives your father indigestion."

"No problem."

"Stop bossing the girl around, Elizabeth," Grandma Rosie said. "She's nearly thirty years old. She knows how to make a salad."

Mama turned from the stove, blinked a few times at her mother and said, "Of course. You're right. Do whatever you feel is best, Melina."

For a moment I contemplated putting in giant lettuce leaves and filling half the bowl with cucumber, but decided to be the bigger person even if I wasn't the one who'd been out-mommed.

"Have you been ill, Norah?" my mother, Queen of Tact, asked. "You don't look well, dear."

Norah shifted uncomfortably. "No. Not exactly ill, just a little under the weather, I guess."

"Have you seen a doctor? I'm sure Melina could find you someone at that hospital of hers. She'd know who was good and who wasn't. What about that emergency room doctor? The handsome one with the dark hair?" My mother had been to the hospital once and had run across Alex. He'd made an impression.

I stiffened. Mom kept whisking the gravy. Sometimes I wondered exactly what my mother knew and didn't know. After all, I'd thought I'd had Norah fooled for years and hadn't. Well, I'd had her a little fooled. Just fooled enough so that when she was completely in the know, she went into an emotional nosedive that I wasn't sure she was ever going to come out of.

I looked over at her now. Her eyes were big as saucers. I certainly could introduce her to a doctor or two. That was exactly what had gotten us into our current problems, after all.

"Where's Patrick?" I asked, changing the topic. Patrick is my little brother. I use the term *little* loosely. He is around six foot two, which is noticeably taller than me.

"He'll be here in a few minutes." Mom glanced at her watch. "His last class gets out at four thirty and you know how traffic on the causeway can be on a Friday."

My brother attends UC Davis, whose campus is a stone's throw from Sacramento, if you can throw a stone twenty miles or so. He's majoring in molecular biology. He hasn't decided if he's going to go the PhD doctor route or the MD doctor route. Either way, he's pretty much the apple of my mother's eye.

I don't blame her. Patrick is so incredibly normal. He went to just enough school dances and played on just enough sports teams to reassure my parents that he was well-liked without being one of those too-popular kids that can turn mean. He got great grades and is kind to animals. They caught him smoking weed once, but it was during the Perseids meteor shower, and I think the hardest part for my parents was not asking if they could have a hit and watch the stars fall with him. He doesn't disappear on inexplicable errands, attract strange phenomena or generally act as a force of chaos in their lives. If he was my kid, he'd be my favorite, too.

He showed up as we were putting things on the table. "You have to help clear because you didn't help set," I told him.

"Hey, big sis." He grabbed me in a hug and nearly squeezed the air out of me.

"Hey, yourself. I wasn't joking about the clearing," I wheezed.

"We'll see about that," he whispered in my ear.

I glared. I will grant him his role as Golden Boy. He walks the walk, so he deserves it. I despise the fact that he can get out of kitchen chores with a smile and a few flutters of his eyelashes.

Mom herded everyone to the table, lit the candles, circled them with her hands three times, covered her eyes and said the prayers. Then we all dug in. Once we were eating, conversation pretty much stopped. My mother is good with a chicken. She'd stuffed and grilled portobello mushrooms for Norah, and even those smelled and looked tasty.

"So what's new, Melina?" Patrick asked, as he dished up a third helping of mashed potatoes. Mama pushed the gravy toward him without his even asking.

I smiled. "Not much." I wondered what everyone would have done if I'd said that I was pretty sure I'd recently been the agent of two men's deaths and had had to chase a Basajaun out of the dojo. "I'm getting some new mats at the karate studio."

"Cool." The conversation moved on.

Yeah, cool. I reached for the bowl of mashed potatoes.

"Do you really need that, Melina?" my mother asked, without looking up from her plate.

I set the spoon back in the bowl and took seconds on green beans instead.

AFTER DINNER, I ENDED UP CLEARING THE TABLE BECAUSE PATrick and my father just happened to get into a good-natured argument about who actually wrote the song "Summertime Blues," with my brother firmly in The Who camp and my father adamantly taking the part of Eddie Cochran. They had to go and look it up on the

Internet in Daddy's office. Patrick blew me a little kiss as he followed Daddy out of the room. I stuck my tongue out and crossed my eyes.

"Stop it, Melina. You're too old for that kind of behavior." Mama bustled past me with a stack of plates. My mother had never been one of those mothers who would tell you that your face would freeze that way. She didn't believe in lying to children. She felt stories like that eroded children's trust in adults and would lead to lives of crime and drug abuse. Throughout my childhood, if a shot was going to hurt, I knew about it in advance.

I might not have always liked what my mother told me, but I could always rely on it. I didn't feel too old to make faces at my brother, but apparently I was mistaken.

As I trooped out of the dining room, balancing several wineglasses and a couple of salad plates, my grandmother smiled at me, crossed her eyes and stuck out her tongue. I snorted.

"Melina, do you have a cold?" my mother asked from the kitchen.

"No, Mama," I called. "I'm fine."

I found Ted sitting out on the back deck, his half-empty beer bottle dangling between his fingers. The stars starting to come out. I sat down next to him and leaned my head on his shoulder. I breathed in the sweet, spicy scent of him, now against a background of my mother's roses with just the faintest hint of roast chicken thrown in. "I'm sorry," I said.

"What for?" He looped his arm around my shoulder.

"For them. For them being so . . . weird."

He chuckled. "Hello, Pot. Have you met Kettle?"

I punched him in the shoulder, but I totally pulled it. "Maybe that's the problem. Maybe they're way too normal."

"They are pretty normal."

"Distressingly so, sometimes."

"You don't know how good you've got it." He leaned back on

his elbows and looked up at the stars. "Your mother will warm up to me. Moms always do."

"Is that so? I warn you. My mom is not easily manipulated." In fact, my mother was nearly manipulation-proof.

"Not like you, huh?" he said, and pulled me onto his lap.

"I am not easily manipulated either." I protested.

"And I am the King of France." He kissed me.

I wiggled out of his grasp, but not too far. "Well, your majesty, I came out to tell you that dessert is being served."

He froze for a second. "What is it?"

"Cheesecake."

"With strawberries?" He sounded like a little boy. Ted loves cheesecake. He especially likes it with strawberries, although he will accept raspberries and won't turn his nose up at blueberries.

"Yes."

He shoved me off his lap and stood up. "Told you she was warming up to me."

I followed him into the house, wondering if he might be right.

WE TOOK GRANDMA ROSIE HOME AT THE END OF THE EVENING. She hobbled out to the car, one hand firmly tucked into Ted's arm and the other firmly on her cane. She'd had two glasses of wine, which was pretty much a bender for her, and wasn't as steady on her pins. Ted helped her into the Buick. My mother tried to help, but Grandma slapped her hands away. "Let the boy do it, Elizabeth. He's young. It won't hurt his back."

My mother had backed off a little, hovering nearby, but she'd let Ted get Grandma into the car. Grandma had then fallen into an instant sleep the second Ted turned on the engine. Norah dozed off by the time we hit I-5. Ted reached over into the backseat and took my hand. We rode in silence. Well, as silent as you can be with two women snoring in an enclosed space. They both woke, startled, as we pulled into the driveway of the assisted-living facility.

"Did I fall asleep?" they asked, practically in unison.

"Yes," I said, just as Ted said, "No."

Ted helped Grandma out of the car and I walked her back to her apartment. I unlocked the door for her and followed her in. As I helped her off with her coat, she said, "They'd understand you better if you let them."

"Excuse me?" It sounded like one of those Zen koans, but that wasn't really Grandma Rosie's way.

"I know you feel like none of us understand you, and we probably don't. It's not our fault, though, dear. You don't let us."

I made myself busy hanging up her coat while I figured out what to say. I couldn't let them understand me. It was part of the gig, to be alone.

"You know me better than anyone. You're my family." I turned to face her.

"We know that you got new mats for the karate studio. That's not knowing a person." She waved me away. "I get it. You don't think we could possibly get it. You think we would be shocked. Let me tell you something, Melina. I'm eighty-one years old. There's nothing that shocks me anymore."

That was true. Grandma Rosie took pretty much everything in stride. A few things made her press her lips together in disapproval, but she was rarely surprised. That said, I was pretty sure that finding out her granddaughter regularly associated with denizens of the night, cavorted with werewolves and was on a first-name basis with several goblins and trolls would at least make her raise her eyebrows, if it didn't make her tell my mother to lock me up in the loony bin.

"Grandma," I started, but she cut me off.

"No, Melina. I can tell. You're just going to make some excuse. I love you, dear. When you're ready to let us in on whatever your big secrets are, I'll be first in line." She paused. "No. I take that back. I'll be second. Tell your mother first. She's dying to know."

NORAH AND TED WERE WAITING PATIENTLY FOR ME AT THE Buick. Honestly, I don't know how they did it. It was hard enough for me to walk next to Grandma down the hall without hustling her along. To just sit in the car and wait? I'd probably claw my own eyes out.

Not them, though. Oh, no. Ted just stood, leaning against the Buick, arms folded across his chest, legs stretched in front of him. Still as a magazine ad. Norah was asleep again in the backseat. She'd had more than two glasses of wine, and as skinny as she was these days, it didn't take much.

Ted opened the front door for me and I climbed in. He gave me a kiss before he shut the door. I waited until he got in to start talking.

"Do you think my grandmother knows what I am?" I asked.

"Maybe," Norah said from the backseat, suddenly awake. She popped up, leaning her chin on the front seat between us. I used to do the exact same thing when I used to ride in the backseat of this car with Grandpa driving and Grandma riding shotgun. "She's a wily one, Rosie is."

I had to grant her that. "What about my mom? Do you think she knows?"

"Definitely not." Norah sank back into her seat. "Elizabeth would have you in some kind of twelve-step program or rehab thing so fast your head would spin."

She was probably right about that. It was precisely what I'd always thought.

"Of course, we could be completely wrong. She might totally embrace it. Maybe it'd be like when your brother was playing soccer. Remember how she'd go to every game and cheer her head off? She didn't understand that either and she got totally behind that," Norah said.

"I don't think you can equate delivering axes to dwarves with playing outside mid for a Select soccer team." Although, she had a point. My mother would probably understand what I did about as well as she grasped "offsides," which was not at all.

Ted pulled into a parking place less than a block from our apartment. He had some strange parking karma. It wasn't the first time I'd wondered if he had something magic to him that I'd yet to detect. I sniffed at him. Nope. Nothing numinous, just a faint scent that reminded me of muffins.

"Why are you sniffing him?" Norah asked, as she unfolded herself from the backseat.

"Because I found a good parking place." Ted locked the car and we started down the street.

"That makes no sense." Norah hurried after him.

I trailed along behind the two of them, listening to Ted trying to explain my suspicions of his good parking karma. That was probably why I didn't hear the guys coming up behind us until right before they started swinging.

I DIDN'T FEEL A TINGLE. THESE GUYS WERE JUST GUYS. THAT was something to be grateful for. "Ted," I yelled, as I whirled to face the footsteps I heard coming up behind me fast.

I ducked and his first punch swung wildly over my head. Never underestimate the power of a good, fast ducking reflex. It has saved my jaw more than once. Plus, from my crouched pose, I could give the fist strike that I landed on his jaw a lot of power. I've got strong legs and they can propel me into quite the attack.

The first guy went over backwards. That's when I felt it. Not a big tingle. Just the smidge of a vibration. Whoever he was, he wasn't magical, but he had something magical with him. A talisman, maybe? An amulet? There was no time to investigate because there were two more guys behind him, all of them wearing balaclavas. They launched their attack at me, but Ted was already by my side.

"Norah?" I asked.

"Running for the apartment," he answered.

I didn't have time to comment because our next two attackers were on us. Honestly, I almost felt bad for them. They weren't street fighters. Thug Number Two telegraphed all of his punches so far in advance it felt like he was sending me an engraved invitation to duck under his arm and pummel his rib cage. He doubled over and I landed an elbow strike to his kidney area. He went down. I whirled to see how Ted was doing.

His guy was a little savvier. I guess they must have thought it would be better to send their better fighter after the man in the group. On top of that, Ted was still favoring the arm with the cadejo bite. As Thug Number Three began to back Ted up the sidewalk, I slid in and swept his legs from underneath him.

He never saw it coming.

By now, however, Thugs Numbers One and Two were back up. One managed to nail me right in the kidneys. You have no idea how much I hate that. It completely takes my breath away for a moment. While I gasped for breath, he whispered in my ear, "Stay away from Elmville, bitch." He drew his arm back, readying for another punch.

The thing is, while a punch to the kidneys takes my breath away for a moment, when I catch my breath afterward, I am seriously pissed off. I reared back, smacking his nose with the back of my head. I heard a satisfying crunch. He let out a howl that distracted Thug Number One as he went after Ted.

Ted landed a beautiful uppercut to One's solar plexus. I could hear the air whoosh out of his lungs over the pounding of blood in my ears.

Within seconds all three of them were running. "You stay away," I yelled after them.

"Witty comeback," Ted observed, shaking his hand out. I looked at the knuckles. They were so going to bruise.

"It's all I had at the moment. Not everyone can come up with things like 'bad dog,' you know."

"True that." He looped his arm around my shoulder and we walked the rest of the way to the apartment leaning on each other a little more heavily than usual.

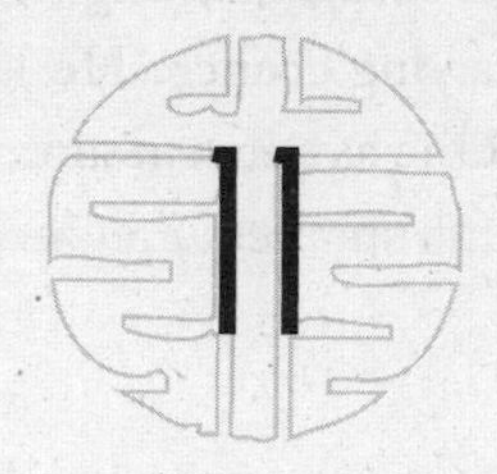

11

"THERE'S BLOOD ALL OVER THE BACK OF YOUR HEAD!" NORAH let us into the apartment. "Are you okay? Do we need to call Alex?"

"It's not my blood. Unless Alex is going to lick it off my hair as a snack, I don't think we need to call him." I was going to have a fairly large bruise on my side, but it would heal quickly. "Ted needs some ice for his hand, though."

Norah ran to the kitchen. "I've got arnica for his bruise, too."

"That's great, Norah. Thanks."

We both lowered ourselves gently onto the couch. Just because we kicked some ass didn't mean our own weren't sore.

"Who were those guys?" Norah brought the ice to Ted in a bag. He wrapped it around his knuckles and leaned back against the couch.

"I'm not sure. They were just guys. They weren't anything special. But they had something with them. I think maybe an amulet.

It had that kind of feel to it. I didn't have a chance to focus in on it, though."

"They were special enough," Ted observed, holding up his bruised hand.

"What did they want?" Norah pressed.

"Apparently for me to stay out of Elmville." Fat chance of me doing that now.

"Why?" Norah asked.

"How did they know how to find you?" Ted asked. "Why did they want to find you? Melina, what are you getting yourself into this time?"

I didn't know. All I knew for sure was that I would be going back to Elmville to find out.

Boy, did their plan backfire.

I WASN'T GOING TO BE GOING TO ELMVILLE ON SATURDAY morning, though. Saturday morning belonged to the Little Dragons. This morning, there was no buzz as I walked into the studio. I was grateful for that. Sophie was there, hair neatly pulled back into a ponytail. Ben was helping her sweep.

"Hey, guys," I said as I walked past them into the office. "Anything I need to know about?"

They glanced back and forth at each other and said, "No." In unison.

I froze for a second. Clearly they were lying. I'm not so far out of teenagerdom that I forget what that looks like. I considered browbeating it out of them, but decided I had more on my plate than I could handle at the moment. Speaking of which . . .

"Will you be taking the axe up to Ginnar on Wednesday?" I asked.

Sophie nodded. "Yep."

"Great." The kids began to bounce in. In some cases, literally. I watched Miguel jump his way in, his whole body making the effort. It made my calves hurt. In fact, a lot of me hurt. Thugs One through Three had landed a punch or two last night and I hadn't finished healing yet. Norah had slathered me with arnica again. I think it made her feel better, but it didn't seem to help me at all. I sighed. I love teaching the Little Dragons. There are moments when the only thing that restores my faith in humankind is their sweet open faces, their excitement and enthusiasm, and the smell of their bubblegum shampoo. There are also moments when I would give anything not to hit the mat and worm crawl with them.

Just because I seem to be aging a little more slowly than most people doesn't mean I'm getting any younger. Then it hit me. I wasn't younger, but Sophie was.

"Sophie," I called to where she and Ben were leaning against a wall next to each other. "Would you take the Little Dragons through their warm-ups?"

She came to full attention. "Me? Do the warm-ups?"

"Yes, please."

"Yes, sensei," she said, and sprang onto the mat.

I'd almost forgotten this part of what Mae had done for me. Yes, she'd kept things from me and leaked information to me like it was more precious than liquid gold. She'd also given me responsibilities. She'd made sure that I had work to do. She'd made sure that I was needed. I could do that for Sophie. Not only could I make sure that she felt needed, I could let myself rely on her a little. The more I gave her to do, the more she'd be able to do. Just like Mae and me.

I'd been chafing at all the responsibilities that seemed to rest on my shoulders now, all the people and things I was suddenly responsible for. Was this really any different? Mae had simply left me more responsibilities. I needed to learn to rise to them. It wasn't always going to be easy, but I knew the satisfaction it would bring me in the end, just as I could see the pride and satisfaction on Sophie's face right now.

I FOUND ALEX UP ON THE ROOF OF THE PARKING GARAGE when I got to the hospital. He was standing on the very edge of the ledge. The moonlight shone off his hair. He stretched his arms wide and threw back his head. Then he stepped off the ledge and turned to face me. "She told you, didn't she?"

I nodded.

"I'm guessing she didn't like the flowers."

"I don't think she minds the flowers themselves. It's the method of delivery that has her creeped out."

"How about you?" He cocked his head to one side, as if he were truly interested in my take on the situation.

I was happy to provide it. "Yeah. It creeped me out, too. I checked her over. You know, just to see if you were using her for a late night snack."

He winced. "I doubt that helped any."

"Nope. Not really. I think it might have creeped her out more." It hadn't exactly thrilled me either.

He nodded. "I can see that. So now what?"

"So now you cut it out." I crossed my arms over my chest and steeled myself. I'd expected an argument. I'd expected protestations of innocence. I hadn't expected him to stand there looking like a lost schoolboy.

"I'm not sure I can." He smiled at me, and not with his way-too-charming grin that made everybody in the hospital, including me, run to do his bidding. It was a sad smile, if that makes any sense.

"What does that mean? How come? Why can't you just stop?" He had way more control than most vampires I know. He could control this. I was sure of it.

He sat down on the ledge, as if he were suddenly very tired. "I'm not sure how to explain."

"Try. Use small words." I came over and sat down next to him on the ledge.

"You know, I first started charming your Norah mainly to piss you off." He glanced at me.

"I'm aware." Alex liked to needle me a bit here and there. I wasn't exactly sure why. It reminded me a little bit of my brother, so I took it as a sign of affection, in an odd way.

"But there's something about her." He frowned now. "It's subtle, but there's something there. Sort of a glow."

Also something I was well aware of. "I think she's good. I've wondered about it a few times. She doesn't have any powers. Honestly, even now that I've given her the grimoire and she's trying to cast protection spells, she totally sucks at it. She's making an unholy mess around the windowsills and door frames, but that's about it."

He chuckled. "You gave her a grimoire?"

"Yeah. She's been scared spitless for so many months. I figured it was better for her to know what was really out there to be scared of and what she could ignore."

"Then she knows she should be scared of me." He sounded so sad.

"Yeah. She knows." It wasn't nice, but a little fear of Alex and his kind wasn't a bad thing. I was still a little frightened of him. Only on occasion, but still frightened.

He stood up and reached back to help me to my feet. "I usually have better self-control than this. Sometimes a guy just gets a craving."

I swallowed hard. I did not like the sound of that. "What kind of craving?"

"You know how sometimes you just want a pepperoni pizza and nothing else will do? Not a hamburger. Not a salad. Not even a sausage pizza."

I nodded. "You have a Norah craving and nothing else will do?"

"Apparently."

"Any idea why?"

He nodded. "I guess I'm tired of junk food and in the mood for something good."

"You can't have her, Alex."

His head snapped toward me and his eyes glowed red. "You know that's not true, Melina."

I felt myself taking a step toward him against my will. My head fell back and exposed my neck. My heart pounded a mile a minute, but I couldn't move. Then just as suddenly as he'd snapped me under his control, he let me go. I stumbled backward several steps. My hands flew to my throat.

"Luckily, I don't want her like that. I don't even want to take her the way I usually take my women. I want her . . . I need her to know who and what I am and accept me on those terms. I'm not sure anything else will do. I don't want to simply charm my way into her arms."

I'd seen how that worked, too. If Alex Bledsoe decided to charm you, watch out. I don't think many women could resist him.

"So, you're not eating at all?" That didn't sound like a good idea.

"I'm eating, but I'm not . . . feeding."

It took me a second to suss out the difference. "What, do you just go down to the blood bank and order up a pint of O?"

He smiled. "You'd be surprised. There are . . . places that one can go."

I shivered a little.

"Cold, Melina?" He sounded amused. I wasn't.

I needed some time to think. "A bit. I think I'll go in now."

He nodded.

I couldn't stop myself from making one straightforward plea. "Please, Alex, stay away from her."

"I can't make any promises."

I didn't like the sound of that. Not one bit.

I WAS PRETTY POOPED BY THE TIME I WANDERED BACK TO MY car at seven A.M. Not too pooped to notice the package sitting on the hood of my car, though. I stopped a few feet away and considered it from a distance. It was roughly the same size and shape as the packages that had gone to Bossard and Rawley. It was covered in the same brown paper wrapping, too.

I took a few more steps forward. Yep. Same little buzz of power came from it as well. I sighed. There was nothing for it. I walked over and picked it up. It had the same neat block printing on the front of it. This one was addressed to John Littlefield. Well, it had his name on it. No actual address, though. What a shocker. It was the kid who'd been thrown out of the Bossard's house just before I was. The one who was sure he was cursed. The one who was probably about to be cursed, assuming I delivered the package. Which I would. Because that's what I did. I was a Messenger and I delivered what was given to me to whomever and wherever it was supposed to go. The thought of another dead boy made me unbelievably weary.

I tossed the package into the Buick and drove home.

I TOOK THE BOX INTO THE APARTMENT WITH ME AND SET IT ON the kitchen counter. I sat and stared at it for a little bit. I was pretty sure I knew what was in there, but I wanted to be sure.

I had no idea what would happen if I opened that box. I'd never done it before. Would it blow up in my face? Would poisonous gas seep out of it? Would I be hexed or cursed or reviled through all time?

Turns out, if I open a box that I'm supposed to deliver, nothing happens. The icky little voodoo doll lays there staring up at me, cross-eyed and roughly sewn, with bits of stuffing leaking out of tricky sewing spots, like its armpits and crotch.

It looked a lot like the one I'd found under Neil Bossard's bed, except its head was on straight and there were matches taped to its back. I so did not want to deliver this thing. There was a price to pay when I didn't make deliveries, though.

I'd only not made a delivery one time. I was in junior high and at the peak of my sullen and sulky period. The moment that I'd shoved that box under my bed, I'd entered a teen girl nightmare. Pimples, busted zippers, gym uniforms gone awry. It had been an ever-worsening gauntlet. I'd fished the stupid thing out from under the bed, biked it downtown and never failed to make my appointed rounds again.

I didn't want to imagine what the grown-up girl version of those punishments would be. At this point in my life, there are a lot worse things than nose zits, not that I particularly want pimples. I just know they're not the end of the world that they were back when I was thirteen. I stared down at the nasty little thing and wondered how I could protect myself from the slings and arrows of outrageous fortune and not send John Littlefield to an early grave.

I called Meredith and asked her if I could stop by with my putrid little poppet. She suggested we meet at the usual place and time. It was as good as things were going to get.

I couldn't sleep right away, though. I would need some kind of plan. It seemed pretty obvious that Emilia Aguilar was some sort of relative of Jorge's. Aguilar isn't the most uncommon Latino name, but it was just too much of a coincidence. What made no sense to me was why she would give me another doll to deliver if she also sent those boys after Ted and me to warn us away from Elmville. There was more going on here than a simple revenge curse. That might be the only thing I was sure of at the moment.

It's hard not to feel like you're drowning when the only thing you feel you have to hold on to is a sign saying that you're in over your head.

I put the doll back in its box and the box back in my car, crawled into bed and went to sleep.

MEREDITH AND I WERE SITTING AT THE BAR AT MCCLANNIGAN'S looking at my latest delivery. I poked it with a swizzle stick. "Can you take the mojo off of it?"

She looked at it lying on the bar and then up at me. "No. If the last doll was any indication, there's a lot of nastiness packed in there. There's not enough sage in California to smudge the mojo out of it. Besides, it doesn't really work that way. You can't really uncreate something and it can be tricky to try and turn something evil into something good. Can you just not deliver it?"

I put my head down on my pillowed arms and said, "No. I have to deliver it. It's my job."

I looked up as Paul walked toward us. "Problems, little one?" He actually looked sympathetic.

I nodded. "If I deliver this box the way I'm supposed to, I'm pretty sure someone is going to end up killing themselves in some kind of hideous fashion. If I don't deliver it, nasty things will happen to me."

"Could you deliver it and then have Meredith destroy it?" Paul asked. Paul poked at the doll with a stick. He clearly didn't want to touch it either. "She destroyed the last one, right?"

I looked over at Meredith. "That might work," she said.

I thought for a moment and couldn't remember any warnings about destroying items after delivery. "It's worth a try," I said. "So are you willing to go on a road trip?"

"Absolutely," she said.

"I can be ready to go by nine tomorrow morning," Paul said.

We both turned to look at him.

He stared us both down. "You think I'm letting the two of you traipse off like that without some kind of protection? You're both out of your heads."

I was pretty sure he was right about that.

Ted was pretty sure of it, too, when I filled him in on our plans later. I waited until we were cuddled up in bed together.

"I have another delivery to make. The box looks just like the boxes I delivered to Bossard and Rawley and it, uh, feels the same, too. It was addressed to Littlefield," I told him.

He stiffened. "When did you find it?"

"This morning. It was sitting on the Buick's hood when I came out of the hospital."

He stayed very still. "Are you going to deliver it?"

"I don't have a lot of choice in the matter. It's one of the mandatory parts of being a Messenger."

"What happens if you don't?" He turned on one elbow and looked at me.

"Nothing good." I related the story of the box under my bed when I was thirteen to him.

"You don't even take gym class anymore." He pointed out.

"I know. I'm pretty sure it would be something different this time, but no less embarrassing and unpleasant. I have another plan. Meredith and I are going to deliver it together, then she's going to destroy it." A brilliant plan. What could possibly go wrong? A witch, a werewolf and a Messenger walked into a bar . . .

"Isn't that kind of one of those letter of the law rather than the spirit of the law things?" His forehead creased as he thought it through.

"Maybe. It's worth a shot, though." Plus, I hadn't come up with anything better in the meantime.

He nodded as if he'd come to the same conclusion. "Are just you and Meredith going?"

I wasn't sure how he was going to take this part. "No. Paul insisted on coming with us."

"Oh."

I couldn't tell if that was a good "oh" or a bad "oh." I waited.

"Well, as long as you have someone with you, I guess it's okay. Do you want me to come with you, too?" I knew he'd offer.

I could not begin to describe the ways I did not want Ted joining our merry band, but telling him that didn't seem like a good idea either. "I think we'll be okay. This way you'll be available to make our bail if something goes wrong."

"Don't joke about that stuff, Melina."

If only I was.

I HADN'T BEEN ABLE TO FIND AN ADDRESS LISTED FOR JOHN Littlefield. I had been able to find one for Kurt's mother, Ginny Rawley, though. I figured she would probably know where to find Littlefield. He'd been one of her son's friends, hadn't he? I wasn't quite sure how else to find him.

It pains me to say that Ginny Rawley was not thrilled to see me. I believe her first words were, "Get out of here or I'm calling the cops. Again."

It was not what I considered a warm welcome. I persevered. "Mrs. Rawley, I just want to ask a few questions. I want to help. I think someone wanted to hurt your son and I want to make sure that person doesn't hurt anyone else."

She stopped in mid-door-slam. "Who are you?"

"My name is Melina Markowitz and these are my friends, Meredith and Paul." I could feel their presence at my back, warm and comforting.

Rawley's eyes narrowed. "Why would you all be interested in my son?"

I opened my mouth, hoping that a plausible lie would come out, but was saved the trouble by Mrs. Rawley herself.

She held up her hand. "Never mind. I don't care why you're here. I'm just glad someone finally cares enough to listen to me. Come on in." She opened the door.

The inside of the place definitely lived up to the charm promised by the outside. The walls were gray and dingy, and the carpet had definitely seen better days. The mismatched collection of furniture in the living room spoke of people's cast-offs and a little judicious Dumpster diving. In other words, it wasn't all that different than my own apartment. I plopped down on the couch, feeling right at home. A spring poked me in the back in welcome.

"What was it that you were trying to tell people that they wouldn't listen to?" I asked. Meredith settled on the couch next to me, but with a more cautious movement.

Paul came in slower, looking around as he walked in, and sat down next to me. I think it's a werewolf thing. They can't just walk in. They have to check everything out. If he could have gotten away with sniffing everything, he probably would have.

"I know my Kurt committed suicide," Mrs. Rawley said, her chin quivering slightly as she spoke. "I know that, but I also know that someone drove him to it."

I leaned forward. "I think so, too, Mrs. Rawley. Who do you think did it?"

Her eyes popped open. "You do? You think so, too?"

"I don't just think it. I'm sure of it. The day that you caught me poking around in your house, I found . . . something. Something that made me really suspicious. I want to hear more about your thoughts, though."

"I can't believe someone believes me." Tears formed in her eyes now and she pressed a tissue against her mouth. "I've been talking and talking and talking, and everyone just kept patting me on the back and mumbling about the grieving process and accepting it. I've accepted it. My boy's gone forever, but I know someone pushed him to it."

"How do you know? What made you think that?" Meredith asked.

"He wasn't himself that last week. He was jumpy and nervous. I know it was strange being home after all those years away. I figured it was a little like when a soldier comes home from the war. It takes them a while to acclimate, to realize no one's going to be shooting at them anymore or trying to blow them up on the side of the road. I figured it was like that." Mrs. Rawley pressed a tissue against her lips.

PTSD. Post-traumatic stress disorder. It wasn't a bad diagnosis. I nodded my head.

"Then the stuff with the bugs started. He said they were crawling on him, biting him all the time. I bought him all new sheets and blankets. He still thought they were biting him at night. So we bought a new mattress. That didn't help either. Then we started with the doctor appointments. The regular doctor. The dermatologist. Finally, the shrink." She leaned forward and whispered, "My boy wasn't crazy. Or at least he wasn't until they made him that way."

"Who? Who made him crazy?" I asked. "Who did this to him?"

She sat back again. "I'm not sure. At first I thought it was those Latinos. They've got all kinds of witches and curses they can throw at you, but they don't do nothing for free. If it was one of them, somebody was paying them to do it."

I glanced over at Paul. He was looking straight ahead.

"I think maybe it was Littlefield," Mrs. Rawley whispered, glancing around as if someone might be listening.

"The third boy?" I asked.

"He's the only one that's still alive that killed that Aguilar man. He was the one that rolled on the other two. Then Kurt said he got religion while they were in lockup." She pressed her lips together. "I don't believe it, though. It was nothing more than a cover. Make himself look all pious and contrite. He was a sneaky one. I never liked him."

"So the boys were friends before this all happened?" I asked.

"Oh, sure. They were all on the basketball team together. It was just JV, but they were good. Afterward, well, they weren't such good buddies anymore."

Mrs. Rawley gave us John Littlefield's address and we stood up to leave.

"What did you find in my house that made you think Kurt didn't do this?" she asked, as she walked us to the door.

I put my hand on her arm. "I'd rather not say right now. I don't know how this is going to play out and it might be better if you didn't know too many details."

She nodded, eyes again wide. "Got it. You need anything else, though, you just let me know."

Then she threw her arms around me and hugged me. "You know, you're not at all bad. I'm kind of sorry that I called the cops on you."

I extricated myself from her embrace. I'd forgotten about that. "What did you tell them?"

"I gave them your license plate number. I was so upset about seeing you poking around at the house. I don't know who I thought you were, I just knew you didn't belong. Then I ran into Drew Bossard, Neil's little brother? And told him that I'd seen you. He suggested I call the police. You know, just to make sure they knew where to look if there was any trouble. Anyway, I'm sorry about that."

Fabulous. That was just what I needed. Something else bothered me, though. Mrs. Rawley's apartment was a solid half-mile from her old house. "How did you know I'd been in your house that day?"

Her brow furrowed a little. "I got a phone call."

"From whom?" Meredith asked.

She shook her head. "I don't know. It was a woman, though. She said I'd better go check on the place, that someone was sneaking around it. I didn't ask any questions. I just ran."

WE WERE PARKED IN FRONT OF LITTLEFIELD'S APARTMENT BY a little after ten. He wasn't home. John Littlefield's apartment wasn't even as nice as Mrs. Rawley's. According to Mrs. Rawley, his parents had moved away soon after his conviction. Why he'd come back to Elmville instead of going to wherever they were living wasn't something she understood. She said Littlefield was spouting some nonsense about making amends and repenting.

"How much longer?" Paul demanded from the backseat. "Can we open a window? I'm suffocating back here."

Note to self: werewolves—even when they are in human form—suck at surveillance.

"The right time will present itself. We have to be patient," I explained. Again. "Read a magazine."

"I'm hungry."

"Eat a snack." I shoved the tote bag full of food that I'd packed at him.

He shoved the bag back. "Cheese sticks and grapes are girl food. Worse yet, they're human girl food."

Meredith twisted around in the front seat. "Pretend you're hunting and you're lying in wait."

Paul leaned forward so that they were almost nose to nose. "If I was lying in wait for this guy, I'd be out in those bushes behind the apartment and at least I'd be able to breathe."

I sighed. "Here he is."

Littlefield rode up on a bicycle. I grabbed the rewrapped box and got out of the car. Meredith and Paul followed me.

"Excuse me," I called. "Mr. Littlefield?"

He looked up from where he was locking his bike to a rack. "That's me. What do you want?" He backed up a little.

I didn't blame him. Alone, I'm not immediately intimidating. With Paul and Meredith walking up behind me like we were the Usual Suspects, I probably looked a little more like trouble. Sadly, I was. "Could we talk for a moment, Mr. Littlefield?"

His back was against the wall now, literally. He glanced from side to side, but there wasn't really any place to run to. "What about?"

"Please, Mr. Littlefield, I'd rather have this conversation in private. Can we go inside your apartment?" I smiled and tried to look unassuming.

He looked from me to Meredith to Paul and back to me. "Okay, then. My apartment's this way."

We followed him in. To say the place was Spartan would be an understatement. The apartment was a single room. There was a mattress—neatly made—in the corner and a chair against the wall, with a box that was clearly being used as a table next to it. There was a bowl and a spoon and a mug drying in the rack next to the sink. That was pretty much it.

"I like what you've done with the place," Meredith said, looking around.

Littlefield closed his eyes and said, "'If anyone would come after me, he must deny himself and take up his cross and follow me. What good will it be for a man if he gains the whole world, yet forfeits his soul?'"

"Matthew?" Paul asked, with a raised eyebrow.

Littlefield nodded. "Chapter sixteen."

"Well, okay then." Biblical quotes were so not my thing. Apparently Paul was good at them. Who knew? We had ourselves a brand-new parlor game. "Mr. Littlefield, I have a delivery for you."

"What kind of delivery?"

"I'm glad you asked. I've made two other deliveries in your town recently. One to Neil Bossard and one to Kurt Rawley. I'm pretty sure you know those two young men?"

Littlefield nodded, his eyes growing wider.

"I'm also pretty sure you know what's happened to them." I didn't want to spell it out if I didn't have to.

He nodded again and sat down in his chair with a thump. "They're dead. They took their own lives. It's a sin, you know."

"I have to make this delivery. I have to give you this box," I said as gently as I could. "But Meredith here can destroy its contents after you open the box and I think you'll be okay."

He glanced at Meredith and then his gaze flickered to Paul. "What does he do?"

I looked over at Paul, too. "He, uh, helps us and makes sure we stay safe." I figured that was as good an explanation as any. Saying that he ripped the throat out of anyone who looked cross-eyed at his woman didn't seem like a good idea.

"Do you know what's in the box?" Littlefield asked.

"I looked." There. I admitted it. I waited for lightning to strike. None came.

"And it's the same kind of thing you delivered to Neil and Kurt?" He gnawed at a thumbnail.

"Pretty much." As in exactly the same.

"I don't want it." He crossed his arms over his chest.

I felt a pang of sympathy. "I'm sorry. I don't have a choice. I have to give it to you. It's my job."

His brow creased. "'Work hard and become a leader; be lazy and never succeed.' Proverbs." He held out his hand.

I took that to mean that he understood and handed him the box.

He unwrapped it, careful not to rip the paper. Then he opened the box and saw the little doll inside. He dropped the box on the floor, as if it had suddenly become hot, leapt out of his chair and scrambled away. "What is that thing?"

"It's kind of like a voodoo doll," I said in a tone that I hoped sounded calm and reassuring.

"Get it away from me." He had backed all the way up against the wall again. His voice had gone up a register or two.

"That's where Meredith here comes in. Would you like her to destroy it for you?" I asked, not making a move toward the doll yet.

"She can do that?" He turned terrified eyes to me and then to Meredith.

"She can," I assured him.

"How?"

"She has, uh, special talents." Bringing up witchcraft seemed like a bad idea at the moment. Littlefield was freaked enough already.

Suddenly his eyes narrowed. "Special talents like the person who made that thing has? Those kinds of talents?"

"Similar."

He looked from one to another of us now, his breath coming faster and faster. Then he pointed at Meredith and screamed, "Witch!"

See. I knew bringing up witchcraft was a bad idea. Meredith took a step back. Littlefield started to advance.

"Mr. Littlefield, John, Meredith is just here to help you." I started toward him.

"Witch!" he screamed again and shoved me aside.

I heard a quiet growling noise behind me. It would be way better for everyone if I dealt with Littlefield rather than Paul. I shoved Littlefield back against the wall. I didn't try to be gentle.

He stared at me. "What are you? Are you a witch, too?" My shove is significantly more powerful than most people would assume.

"Not exactly." I relaxed my grip, trying to figure out how to explain what and who we were. Big mistake.

Littlefield slipped out of my grip and made a beeline for Meredith. He shoved her hard and screamed, "'Thou shalt not suffer a witch to live!'"

Meredith stumbled backward and went down hard. Littlefield was on top of her in an instant. My reflexes are quick. Cat quick. Even so, Paul beat me to him and plucked him off of Meredith like a pesky Chihuahua.

There are a lot of myths about how werewolves change and when they change. Most wolves don't need a full moon, although the moon does call them. A new and inexperienced wolf will have an easier time changing the closer it is to the full moon. Even an experienced wolf will be more likely to change when it's that time of the month.

Basically, though, a werewolf can change any time he or she wants to change and Paul was going to change right now. He hadn't even taken off his clothes, which meant that they were going to rip and burst as his body transformed. The expense of constantly buying new wardrobes was just one of the reasons that most shapeshifters had absolutely no sense of modesty whatsoever.

The more emotional the reasons for a werewolf's change, the more violent the change. Apparently threatening a werewolf's woman was a pretty emotional reason for making the change, because even I cringed as Paul's jaw line lengthened and his bones began to pop and snap. And I'd seen it before.

Paul shook Littlefield like a bad puppy and I was afraid he was going to break his neck.

"Paul, no. Set him down." I grabbed his arm.

Paul glanced at me and growled a warning. I backed away. As

much as I didn't want him to kill Littlefield, I really, really didn't want him to kill me.

Paul's shirt ripped as his back began to arch.

Littlefield started screaming. "'Beware of false prophets, which come to you in sheep's clothing, but inwardly they are ravening wolves.'"

Fabulous. This guy had a bible quote for everything, even werewolves.

Meredith grabbed Paul's arm now. "Set him down, Paul. I'm okay. He didn't hurt me. Set him down."

Paul growled again, but Meredith is apparently way less of a chicken than I am. She didn't back off.

"I'm fine, Paul. He didn't touch me. I'm safe. Set him down," she repeated.

That was when I heard the sirens in the distance. Fantastic. Someone must have heard the commotion and called the cops. We really needed to get out of here. I realized Meredith hadn't heard the sirens yet. I wasn't sure that Paul had either over his rage.

"Cops," I said.

Everyone froze.

"Let's go." I headed toward the door.

Paul dropped Littlefield and followed me to the door, with Littlefield screaming after us, "'Go your way; behold, I send you out as lambs among wolves.'"

"Look! We're the good guys!" I protested.

"How do I know that? How do I know you're not emissaries of Satan sent here to tempt me?" he demanded.

"Because I'm pretty sure the ones who say they're going to help you stay alive are always the good guys." That seemed obvious to me.

"Then you don't know a lot about heaven." Littlefield glared.

He had a point. I didn't. I wasn't entirely sure I believed in it. Or in hell. I did believe in staying alive, however. "Maybe not. I'm offering to help you not visit before you're supposed to, though. Doesn't that count for anything?"

"Not when you're going to use witchcraft to help me. Get out, witch. Get out, both of you."

We got.

I headed toward the Buick. "We can't get him back in the car like this," Meredith said, gesturing to Paul, who was halfway to full werewolf form.

"Then what?" I asked. The sirens were getting louder. We didn't have long.

"I'm going to go with him to that field back there." She gestured to an open area behind the apartment complex. "He can change the rest of the way and get home in wolf form."

"What about you?"

"I'll figure something out. Now go. Get out of here. Even I can hear the sirens now." Meredith gave me a little shove toward the car.

"I'll drive around and meet you on the other side of the field, okay?"

"Whatever. Just go."

I ran to the Buick.

APPARENTLY I'M NOT SO GOOD AT RUNNING FROM THE LAW. I did manage to pull around to the other side of the field and pick up Meredith. She picked her way through the grass, carrying Paul's wallet, keys and cell phone and the ripped up remnants of his shirt and jeans. I opted not to mention the lack of underpants. Leave it to a werewolf to go commando.

Meredith shoved the wallet, phone and keys into the glove box and the ripped clothing under the seat. I turned the Buick around to head back to 120 and get the hell out of Dodge without breaking the speed limit or running a stop sign, but the police pulled us over when we were still two blocks away from the highway and miles from home free.

"How do you want to play this?" Meredith asked, as I pulled to the curb.

"Dumb." I really, really needed a new fallback position.

"Is that what you usually do?" she asked, brows arched.

"Yep."

"And it works?" She looked like she was starting to laugh.

"Most of the time." Not as much as it used to, though.

"You need a new fallback position." She settled back in her seat.

"Tell me about it."

Then the uniform was knocking at my window. I rolled it down and smiled. "What can I do for you, officer?"

He didn't smile back. "Step out of the car, please."

I stayed put. "Is there a problem?"

He stepped back from the door. His hand hovered over his weapon. "Step out of the car, please," he repeated.

The hand near the gun was making me nervous. "Sure thing, officer." I glanced at Meredith and got out of the car, hands to my sides and away from my body.

The uniform glanced in the car. "You, too, ma'am," he said to Meredith.

Ooh. She wasn't going to like that "ma'am," although in all fairness the officer looked like he was barely out of high school. I glanced at her again and could see the start of static in her hair. I hoped he didn't over-"ma'am" her. He'd be likely to get a good zap if he did and I wasn't sure how we'd explain that.

"I'm going to have to ask you ladies to come with me," he said.

"On what grounds?" I asked, looking for a loophole.

"We had a report of a disturbance," he said, Adam's apple bobbing.

"What kind of a disturbance?" I asked. More information in these situations was always better. Who knew what the person who had called this in had heard?

"We can discuss this down at the station." He grabbed my arm and started to march me toward his car.

I could have run. It would have taken nothing to slip away from this guy and jump in the Buick. It wouldn't have done me much good. Even I can't outrun radio waves and I knew they had my license plate. Plus, I wasn't sure if I could get Meredith in the car fast enough and I wasn't going to leave her standing on a curb in Elmville with Officer Friendly when she was only there to do me a favor.

"Is it okay if my friend follows in the car?" I asked.

He looked confused for a second. "I can't see why not," he said, trying to sound gruff and not quite pulling it off.

"Keys are in the ignition," I called to Meredith, as my new buddy put his hand on my head and shoved me into the back of the cop car.

I AM NOT NEARLY AS CLAUSTROPHOBIC AS PAUL AND I PRETTY much wanted to claw my way out of the back of the squad car.

It didn't smell nice back there, plus it was stuffy. I figured making a list of demands starting with "Could I have some air back here?" would not make me more popular, so I practiced some deep-breathing exercises and tried to be calm.

Elmville is not that big, so it didn't take long to get to the station. As we walked in, I saw Meredith pulling the Buick into the visitor parking area and breathed a little sigh of relief. At least somebody knew where I was.

I was marched in through the back, but at least no one had handcuffed me yet.

"What's up, Lopez?" the desk sergeant asked, as we walked in.

Officer Friendly, as I'd christened him in my mind, said, "Chief wants to talk to her."

The desk sergeant nodded at a bench and said, "Wait there."

Lopez walked into a back room. I sat down and pulled my cell phone out of my pocket. Before I could dial, the desk sergeant looked at me, shook his head and pointed at the sign that had a cell phone in a big red circle with a line through it. I sighed and stuffed it back into my pocket. At least he hadn't taken it away from me.

About five minutes later, Lopez came out and said, "Chief's ready now." He gestured for me to follow.

I got up and walked in after him to the chief's office.

I don't know what I expected. Maybe Carroll O'Connor in *In the Heat of the Night*. Or Hal Linden from *Barney Miller*. Instead I got Susan Dey in a police uniform.

"Hello, Ms. Markowitz. I'm Chief Murdock." She didn't stand up from behind her desk. In fact, she didn't look away from her computer screen at first.

I sat down in the chair across from her desk and waited until she swiveled in her office chair to look at me.

"So why am I here?" I asked, figuring I'd cut to the chase. I did it with a smile, though.

"We've had several reports of your car being in the area." Chief Murdock smiled back at me. I didn't feel like she meant it, though.

"And that's a crime of some kind?" I asked, still smiley, as if I were just asking for information, which I suppose I was.

She leaned forward on her desk, bracing herself on her elbows. "Why would you think that? Did my officer put you under arrest?"

"No, but he did bring me to the police station in a squad car." *That smelled really bad*, I added silently.

Chief Murdock steepled her fingers and watched me for a moment. I watched right back. "What exactly brings you to Elmville, Ms. Markowitz?"

"I'm thinking of moving here. I wanted to check it out." I'd had a few minutes to come up with some reasonably plausible sounding stories in the back of the squad car while I was deep-breathing through my mouth.

"Do you have family here?" she inquired.

"No." I kept that smile plastered firmly on my face.

"Friends?" She pressed.

"Not yet." But I was making new ones every minute. I could tell by the look on Chief Murdock's face that she was looking forward to watching the *Sex and the City* movie with me while we drank cosmos and ate low-fat popcorn.

"Why Elmville, then?" She leaned back in her desk chair.

"Why not?" I countered.

Murdock kept leaning back, eyeing me carefully. I didn't say anything. It was her move, as far as I was concerned.

"The reports of your car have been in particular areas," she finally said.

"Really? I feel like I've been all over town." I had, too. Luckily, the Elmville Three hadn't all been from the same socioeconomic bracket.

"I didn't mean a particular geographic area. I meant areas associated with certain persons."

I didn't say anything to that. It wasn't a question. I didn't feel like I had to answer.

"Ms. Markowitz, certain people in this town did a terrible thing a few years back. What they did was wrong, but they have paid their dues. They did their time and took their punishment. Any further punishment would be considered harassment. I will not tolerate harassment in my town. Not of anyone. Even if they did do something bad."

"I'm not sure what people you're referring to." I looked her right in the eyes. My heart didn't flip-flop looking at her and it was way more easy to lie to her than it was to Ted.

"Let me cut the bullshit, then." Murdock came out from behind her desk, walked around and perched right in front of me. "If I find out you had anything to do with those two boys' suicides, I will be on you like ugly on an ape. And if anything—and I do mean anything—happens to John Littlefield, you will be my first person of interest. Do you understand?"

I looked up at her. "Got it. Can I go now?"

"As long as we're clear."

"Crystal," I said, and got up.

I breathed my sigh of relief just a moment too soon. I wasn't quite past the desk sergeant when a young man walked in. I recognized him instantly. He was the kid who'd caught me fishing the voodoo doll out from underneath Neil Bossard's bed. There was something else about him. Something else familiar, I just wasn't sure what.

"Hey," he said to the desk sergeant. "Where do I go to pay this parking ticket?"

Then he turned and I was pretty sure why he seemed familiar. He had a heck of a bruise on his chin. It looked as if someone had landed a solid first strike to it. Maybe she'd done it after she'd been attacked while walking from her car to her apartment.

I'm not perfect at remembering people. We get so many students in the dojo and their parents that I start to lose track of the people I meet. Add to that the steady stream of patients in and out of the emergency room at Sacramento County and I see a stream of faces every week. I can't possibly keep track of them.

Someone who has attacked me, though? That person has my attention. And whether or not I've seen their face, it's part of what I do to know a person's physique. It often gives clues on who to attack and what their weak spots might be. I was pretty positive that Drew Bossard had been Thug Number One.

I ducked my head, hoping I could make it to the door before he noticed me. No such luck.

He turned to head to the drop box for tickets and he spotted me. "Hey! You're the woman who was crawling under my brother's bed at the memorial service. What are you doing here?"

Chief Murdock gave me a baleful look, spun me around and marched me back toward her office.

"YOU CRASHED A MEMORIAL SERVICE?" MURDOCK WAS BACK on her perch on the front of her desk, with me craning my head to look up at her. My other choice was to look at her gun, with which I was eye level. Neither choice made me comfortable. I opted to crane. Guns make me nervous.

"When you say it like that it sounds icky," I protested.

"It is icky," she shot back. "Those people were grieving. Their son was dead. By his own hand. And you came in and crawled around under his bed. Looking for what?"

"You've got it all wrong, Chief! I was just driving around looking at neighborhoods. I saw people walking into the house with casseroles. I thought it was an open house. Then when I got in there, I had to go to the bathroom. I got confused, ended up in a bedroom, dropped my earring and that was when that boy walked in."

"Girl, you lie like a rug. It's totally effortless for you, isn't it?" She shook her head in amazement.

That was completely unfair. It wasn't effortless. It was a skill. I'd practiced it and polished it nearly as much as I had my roundhouse kick. If I had to choose between the two, I'd probably pick the roundhouse, but it seemed inappropriate at this moment and quite counterproductive. "Listen, could you just call Ted Goodnight from the Sacramento PD. He'll totally vouch for me."

"Honey, I don't care if he'd totally tap dance and whistle 'Dixie.'" She stared at me hard for a few minutes. Then she stood up, walked back around her desk and sat down in her chair. "Ms. Markowitz, with all due respect, get out of my town and stay out of my town."

She didn't need to tell me twice.

MEREDITH WAS WAITING FOR ME IN THE PARKING LOT WITH the Buick. "Hey," she said as I walked up. "I was just wondering if I should call Ted. Paul's got him on speed dial."

"I'm glad you didn't, but it was touch and go in there for a few minutes." I rested my hands on top of the car and took a deep breath.

She tossed me the keys and I slid into the driver's seat.

"So what now?"

"I'm to get out of town and stay out of town." I started the engine and gave the dashboard a little pat. The Buick purred like a great big cat.

"And are we going to do that?"

"Absolutely." I paused. "With one little stop first."

I pulled out of the parking lot and headed back to John Littlefield's apartment. We parked down the street a little ways. We couldn't see the door to his apartment, but we could see his bike.

"What are we watching for?" Meredith asked, as I settled in.

"I'm not sure. Are you going to go all antsy on me like Paul?" I looked over at her and we both started to laugh.

"It's adorable, isn't it? He just can't stand enclosed spaces for very long." She wiped a tear from her eye.

Adorable hadn't been the word I would have used, but then again, I wasn't sleeping with the big bad wolf. "Just remind me never to bring him with me on any kind of surveillance again."

That was the moment that Littlefield walked out of his apartment complex. He looked up and down the street, and both Meredith and I instinctively slunk down in our seats, although I was pretty sure he couldn't see us where we were parked.

He walked over to the Dumpster carrying a little box.

"That's our box, isn't it?" Meredith said, squinting.

I didn't need to squint. "Yep."

He threw the box into the Dumpster, slammed the lid shut and walked back into his apartment, brushing his hands on his jeans.

I turned on the engine and pulled out of our parking space. "Well, that's not going to work at all."

"No. It's not," Meredith agreed. "So I want to see this witch of yours. Take me by her house."

I drove Meredith into the neighborhood where Crying Woman—or Emilia Aguilar, as I suppose I should call her—lived. It just wasn't nearly as romantic a name.

"How convenient," Meredith said dryly, as I drove past the cemetery. Even I, witchcraft washout, knew what she meant. A little graveyard dirt added a lot of punch to a spell. Having a house by the cemetery was a little like living down the street from the supermarket.

It took me a minute or two to find her house again, but I knew it the instant I saw it. It definitely had a certain feel to it. It was an entirely different vibe than I got off the voodoo dolls, though. "Here it is," I said. "This is where Crying Woman lives. I don't know what she's up to, but she's got me completely confused." I pulled over a little ways down the street from the house.

"What did you call her?"

"Crying Woman. The first time I saw her, she was crying behind a tree at the cemetery."

"Hmph." Meredith got out of the car and leaned against the Buick door.

"Is that significant?"

"La Llorona," she said.

My Spanish pretty much sucks, but living in California one does pick up a little here and there. "Something about crying?"

"The Crying Woman. She was Hernando Cortes's mistress. She murdered both her children by him, drowned them. People have seen her all over Mexico, crying for her children." A breeze had begun to pick up and Meredith pulled her hair back into a ponytail.

I shivered. "I haven't seen any children."

"Before she was La Llorona, she was La Malinche. Because she was Cortes's consort, her name became a symbol of betrayal. There's more happening here than meets the eye, Melina. I don't know what you've gotten yourself into this time, but I think it's going to be ugly."

I DROPPED MEREDITH OFF AT HER PLACE. "YOU'LL CALL WHEN you hear from him?" I didn't have to say which him I was talking about. Nor did I mention that I'd noticed her holding his cell phone in her hand the entire way home, as if she could forge a connection to him through it or could make it ring just by holding it close to herself.

She nodded. "Even if it's late."

"He's going to be fine," I said, as much to reassure myself as to reassure her.

"I know he will be. There's not much that can take him in human form. In wolf form? Well . . ." She smiled and shrugged.

We both knew that Paul was strong and powerful and smart. We also both knew that sometimes that wasn't enough.

Meredith gave me a hug and then took a long hard look at me. "Go get some rest. You look like hell."

"Thanks." You would think having friends would boost my self-esteem. My life never did take straightforward paths.

"You know what I mean. Take care of yourself."

"When? While I'm running the dojo? Or filing at the hospital? Or trying to figure out why the people I make deliveries to keep dying? Or teaching Sophie how to be a Messenger?"

"You have to make time, Melina."

"No one can do that, Meredith, and you know it."

She nodded. "You're going to have to try and you know that."

I LET MYSELF IN TO THE APARTMENT, WHICH WAS AGAIN UN-chained. I gave myself a little pat on the back. I'd done something right. I'd helped Norah be less afraid. I could cross something off my list.

Then I noticed the packing boxes open in the living room.

Norah came out of her bedroom carrying an armload of books and put them in one of the boxes.

"What are you doing?" I walked over and looked in the box. Maybe she was just putting together some stuff to take to Salvation Army. She went through occasional feng shui periods, where everything that wasn't immediately useful had to go. She'd put in her copy of *The Moosewood Cookbook*, her dictionary of rune symbols and a guide to finding your animal spirit guide. Those were some of her favorites. I took the cookbook out. I looked up at her, confused.

"I'm packing," she said, a little defiantly.

I blinked a few times. "To go where?"

"I'm not sure exactly where. Maybe my parents' house for a little while. It just has to be somewhere where I haven't, you know, invited him in." She took the cookbook from my hands and put it back in the box.

I took it back out. "I talked to him, Norah. I swear I did."

"I believe you. It just didn't make any difference." She walked back toward her room, leaving me holding the *Moosewood*. I followed her. She pointed at the vase. "He left another one."

"When?" I sat down on her bed, clutching the cookbook to my chest.

"Last night. While I was asleep." She opened up a drawer, pulled out some clothes and dumped them in a suitcase that was open on the floor.

"I'll talk to him again," I said. This wasn't happening. I know I took Norah for granted all the time, but that didn't mean she wasn't important to me. She'd always been there for me, through being the weird kid in grade school and the sullen, silent girl in junior high and then through the horror that was high school. She's always been there with her sweet smile and her accepting ways. I couldn't let her go now.

Besides, who would pay half the rent?

"It won't help. You know it. I know it. He'll do whatever he wants. We can't stop him. I didn't realize when I invited him in that night. I didn't know what it would mean. I can't stay here, Melina. I have to go. One of these nights, I'm going to wake up while he's here and I don't know if I'll be able to resist him. I don't know if I even want to resist him." She pulled a black T-shirt out of the suitcase and held it up to me. "Do you want this? I never wear it."

I shoved it back at her. "No. I don't want it. I won't do this. Put it back in the drawer."

"Oh, Melina," she said, and wrapped her arms around me.

I shoved her away. "Don't. Don't do that. Not if you're not staying." Then, to my horror, I started to cry. "I can't do this. I can't lose one more thing. I can't have one more thing change. Not right now."

My chest felt so tight I didn't think I was going to be able to get any air sucked down into my lungs. "Don't leave me."

"But I can't stay, Melina. I know you can see that." She stood there with her stupid black T-shirt that I sort of wished I'd taken because it was kind of cute balled up in her hands.

"Give me one more chance. Let me talk to him. Let's talk to him together."

She shook her head.

"Please, Norah, just one more chance. One more night. Please."

I don't know if it was the tears or the outright begging, but after a few minutes of standing there with a frown on her face, she finally nodded. "One more night, but if I get one more rose, then I am out of here. *Capisce?*"

"*Capisce*," I said.

I felt the air returning to my lungs. Of course, what I was going to do with this one more night to change her mind, I didn't know. I did know how to start, though. I walked out of her room and dialed Alex's number on my cell phone. I got his voice mail.

"Get your undead ass over to my apartment the second the sun sets or I will come to your house and stake you myself."

13

TED AND ALEX ARRIVED AT THE SAME TIME. I WONDERED IF Alex had called Ted to find out what was up. Whatever. I didn't care. I needed this dealt with in a way that had Norah staying in the apartment where she belonged and it needed to happen now.

I'd put the chain on the door so that they had to knock.

"Why, come in, Alex. Of course, you would if you wanted to regardless of what I said right now, wouldn't you?" I hoped he heard the sarcasm in my tone. Who am I kidding? A deaf ogre could've heard the sarcasm in my tone.

He shot me a look. "Is that what this is about?"

"Yes, Alex. It is. It's about you creeping everybody out. It's got to stop. Norah's moving out." I'd meant to sound stern and angry. Unfortunately, my voice wobbled a tiny bit on the last sentence. Norah put her hand on my shoulder. I grabbed her hand and held on. I couldn't lose Norah. I wouldn't lose her.

His head came up.

Ted put his arm around me. "Really?"

"Yes. Really. If Alex doesn't stop sneaking in here at night and watching her sleep, she's going to leave me." I heard the catch in my voice again and wanted to scream. When had I become a crier? This was ridiculous.

Alex sat down in the living room. "Let me try to explain."

"That would be nice," I said, and we all trooped in to see if he could make it right. He damn well better.

"I've been a vampire for three hundred and seventy-eight years." He said it quietly, without a lot of fanfare, as if announcing that he liked the curly fries at Redrum Burger. Like it was just another not-so-interesting personal tidbit of information.

I wasn't particularly surprised. I'd figured he'd been around about that long. I knew he wasn't a new vampire and the guys who'd been around for five or six hundred years had some odd airs about them. Alex was gentlemanly but not courtly, if you know what I mean.

"When I was first . . . made"—he stumbled a bit, but then went on—"I was horrified. I was supposed to be a man of healing, a physician, instead I'd become a monster, a thing whose very existence depended on sucking the lifeblood out of another human being. I disgusted myself."

"Why didn't you just . . . I don't know, walk out into the sunlight?" Norah asked. Her face stayed grim.

I started to protest. Alex held up his hand to shush me. I bit my tongue. It was a rude question, which was unlike Norah. I supposed she'd been pushed to it, though.

"I considered it. Here's one of my many problems with living as . . . what I am. Most days, most times, I hate it. The idea of taking humans as my prey, even when I dress it up in a pretty, seductive package"—he smiled a little—"it sickens me. But the pleasure I get from it? You have no idea, no clue, the intensity of the gratification. Nothing I ever experienced as a human can touch it. Except . . ."

"Except what?" Norah asked.

We'd all leaned forward. I was pretty sure Alex wasn't using even a shade of his command voice on us, but it almost felt like that, as if we were drawn to him despite knowing so much better.

"Except the pleasure of being fed upon." He stared right at her.

She backed away.

"You're a smart girl, Norah. That is the correct reaction to me and to all things like me. You figured that out when you saw the *kiang shi* in action, didn't you?" Alex leaned back in his chair and crossed his legs, one ankle carelessly resting on the opposite knee. He looked relaxed, but I could feel the tension in him. It thrummed through the room.

Norah nodded. "They were monsters."

"Like me," he said flatly.

"Like you," she agreed.

"I saw it that night in your eyes. I saw reflected back at me what I'd felt about myself all those years ago. I'd pushed those feelings so far down, I'd almost forgotten they existed. Seeing your fear and disgust brought it rushing back like a tidal wave." He shook his head. "It was almost unbearable."

"And now?" she asked. "How do you feel now?"

"Not much different. I've been trying a different way to feed. I found a . . . source for blood, enough of it to keep me going, but it's not the same. It can sustain me, but it does not . . . nourish me." He rubbed a hand over his face.

"So?" Norah asked, still hard-jawed but now leaning toward Alex.

"So nothing. I'll be able to go on this way for a while. Eventually, the hunger, the desire for more than being sustained, will become too strong for me to ignore." He put his hand back on his thigh and looked right at her.

"And what will happen then?" She was relentless.

He stared her right in the eye. "I'll find someone. Either willing or unwilling, and I will feed from them. I will do my best not to drain them and leave them dead or, worse yet, undead like me. It will be a struggle, though."

"And it's always been like this? All three hundred and seventy-eight years of it?" Norah had moved even closer to him. He could have her throat in less than a second. For as much as she was frightened of Alex, I didn't think she still fully appreciated the danger she was in. I started to stand, to move between her and Alex, but he held up his hand and gestured for me to sit back down. Again, it wasn't a command, but something in his face made me obey.

"No. No, there was a respite. Now it seems impossibly brief, but at the time, it seemed like it could be like that forever." He smiled for a moment, but it faded quickly.

"How did you get that respite?" Norah inched even closer to him.

Alex didn't move, but his gaze did not leave Norah's face. "I found respite because of a woman."

I had the disturbing impression that as far as Norah and Alex were concerned, there was no one else in the room. I stayed as still as I could. I glanced over at Ted. He was like a statue, but his eyes were bright and alert.

"How did she give you respite?" Norah ran her tongue over her lips, as if her mouth were suddenly dry.

"By seeing me, seeing the monster I was and accepting me, all the same."

I saw Norah swallow and watched Alex watch the movement of her throat. "Did you feed from her?"

He nodded. “I did.”

“She allowed it?” Norah’s heart was beating so fast, I could see the faint pulse in her neck.

“She welcomed it.” Alex steepled his hands in front of himself and leaned toward Norah now.

She didn’t draw back. “Only one woman was ever able to be like that with you?”

He smiled gently. “I have had many lovers. I have fed from all of them. But she was special. There was a light in her. A glow, if you will.”

“She was good.” Norah nodded.

“As good as I was evil.”

“And her goodness made you less evil?” She cocked her head to one side, as if considering the information carefully.

“I think it did. It at least allowed me to live with my evil and keep it in check.”

“Have you ever met anyone else like her?”

He reached out and caressed her jaw. I saw her stiffen the tiniest bit and then relax against his hand. “Not until very recently.”

“She wanted you. For yourself. Not because you made her want you.” It wasn’t a question.

Alex answered her anyway. “Yes.”

“The way that I want you.” Again. There was no question asked. This time, Alex merely nodded.

“You’re not making me feel this way with some kind of special vampire power?” Finally! An actual question!

“No. And trust me, if I could make myself stop feeling this way, I would. It has not been . . . pleasant.”

“If I do this,” she said, and it took all my willpower not to gasp out loud. “If I do this, we need to set some ground rules.”

Alex tilted his head. A smile quirked at the edge of his lips. "Of course."

"No more sneaking into my room and watching me sleep. That's creepy, stalker-type behavior and it's not okay."

"Got it."

"No bite marks where they're going to show. I don't want to have to wear a turtleneck when its one hundred degrees here."

"A reasonable request. Not a problem."

"You let me drive the Porsche some time."

He did laugh then. "Of course."

Norah reached up and took Alex's hand. She turned and walked toward her bedroom, leading him behind her. I heard the door to her bedroom open and then, as if in case there were any doubt in anyone's mind what she intended, she said, "Please come in."

I heard the door click shut behind them.

TED AND I WENT TO BED A LITTLE BIT LATER. WE WAITED A bit. I am not proud to admit that I got a stake I just happen to keep on my closet floor—behind a pair of red ankle boots, which Aunt Kitty talked me into buying, that I can never get up the nerve to wear, despite the fact that they're fabulous—and waited outside Norah's bedroom door for a little bit of that time.

I trust Alex. I really do. Except when I don't.

This was one of the times that I didn't. I'd seen the hunger glittering in his eyes, but that was nothing new. What I wasn't sure I'd seen was the desire. Oh, sure, I'd seen him turn on the charm and seduce pretty young residents into the supply closets, but that had seemed almost more of a game. Nothing of Alex had truly been invested in that.

Whatever was happening in that room was silent. I couldn't hear a peep. After about a half hour, Ted, just as silent as Alex and Norah, led me down the hall.

He shut the door behind us and backed me up against it. I didn't fight back. With his gaze locked on mine, he started to unbutton my blouse, one agonizing button at a time. He slid it off my shoulders and I let it drop to the floor.

A cold heat swept through me, making my knees feel unsteady as he traced his fingers along the lace edge of my bra. He undid my jeans and peeled them down my legs, gliding his hands back up my inner thighs as he stood back up. I almost toppled over, desire surged through me with such strength.

Then I froze. "Stop," I whispered.

"Are you sure?" he murmured into my ear, making me shiver. "I'm pretty sure you're liking this."

"I am," I said. "Maybe a little too much."

He stopped then. "I'm not sure there is such a thing as liking this too much."

"I am. When it's not just us."

He looked around him. "What's there? Is there something there I don't see?"

Ted can see Alex just fine and Paul, for that matter. He can't always see everything that's out there, though. The first time he kissed me, a goblin bit my leg. Ted never saw a thing.

"No. At least, nothing I can see either."

"Then what is it?" He relaxed. His fingers now trailed along the edge of my panties.

I could barely control my breathing. "I think we're catching some of the, uh, spill-off."

"Spill-off? From what?" He nuzzled my neck.

"Not what. Whom. I think we're catching vibes from Norah

and Alex." I pushed him away, pulled my jeans back on and grabbed my shirt.

Ted backed away. "So I'm only horny right now because of what they're doing in the other room."

"I'd like to think there might be some other factors," I said a little angrily, as I wrapped my shirt back around myself.

Ted sat down on my bed. "You know I think you're beautiful." He grabbed me around my waist and pulled me to him so that I stood between his spread legs.

"But not that beautiful." I braced my hands on his shoulders and pushed away from him, although every fiber of me wanted to plaster my bare skin against his. My shirt fell open.

He didn't let me move away. Instead, he nuzzled my bare midriff. "Every bit that beautiful. Let me show you how beautiful." He started kissing his way south toward the top of my panties.

"Ted, this isn't just us."

He stopped kissing and looked up at me, the calm steady blue of his eyes nearly eclipsed by his pupils. "Melina, I wanted you last night and the night before and the night before that. Alex was nowhere near here. I will want you tomorrow in the morning, at noon and at night regardless of what's happening in any other room of any other apartment on the planet. Now shut up and take off the rest of your clothes so I can prove it to you."

How is a girl supposed to argue with that?

I CREPT OUT OF BED INSANELY EARLY THE NEXT MORNING, sore in all the right places. Ted had left well before dawn. He'd needed to get home and get his uniform before heading into work. I made my way quietly down the hallway. Norah's door was ajar.

I stood outside and listened. All I heard was a faint snore. Not a big snore, just a little snuffle. I sniffed the air. No blood. I smelled a lot of other things: sex, incense, more sex. But no blood.

I took a deep breath and opened the door a little more. Norah was sound asleep, facedown on her mattress, sprawled and peaceful.

I walked down to the kitchen. By the coffeemaker—where I'd be sure to see it first thing—was a note from Alex. It read, "She's fine. I'm not a monster."

I folded it up and put it in my pocket. We'd see about that.

SOMETIMES I WONDERED WHY I EVEN HAD A JOB. THINGS ended up finding their way to where they were supposed to be. It happened all the time. Because I had a vested interest, I decided to wait and watch to see how this one would work out.

My phone rang while I was still on the road. It was Meredith. "He made it back to the Pack."

I felt my load lighten a little. "Is he okay?"

"He sounded . . . fine." She sounded unsure.

"What does that mean?"

"He wasn't hurt. He was clear on that. He's taking a break from McClannigan's for a while. He'll be sticking close to home for a bit."

"Meredith, is he in trouble?"

She sighed. "Maybe. Maybe not. I don't know how serious it is yet. I don't know if I can even find out. I'll get back to you when and if I know anything, okay?"

"I'll see what I can find out, too." Nice offer considering that Paul was my favorite source of information. "Are you okay?"

There was a pause. "A little sad. I'll be fine." She didn't really sound like she believed it, though. I wasn't sure I did either. About either of them.

We hung up.

John Littlefield's garbage pickup day was Tuesday. At the risk of pissing off Chief Murdock, I went back to Elmville to see how that was going to go. I figured the best way to blend in would be to show up before it was light, so I found my spot on the street freakishly early. I figured I could doze in the car. I'd be hard-pressed not to be woken by the racket of the garbage truck.

When they came for Littlefield's Dumpster, the street was still pretty empty, although a couple of people had left for work. Mainly it was still gray and quiet. The truck rumbled as it came down the street, then let out its piercing beep as it backed into the parking lot. One man jumped down from the truck and directed the driver so that he backed directly up to the Dumpster. The big metal forks lowered down, slid under the Dumpster then lifted the whole thing up to be dumped into the back of the truck.

Maybe I was wrong. Maybe the doll would end up in the landfill and rot away harmlessly. Maybe unicorns would fly, too. Anything was possible.

The Dumpster lid flapped open as it was lifted into the sky and the garbage dumped into the back of the truck. But like trying to get a baking sheet of Tater Tots to all go into a serving bowl, a few items didn't quite make it. Some paper scattered. Something that looked like a partial head of cabbage bounced onto the asphalt of the parking lot and rolled a few feet.

A little box hit the edge of the truck, flipped over its side, bounced a couple of times and came to rest right next to John Littlefield's bicycle.

The guy on the ground whistled and made a hand motion and jumped back onto the back of the truck and it rumbled off down the street.

I sighed. I would have liked to have been wrong this time.

JOHN LITTLEFIELD DIDN'T COME OUT OF HIS APARTMENT UNTIL close to noon. All I can say is that it is a very good thing that I have excellent bladder control. John looked like he might need to work on his bladder control when he saw the little box sitting next to his bicycle.

He didn't pick it up at first. He stood and stared at it. He did a quick scan up and down the street. I slumped down in the Buick. My eyesight was good enough to see him at the distance I'd parked, but I was pretty sure his wasn't good enough to see me. He nudged the box with his toe.

Nothing happened.

He pulled out his cell phone and made a call. He paced up and down in the parking lot, talking and waving his arms. I cracked the window of the Buick but could only catch bits and pieces of what he was saying. I caught the words *witch*, *curse*, and *doomed*. I wasn't sure who he was talking to, but the subject matter was pretty clear.

He shook his head violently several times. Then his shoulders slumped. Finally, he hung up, picked up the box, shoved it into his pocket, got on his bicycle and pedaled away.

I waited for a few moments and then followed.

Following a guy on a bicycle when you're in a car can be tricky. They can go places you can't. They can go the wrong way down one-way streets, cut through alleys, hop up on sidewalks and disappear into parks. Littlefield did the one-way street thing. I swore to myself and screeched around the block as quickly as I could without risking running over a small child or attracting the attention of one of Chief Murdock's minions. I could afford a ticket. I didn't think I could afford the time to go back to the station house. With Littlefield having the doll in his possession, his time was limited. I knew how much the dolls affected me and they weren't even meant for me. Emilia Aguilar made a powerful poppet, as Meredith had said. It would be even more powerful when it was in the hands of the person it was intended for.

As I sailed around the corner, I saw Littlefield drop his bike on the lawn of a church and run inside. He didn't even stop to lock it up. Granted, it was kind of a hoopty bike, but it was his only means of transportation. As he ran, he took off his jacket and grabbed at his back.

I had an idea of what he was feeling. He was grabbing at the area that would correspond with the place on the doll that the matches were taped. It was my guess that he felt like that place on his body was on fire.

I parked the Buick a little ways down the street and made my way quickly and quietly to the church. I hadn't even made it to the lawn when I heard Littlefield's voice.

"You've got to help me," he pleaded. "Help me destroy this thing."

"That thing only has power over you if you allow it to have power over you, John," a male voice said in a very reasonable tone.

Ha, I thought. Spoken like someone who'd never been cursed by a *bruja*.

"Help me not to believe, then," Littlefield begged.

"Of course. How about we read some Bible verses together," the other man suggested. "I think we might find some words to comfort you in the Psalms."

No wonder Littlefield could come up with a verse for every occasion.

"'The Lord is my light and my salvation; whom shall I fear? The

Lord is the stronghold of my life; of whom shall I be afraid? Though an army encamp against me, my heart shall not fear; though war rise up against me, yet I will be confident,'" the man intoned.

"It still burns," Littlefield said. "Can you help me with this?"

By now I'd made my way to the door of the church. I slipped inside. Littlefield was kneeling before this man and proffering up the voodoo doll.

"Let's throw it out." The preacher took the doll.

"That won't work. I tried to throw it out, but it came back to me." Littlefield was nearly babbling.

"What do you mean it came back to you?" The preacher looked confused. "How could it come back to you?"

"I put it in the Dumpster yesterday, and then it was underneath my bike this morning." Littlefield wrapped his arms around himself. I could see him shaking from far back in the church.

True enough. I'd watched it happen.

The preacher rubbed at the back of his neck. "Is it warm in here?"

"It's the doll," John screamed. "It's getting to you, too. Do something!"

"Don't be ridiculous," the preacher said. "It's cloth and thread. It can't do anything."

His words sounded good, but he had started shrugging his shoulders, as if his back were uncomfortable.

"I feel like I'm on fire," Littlefield said. "Right on my back. Right where those matches are taped."

The preacher looked uncomfortable. I'm guessing he felt it, too, but didn't want to tell Littlefield that.

"It's the power of Satan, John," he said. "He has no power if we don't give it to him."

"Help me stop him, then. Please, help me. I don't want evil in my life. I want to do good." Littlefield had started to cry.

"I know that, John."

I was actually starting to feel sorry for Littlefield. The preacher knelt down next to him and they started to pray.

John leapt up. "It's not working. It's not helping. I need more than words." He ran to the font, grabbed a handful of water out of the basin and threw it onto his own back.

I could hear the sizzle at the door and the smell of burnt flesh tickled my nose. Littlefield's back steamed like a pan that was being deglazed.

The preacher fell back on the floor. "Devil," he whispered. And then louder. "Devil. I cast you out, Satan. I cast you out."

Littlefield whirled, wild-eyed. He ran at the preacher. "Give me your keys," he yelled.

The preacher cowered back.

"Your keys," Littlefield screeched. "Now!"

With shaking hands, the preacher pulled his keys from his pants pocket and handed them to Littlefield. Littlefield grabbed them and sprinted out the side door of the church.

I ducked back out the front and sprinted for the Buick. Littlefield came tearing out of the parking lot in a blue Camry. I leapt into the Buick and followed.

Littlefield careened around the corners of Elmville, headed in a generally eastern direction. He was driving so fast I didn't even bother trying to be discreet. I just stayed on his tail. We were out of the town in a matter of minutes. He must have known I was right behind him. We were the only ones on the road. He didn't seem to care.

I could hear the faint sounds of sirens in the distance, but they were miles back. They'd find us eventually; the road was long and straight without any place to turn off. They were still quite a few miles back.

Wherever we were headed, it was remote. There was nothing around us now. Littlefield sped ahead. I pressed down on the accelerator.

The road dead-ended in the parking lot of a reservoir. Littlefield fishtailed into the parking lot, leapt out of the car and ran toward the water, leaving the car running and the door hanging open.

I pulled in behind him and ran, too, shedding my shoes as I raced behind him. He was headed straight for the water. He ran down the boat dock and plunged headfirst into the water. I had closed a fair bit of distance between us. I'm pretty fast when I pour it on and I was pouring with all that I was worth. I wasn't more than thirty seconds behind him as I dove in after him.

The water was dark and murky. I couldn't see more than a few feet in front of my face. I broke through to the surface. Littlefield bobbed up yards ahead of me and to my left. I kicked hard and sent myself in his direction. He ducked under the water again. I dove down after him.

Knowing which direction to look helped a lot, but it was still hard to find him under the water. I swam as hard as I could to where I thought I'd caught a glimpse of him, but he was already gone when I got there. I surfaced again and gasped in air.

A wave slapped me in the face. I sputtered and treaded water, catching my breath. I turned, doing a full three-sixty and saw nothing. I sucked in air and dove under again. I tried to stay still, to see if I could sense movement. Littlefield had to be doing something to keep himself underwater.

I didn't see anything, but I did sense something. A little flicker of power. It had to be the voodoo doll. Littlefield must have carried it with him. I surfaced again to get more air and then dove down and tried to follow the flicker.

It's hard sometimes to trust your senses. Your eyes can play tricks on you. You don't always hear things correctly. How many times have you thought for a second that you smelled brownies baking and then realized your brother just farted?

The pull of an object of power, on the other hand, doesn't often lie. I ignored the fact that my eyes told me nothing and my ears told me less. I followed the pull of the power down into the water. I was not thrilled about how far under I was going. I'm a strong swimmer with a reasonable set of lungs. I am not, however, immortal and do need to suck in oxygen on a very regular basis to keep myself functioning.

Why hadn't I brought Ted with me? He was so much better at the holding-your-breath thing than I was. Oh, yeah, he would have killed me if he'd known I was here.

I kicked harder and practically plowed into Littlefield. He was in a dead float, arms outstretched, face down. I grabbed him under the arms, flipped him on his back and began kicking my way to the surface. He was dead weight and I was already tired. Spots started forming in front of my eyes. My lungs burned like they were on fire and my heart pounded so loud it was deafening. I kept kicking for the surface, though. A dim circle of light appeared. It seemed impossibly far. I kept swimming and pulling Littlefield up toward the circle of light with me.

I broke the surface, gasping for air. I made sure Littlefield's mouth was out of the water, but he stayed desperately still. I lay back in the water. I'd been too late. I hadn't been fast enough. Tears started to form in my eyes. Someone's life had been on the line and I hadn't been good enough. I hadn't saved him. What's more, I was going to be totally up shit's creek without even the slightest hint of a paddle because of it. I was reasonably certain that Chief Murdock hadn't been joking about arresting me if anything happened to Littlefield.

Littlefield twitched in my arms. I kicked upright. He twitched again and took a sputtering breath and then began coughing like crazy. I almost whooped. He wasn't dead. He was breathing.

I made sure I had a good grip on him and started kicking toward shore. He reached around and punched me in the jaw. Hard.

"What the hell?" I nearly dropped him. Then I remembered being told that drowning victims often fought their rescuers. They were desperate. Terrified. They didn't know what they were doing. I made sure my grip was solid again and swam.

Littlefield punched me again.

"Cut it out! I'm trying to save you!"

"Let me go!" He screamed right back.

"No! You'll drown." Lifesaving is generally not my thing. Mae didn't train me to do it. She did, however, train me to respect it. Life, that is. I wasn't sure I was crazy about John Littlefield. I didn't like who he'd been and I wasn't really enamored of what he'd become. I still didn't want him to die and that was completely separate from the fact that I was highly likely to get blamed if he did.

"I don't care. I'm on fire. I need it to stop. I need to go back under." He struggled against me.

I held tight. "If you go back under, you'll drown."

"I don't care. I just want to make it stop. Please let me make it stop." He was begging.

"I can make it stop. I can help. My friend can help. We can get rid of that doll." A wave slapped into my face and water poured into my mouth. I coughed and sputtered a bit. I must have loosened my grip.

Littlefield shoved away from me, reared up and smacked me in the nose with his elbow. "Witch!" he screamed.

For anyone who's never been hit in the nose, it's probably hard to understand how it can totally take a person out. There's a moment, just after impact, where your eyes water so much that you can't see anything but the nearly cartoon-like stars swirling in front of you. Add to that the blood that's likely to be pouring down your face and it's a great distraction, too. It's totally incapacitating, which is why a palm strike to the nose is such an effective way to stop an attacker. I don't know if you can actually kill a person with an upward palm-heel strike to the nose or not. It might be an urban legend. It might not. I don't want to try and I sure as shooting don't want anyone to try it on me.

Littlefield didn't kill me, but he damn sure made me lose my grip on him. He followed up his elbow to the nose with a kick to my gut as he dove back underneath the water.

I went under, too. I doubled over as the air left my lungs. For a second, I was completely disoriented. I wasn't sure which way was up and which was under or whether I'd be able to head the right way once I figured it out. My usual first step to calm myself—deep breathing—wasn't going to help this time. I did my best to still my panic while holding my breath.

When I could finally straighten out and breathe, I tried to dive back under the water for Littlefield. My nose was clogged with blood and I could feel my eyes starting to swell. I heal fast, but not fast enough to overcome a broken nose in time to save Littlefield from drowning himself.

I found him on my third dive. This time when I hauled him up, he stayed dead weight. There was no miraculous stirring as I swam toward shore. He didn't breathe. He also didn't smack me in the head, but I'd almost prefer that he had. This hero stuff was turning me into a masochist. Who was I kidding? This hero stuff was all about masochism. I swam to shore as fast as I could, pulling his dead weight with me. If I hurried there might still be time. I got to the beach and dragged him up onto the solid ground.

Everyone in the hospital gets CPR training. We get recertified every two years whether we want to or not. Generally, it irritates me. I have never once used CPR at the hospital. I can't imagine a moment when someone might need CPR when someone much more qualified than me to administer it isn't within shouting distance. The class is the same every time. I can go through the motions of it practically in my sleep.

As it turns out, that might be a good thing. I didn't have to stop and think as I cleared Littlefield's airway, positioned him on the hard sand and tried to get him to start breathing again.

Unfortunately, being well trained does not guarantee success. I didn't bother trying to call 911. I was pretty sure my cell phone was toast. I might have some magical protection, but that didn't mean my electronic equipment did. My cell was in my pocket and my guess is that the water had totally fried it. It wouldn't be my first one. There was a reason that I always purchased the insurance.

Besides, I could hear the sirens. Help was on the way.

I heard something else, too. I heard crying. I looked up to see Emilia Aguilar crouched at the edge of the lake, whimpering. I felt rage building up in me and rising up from my gut.

"What the hell are you crying for? This is what you wanted, isn't it? It's what you've been working for." I yelled at her between compressions.

She turned to me, cheeks wet with tears and smeared with dirt. "No," she shouted. "Yes. I don't know. I'm so confused."

She began to sob for real.

Confused, was she? Well, that made two of us.

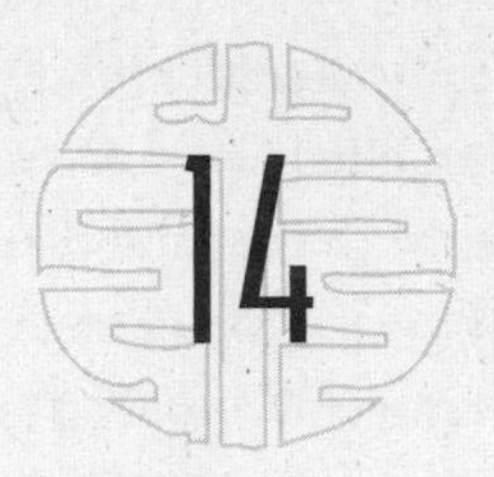

THE CAVALRY ARRIVED AND I WASN'T SURE THAT WAS GOOD news. I kept doing CPR on Littlefield, even though I was pretty sure it wasn't going to help matters any, until I let two police officers haul me off of him. I didn't fight them, so I felt like the two on one deal was a little bit of overkill, but frankly I was grateful that someone else was taking over and didn't feel up to making a fuss. Maybe they'd have better luck than I had.

I watched them start to work on him. It didn't look like they were going to have any more success than I had had. I suspected that if Littlefield had wanted to live, he might have made it. I shivered in my wet clothes as I watched them work and listened to Emilia sniffle next to me.

"Someone get her a blanket," Chief Murdock barked, as she marched onto the scene.

A female officer scurried off to the cars. Murdock just stood and looked at me. I stared right back into her eyes. I was wet and cold and dispirited, but I'd be damned if I was going to let her intimidate me. Or, I suppose, let her know that she intimidated me more than she already had.

I felt the blanket hit my shoulders and wrapped it around myself. It was scratchy and smelled like mildew and tobacco, but it was at least a little protection from the wind that had picked up and was making my clothes turn to ice around me.

"You couldn't take a hint, could you?" Murdock said, shaking her head. "You know I'm going to have to arrest you now, don't you?"

"For what? Trying to save someone? You guys ever hear of the Good Samaritan law down here?" I countered, even though just the sound of the words *arrest you* made me shake in my boots. Of course, I was shaking in them anyway. I was freezing.

"Drowning a man doesn't sound like being much of a Good Samaritan to me." Murdock clasped her hands behind her back and put her face right into mine. She had lovely skin. Practically poreless. I didn't think it was the moment to ask her about her beauty regime, though.

"She didn't try to drown him. She tried to save him," Emilia piped up beside me.

Now there was help from an unexpected quarter. Of course, Emilia had me pretty darned confused anyway.

Murdock shifted her attention. "And I should take the word of the cousin of the man that the dead guy murdered on that subject?"

Emilia stood up. It wasn't terribly frightening. She was an itty-bitty thing. Still, it showed presence and some definite backbone. I could respect that. "Yes. Yes, you should."

"May I ask why?" Murdock smiled, but it was a little like the smile of a crocodile. She was just getting ready to snap.

"Because it's the truth. That's why." Emilia squared her shoulders and looked Murdock in the eye.

Murdock's smile grew. "That is so sweet, Emilia. Is there any reason I should believe you? Any reason at all?" She cocked her head to one side and looked at her with her squinted eyes. "What are you doing here anyway? How'd you end up here just as your cousin's murderer was drowned?"

Emilia took a deep breath. "I was called."

Murdock leaned back. "Called? Who called you?" She turned and looked at me. "Did you call her, Markowitz? Are you two in cahoots?"

Cahoots sounded like such a sweet word for what Chief Murdock was actually accusing us of. I shook my head. "I didn't call her. I didn't call anybody."

"So how did you end up here?" Murdock asked me.

"I followed him." There it was. The plain truth. Who knew it could even come out of my mouth?

"After I told you to leave him alone?" Murdock pressed her lips together in a thin line.

I shrugged. "And threatened me that if any harm came to him, you'd arrest me. I didn't see anyone else protecting him, so I figured I was it."

A flicker of doubt crossed Murdock's cool gray eyes, but it was only a flicker. A brief light of possibility and then—poof!—gone again, suspicion in its place. "Where did you follow him from?"

"Some church over on Patwin Road." I nodded my head toward the Camry. "That's the preacher's car. Littlefield took it."

Murdock twisted her lips. "I'm aware. I'm also aware that he apparently steamed when holy water was thrown on him and was possessed by Satan."

I shrugged. I figured it was better to neither verify nor dispute that. "He ran out here and jumped into the water with all his clothes on. I jumped in after him. I pulled him up once, but he fought against me and popped me in the nose. I lost my grip on him and he went under again. It took me too long to find him the second time." Horrifyingly, my voice started to clog up as I told the final part of my story. I coughed and tried to pretend that it was water in my throat.

Murdock stared at me for a few seconds and then turned her attention back on Emilia. "And you were called here. Who did you say called you?"

Emilia tilted her chin up. "I didn't say. It wasn't a who. It was a what. I was drawn here. The universe called me. I answered."

"The universe, huh? Must be one heck of a phone bill." She looked from one of us to the other for a second and then turned. "Arrest these two," she barked at the closest uniform. "And call a bus for the dead guy, will you?"

"Arrest them for what?" Bless his heart, he actually looked confused.

"I don't know. Find something. Maybe Markowitz here has got a broken taillight." She marched back toward her car, saying over her shoulder as she went, "Find something that we can hold them on until I can book them for murder."

I didn't exactly feel like I'd made a new friend.

THE GOOD NEWS WAS THAT I WAS IN AN INTERROGATION room. That meant that they hadn't found anything to charge me with. Yet.

The bad news was that I'd been there for two hours in my soggy clothes and I was getting pretty bored. I do not have the world's longest attention span. I need stimulation. I like books and TV and the radio, and I like them pretty much constantly. Sitting here in an empty room with its industrial-grade carpet embedded with the smell of fear and desperation without so much as a piece of paper to doodle on might well make me go crazy.

Chief Murdock was a wily one. She knew how to soften a girl up.

I laid my head down on my folded arms. If I hadn't been so damn uncomfortable in my wet jeans and if my nose hadn't been throbbing like the bass beat at a Sublime concert, I might have taken a nap. I closed my eyes and tried to drift off.

I wasn't sure how long I'd been like that when the door opened. At least they'd brought me something to eat. It smelled yummy. Kind of like an apple cinnamon muffin.

"Hey, you wanna go home?" a very familiar voice said.

My head shot up. "Ted? How did you get here? They haven't let me make a phone call yet!"

Maybe I was dreaming. I'd had worse dreams. I didn't remember ever being able to smell something in my dreams, though.

Maybe we'd become psychically linked and he could sense my dismay and danger. I'd heard that happened to werewolves once they were part of a pack. They could sense when one of their members was in trouble.

Maybe Littlefield had hit me harder in the head than I realized and I was hallucinating.

They were all possibilities.

Ted came the rest of the way into the room and sat down across from me at the table. "We got a request for information from the Elmville Police Department."

"About what?" I was definitely not thinking straight. This made no sense to me.

"About you. To see if you were a person of interest in any investigations. Or had come to our attention in any way. Your name is mentioned in my report on the gang troubles last summer." He arched a brow at me and touched his lips with his finger, as if I didn't have enough common sense not to start babbling about Chinese vampires and hydroponically grown marijuana in an interrogation room that could very well have a tape running somewhere. "That's how I knew you were here. I tried your cell but didn't get an answer."

"It was in my pocket when I went into the reservoir." I explained.

He nodded slowly. "You went into a reservoir. Fully clothed, I take it."

"There wasn't really time to change into a more appropriate outfit." I smiled at him, but it made my face hurt.

"And was this before or after you broke your nose?" He reached out and tilted my chin.

"Kind of concurrent."

He stood up. "Let's get you out of here." He held his hand out to me.

I took it. I wasn't feeling all that proud at the moment. We started to walk out of the room. "Ted?"

"Yeah?" His voice sounded a little rough.

"Have they let Emilia go yet?" I couldn't leave without her. She was the key to everything. Maybe it was all over, now that Littlefield was dead, but I didn't think so. Plus, I still didn't understand, and that rankled with me.

"Who?"

Not a good sign. "Emilia. The woman they brought in with me."

"I don't know."

"Ted, we need to get her out, too." I knew I was asking for a lot. I knew he was probably ready to kill me. I knew I couldn't leave her here, not if I wanted answers.

"Melina, I don't think you appreciate what it's costing me to get you out." He kept his voice even, but there was definite stress in it.

"I'm so sorry. I will try to find a way to make it up to you. But I can't leave here without Emilia." I stopped walking.

He sighed and looked down at me. "Who exactly is this person, now?"

"Her name is Emilia Aguilar, and she's the one who's been killing all these people, and I'm not leaving without her." I looked back up at him. At least I wasn't lying anymore.

He closed his eyes and I was pretty certain he was counting under his breath. "Then we'd better go find her."

THEY HADN'T CHARGED EMILIA WITH ANYTHING YET EITHER. IT took another fifteen minutes or so, and all three of us were walking out of the Stanislaus County Jail together.

"Thank you for helping me," she said, as we walked to Ted's truck. "I don't know how long they would have kept me in that room if you hadn't."

"Not much longer," Ted said. "Eventually they either have to charge you with something or let you go."

My feet squelched as we walked across the pavement.

"We need to get you some dry clothes," Ted and Emilia said, nearly in unison.

"Please," Emilia said. "Come to my home. I'll get you some dry clothing and some food. You're hungry."

As if on cue, my stomach growled.

We rode the rest of the way in silence, although Emilia kept turning to look out the back window. Ted parked the truck at the curb and we all piled out. Emilia led the way into the house. It was cozy inside. I'd half expected it to be covered with shrines and Day of the Dead figurines. It was mainly distressingly normal.

"Come with me," Emilia said. "I'll get you some dry clothes."

I looked at her. "I don't think anything of yours will fit me." I was five or six inches taller than her and we don't even need to start talking about issues of width. Maybe Paul was right. Maybe I needed to hit those diet drinks a little harder.

"I have some things I keep for clients, just in case." She led me to a bathroom, disappeared down the hall for a minute and then came back with a set of sweats. "These should fit you. Bring your wet things out when you've showered and changed and I'll wash them."

She shooed me into the shower and walked out.

I turned on the hot water and stepped into the tub. It was such a relief to be warm again. I found a bottle that smelled like shampoo on the side of the tub and used it to wash the reservoir smell out of my hair. There was a bar of soap and I scrubbed down with that, too.

By the time I stepped out of the bath, I could smell something delicious. I towel-dried my hair, combed it out with a brush I found by the side of the sink and pulled on the sweats. They were old and a little worn, but that just made them feel soft against my skin.

I padded down the hallway and found Ted already shoveling food in at the kitchen table.

He looked up a little sheepishly when I walked into the room. He washed down the bite he was chewing with a swig from the bottle of beer by his plate. "Sorry, babe. I couldn't wait. It smelled too good."

I put a hand on his shoulder. "I'll forgive you if I can have a bite."

"Have a whole plate." Emilia set two plates down at the table and sat down at the one across the table from Ted, leaving me between them. I sat down, too. It did smell really, really good. I wondered if it was poisoned. I looked over at Ted. If it was, it didn't seem to be having any ill effects on him.

I dug in.

You can order tamales at a restaurant. You can buy them at a store. But until you've had homemade tamales made by someone who knows what they're doing, you have not had tamales. Emilia knew what she was doing with a corn husk. No one talked for a few minutes, although Emilia scratched at her leg periodically. I noticed a series of red angry bumps, like mosquito bites, marching up her calf.

Finally, Emilia pushed back from the table and said, "Let me explain to you why I killed those boys."

I'M NOT SURE I'VE EVER SEEN TED MOVE THAT FAST AND WE spar together pretty often. He had pushed back his chair and leapt up from the table and had his hands out in front of him in a split second. "Don't tell me anything that will make me have to arrest you, Emilia. I'm a cop. I'm duty bound. Get a lawyer. Turn yourself in. But, please, don't make me have to arrest you right now. Especially right after I sprung you out of the county jail."

Emilia leaned back in her chair, a rueful smile playing on her lips. "Nothing I tell you will lead to my arrest. My actions won't be judged in your courts, Officer Goodnight. There are other places where I will be judged." She dropped her head and wiped at her eyes.

I took one last bite of tamale and shoved my plate away. "So let's hear it, then, Emilia. What's your excuse?"

"My excuse?"

"We all know why you killed them. They killed your cousin. You wanted revenge. You've got it. Save the crocodile tears for someone who might buy them." Good tamales will buy you some listening time with me, but not a lot of sympathy. I might be cheap, but I am not easy.

"You don't understand how it was." She looked up at me now, directly into my eyes. A tear or two still glittered there, but there was fire also. That was fine with me. I'd much rather play with fire than drown in tears.

Which explains a lot about me. I know.

"So explain it." I turned to Ted. "Sit down. There is really nothing she's going to tell you that you'll be able to book her on."

Ted sat down reluctantly. "Fine. But only if I can have seconds."

Emilia took his plate and dished up more tamales, beans and rice. She pulled another beer from the refrigerator, but he shook his head. My Boy Scout. He'd be driving tonight. One beer was his limit.

"It was never my intention to kill them," Emilia said quietly, as she sat back down at the table.

"You made voodoo dolls of them as special birthday presents? To commemorate their twenty-first birthdays?" Right. That's how I celebrated all my friends' transitions to adulthood, by giving them lethally cursed toys. It's what all the cool kids were doing.

She shook her head. "Of course not. They were for me. They were like . . . therapy. A way to express my anger."

"I think you expressed it pretty clearly." I crossed my arms over my chest. This was going nowhere. "So if they were just for you, how did they end up sitting on top of my car for me to deliver, with carefully written addresses on their little boxes?"

Emilia's brown eyes opened a little wider. "You delivered them? All of them?"

"Of course I did. It's what I do. I'm a Messenger. I deliver things." I leaned forward on the table. "But you knew that, didn't you?"

Emilia shook her head again. "I knew there was . . . something about you. Something others probably don't see, but that happens a lot with me. I see . . . things."

My eyes narrowed. "What kind of things?"

"Some pretty run-of-the-mill things, I think. Auras, you would call them. By the way, I think I could help with yours." She reached out a hand and placed it on my forearm.

I jerked back, but not before I felt a little zing. "What are you?" And what the hell was wrong with my aura?

"My people call me *bruja*. Or sometimes *curandera*. More the latter." She put her hand back in her lap.

"Witch?" Ted asked.

Emilia shrugged. "Roughly translated, yes. A witch. But more of a healer."

"You weren't doing a lot of healing with those dolls," I pointed out.

Her lips tightened. "Please, let me explain."

I leaned back in my chair. "I am all ears."

She smiled. "You Americans. You say the cutest things."

I gave her a baleful stare.

"Fine. This is how it was. I moved to Elmville three years ago to take care of my aunt."

"Rosita Lopez. The one who owned this house? The one who Jorge was living with when he was killed?"

Emilia nodded. "She was my mother's sister. She had no children of her own. When she became ill, my mother sent me. I had already had some success in healing in Mexico and even if I couldn't help her in that way, I could help with other things. Housework. Cooking. Shopping. I could help with the pain." Her eyes clouded.

I'd seen plenty of people dying of cancer at the hospital. I knew all about the pain.

"Three years ago, Rawley, Bossard and Littlefield were all locked away in a California Youth Authority facility," I said.

"Exactly," Emilia agreed. "They weren't here. Very few people talk about what happened to Jorge around here. Some don't want to stir up trouble. Others are ashamed. Most want to forget it ever happened and go on with their lives."

"But not you," I said. "You didn't want to forget and you definitely didn't want them to go on with their lives."

She shook her head, her long dark hair spilling over her shoulders. "No. You still don't understand."

"I'm trying." But my patience was getting very thin.

She looked at me, eyes narrowed. "No. You're not. You are closed here and here." She gently touched my forehead and my chest.

I snatched her hand and held it by the wrist. "Don't touch me."

"You don't need to fear me." Our eyes met, and I felt my hair begin to rise as if electricity flowed between us.

"Tell that to Bossard, Rawley and Littlefield."

"So much anger. How can I get through to you when there's this wall of anger between us?" she demanded.

"I've been used. That tends to piss me off." Which might explain why I spent so much of my life angry. I stored that thought away for later contemplation.

"I was not the one who used you, Messenger." Her eyes narrowed.

I countered. "Then who was?"

"I'm trying to figure that out." She sounded almost as exasperated as I felt.

I turned her hand over. A burn stretched from the inside of her wrist nearly to her elbow. "What happened to your arm?"

"An accident at the stove."

It must have been one heck of an accident. The burn looked nasty. "At the restaurant or here?"

Ted broke in. "Melina, maybe you should listen to her, hear her story and then ask questions. Otherwise, we're going to be here all night."

I scowled at him and then realized that Emilia was giving him a beatific smile, which made me scowl harder.

"You are not closed," she said to him. "Not there or there or anywhere." She pointed to his head and chest. Luckily, she didn't touch him as she had me. If she had, she might be pulling back nothing but a bloody stump. He's my man, after all.

Oh, great. Jealousy. How girly was I going to get?

"I'm listening," I said, and sat back again in my chair. I took some deep breaths and stilled myself. Emilia was right and I knew it. My heart and head were closed to her. I tried to open them. If anyone knew better than to judge based on appearances, it should be me.

"I loved it here. My aunt was very kind. Her home was very nice. In America, there is so much of everything. Food. Clothing. You don't know how grateful you should be. Then I met another woman, an older woman, a *bruja* who wished to mentor me. She recognized what I had inside me and started teaching me how to tend it and nourish it. I felt as though I came here and . . . blossomed."

"Fabulous. Blossoming. It sounds terrific." So maybe she had only paused to take a breath, but it seemed to demand a comment and I am pretty much always ready with a comment.

"I learned so much from my *mentora*. People began to come to me to be healed. I still have to work at the restaurant, but every day I come closer and closer to being able to make my living helping people." Her face took on a glow.

"It's an amazing feeling, isn't it?" Ted said.

"Yes. Yes, it is," she said.

I rolled my eyes. How had I gotten here in a room full of saints? Most days, all I wanted was to make it through without getting hurt or scratching the Buick.

"And exactly where in this blossoming healing thing did you start killing people who pissed you off?" I asked.

"Melina." Ted put his hand on my arm and I quieted.

Emilia held up her hands. "It's all right. I'm getting to it. It started when the first one came home. Rosalinda, my *mentora*, called me. She'd seen him downtown. She called to warn me to stay home. I wish I'd listened."

"So you didn't listen. You went to see him?" I asked.

She nodded. Her jaw tightened. "There he was, out on the streets, laughing with people his age. Walking with a girl. Drinking. And where was Jorge? He was where Rawley put him. Cold and in the ground, that's where. Why was Rawley walking around while my cousin was food for the worms? Where was the justice in that? I became enraged."

Ah, now we were getting somewhere. Rage. I knew that emotion, especially the pointless kind that rails against the universe with puny arms and weaker powers. It was one of my specialties. I also knew how desperate it could make someone. "So what did you do, Emilia? What did you do with all that anger?"

"I stared at him. I let the hatred I felt for him and his kind flow through me into the universe, into the world. As I watched, he stumbled and fell. For a moment, on the ground, it looked as if he could not breathe. It made me glad. Then, it frightened me. I had grown more powerful than I'd known. Maybe even more powerful than my *mentora*. But what good was all that power when a man like that could walk the streets when Jorge would walk no more."

"Frustrating, isn't it?"

"For two days, I screamed. I cried. I beat against the wall with my fists until my hands bled. And the worst part of it? I knew. I knew the other two would be coming out soon. They, too, would be walking down the street in the sunshine, girls on their arms, drinks in their hands, lives to live, while my Jorge, my sweet Jorge, lay buried in the cold, hard ground." She turned her face from us, her shoulders heaving.

Ted and I exchanged glances. He raised his eyebrows. I shook my head. He stayed still in his chair.

A few seconds later, Emilia turned back to us, composed again. "I went to my *mentora*. I cried to her. What should I do? Who could I heal with all the pain and hatred inside me? How could I move through it? That's when she told me about the dolls and how to make them." She sat back in her chair, as if reliving those moments had exhausted her.

"So your teacher, your *mentora*, put you up to this? She taught you how to kill those boys?" That was one hell of a mentor. What was the next lesson? How to smite people?

"She taught me how to make the dolls. They were never meant to kill. They were to be . . . cathartic. They were a place to pour my rage and pain and anger and hatred. The idea was that I could put all of it into the dolls and then we would bury the dolls and thus bury my anger. I would be free of it without causing harm."

"Well, that didn't exactly work out, did it? What made you decide not to bury the dolls?" I asked.

She threw her hands in the air. "Nothing. I did bury them. Under the full moon, with a layer of graveyard dirt over them."

That made no sense. "So how exactly did they end up on the hood of my car?"

"That is what I don't know and what I think I need to find out."

She stood up and began to clear our plates. Ted looked after his wistfully as she took it away. I felt another pang of jealousy. He'd never looked like that after anything I'd made him. Of course, I couldn't remember the last time I'd cooked.

I sat with that for a moment and then asked, "Why? It's over now. All three of them are dead."

"I know. When Kurt Rawley died, I thought maybe, maybe it's just a coincidence."

I heard Ted growl a little next to me. I put my hand on his knee. I didn't believe in coincidences any more than he did. But now wasn't the time to bond over that. I could see why she would think that, though.

"Then Bossard died." She swallowed hard. "I knew then. I knew it was not just a coincidence. I didn't want to admit it, but I knew."

"I saw you at the funeral," I said. "Crying behind a tree. But I could still feel the hatred rolling off you in waves."

Emilia put her face in her hands. "You don't know. You just don't know. I did. I hated those boys. I hated them for their hatred. How wrong is that? Still, for me to kill another? With my powers? It was never something I meant to do. Never something I wanted to do. And there are repercussions for doing things such as that. There are consequences."

I took her hand again and turned it over. "Like this?" I asked, pointing at the burn.

"Exactly like that." Her face grim, she went on. "As much as I didn't want to know that it was I who caused the deaths of Rawley and Bossard, I knew I had. I knew I had to try to stop Littlefield from dying, too."

I understood that. "Not so easy to help someone who doesn't want to be helped, is it?"

She shook her head and gave me a wry smile. "No. It is not.

Particularly one who has become so afraid of witchcraft that he cannot discern good from bad or help from evil intent."

"If it makes you feel any better, he didn't want my help either."

"I noticed." She cocked her head to one side. "Your nose is healing very quickly. The swelling is almost already gone."

My hands flew up to my face. My nose was still tender, but it didn't feel like I'd borrowed it from Jimmy Durante anymore. "Good genes," I said.

"Yes, I sensed that." Emilia smiled and I could tell she was getting more curious about who and what I was.

"So it's over now, right? All three boys are dead. Whoever dug up your voodoo dolls got what they wanted and it's over." Except for the part that local law enforcement was looking to pin the deaths on yours truly, of course.

"I don't think so," Emilia said. "I told you that there are repercussions for using one's magic for these kinds of purposes. Since my specialty is healing, it's never been a problem for me before. Now, however, now it's a problem."

"The burns and the bug bites on your legs?"

"Yes, and the sense that I am always being followed. I don't think the boys' deaths will make those things go away. They might just make them worse. Also, remember how you said you didn't like being used?"

I nodded.

"I am not exactly wild about it myself. Someone used me. Someone used my skill. Someone used my magic. I don't know why. To me, these deaths are senseless. Yes, I hated what these boys did and what they stood for, but they had been punished and I knew that they would have to live their lives with the knowledge of what they had done. I myself cannot imagine that kind of torture, to have to look every day into the mirror and know I was the kind of person who would beat an innocent young man to death merely because I didn't like the color of his skin. But to kill them? And in such a way? It makes no sense to me. No sense at all."

I looked over at Ted and he looked back at me. "Somebody wanted those boys dead. It shouldn't be that hard to figure out who."

"You can't be poking your nose into things down here, Melina. Chief Murdock has a serious hard-on for you. She will bust you if you so much as jaywalk," Ted said.

"So I won't jaywalk." I shrugged, trying to look more nonchalant than I felt.

"This is serious, Melina." He gave me a hard stare.

"I'm aware." I stared right back.

He sighed, some of the starch leaving his shoulders. "Leave it alone."

"You know I can't." I put my hand on his arm.

"I don't know any such thing. Right now, no one has brought any charges against you. We can get in my truck, pick up your car, drive back to Sacramento and pretend that none of this ever happened." He put his hand over mine.

"But it did happen."

"I know that, Melina, but you're making my head hurt."

Emilia broke in. "It's late. Why don't we all get a good night's sleep? I have plenty of room here. There's no need for you to drive back tonight. It's been a long day."

She was right. I had no desire to get in my car and drive back. I looked over at Ted, ready to do whatever he wanted. See how good I am at compromise?

He nodded. "Fine. It would be safer if we got some rest before we drove back."

15

IT WASN'T DAWN YET WHEN AN INSISTENT BEEP BEEP BEEPING woke me. I spent a few seconds trying to figure out where I was. Emilia Aguilar's house. Then I looked around to see what might be beeping. I can see pretty well in the dark. It wasn't anything in the room. It was coming from the hall.

I slipped out of bed and walked toward the door. That's when I smelled it. Smoke. The beeping was a smoke alarm. I shook Ted awake.

"Ted. Something's wrong. I think . . . I think the house might be on fire."

Apparently, saying something like that is not the kindest, gentlest way to wake a man from peaceful slumber. Ted exploded out of the bed. He jumped into his jeans and raced to the door.

He stopped and rested his face against the door, feeling the doorknob. "It's not hot. We can get out," he said.

"What about Emilia?" I asked, pulling on clothes.

"We'll get her out, too, but first we have to make sure we have a way out." He shook the pillows out of the pillowcases, ducked into the bathroom that connected to the room and the other small bedroom on the other side, ran them under the faucet and handed me one.

I looked at him questioningly.

"To cover your face with, in case there's a lot of smoke. Stay low, okay. And, Melina"—he took me by the shoulders and looked into my eyes—"please stay with me."

I nodded.

"Grab my belt," he said.

I did and he opened the door. The smoke was thick and getting thicker. I put the pillowcase over my mouth and nose, and we headed into the hall.

Ted ducked down and I ducked with him. We went down the hall and into the living room. The smoke was getting thicker by the second. I could see the source. It was coming from the kitchen. The kitchen that was between the living room and the master bedroom, where Emilia was sleeping.

I started that way. Ted grabbed me, shook his head and steered us both out the back door onto the porch.

I gasped in air and whirled around. "We have to go back in. We have to get Emilia."

Ted grabbed me. "Not from in there. Which one's her room? Let's see if we can get her from out here."

I looked around and pointed. "That end of the house."

We ran around the porch. A door opened onto the back deck. It had to be from Emilia's bedroom. I grabbed the doorknob. It didn't turn. It was locked from the inside.

Ted pushed me behind him. "Stay back." He kicked the door. It gave a little but didn't open.

"Let me," I said.

He shot me a look. I doubt it's easy to have a girlfriend who has certain strengths, or lots of strength, actually. It's probably especially not easy when you're the kind of guy who generally rescues everyone else. There wasn't time at the moment to pander to anyone's ego, though. I could hear the flames crackling and the heat from the house was rising.

He gave way. "Fine. I'll call in the fire."

The flying sidekick took me months to master and probably a year or more to perfect. It's not an easy kick to do well. There's also not much call for it. It's a flashy kick, not much good in a fight. You're vulnerable when you're in the air. You might use it to finish off an opponent once you knew you had them where you wanted them. It would be a little demoralizing. It would, however, be perfect for smashing in this door.

I backed up, took a few running steps, launched myself off my left leg and bunched my right leg up to my chest. I thrust my right leg out when I reached the peak of my jump, hitting the door with my heel. It exploded inward. I landed in a crouch.

Ted rushed through the door ahead of me. Seconds later, he was hauling Emilia's still body out through the door onto the porch.

"Is she . . . ?" I couldn't bring myself to say it. Was I too late again? Had another person died while I stood by, impotent to help?

"She's alive, but she's inhaled a lot of smoke. We have to get her away from the house." Ted barely stopped to explain as he hauled Emilia away from the thickening smoke.

I heard the sirens coming. "Help's on the way."

Ted glanced at me. "Sirens?"

I nodded.

He laid her down in the grass. Her eyes fluttered open and she tried to sit up but fell back on the grass. "What happened?" her voice was hoarse. Her hand went first to her throat and then to her head.

"There's a fire," I said, feeling like I was stating the obvious.

"My house?" Again, Emilia tried to sit up. This time she was more successful. Her hands flew to her heart. "My house."

"I'm so sorry," I said. I looked over my shoulder. The sirens were getting closer, but the flames were moving quickly. They'd better get here quick or it was going to end up spreading to the other houses.

Tears began to trail through the soot on Emilia's cheeks. "Where will I go? What will I do?"

"We'll figure something out," Ted said. He headed out to the street to meet the firefighters as they arrived. I heard them ask if everyone was out and a few other questions.

"It's my own fault. I brought it on myself." She began to weep.

Wasn't that true about pretty much all of our own troubles? In this case, though, not entirely. "With a little help from someone else," I reminded her.

She sat with that for a second. "It doesn't change the circumstances. Where do I go now? What do I do?"

"Have you ever slept on a futon couch before?" I asked.

IT WAS A FEW MORE HOURS BEFORE WE COULD LEAVE ELM-ville. The paramedics had to check us over. The fire chief had a question or two. But it still wasn't quite light yet when we left what was left of Emilia's home. It wasn't pretty. It looked and smelled as bad as Kurt Rawley's house had.

"Looks like something was left on the stove," the fire chief told Emilia.

"No," she said. "That's not possible. I didn't leave anything on."

He looked uncomfortable. "Well, now, people sometimes forget. Maybe they put a kettle on for tea. Or maybe they start something for the next day. They walk away and forget. Especially if, well, maybe they've had a drink or two."

"I wasn't drunk. I didn't leave anything cooking on the stove." Emilia's jaw clenched.

I didn't blame her. I was also pretty darn certain that she hadn't left anything on the stove. I'd watched her shut the kitchen down. If something had burned on the stove, it wasn't because of her forgetfulness and neglect. Arguing with the fire chief at that moment, however, was getting us nowhere. "Come on, Emilia," I said. "Let's go."

"Listen to your friend," the chief said. "Be grateful you got out alive. This was a nasty one. I'm not sure I've seen one of these houses go up this fast. You're lucky you got out when you did."

Emilia started to open her mouth. While I don't generally have a good sense as to when to keep my own mouth shut, I do often recognize when other people should stop talking. I grabbed her and said, "Let's go. I'm hungry and tired and I smell bad. I want to go home."

She followed me reluctantly.

"Can we at least please stop at Rosalinda's house? She should know what happened and that I'm okay and where I'm going. She'll see the house and worry. She lives just a mile or so that way." Emilia pointed west.

"Of course," I said. We piled into Ted's truck and Emilia directed us through the streets to her *mentora*'s home.

Dawn was just breaking as we arrived. A few birds chirped in the streets as the light began to stream over the horizon. Ted pulled the truck over. Just as Emilia started to get out, I noticed movement by the front door.

"Wait," I said. "Get down."

Not many people leave their homes right at dawn. A few runners I know, but they're certifiably insane. Generally, people slipping out of doors at the crepuscular times of day are hoping not to be noticed.

Whoever was leaving Rosalinda's home was a big person, definitely male and without a shred of magic to him. I squinted in the dim light. He looked familiar. I'd definitely seen him before.

It took me a few seconds, but it finally dawned on me. It was Neil Bossard's brother, the one who'd caught me in Neil's room trying to fish the voodoo doll out from underneath the bed. The one who'd gotten me thrown out of Bossard's memorial service. The one who'd gotten me hauled back into Chief Murdock's office. The one who'd told Kurt Rawley's mother to make a police report about my being in her house. And, last but not least, the one who'd tried to beat the crap out of me and told me to stay away from Elmville.

The one whose parents had spent all their money trying to keep his older brother out of jail.

As we watched, a woman came out. She was wrapped in a bathrobe, but not one of those dorky terrycloth ones or even one of those flannel zip-up-the-front ones that my mother gives me for Hanukkah. This was more of a slinky negligee-type of bathrobe. She danced out barefoot and caught Drew Bossard by the shoulder. He turned and took her in his arms and gave her the kind of kiss that makes a promise to a woman.

"Ewwwwww!" Ted and I said in unison.

Emilia said nothing.

"Do you know who the kid is?" Ted whispered.

"It's Neil Bossard's brother."

"What the hell is he doing here?"

"I have some guesses."

"Me, too," Emilia said. "Way too many."

WE RODE OUT OF TOWN AS SOON AS WE WERE SURE BOSSARD'S brother was gone and Rosalinda was safely back in her house. I have to say, I was pretty glad to see Elmville in my rearview mirror. I had a bad feeling that I'd be back, though, and much sooner than either I or Chief Murdock wanted me to be.

"How are you going to explain her to Norah?" Ted asked, gesturing to where Emilia slept in the backseat.

"What's to explain? She's a friend who needed someplace to stay. Norah would take in every stray on the block if she could." I fiddled with the heat. I can never seem to get it exactly where I want it. It's either blasting so much heat that I can feel my eyeballs start to dry out or I'm freezing.

"A cursed friend." Ted pointed out.

True enough. "I wasn't necessarily going to lead with that."

"Norah's not stupid. She's going to figure it out when there's an infestation of cockroaches or the apartment catches fire." He slapped my hand away from the temperature controls and set it himself.

"We'll figure out what Rosalinda and Drew are up to before that happens," I said, with much more confidence than I actually felt.

"And then what?"

"What do you mean 'and then what'?" It wasn't quite warm enough. I reached for the fan dial.

"Give it a second. It's a temperature control, not an on/off switch." Ted slapped my hand away again. "Once you find out, what will you do? And will it make any difference?"

"I'm not sure, but I don't see that we have any choice."

"This isn't your fight." Emilia's sleepy voice came out of the backseat. "It's mine. You should take me back to Elmville before it's too late."

We had been having variations on this basic conversational theme for a while. I couldn't see leaving Emilia to the tender mercies of whatever fate had in store for her. Plus, I was pissed as hell that someone she trusted was using her and had used me. I was a little tired of being a pawn in someone else's game.

"Not gonna happen." Something was wrong. I was comfortable. I looked down at the temperature dials and over at Ted. "How did you do that?"

"It requires a little patience." He leaned back in the seat and smiled at me. "You'll never be able to do it."

I didn't argue. So I asked the question that had been bothering me the most. "Emilia, why would your *mentora* want to screw you over like this?" Because there was no doubt in my mind that that was exactly what was happening.

Who had guided Emilia to make the voodoo dolls? Who knew where they were hidden? Rosalinda.

The question was why. And what was she doing playing tonsil hockey with a boy half her age?

I HAD BEEN RIGHT ABOUT NORAH. SHE'D HAD NO PROBLEM with the idea of letting Emilia stay with us. I'd even come completely clean about the whole being-cursed thing.

"I'll look some protection spells up in the grimoire. Maybe I can help keep us all safe." She spread a thick layer of organic natural peanut butter on a piece of whole-grain toast. It did not look appetizing. It looked bumpy. I don't like my sandwiches to be bumpy. But she was eating, which was nice.

"Thanks." I hesitated, not sure how to bring up what had happened here in the apartment. "How are you doing?"

She licked the peanut butter off her lips and smiled. "I'm fine. Never better."

"Really?" I pressed.

"Really. It's a little like finding out that ice cream is actually good for you."

I raised my eyebrows, not sure I understood.

"You know how much I love ice cream?"

I did. Norah adored ice cream. It was one of her only vices. She fought it like the devil, but sometimes she just couldn't take it anymore and she'd dive into a half gallon of Super Fudge Chunk or Rocky Road and not come up for air until it was gone. She'd moan about it for days afterward.

"I wanted him like I want ice cream. I fought wanting him. I didn't want to want him, but I did, Melina. Desperately. It terrified me. You know I can't fight the ice cream craving forever. I was afraid it was going to be just like that, but this time the regret was going to be much, much worse."

I could see that.

"But it's not like that."

"How is it, then?" I asked.

"It's . . . sweet." She smiled.

Sweet had not been what I expected. Hot. Steamy. Erotic. Dangerous. Those I'd expected. Not sweet.

She threw her arms around me and gave me one of her warm hugs. "I'm okay. It's okay. You don't have to worry."

It was a little like telling me I didn't have to breathe, but I'd give it a try.

We went out to the living room, where Emilia and Meredith waited for us.

"Have you heard anything more from Paul?" I asked Meredith.

She shook her head. "Tell me a little more about this *mentora* of yours." Meredith sat down on the futon couch.

"She's a very powerful *bruja*. Very wise and very strong. She's taught me so much." Emilia's eyes began to fill with tears. "I don't understand why she's doing this to me."

Meredith took Emilia's hands in hers. I saw her jump a bit and then settle down. "You're quite powerful yourself," she said.

Emilia smiled. "It was like a miracle when I met Rosalinda. Always I'd had these feelings inside me, this sense of things that needed to burst out of me. Sometimes they were so strong, but I had no idea what to do with them. She taught me how to channel that energy, how to use it, how to help people with it."

"How did you find her?" Meredith wasn't letting go of Emilia's hands.

"She came into the café where I work one day. I waited on her. When she was leaving, she asked me if I knew what I was. She left her card and said that if I wanted to know, I should call her. If she hadn't stopped in when I was working, I don't know if we would have ever met. It has been the happiest coincidence of my life."

Meredith took a deep breath in and let it out, then she released Emilia's hands. "I doubt it was a coincidence. I'm also surprised she didn't chase you out of town right away."

"Why would she have done that?"

"Emilia, you must know, you're a very powerful witch. I have a feeling that your Rosalinda doesn't like to share much and you're in her territory. Has she ever had any other students?"

Emilia shook her head. "Not that I know of."

Meredith made a funny noise in the back of her throat. "Is Rosalinda a healer like you?"

Emilia's eyes flew open. "How did you know I was a healer?"

Meredith smiled. "I can feel it from you. Can you tell what I do best?"

Emilia shut her eyes. Then she smiled. "You protect things, don't you?"

"I do, indeed." Meredith smiled back at her. "What does Rosalinda do? What's her specialty?"

"Mainly potions, but she's done a bit of everything."

Meredith turned to me. "And you saw her with a much younger lover?"

"It sure looked that way to me. He's no more than seventeen or eighteen and she's a woman near forty. What does that mean? Besides the fact that Rosalinda is totally skeezy." And has terrible taste in men. Teenaged boys? Eesh. I remember what my brother and his friends were like at that age. Let's just say that hygiene wasn't high on their list.

Meredith chewed on a fingernail. "Relationships like that don't tend to be equal. One participant is always the student and one is always the teacher. There's an imbalance in power. When a sexual relationship is imbalanced, well, skeezy is the least unpleasant thing it can be."

"Do you think she's abusing him?" I asked.

"I think the relationship is abusive by its very nature. I also think that Rosalinda is very interested in making sure she's always the one in power in all her relationships." She turned back to Emilia. "She knew you were in her town. She didn't show up at the café when you were working by accident. She felt your presence, as you would feel the presence of a powerful witch moving to your town. She was seeking you out."

Emilia thought about that for a moment. "And if she was? Why is that so bad?"

"It wouldn't have been if she'd been honest with you and told you that. Instead she began your relationship with subterfuge and I doubt anything much has changed."

Emilia started to protest. Meredith held her palm up to stop her. "She wasn't there to teach you. She was there to control you and I'm guessing you've gotten to be more witch than she can handle."

"Do you think it was her plan from the start?" I asked. "To get Emilia to kill those boys?"

Meredith shook her head. "No. I'm sure she was looking for Emilia's weakness from the start. She was undoubtedly looking for ways that she could manipulate her or things that made her weak, like her anger and hatred for the boys who killed her cousin. But there's a piece to the puzzle I'm sure we don't have yet, something that put everything in motion. It doesn't matter, though. We need to figure out a way to turn Rosalinda's manipulations back on her before Emilia ends up dead."

"I won't curse someone again," Emilia said quietly.

"Of course not," I said. I gestured toward her burned arm. "We've all seen how great that works out."

"It's not just that. When I made those dolls . . . I found a darkness inside myself, one I didn't know existed before. When I poured all that hatred into those dolls, I felt that darkness grow."

Meredith took Emilia's hands again. "We all have some darkness in us. Don't be ashamed of it. It's part of all of us. Without the dark, there can be no light. The important thing is that you know it's there. You can learn to use its power—and, make no mistake, it is very powerful. You can't let it reign over you, though. Not without ending up like Rosalinda."

"So what do we do? How do we counteract what Rosalinda is doing?" I asked.

Meredith sat back in the papasan chair and chewed on her lower lip. Emilia sat and looked at her hands.

Norah said, "I have an idea. What if we tried to counteract it with love?"

I put my head in my hands. It was such a typically Norah suggestion. In some ways, I was relieved. She was getting back to being herself. It's what I'd wanted, after all, for things to be like they used to be. On the other hand, her charmingly naïve view of the world still made me want to weep. I looked up, trying to figure out a nice way to tell her that that was one of the stupidest ideas I'd ever heard, to find Meredith and Emilia staring at her, mouths agape.

"Out of the mouths of babes," Meredith said.

"*Claro que si*," Emilia said.

I stared at all three of them and tried to figure out if the entire world had gone crazy.

Which was when my door flew open and Sophie ran in, threw herself in my arms and started to cry.

IT TOOK FIVE MINUTES TO CALM SOPHIE DOWN ENOUGH SO that she could talk. "Are you hurt?" I asked her.

She shook her head.

"Angry?"

Again, a negative.

"Sad?"

Nope. That apparently wasn't it either.

Emilia came in with a cup of tea and handed it to Sophie. She took two sips, sat up straight and said, "I made the delivery."

It took me a few seconds to remember. It was Wednesday. The day she was supposed to go back up into the mountains to deliver the axe to Ginnar.

Meredith sat down next to her. "Tell us all about it."

"Well, I did it just like I did last time. I let the axe guide me. It didn't take me to the same clearing." She looked over at me.

"It's fine. If it worked, it was fine," I reassured her.

She gave me a quick nervous smile. "It worked. It worked great. This time, I set it on the ground like you said. It took about an hour, but he came and got it. And you're not going to believe this part!"

I didn't believe that anything happened that I wouldn't believe. I've been doing this for a while. I've seen a few things. "I'm listening."

"He said thank you!" She clapped her hands together.

I couldn't help but laugh. "You did a great job, Sophie. Just great."

She sprang up and gave me a quick hug. "I've got to go. I've got a Spanish test tomorrow I have to study for."

She was out the door in a flash. We all sat for a moment.

"I have a plan." Emilia said it so quietly, it hardly seemed like much of a declaration, but it stopped all of us in our tracks.

"Do tell." I sat down on the futon couch. I was all ears because I pretty much had nothing. Just because I could figure out how a Messenger should deliver an axe, didn't mean I could figure out how to take down a *bruja*.

"Rosalinda has done her damage. Bossard, Rawley and Littlefield are dead. I can't change that now." She sunk the heels of her hands into her eyes then started to speak again, although her voice was rusty. "I won't let her get rid of me, though. Not this way."

"Okay. But how are you going to make it stop? I don't think we can just tell the cosmic forces that you didn't mean any harm with those dolls. You can't just go into the cemetery at midnight and yell out a 'my bad' and have them say okay."

"I know. I need to put out a different energy to the world. I put a lot of hatred into those dolls. What if I filled a doll with an equivalent amount of love and put that out into the universe? Just like Norah suggested. Maybe it would balance out the hatred."

I looked over at Meredith.

She took a second to think it over, biting ever so gently at her lower lip. Finally, she said, "I've heard of worse plans. Who would you give the doll to?"

"Rosalinda," Emilia said, with no hesitation.

A slow smile spread across Meredith's face. "I like it. Not only are you sending love out into the world, hoping it will come back threefold to yourself, you're also neutralizing some of her hatred and envy by deflecting it with love."

"And respect," Emilia added.

"It's diabolical in its niceness." Meredith chuckled. "What do you need for the doll?"

"Not much," Emilia said. "Some muslin, some thread and some felt."

Fabulous. I could pick all that up at Jo-Ann Fabrics. Maybe they would start a special voodoo doll section over by the scrapbooking supplies.

"What kind of tools will you need?" Meredith asked.

"Not much," Emilia said. "A knife, an egg, some candles. Nothing fancy."

"Any special kind of knife?"

"Not really." She grinned. "Our practices grew under the watchful eye of the Spaniards. We were better off if our tools were things you could find in any kitchen anywhere. It made us safer."

"Anything else?"

She bit her lip. "Yes. I need something of Rosalinda's. Something truly of her. A lock of hair. A fingernail."

"That's going to be fun to get. I don't suppose you have any suggestions on an easy place to pick those items up," I said.

"Sadly, no. Rosalinda is very careful with items from her person and warned me to do the same. It wouldn't be good to have a *bruja* fall under someone else's influence. We'll have to break into her house to get what we need."

I dropped my head back against the couch. "I am so sick of making that drive."

"You're not making it again," Ted said.

"I have to get there somehow." Trust me, if I could teleport or something cool like that, I would do it in a heartbeat. I wouldn't get rid of the Buick, though. I love that car.

"No, you don't. It's a bad idea. You need to stay out of Elmville." Ted was shaking his head.

"I would love to stay out of Elmville. I want to go to Elmville about as much as a vampire wants to go to Gilroy during the Garlic Festival. I don't see that we have a lot of choice."

"You can't go back to Elmville. If Chief Murdock catches you—and make no mistake, she will be watching for you—you are going to end up in jail. If she has anything on you, and I do mean anything, I won't be able to help you. You can't go back there." A vein was pulsing in Ted's forehead. He bit off his words and spit them out, as if they were bitter to the taste.

"Fine. You go, then. When they catch you breaking and entering into Rosalinda's house, how's that going to go down with the powers that be at the Sacramento PD? How high do you think you're going to go in the ranks with a B and E on your record?" I was every bit as steamed as he was. I'm not crazy about being told what I can and cannot do. It's especially frustrating when there's nothing more I'd like to do than take his advice and I know that I can't.

"How do you think it's going to go down when you get caught? Do you really think it's going to be any better?" He threw his hands in the air in exasperation.

I stuck my face right into his. "I'm not going to get caught."

"How do you know?" He wasn't backing down. Not an inch.

"Because I know how to get in and out of a place without anyone noticing me." I have been making deliveries of one kind or another for more than twenty years. While it's often okay to stroll in and hand an item over to whoever's expecting it, it's often wiser not to be so obvious. There is the matter of not everyone wanting my special deliveries. Then there's also the matter of whatever 'Danes might be hanging about. Most 'Danes can't even see a lot of what's around them. Goblins scurry by. Elves and brownies dart in and out. People catch a flicker in the corner of their eye and think they've had their contacts in for too long.

If they see me actually handing an item over . . . well, things become confusing and not in a good way. It's often best if I slip in and out with no one the wiser, 'Cane or 'Dane. I've gotten good at it. As far as I'm concerned, sneaky is the new black.

"Melina, there's got to be a better way."

"There isn't. I will be in and out before anyone even notices that I'm around. Nothing's going to go wrong, and if it does, I will get myself out of it, like I always have."

"Always? Really? Are you forgetting I was there when Alex and Paul took out those Triad hit men?"

"Fine. Almost always," I said. "This is one time that I think a daytime hit is probably a better choice than a nighttime one. I'm going to bed. I think I'm going to need an early start tomorrow."

16

WHEN ALL THIS WAS OVER—AND THAT HAD DAMN WELL BETTER be soon—I was never going to drive to Elmville again. In fact, I might go through all my maps and black Elmville out. Or even cut it out. Then I could burn the little fragments. Norah used to occasionally do that with photos after she broke up with a boyfriend. It seemed to really help her forget them.

I totally wanted to forget Elmville.

I was pretty sure that Elmville totally wanted to forget about me. Perhaps it would be cutting up little photos of me and burning them. More power to it.

I try my best to make my errands as little work as possible. I park as close as I can without crowding the disabled and I very much like the shortest distances that exist between two points. That wasn't going to fly this time.

I needed to not be noticed. The first thing I did was leave the

Buick in the parking lot of the Walmart at the edge of town. The parking lot was big and almost always at least half full. You'd have to be looking for my car there to find it. Sadly, the Walmart was a solid five miles from Rosalinda's house. It was what it was. I threw my backpack on and started to trudge my way along.

I'm a good runner. I'm not a happy runner, but I am a good one. I'm tall enough to have a nice long stride and I can clip along at a pretty decent pace. Running along a road in street clothes with a backpack, however, was going to make me conspicuous. I was all about not being conspicuous at this point. That was going to require some patience, not my strongest suit. I had, however, managed to set the temperature in my car at a comfortable spot on the way down. I could so be taught.

I walked. It wasn't so easy. I kept my head down and the collar of my jacket up. When I got to Rosalinda's neighborhood after what felt like a lifetime of walking, I slowed my steps down. As I walked along, I opened my senses wide. If Rosalinda was home, I thought I'd be able to catch a sense of it before I was on the lawn.

The second I let down those mental walls, I was hit with a wave of something completely foul. Instinctively I slammed the doors of my mind shut again. Hard. Even so, I found myself swaying on my feet, barely able to stand. I looked around. I saw nothing. No one.

I took a few deep breaths to steady myself. Whatever was in that house didn't like me much. Well, maybe not me personally. I didn't get a sense that it was targeted at me in the few brief seconds that the negative energy had rushed through me like a nasty choo-choo train speeding to keep its schedule.

I opened myself again, but this time only a fraction. It was all it took. Rosalinda had certainly armed her home well. I forced myself to not slam shut again. It was a little like trying to breathe through your mouth in a particularly smelly public restroom. It didn't help nearly as much as I needed it to. Being prepared for it did help a little, though. The first wave had been a shock.

I took a few seconds and let myself become accustomed to the trickle of foul and fetid energy rolling out of the house. I didn't sense anything alive, 'Cane or 'Dane. That was something, I guess.

I looked around the neighborhood. It was one of those solid lower-middle-class areas, with tidy ranch houses on well-kept lots. Rosalinda's house was brown, with a brown tile roof, an attached garage and a driveway to the left of the main entrance. There were probably three houses on the block exactly like it. A few certainly looked like they had the same floor plan.

I wondered how many people walked and drove past it every day and never felt the wave of energy I'd felt emanating from it. In the general population, I'd say roughly 8 to 10 percent of people are sensitive to magical and supernatural forces. They may not know how to interpret them or even want to know what they mean, but they feel them.

Even the least sensitive person gets the occasional unexplained chill, which I could probably easily explain to them. Or maybe there's a corner in the basement that they don't like going near or a spot in the park that makes them feel uneasy. They don't know why, but they feel it.

Rosalinda's house was like all those places rolled together. I glanced around her neighborhood. If someone told me that the rate of divorce was higher in this neighborhood than most, I wouldn't be the least bit surprised. I'd bet there were more domestic violence calls, too. I shook my head. How could Emilia have come here without sensing this? What's more, how could she have sent me into it without a warning?

I sighed and trudged around the block, looking for my best way to perform a little breaking and entering while attracting the least amount of attention.

The neighborhood seemed deserted, which was what I'd hoped for. Everyone was at work or at school. Still, discretion would be the better part of valor. There was no need to call any more attention to myself than necessary. Once I'd satisfied myself that no one was watching, I circled back around to Rosalinda's house and slipped up the driveway to the back of the house.

The backyard had a large herb garden. I recognized some of the plants. Even in October in California, a person could still have sage, rosemary and mint growing, and Rosalinda did. A witch's winter garden. How perfectly lovely.

I glanced around. Maybe I wouldn't have to enter the house at all. People left plenty of bits and pieces of themselves around a garden. You can prick yourself on a thorn and leave a few droplets of blood. A hair can snag on a branch. A nail can break while you dig in the soil. There were probably mounds of Rosalinda detritus all around me. I just needed to find them. I opened my senses a tinier crack more.

Apparently I was becoming accustomed to the energy fields around the house. They made me a little nauseous, but I didn't feel like they were going to pound me into the ground anymore. I scanned the garden, hoping to find some sort of witch waste, but nothing presented itself to me and I didn't dare open my senses any wider. If the small amount I was allowing in was making me feel like I'd had one too many margaritas the night before, then opening myself enough to try and find shreds of Rosalinda would have me retching in a corner.

I turned toward the house. I could be in and out in a few minutes. I'd find the bathroom, grab some hair from a hairbrush and be gone before the creepy-crawly sensations seeped into my bones.

At least, that's what I told myself. It wasn't like I had a lot of choices.

Rosalinda had locked all the doors and windows to her house, but she hadn't braced the slider. There's apparently some kind of rule in California that all bedrooms must have sliding doors out onto the back porch. I tried to think of a single solitary house, no matter its size or neighborhood, that didn't have this feature. I failed. It didn't take much to pop the slider off its tracks and slip into Rosalinda's bedroom. A simple broom handle stuck in the track would have made my life significantly more difficult. It also seemed that any witch worth her weight in eye of newt would have a spare broom handle lying around. As it was, I managed to get in with only a broken nail. I'm not exactly a mani-pedi kind of girl anyway. I figured I'd live.

All the blinds were drawn and heavy curtains had been pulled over those. Despite the sunshine outside, the room was dark. I stepped inside slowly. My feet crunched on something in the dim light inside the bedroom. I crouched. There was a powder on the floor. I dabbed a bit up on my finger, sniffed it and then tasted it.

Salt.

My tongue tingled. Not just salt. Salt with a little something extra to it. Rosalinda had been sealing her home against demons. She'd been doing a hell of a better job of it than Norah had been with our apartment, too.

The same 8 to 10 percent of the general population who could sense the supernatural around them could also probably be trained to do some magic. I'm not talking card tricks at kiddie parties either. Something in them, something special, allowed them access to the various forces and powers around us. The other 90 to 92 percent of us—and I include myself in that bunch—couldn't cast a ward to save our lives. Norah was firmly in the no-magic bunch. It's a little like being one of those people who don't have the right enzyme to taste cilantro correctly, except there are more of us and most of us are less aware of it than we are of cilantro.

I hadn't had the heart to tell Norah how completely worthless her protections were. She was doing her best. There was no magic in her, though. None. Zippo. Zero. Nada. Zilch. And along with the other 90 or so percent of us, she could pour salt around our doorsills from now until the end of time and demons would be able to waltz right over them with no problem whatsoever.

Rosalinda's salt, however, was a whole different can of Morton's. It made my tongue tingle. I'd bet it would make something truly demonic writhe in agony. What exactly had she been messing with that she needed this kind of protection at her home? Or was it just a routine security thing for a *bruja*? I'd have to ask Emilia when I got home.

Normally I would have given my eyes a few more seconds to adjust to the lack of light inside the house, but I wanted out of there as fast as I could. I was keeping all the negative forces at bay, but it was costing me. It was a constant fight to keep myself sealed off, allowing only a trickle of what was there in. It was a little like wandering blind through a forest. The likelihood of me bumping into something I didn't like was high. Still, I didn't want to linger.

I made my way toward a door that I hoped was to the master bathroom. It would be the best place to find some bits and pieces of Rosalinda to take to Emilia for her doll. Something snagged at my hair. I sprang away, landing in a fighting crouch.

A dreamcatcher hung in the doorway. I nearly laughed. Of all the cheesy tourist trap items to find in a bona fide *bruja's* house. A dreamcatcher. You could buy one in almost any store anywhere near any Native American population. Half of them were probably made in China these days. They were nothing but a meaningless gesture meant to reassure little children that they wouldn't have bad dreams. I knocked it to one side and went into the bathroom.

Jackpot.

It was like a cornucopia of Rosalinda remnants. There was hair in the hairbrush and nail clippings in the trash can. I thought about taking a toothbrush for good measure, but then decided against it. She'd miss that. I was pretty sure I could put the slider back on its track, and if I could, it was possible she'd never even know I'd been there. I gathered up my booty and headed out.

I ducked past the dreamcatcher and stepped over the salt. I was popping the slider back into place when the first crow hit the window next to me. With most of my senses shut down tight, I hadn't had any warning. Just a sense of something flying way too close to my ear and then the thud as it hit the glass. It was dead before it hit the ground, its head canted at an unnatural angle.

I was still staring at it, lying dead there on the porch, wondering if it meant something, when the second crow headed straight at my head. I ducked. It hit the glass, too, also with enough force to kill it instantly.

Not everything in life is an omen. Weird things happen. Funny coincidences occur that mean nothing. Little synchronicities pop up, but they signify nothing. One of the dangers inherent in being a Messenger is to read too much into what's going on. A black cat crossing your path might mean that the cat wanted to go lie in the sun on the other side of the street. Not everything means some nefarious goings-on are about to come to a head. Sometimes birds fly into windows and break their necks.

Occasionally two birds fly into a window and break their necks. Rarely, rarely, do three birds fly into windows after only missing your head because you have damn fine reflexes and know how to duck after hours of your sensei swinging kendo sticks at you and then break their necks.

I had a feeling that I hadn't made it in and out undetected. So much for my super-secret Messenger moves. I wondered if I'd be able to get out of this without telling Ted. Then another bird flew at my head and I stopped wondering about anything except the fastest way to get to the Buick without getting my eyes pecked out.

I stopped worrying about being inconspicuous, too, and ran. On my way past the garden, I grabbed a stake and began swinging it around my head to ward off the cloud of crows that had descended into Rosalinda's yard.

I jumped over the gate and onto the street and took off, still waving the garden stake. I hit the corner and turned. The birds were flying after me. I took a moment, choked up my hands on the stake, made sure my right elbow was level and started swinging.

I hadn't played Little League but Patrick had, and Dad used to take us to the batting cages now and then. Patrick needed to work on his swing, and I thought it was fun. This was totally the same deal but without the warm summer night vibe and I doubted anyone would buy me a sno-cone afterward. I took out at least fifteen birds in quick succession and then when there was a break in the flow, I turned and ran again.

There were fewer crows, but I still had at least two miles to go to get back to the Buick. I went to my next turn and then whipped around to face the birds. I brandished my garden stake and I could swear the flock slowed a little. Then another one charged. I took it out. The next two came together, though, requiring me to go with a forward swing followed by a backhand. Why, oh why, had Patrick not taken up tennis?

Three charged me at once now. I took them all out, but one of them managed to slice at my face, drawing blood. I wasn't going to wait around for them to get even smarter. I turned and ran faster, my backpack bouncing against me, my stake still waving in the air.

I turned again at the next turn. After this, I'd only have one more turn before I got back to the Walmart parking lot. The flock was gone. There was nothing behind me. It was just me, in batting stance with my garden stake, blood dripping from my cheek and feathers in my hair.

That's when I heard the sirens.

I WAS BACK IN THE INTERROGATION ROOM AT THE STANISLAUS County Jail. I wasn't thrilled with the place, but I really appreciated the lack of windows in the room. The last thing I needed was to be questioned while crows flung themselves against the windows, trying to rip my flesh off my bones while I still breathed.

"I thought I told you to stay out of my town." Chief Murdock had a funny smile on her face. If I hadn't known better, I would have sworn she had something to do with that crowd of crows.

"I don't think you're allowed to do that," I said, trying to sound reasonable in what was clearly not a reasonable situation. "I think you have to have actual legal grounds to ban a person or to create a restraining order."

"You're right. I don't have the evidence I need to do that. However, I seriously don't like you and really don't want you in my town." She said it with just a bit of a smile. If you watched our conversation on mute, you might think she had actually said that she liked my haircut. Which was unlikely, considering what battle with a flock of crows can do with a girl's do, even if it's a relatively simple braid. I'd had a nice neat braid running down my back when I'd started. I now looked like one of those pictures of models in those books that they have at the hairdressers, the ones that make you wonder why on earth anyone would allow someone else to do that to their hair.

In addition to having bad hair, the remark stung. What was there not to like about me? I bathe on a regular basis, brush my teeth, say please and thank you. I'm a doll. "Well, I like you, Chief Murdock, and I think if we tried, we could be friends."

"What were you doing at the intersection of Baker and Third?" She glanced at her notes to get the street names. "And why were you being attacked by a flock of crows?"

"I was walking back to Walmart . . ." I began.

"From where?" She interrupted.

I sighed. It was a good question. I would have asked the same thing. "Around," I said, which I thought was a stellar answer, given the circumstances.

"What were you doing walking around Elmville? I told you to stay out of my town." She didn't look very friendly now. She had her lips pressed together tighter than a lid on a leprechaun's pot of gold.

"And I thought I explained that you are on pretty shaky legal ground," I answered.

"Are you always this much of a smart-ass?"

I thought for a second. "Pretty much. Yes."

Murdock dropped her head in her hands. "What was the business with the crows? We had at least three phone calls about a woman being chased down the street by a flock of crows."

"That I can't tell you. Apparently I'm irresistible to certain kinds of wildlife in your town."

That's when things got weird. Chief Murdock started to giggle. "Did you really bat them out of the air with that garden stake you were carrying?"

I was glad she was finding it amusing. Confused, but glad. I nodded.

"Percy Bainbridge thought we ought to get some scouts for the Giants out here. He said you were taking them out two or three at a time." She gasped out between brays of laughter. "He thought you could take Frank Lewis's place in the lineup."

"I did what I could."

Now she was banging the table with the flat of her hand. "Kept your eye on the birdie, did you?"

There was something so infectious about Chief Murdock's laughter that I found myself starting to snicker, too. "It's not funny," I protested, still giggling. "They were going for my eyes."

That sent her over the edge. She rocked back and forth, laughing while tears ran down her face. "Why?" she finally asked. "Why me? Why my town? What the hell are you and how can I get you to go away?"

The question seemed rhetorical, so I opted not to answer.

IN THE END, CHIEF MURDOCK LET ME GO WITH NOTHING MORE than a warning, gasped between wild gales of laughter that I felt had a touch of a hysterical squeal to the tail of them. She would not dispatch a car to take me back to the Buick, which I thought was the tiniest bit spiteful, especially since she had clearly told everyone to keep an eye on me. I couldn't even run back to the car because a squad car was lurking behind every other corner.

Well, lurking would imply a certain amount of subterfuge. They were sitting there, watching me walk back to my car.

It did, however, give me a little time to think.

Once Emilia made the doll, it was going to be tough to deliver. Obviously Rosalinda was prepared for any kind of attack. It was definitely going to be a tricky one.

To save me from having to drive all the way back to Sacramento with my spoils, Meredith and Emilia were waiting for me at a hotel in Modesto. I knocked on the door and they let me in.

"You got it?" Meredith asked. "All of it?"

I nodded.

"What happened to your hair?"

"You don't want to know," I said. I'd tried to brush it out once I got to the Buick, but it was going to take a good, thorough shampooing to make it right again. "I promised Ted I'd call in."

I dialed his cell. He picked up on the first ring.

"How did it go?" he asked.

"It wasn't the smoothest operation I've ever pulled off, but it's done."

There was a hesitation on the other end. "What went wrong?"

I gave him a quick summing up of my morning's adventures. When I got to the part about the crows chasing me down the street, Meredith was slapping her hands on the hotel desk and snorting. It was not one of her more ladylike moves.

"You're not delivering the doll," he said flatly, when I was done.

That wasn't happening. "Of course I'm delivering the doll. This whole exercise will be pointless if I don't."

"I didn't mean it wasn't going to get delivered. I meant that you weren't going to be the one who delivered it. I'll do it."

"We've been over this before, Ted. It's not your job. It's mine."

"Not this time. It's not like I'll be breaking into her house, anyway. It won't be a big deal. I'll drop it on her doorstep and it will be done."

"What about Drew and his thugs? What about Chief Murdock?" I countered.

"Melina, you're not seeing this clearly. They're all focused on you. I'm collateral damage. If you're not there, nothing's going to bother me."

I was too tired to argue with him anymore. Plus, I had bird poo and feathers stuck in my hair. That tends to make me cranky. I hung up the phone, took a shower and then crawled into one of the beds to take a nap while Meredith and Emilia worked on the doll. Their murmurs were actually comforting. As I dozed off, the room seemed to fill with warmth. Not that horrible hotel room heat, either. More like the heat of a warm bath.

I woke up with Meredith shaking me. "It's done," she said, beaming. She gave my forehead a little kiss.

I was about to protest, but when I looked up at her, my heart was filled with such gratitude for having such a wonderful friend, I decided to let it go. "It's ready, then?"

She nodded.

"Okay. I'll get dressed and deliver it. The sooner, the better."

"Hang on there, Tiger," Ted said.

I blinked a few times. Ted was here. "How long have I been asleep?" I was getting a very Rip Van Winkle-ish vibe.

"A couple hours," Emilia said. "You looked very sweet as you slept, almost angelic."

I started to roll my eyes and then didn't. It was nice of Emilia to say that. She was such a sweet person. Really, I was lucky to have met her even though the circumstances weren't ideal.

Then it hit me. "Wait a gosh-darned minute," I said. "Is that love doll in here?"

All three of them smiled at me and nodded. "It came out really well," Meredith said. "Emilia's very talented."

"Get it out of here." I got up out of the bed and started getting dressed. "Put it out in my car. Wrap it in something first."

Meredith blinked several times. "Why?"

"Don't you see? It's getting to us. The doll is messing with our feelings. I'm filled with all these thoughts of warmth and love and respect for all of you. Get it out." I went to the sink to splash water on my face.

I turned around and they were all still standing there smiling at me. "You're so cute when you're riled up," Ted said.

I rolled my eyes and got my car keys. "Give me the doll. I'm going."

"I don't think so." He held up his hand like he was stopping traffic. "We've decided. I'm going. I'll be back in an hour, maybe less."

He was already holding the doll. I weighed my options. I could take him. I knew I could. I could get the doll from him and be out the door before any one of the three of them could do anything about it.

It would hurt Ted's feelings terribly, though. What damage would it do to our relationship? I couldn't risk it. I held up my hands in surrender.

"Okay. You take it. We'll wait here."

I DIDN'T START GETTING NERVOUS UNTIL TED HAD BEEN GONE for two hours. "He should be back by now. It's only thirty minutes there." Even allowing for a difficult delivery, he should have been back a half hour earlier.

"Stop pacing, Melina. It's not going to help anything." Meredith patted the bed next to her. "Sit down."

"He could be in trouble. We should go." I started pulling on my boots. I looked out the hotel room window. It had started to get dark. I missed summer, when it would stay light until late in the evening.

Meredith put her hand on my arm. "What kind of trouble?"

"I don't know! Chief Murdock. Flocks of crows. Teenaged thugs. There are a lot of choices here." Who knew what kinds of things Rosalinda could cook up? "I should never have let him go. It was that stupid doll. It was filling me with all kinds of feelings of respect and love."

Emilia looked at Meredith. "She's right. It's been too long. Maybe we should go."

I stared at her. She'd been quiet for a long time. "What's wrong?"

She shook her head. "I'm not sure."

"But something is."

"I'm afraid so. Something has gone wrong."

"How do you know?"

Emilia sighed. "When you make a doll like that, it's not just part of the other person that gets put into the doll. Part of yourself is in there, too. When something happens with the doll, you . . . feel it."

"You felt some of what happened to Bossard, Rawley and Littlefield?" I asked.

She nodded. "And I feel something now."

"That's it. We're out of here."

Meredith didn't try to stop me this time.

17

WE DROVE BY ROSALINDA'S HOUSE. IT WAS EMPTY. NO CARS in the driveway. No lights in the window. No sense of anyone or anything in it.

It was fully dark now and the wind had picked up. I felt chilled and not just physically.

"The cemetery, I think." Emilia looked at me. "I'm so sorry."

"If she's there, we can't just barge in." The cemetery would be a place of power for Rosalinda. She drew some of her magic from there and being there would make her even stronger. "We need a plan."

Emilia nodded. "Let me go in first. I'll walk in so she sees me. It will distract her. You and Meredith can slip in unnoticed and help me if I need it."

It wasn't much of a plan. It sounded reasonable, but my thoughts were clouded with worries about Ted. "What do you think she's doing?" I asked.

Emilia shook her head. "I have no idea, but I don't think it's good."

We parked the Buick a few blocks away from the cemetery and made our way separately on foot, with Emilia walking in the front gates bold as brass. Meredith and I split up. She was looking for a side gate. I didn't bother. I vaulted into the cemetery over the fence. My fear for Ted was growing by the second.

I crept from tree to tree, ducking behind the large monuments, staying close to the ground. I could hear Emilia marching her way in, making no attempt at subterfuge. I hoped the noise she made masked any sign of my entrance and Meredith's as well.

It only took a few minutes to figure out which direction to go. I could see a little pocket of light ahead of me and to my right. I made my way toward it as silently as I could.

Cemeteries at night are always creepy. It doesn't matter how modern the cemetery is, how uniform the graves are or anything else. They're just creepy. They always are. I am used to ghosts and goblins, and I am well aware that just because a person is dead doesn't mean they're out to get you and I still avoid going into cemeteries at night.

Cemeteries are even more creepy when someone has lit a ring of black candles on a relatively fresh grave site and has placed a skull with a candle jammed into it in the center of that circle. Maybe it's the way the candlelight flickers and casts moving shadows across the ground or the way it lights just a few things, making the pockets of darkness all that much more intense. I don't know. I just know it's creepy.

If the person who made the ring of candles is dressed in a long white robe knotted with a rope and has a young man kneeling before her while she holds a knife to his throat, it ups the creepy factor considerably.

It makes my heart almost stop in my chest when I see my boyfriend lying facedown in the dirt with his hands and feet bound.

Suffice it to say, then, that when we found Rosalinda, her left hand fisted into Drew Bossard's hair as he knelt in front of her and her right hand holding a knife to his throat, all while surrounded by a ring of black candles with a skull in the center of the ring, I was officially creeped out. Gooseflesh stood up all over my body. The hair on the back of my neck stood at attention and my flesh buzzed with recognition of magic in the air.

I watched Ted's back rise and fall, so I knew he was still breathing. I needed to get to him, but there were yards of open space between him and me. My panic rose.

Emilia, however, seemed totally calm. I wasn't sure if that made me feel better or worse.

"I knew you'd come." Rosalinda smiled. The warmth and welcome of her smile chilled me. "I see you've brought friends. Come out, come out, wherever you are."

So much for the surprise attack. I stepped out from behind the tree.

"Nice to meet you in person, Ms. Markowitz."

"I'd say the pleasure was mine, but I'm trying to give up lying." I smiled right back at her, but I kept my eye on the knife. It never wavered from Drew's throat. I couldn't let myself be distracted by her seductive voice, though. I could get to Ted before she could get to him with the knife, but then what? There was no way I could get him away from her before she could get to us with the knife. My focus didn't go undetected.

"Do you like my knife?" she asked.

"It's lovely." What can I say? I like a nice piece of cutlery. "How's the balance on it?" I held my hand out, as if she might give it to me so that I could test the heft.

She laughed. "Really? That's your best effort?"

I shrugged. "Nah. Just an opening gambit. It never hurts to try, you know?"

"I disagree. Sometimes it can hurt quite a bit." She turned the knife ever so slightly and nicked Drew. He cried out. Rosalinda merely tightened her grip on his hair. "Hush, love. Now's not the time to make a fuss."

"Rosalinda," Emilia said. "Let the boy go. Please."

Rosalinda laughed. It was a surprisingly pretty laugh, considering the circumstances. Musical, even. It wasn't an evil mwa-ha-ha or even a hysterical laugh with a squeal at the end. She sounded genuinely amused. Personally, I didn't think it was all that funny. "Why would I do that, Emilia?"

"Because he has no part in this. Not really." Emilia sounded so calm. I was pretty sure my voice would come out a little squeaky and shaky if I tried to speak.

"But he's where it began, Emilia." Rosalinda leaned forward and kissed the top of Drew's head. "Didn't it, Drew? Didn't it begin with you?"

"I'm so sorry. I didn't know." Drew's voice sounded like what I thought mine would sound like, more than a little quavery.

"Don't be like that, sweetheart. No regrets now. That's the best way to live."

She had a point, but I didn't think she meant it quite the same way Aunt Kitty did when she was trying to talk me into buying a pair of boots at Macy's Presidents' Day Sale.

"Drew came to me. His brother had come home. You know the one. Neil Bossard? One of the ones who killed your cousin? I think he may have even been the one who gave the final kick to Jorge's head, the one that truly finished him off." Rosalinda's voice had an almost singsong quality to it. She swayed a little as she spoke. Drew swayed with her as she pulled him back and forth by his hair, the knife right at his throat.

"I know him," Emilia said between gritted teeth. At least she didn't sound freaky calm anymore. It made me feel a little better.

"That's right. You know him quite well. You made him that special doll with his hair and fingernail clippings. It's an intimate process, isn't it, Emilia? It makes a connection between you and that person. Were you surprised by that?" Rosalinda smiled at her.

"You were my *mentora*. You should have warned me. You should have told me." Anger tinged Emilia's voice.

"Where would the fun have been in that?" Rosalinda laughed again. "You have no idea how much I enjoyed watching you suffer through that. Oh, the tears that ran down your face onto those dolls!"

"I thought you were helping me heal myself," Emilia accused.

"I know! Wasn't that beautiful? When all the time I was going to use those dolls to kill you," Rosalinda said.

"Wait a minute," I broke in, and surprised myself with the strength in my voice. "Why did you want to kill Emilia? I thought you were her teacher?"

Rosalinda's face sobered in an instant. "I was. She was a most promising pupil. I knew she would be. I felt her power the moment she came into my town. I knew she would be an incredible *bruja*, strong and compassionate. People would come from miles around for her help."

"So why try to kill her?"

"Because this is my town!" Rosalinda screamed. Her hand clutched tighter in Drew's hair, and he screamed out in pain as the knife bit into his throat for an instant. "My town! I tell you. Mine! Why should I let some simple girl from the backcountry come and take my town from me? That's what she was doing, you know. Taking my town. Taking all I'd worked for for so long. All I heard was how Emilia had helped this one stop drinking or made that one stop beating his wife or cured a rash or calmed an ulcer."

Meredith had been right. It all came down to envy and territory. "You started this because you were jealous?" I asked.

Rosalinda chuckled. "I wish I could take credit, but I can't. This one started it." She yanked on Drew's hair again. He moaned. "Couldn't stand to have big brother back, could you? It was bad enough that your parents had used up every dime of their money trying to keep him from going to jail. Every cent of the money that was to send you to college, to get you out of this town, to buy you fancy cars and computers and trinkets, had gone to their failed effort to defend him. Now he was home and everyone was acting like he was some kind of hero. You didn't kick an innocent man to death for walking with a white girl. You didn't call him a spic or a beaner or a wetback. Where were the dinners in your honor? Where were the hugs and the praise? Like always, they all went to Neil, didn't they? Poor little Drew. He came to me. He wanted his brother gone, out of the way, for good. And I knew just how to do it without getting my hands dirty." Rosalinda looked satisfied.

"You got Emilia to make the dolls that would curse them," I said.

"Oh, yes. I made sure she saw those boys strutting around town as if they owned it. I whispered in her ear about how unfair it was that they should be living and laughing while her poor cousin rotted in the earth. Who wouldn't be angry? Who wouldn't want revenge? Even our sainted Emilia is human underneath it all, aren't you, *cara*?"

"Too human," she said, her voice soft. "I hated those boys. I hated them for what they had done. I hated them for having so much handed to them on a silver platter. I hated them for taking what little poor Jorge had and spitting on it. I hated this town for creating them, for making the monsters that thought it was good sport to kill a boy because his skin was a different color than theirs. I hated that they'd gotten so little punishment in light of what they'd done. I had so much hate."

Rosalinda cocked her head, her face full of sympathy. "You did. You had so much hate. It was poisoning you. You couldn't sleep. You couldn't eat. Your work suffered. Remember when Margo came to you with that rash? It should have been simple for a *curandera* like yourself to heal it, but you couldn't make it go away, could you? It just stayed and stayed, just like those boys staying and staying."

Tears rolled down Emilia's cheeks. "Yes. My hate. It tainted everything I touched. It made my food taste bitter. It gave me dreams of blood and revenge. I came to you, my *mentora*, for help."

"And I did help, didn't I? I gave you someplace to put that hate to get it out of you, out of your system." Rosalinda smiled.

Emilia nodded, tears still streaming from her eyes. "You did. You showed me how to take all that hate and pour it into something else and then you and I came here together and buried them in the cemetery under the full moon. They would rest here with the dead and no harm would come to anyone."

"And on the next full moon, I came and dug them up! It was so simple, so beautiful. All I had to do was have them delivered to their rightful recipients and everything would be set in motion. That's where you came in, Melina. I heard about you. A person who makes deliveries. No questions asked, but that's not how it worked, was it? You started asking questions." Rosalinda made a tsking noise. "See where that gets you?"

Apparently in a cemetery under a full moon, hoping you can

stop the murder of a young, if not terribly innocent, man. "Sorry about that. I'll make sure I edit my ad in the supernatural yellow pages next time."

"Well, as sorry as you are, Drew here is going to be sorrier. You ruined everything, you know." Rosalinda caressed the side of Drew's jaw with the flat of the knife. "The second you made the doll, I felt it. I felt what you'd done. Now he's going to die and it will be all your fault."

"Why does he have to die?" Emilia stepped forward.

Rosalinda laughed. "Because I love him now." She turned the knife and slid it along the side of his cheek. Drew screamed and a long, thin line of red appeared on his cheek.

I ignored the blood. I am not terribly squeamish. Working as a filing clerk in the emergency room will root out the delicate and weak-stomached pretty quickly. As long as the body fluids don't spray directly on me, I'm generally okay.

Cruelty, however, turns my stomach. Maybe it's a general feeling that mean people suck, but seeing someone deliberately inflicting pain on another makes me queasy. Go figure.

"You're upset," Rosalinda said, her mouth pursed. Her face looked sympathetic. It was hard to take her concern as sincere when she was tipping Drew forward to let his blood drip into a bowl set on the ground next to him.

"A little."

"Not nearly as much as Emilia is, though." Rosalinda smiled at her former student again. "You thought you could undo all of what you've done with one little doll?"

"I'll never be able to undo what I've done." Emilia hung her head. "I'd hoped to balance it out."

"Ah, yes, balance and harmony. That's always your goal, isn't it, Emilia?" Rosalinda asked.

Emilia nodded. It didn't sound all bad to me. There were plenty of days I wished I had a little balance and harmony going.

"Here's the thing about balance, Emilia, I believe in it, too. You're always looking at the little details, though. Is the head balanced with the heart? Is the liver balanced with the lungs? You have to look at the bigger picture. Without the darkness, light has no meaning. Without sour, there is no sweet. And without hate, there is no love. Did you think about that when you tried to destroy my hatred, Emilia? Did you think of the consequences of that?"

Emilia shook her head.

"Of course not. You never think in the big picture. You have a lot to learn yet, *mi hija*. Did you think of what it would mean for me to have to love this pathetic excuse of a man?" She shook Drew's head again. He whimpered. "The thought of it disgusts me and yet here I am, feeling a tightness in my chest every time I look at him. His own hate has been sucked dry now. He got his revenge on his brother, on his parents, on his town and it wasn't the tasty dish he bargained for, was it, Drew?"

"No," he whimpered. "No. If I could take it back, I would."

Rosalinda laughed her beautiful trill of a laugh again. "Oh, it's much too late for that, *mi querido*. Much, much too late."

"If you love him, then let him go, Rosalinda. I beg you. Let us stop this. No one else needs to get hurt." Emilia stepped forward.

"It's not that easy, Emilia. You may be able to manipulate my feelings. You may be able to force me to feel this love." She said the last word as if it literally left a bad taste in her mouth. "But I can still see the big picture. I'm not a naïve little simpleton like you. I won't be manipulated like this. Luckily, you brought me access to so much more hatred." She shook Drew by the head again. "Get me the doll, Drew."

He whimpered again.

"I said get it!" She whipped his head back and in a lightning flash cut his other cheek.

Drew screamed and pulled a voodoo doll from his pocket. He held it in front of him with trembling hands.

"Dip it in the blood," she directed him.

Drew lowered the doll's feet into the bowl that held his blood next to him. A second later, I was on my knees. My feet felt as if they'd been burned away from beneath me. I didn't remember shrieking, but the echo of my own scream rang in my ears.

"You left a few souvenirs when you broke into my home, Melina." Rosalinda smiled at me.

I cursed myself. Of course, the dreamcatcher that had caught at my hair. The broken nail when I'd popped the sliding glass door off its track. Not to mention the blood and hair the crows could have brought home.

"You have plenty of hate in you, don't you? Although yours takes such an interesting twist, doesn't it?" She smiled at me and then forced Drew's hand down again so that the doll with my hair and my fingernails dipped into the bowl of blood again.

Even prepared as I was for the pain, I cried out again. I shut down my senses as hard as I could. Still, the pain seared up through my flesh like a fire that burned me from the inside out, sucking the air from my lungs. She let Drew lift his hand and the pain stopped. I fell the rest of the way to the ground, gasping in air.

"You don't like yourself very much, do you, Melina?" she asked, as if she hadn't just reduced me to a puddle on the ground. "Or, at least, you don't like what you are. It embarrasses you. It shames you. Yet it is who you are at your very core. Tricky emotional waters to navigate, certainly, aren't they?"

"Let her go," Emilia said.

"Who's going to make me?" Rosalinda laughed, and now, finally, I could hear the tinge of madness to it.

"I will," Emilia said. She rushed to my side and put her hands on me.

Every place she touched burned. I writhed away from her.

"Self-hatred is a tricky one, isn't it? It's so hard to accept ourselves as we are, with all our faults and foibles. You're much more forgiving of the people around you than you are of yourself, Melina. You should try to use that same compassion for yourself." She dipped the doll again. The pain sliced into me once more, shooting through my body like flames, eating me from the inside until I thought my heart would burst.

"Others love her," I heard Emilia say. "Many others."

"She does her best to deflect it, not to accept it. She keeps them all at arm's length, even her own family."

My mind was going fuzzy with the pain, but even so I knew she had a point.

"I love her," Ted said.

How sad. I was going to hear his voice as I was tortured to death and I wouldn't be able to tell him how much better it had made me feel. I mean, it didn't lessen the pain any, but it somehow made it seem as if it were happening to someone else.

"I love her, too," Meredith said.

I had sort of known that. I had at least suspected that she liked me okay. Loved? Well, I was useful to her. Maybe I was something more?

"I love her, too." Another voice chimed in.

Now that surprised me. Clearly the pain was making me hallucinate. I could have sworn I heard Norah. I didn't expect to hallucinate that Norah was there while I died. In fact, she was about the last person I thought I would wish into the situation, but that was clearly her voice that I was hearing. Or manufacturing.

"Isn't that sweet?" Rosalinda asked Drew, tipping his head back to expose his throat a little more. "Her little friends came here, too. I don't think they'll be able to help much, though, do you? They have no magic. Not a shred. Silly of her to waste her time with . . . what does she call them? 'Danes?"

That was weird. Was Rosalinda hearing my hallucinations? Had she linked herself to me psychically with the doll enough that she could hear my thoughts?

"Then there's me," a deep voice said. "I'm quite fond of her as well."

I knew that voice all too well.

Rosalinda hissed. "Vampire."

"Yep. That's me. Your friendly neighborhood bloodsucker at your service," Alex said.

It began to dawn on me that I wasn't hallucinating. I would totally have read all of them the riot act if excruciating pain wasn't forcing me to keep my jaws clenched.

"Good luck doing anything with that. She's closed tight as a drum," Rosalinda said.

A decidedly leaky drum, since I could feel her magic seeping through.

"She's right," Emilia said. She laid her hands on me again. I cried out in pain. Every spot she touched burned like it was being thrust directly into the flames. "I know it hurts. You have to open yourself to us. We can help you fight her, but not if you don't open yourself to us."

Open myself? Was she crazy? I had all my defenses up at DEFCON 1 and I couldn't even stand up. If I opened myself, I'd be reduced to nothing. I'd incinerate on the ground in front of them. Not only would I be gone, but it would probably scar them all for life. Well, except for Alex, who really didn't have a life. He'd still be really sad.

"You have to, Melina. Stop fighting us. Start fighting her. Use us. Use our love to fight the hatred."

I could feel the four of them battering at my defenses. I shook my head. I couldn't do it. They weren't strong enough. We couldn't defeat her, not when she was using my own emotions against me.

"Please, Melina, let us help." Norah. It was Norah. Poor sweet Norah, who hadn't asked for any of this in her life. Norah, who'd been so scared for the past six months that she'd barely been able to leave the apartment, was in a cemetery during a full moon trying to help me face down a pissed-off *bruja*.

I supposed the least I could do was try to let her help. I let my walls down a fraction. If I had thought the pain was searing before, it was because I'd had no idea how much worse it could get. It thundered at me, through me, around me. My skin stung like a thousand angry bees had covered me. My lungs burned as if I were trying to breathe in fire. A twisting agony roiled my guts. Somehow, though, deep down inside, I found a kernel of peace.

"We're there, Melina. Fight for us. Fight with us," Meredith urged.

"Please, Melina," Ted said. "Don't give up. Stay. Stay with us."

A cold hand touched my forehead. I knew it was Alex.

I dug for the kernel. I fought down through the swirling pain to find it and hold it. It was such a tiny place of peace in the cacophony of pain that hammered at me. How could it do any good? How could it make any difference?

"Don't give up," Ted said. "Stay. Stay here."

Rosalinda laughed and the pain grew in intensity.

"Open the doors, Melina," Emilia urged. "Trust us."

I didn't think I could get myself to open to such agony. If Rosalinda could inflict this much pain when my defenses were half up, how bad could it get?

On the other hand, maybe it would be like pulling off a bandage. The pain would be intense, but only for a few moments. Then either it would kill me, in which case it would be over, or I would be able to fight back, in which case it would be over.

It was a lose-lose proposition turned on its head into a win-win one. One way or the other, I'd be out of pain soon. I grabbed hold of someone's hands. I don't even know whose they were, just that they belonged to somebody who cared about me.

Then I dropped everything.

Every wall to my self was down. Every door and window was open. I let all my defenses drop. Everything. The pain that rushed in was excruciating. Knives twisted in my gut. Fire ran through my veins. My head felt like it would split in two. I was afraid that my heart was going to burst and then I wished it would because the agony would be over.

On some level, I was aware of my friends still around me, but the physical world seemed terribly distant. All I knew was the pain. I gave myself over to it. I let myself swirl down in the dark whirlpool of agony, ready to drown in its choking, reeking maw.

Just as I was about to let go, something pulled me back.

It was that little kernel of peace. Like a bright flickering light at the end of an extremely long, dark tunnel, it beckoned to me. I reached for it with my mind, worried that it was a mirage, some kind of illusion that I had created out of whole cloth. It was there, though. It was real.

It was hard to focus. The pain kept pulling me toward it like a magnetic force. The flickering light so far away receded a little farther. I couldn't reach it. The blackness would swallow me whole. I was sorry that Ted, Norah, Alex and Emilia would have to watch it. I doubted it would be a pretty death. It couldn't hurt any more than what was happening now, though.

I didn't have the strength to fight it, but the kernel of peace did. It reached for me. It grew on its own. I marshaled my forces. I didn't have much strength left. I made one last major effort to reach toward that light and away from the swirling chaos of darkness that wanted to rip me to shreds.

It grew more. The pain receded. It didn't go away. Not by any means. But for a moment I could breathe again. I reached more. It grew more.

Inch by inch, I moved closer to the light and the pain loosened its grip on me. I was so close. I could almost reach it. I stretched as far as I could stretch to touch it.

It's hard to describe what happened next. I touched the light. I touched the kernel of peace that my friends had created to pull me out of the jaws of death and torture.

It was like touching lightning.

Everything around me sizzled and popped. I snapped back into my corporeal self, but now everything was flooded with light. It was as if a thousand lamps had been lit. I stood. The pain was gone. Vanished. As if it had never been. I could feel electricity coursing and snapping through my system as the pain and chaos had moments before.

I turned to Rosalinda and pointed at her. "Back off, bitch." A jolt of electricity shot from me and hit her square in the chest.

Rosalinda stumbled backward, but she didn't let go of Drew's hair or lose her grip on the knife.

I stepped toward her. "I said to back off." I zapped her again.

In the sizzle's aftermath, I heard the faint sound of sirens. Fabulous. Why was it always sirens? Didn't Chief Murdock have anything better to do? Rosalinda still didn't let go of Drew. She wasn't looking so good, though. She was shaking now and a little pale.

"Let him go, Rosalinda." I walked toward her and kicked one of her black candles out of the way. She sagged a little.

"The cops are coming," I said. "They'll be here soon."

"And what?" She sneered. "You'll tell them that I talked Emilia into cursing those boys? I think you'll end up locked up in the loony bin before I end up locked in a jail."

She had a point.

"I think they might want you on charges of kidnapping at the moment," Ted said from behind me. "I doubt Drew's here of his own free will. Are you, Drew?"

Drew shook his head.

I kicked over another candle and kicked dirt over the circles that had been drawn on the ground in salt. "Let him go, Rosalinda."

"And then what?" she asked. "You'll let me go? We'll all walk away from this like nothing ever happened?"

"I don't know." What would happen? What could happen? I couldn't just let her go. She had dabbled in things she shouldn't and it had tainted her. I couldn't allow her to simply walk away.

The sirens were closer now. I kicked the third candle down and squished the flame out under my boot. Drew began to struggle against Rosalinda in earnest now. I'd been right. He had been too docile earlier. The circle had held him in check as much as Rosalinda's knife had.

I zapped her again. She sagged and stumbled but still didn't loosen her hold.

Suddenly Rosalinda was framed in the beam of a high-powered flashlight. "Freeze!"

The cops had arrived. I kicked over the fourth candle. Drew reared back and twisted. Rosalinda let him go, but she still held the knife.

"Set the knife down, ma'am." It was Chief Murdock. I had a bad feeling we weren't going to have a friendly chat about this one after it was over.

Rosalinda smiled. "No," she said. "I won't."

"Just set it down, ma'am. No one will get hurt."

"No." She shook her head. "I don't think so."

"Drop the knife, and we can all go back to the station house and have a nice long talk. I'm sure we can sort this out."

Rosalinda laughed her lovely trilling laugh. "You're sure, are you?"

"Yes, ma'am. I'm sure. I've found there's very little we can't sort out by talking it over, but we can't talk it over while you're holding the knife."

Rosalinda nodded as if she understood. Then she raised the knife and slit her own throat.

THINGS GOT A LITTLE CHAOTIC AFTER THAT. SOMEONE THREW me to the ground and handcuffed me. Norah, Meredith, Emilia and Ted got similar treatment. Alex had disappeared. Sometimes being a vampire was a good thing. Melting into the night was pretty much one of their specialties.

I was hauled to my feet and summarily shoved into the back of a cop car, but no one closed the door. There were lots of cop cars and ambulances. Drew was taken away to a hospital, presumably. I was pretty sure that Rosalinda's knife work was going to leave some permanent marks. He'd carry the scars of his dalliance with her to his grave and not just the ones on his face. There are things that leave marks soul-deep and I was pretty sure that Drew's alliance with Rosalinda was one of those things.

So I waited in the back of the cop car. I wiggled my hands in the air a few times but couldn't come up with much more than some static electricity. I didn't feel any different either. What I felt mostly was tired. Seriously bone tired.

Eventually Chief Murdock came over to chat with me. "Hey, Melina," she said. She sounded remarkably calm.

"Hey, yourself. Everybody okay over there?" I gestured with my chin, since my hands were still cuffed.

"Well, Rosalinda's not. I'm pretty sure she was dead before she hit the ground." She rubbed her eyes and yawned.

"It didn't look good from where I was standing."

She grunted. "I imagine not."

We sat for a second in silence.

"Listen," she said. "I'm not going to even ask you what you were doing out here. You're just going to lie to me and there's not much I can do about it. Drew Bossard was going on about witches and curses and vampires, and now one of my deputies tells me that he saw you point your finger at Rosalinda and zap her. She has some marks on her that look almost like burns. He thought maybe you had some kind of Taser or stun gun on you."

I shook my head. "You guys searched me pretty thoroughly. I'm not packing."

"Yeah." She crouched down and looked me right in the eye. "I want you to tell me the truth just one time, Melina. Do I want to know what went on here tonight?"

Finally, a question I could answer honestly. "No, Chief Murdock, you don't."

She looked at me for a long moment. "Will you be coming back to my town again?"

"Not if I can help it."

She stood and called to her deputies. "Set these guys free. I've got their contact info. They're just witnesses."

Then she walked away.

18

WE SPOTTED ALEX ON THE SIDE OF HIGHWAY 120. HE STEPPED out into traffic and waved us down. He climbed into the truck and apologized. "Sorry. I find it's best to avoid cops whenever possible. Present company excepted."

Ted nodded. "I can see where it could get awkward."

"So what exactly happened back there, Melina?" Alex asked.

It was the sixty-four thousand dollar question, wasn't it? No one else had asked it yet, though. We'd ridden mainly in silence. "I'm not sure," I said. I wiggled my hands in the air. Nothing.

"Has anything like that ever happened to you before?" Alex asked.

"You mean, have I ever started shooting lightning bolts out of my fingers before and not mentioned it? No. I haven't." I huddled down into the seat.

"No need to get snarky. I was just asking a question." Alex sounded amused.

I knew he was. It was the same set of questions I had. What had happened? Why had it happened then? What did it mean? "Sorry," I muttered, as I hunkered down in the seat.

He patted my shoulder. "I'm sure we'll figure it out."

What's this "we," kemosabe? I thought the question, but I didn't ask it. If tonight had made one thing manifestly clear, there was a "we." I was definitely not alone. I could not have survived Rosalinda's onslaught without my friends and I definitely couldn't have fought back against her without their energy channeling through me.

More than just their energy, really. Their love. In the end, it had been love that had defeated Rosalinda and kept me from defeating myself. I reached over my shoulder and patted his hand. "Thanks, Alex."

He leaned back into the backseat and looped his arm around Norah's shoulders.

These people knew what I was, who I was, and still accepted me, even when I wasn't sure what or who I was anymore. I'd spent years with only Mae to truly confide in and with only her to have my back. No one would or could ever take her place in my heart or in my personal history, but her death hadn't left me as alone and isolated as I thought it had.

I might be stuck in the middle as always, a go-between by vocation and stuck in between by circumstances, but I wasn't alone there. I think it wasn't until that moment that that fully dawned on me.

Ted reached over and took my hand, lifted it to his lips for a kiss and then set it on his leg as he drove.

I started to cry.

I PULLED INTO MY PARENTS' DRIVEWAY AND SAT FOR A MOment. The morning had been wind-whipped and foggy, but the sun had come through now. I could tell that my mother had already swept the front patio. She was probably out in the backyard, cleaning up any debris that the morning had tossed around and making sure that her roses were well tended.

I got out of the car, walked around the side of the house and let myself into the backyard. Sure enough, there she was, sun hat on her head and gardening clogs on her feet. She was kneeling on the foam mat that I'd gotten her for Mother's Day, one of the few gifts I'd managed to get her that appealed to her practical nature.

"Hey, Mom," I said.

She looked up, startled, and then smiled. "Melina, what a nice surprise! What brings you here?"

"I just thought I'd drop by." Now that I was here, I was feeling less and less sure about this decision. I scuffed at the brick walkway with my toe.

Mom snapped her pruning shears shut and dropped them into her basket. Then she stripped off her gardening gloves and wiped her hands on her jeans. "Would you like a glass of iced tea?"

"That'd be great."

We spent a few minutes covering the usual stuff. My job. The dojo. Dad. Patrick. Grandma Rosie.

Then we sat down on the steps to the patio in the backyard.

My mother's commitment to neatness and order has meant many things in my life. A lot of my childhood memories are dominated by her telling me to clean up after myself, to keep things tidy, to put things in their place. It had been irritating as hell, but these were also not such bad lessons to learn.

Her neat-freak nature, however, was also the cause of my current condition. After all, if she hadn't been so damn busy scrubbing the tiles of our swimming pool, she would have noticed me slipping into the pool behind her, and I would not have drowned and come back to life, and would not, I am pretty certain, have ever become a Messenger. I used to regularly curse her about this behind her back.

I'm not cursing her so much anymore. Maybe it's not so bad to be who and what I am. Sure, I'm different. But is that really so awful? Of all the kinds of hatred I'd encountered over the last few weeks, I'm pretty sure that self-hatred is the worst and most destructive kind.

I looked over the backyard. It was immaculate. The grass was mowed. The flowerbeds were tidy. Everything was edged and defined. Looking at it gave me a peaceful feeling. There were worse things then a well-tended yard. I leaned my head against my mother's shoulder.

"Mama, there's something I need to talk to you about."

"Anything, Melina, you know that." She looped her arm around me and kissed the top of my head.

It was true. I did know. "Mama, there's something different about me. I think you should know."